THE NIGHT HAG

Also by Hester Musson

The Beholders

THE NIGHT HAG

Hester Musson

4th ESTATE • London

4th Estate
An imprint of HarperCollins*Publishers*
1 London Bridge Street
London SE1 9GF

www.4thestate.co.uk

HarperCollins*Publishers*
Macken House
39/40 Mayor Street Upper
Dublin 1
D01 C9W8
Ireland

First published in Great Britain in 2026 by 4th Estate

1

Copyright © Hester Musson 2026

Hester Musson asserts the moral right to be identified as the author of this work in accordance with the Copyright, Designs and Patents Act 1988

A catalogue record for this book is available from the British Library

ISBN 978-0-00-856565-7 (hardback)
ISBN 978-0-00-856566-4 (trade paperback)

This novel is entirely a work of fiction. The names, characters and incidents portrayed in it are the work of the author's imagination. Any resemblance to actual persons, living or dead, events or localities is entirely coincidental.

All rights reserved. No part of this publication may be reproduced, stored in a retrieval system, or transmitted, in any form or by any means, electronic, mechanical, photocopying, recording or otherwise, without the prior permission of the publishers.

Without limiting the exclusive rights of any author, contributor or the publisher of this publication, any unauthorised use of this publication to train generative artificial intelligence (AI) technologies is expressly prohibited. HarperCollins also exercise their rights under Article 4(3) of the Digital Single Market Directive 2019/790 and expressly reserve this publication from the text and data mining exception.

Typeset in 13/16.5pt Bembo MT Pro by Six Red Marbles UK, Thetford, Norfolk

Printed and bound in the UK [using 100% renewable electricity at CPI Group (UK) Ltd]

THE NIGHT HAG

PROLOGUE

c/o The Post Office
Gledsmuir
Wednesday 20th October, 1886

Dear Dr Lachlan,
   I cannot know how you will receive this letter — with little sympathy, I expect, or at least with a certainty of opinion in line with your profession, an opinion that would sooner close itself off to reason than admit <u>uncertainty</u>. ~~Excuse my~~ However, I read your article in 'The Journal of Mental Science' discussing the origins of hallucinations and challenging the established theory that they must be purely psychological in nature. It led me to look further into your work, and I was heartened to learn that you have also questioned some current ideas about the female constitution, particularly with regards to education. My hope is that you are perhaps more enquiring than some of your colleagues and will approach my complaint from a position of <u>pure medical</u> interest, untainted by worn-out <u>prejudice.</u>
   The affliction I wish to be cured of first troubled me around the age of thirteen and continued until I was sixteen. My situation during those years was not a happy one, and once free of it, I found I was also free of my trouble. For twelve

years I have lived at peace and in comfort, at first as a governess and for the last eight years as a sketch artist and assistant to archaeologists. I was very happy to consign my strange ailment to the past and my unfortunate circumstances, perhaps also to some symptom of adolescence. Two months ago, however, it began again (I am twenty-eight years old). I can see no reason for this, and it is increasing steadily in frequency and intensity. ~~Unchecked, I fear it will end as it did before~~

I think it best if I simply describe what happens. I set down here a typical instance, one such as I experienced last night, or rather early this morning.

I go to bed at a normal hour (alone) and sleep dreamlessly. The 'attack' usually comes in the later stages of the night, and the following occurs:

I wake up. The first thing I know, before I even open my eyes, is that there is something or someone in the room with me. The knowledge is immediate and dreadful. You must have experienced such moments of awful realisation, Dr Lachlan, the kind that strike in an instant – the sudden awareness that a young child is no longer in sight, for example, or that a caged animal has been forgotten, unfed – a flash of horror so intense it somehow includes the full weight of its consequences.

The next thing I am aware of is a hissing sound; the air itself seems to be crackling, and the strangest tingling sensation comes over my skin – as if the flesh is fizzing and the physical integrity of my body is no longer secure. I open my eyes. At the end of my bed is a man, watching me. He is all in darkness, a shape only, but so charged with malevolence, the room feels thick with it. Somehow, I know beyond doubt that he has come for me, that he has been near all my life – perhaps even before I was born. My impulse is to cry out, but I find I can neither open my mouth nor make a sound. Apart from my eyes, I cannot move. I don't know if you have ever been paralysed and *experienced the sensation of screaming in your own head. It is to perch on the very edge of sanity with an eternity pressing at your back, a hair's breadth from falling to one's death.*

The night-mare (as I have come to call it) approaches and climbs onto the bed. I can feel the mattress dip under its weight and hear the springs creak. I <u>hear</u> them, Dr Lachlan. Despite the shrieking impulses of my body, I can do nothing; I cannot raise a finger. In my head I am waging the fiercest battle of my life, fighting with every ounce of my being to stop my mind from pitching over the edge. I know that to stop resisting even for a second would mean to be lost, my reason gone. It is my <u>greatest fear</u> that one night I shall lose this fight. Even writing this, my heart pounds, and my breathing grows short. The night-mare crawls up my body until it is kneeling on my chest and wraps its fingers around my throat. I cannot breathe. The unrelenting pressure threatens to break the bone; please try to imagine the pain of this. I believe I shall die. Every time, <u>I believe I shall die</u>. But in the end, it lifts. It might remain in the room or even resume the attack, but eventually I am released; I can move.

~~For God's sake~~ Writing this, I am frustrated by my poor powers of description, but I hope I have conveyed at least some sense of the terror. Since the phenomenon has returned, the nature of it is volatile, changing almost nightly. Sometimes there is a different man, clearer, older; he sits on my bed and weeps copiously, wild, wracking sobs that shake his frame with dreadful violence, and this somehow terrifies me more than the strangling. I have seen small boys too with frightful, hungry eyes. At other times nothing comes but an awful screaming — I think it is the sound of horses — but always, eventually, the dark figure returns. ~~You have to~~

What I must impress upon you most keenly is the realness of what I see and feel and hear. ~~I fear~~ I cannot pretend to myself, much less to you, that I am not fully awake during these 'attacks', even as I write these words and hear how they must sound to an alienist. It is as real to me as I would be to you if I were speaking these words now, sitting across from you (I imagine you at a desk) and reaching out to touch you.

I expect you will say that I am mistaken, that I am not awake at all, but in the grip of a powerful dream. ~~Nonsense~~ *Then how to explain the time when I was younger and it came to me in the middle of the day in front of witnesses?* ~~Host~~

What I hope you will say is that it is a temporary hallucination, that the same mind that can imagine you, a man I have never met, at a desk that doesn't exist, can equally well create a figure that seems to live outside of itself and terrifies with its vividness. I hope you will say such a mind can be brought to order as simply as an upset stomach may be calmed.

The word night-mare – with the hyphen – as I expect you know, is the old term for a demon supposed to terrorise people at night. I have often come across these stories in my work – they appear in folklore throughout the world, often as hags. The Mara is one, whose very name shares the same root as the 'mare' in nightmare. I use the hyphen because I know I am awake when I see these things; it is not a nightmare in the modern sense of a dream only. But please understand, this does not mean I believe my experience is in any way supernatural. I do <u>not</u> believe in demons or spirits or anything of the sort.

They say only the mad insist on their sanity. All I say is that, as real as these torments are to me, I look upon them with a sceptic's eye and, here, hold them up to a medical one. I wish to be cured of an illness, a physical disorder – oh, for it to be indigestion! – before it does indeed do damage to my mental state. But I know too well what many would think who read these words. For some doctors, to be female is a grave diagnosis in itself; feeble-mindedness and hysteria are merely symptoms that must inevitably follow. Perhaps you are one. I think not, but I am cautious. My fear of being trapped by the blunter instruments of the medical profession, of <u>losing my freedom</u>, compels me to withhold my real name and begs you to direct your reply to the above post office, should you indeed wish to respond to this first, desperately inadequate letter.

    Yours sincerely,
      Miss Gerrard

PS I must add that although my name is a fiction, my financial resources are sound and may be relied upon.

1

Lil woke up. Something had happened. She could feel its wrongness, an echo of violence as if she had been kicked awake. Her eyes opened on total darkness. Raindrops hit the window like a handful of grit; wind gusted, roiling, at odds with itself. The cold was more ice than air against her face. She tried to move, to turn over – and could not. She was pinned. Panic bolted through her that she had woken to *it*, that it was there in the darkness beside her. Eyes peering blindly, she wrenched her body over, fear lending her strength, and the sheet that she had become wrapped in came loose. She would have been flung clean out of bed but for the weight of heaped blankets halting her progress like a snowdrift.

Relief made her breathing loud. Slowly, she disentangled limbs from bedclothes, the cold latching on fast to every emerging inch of skin. She swung stockinged feet to the floor. Hands that could see in the dark reached for matches and candle, and the small, low room flared and spluttered into being. Floorboards and hard chair; boxes of finds stacked halfway to the low ceiling and dissolving into shadow; the table with its papers and pencils, microscope, and jars of acids, balsam and turpentine barely kissed into existence by the light. Lil quietened her breathing, listened for more than the wind, watched the black beyond. The trouble with light was that it made the darkness darker. She reminded herself that these ordinary shadows held no terrors for her, that for so many years it was she who had inhabited them and she alone; it was her hands that had reached out of the black to touch the nape of the neck, the powdered cheek. A child's hands, made cold and spectral. She looked at them now, holding the candle: small and pale still, but showing the calluses of long hours with a trowel, even more with a pencil.

The sound came again.

She started, turned to the window. It had been a crack like a gun going off in a brief lull in the wind. She moved quickly, pulling on her boots and clawing for her jacket and shawl. It took no time; neither of them had fully undressed for weeks. She lit the lamp, chasing the shadows into oblivion, and clattered with it into the kitchen. Nils was already there, filling the cramped space, alarm and sleepiness making a haggard moon of his face. Without speaking, they snatched at greatcoats and hats and plunged into the wild night. Nils tripped on something just outside the door and kicked it to the side.

It wasn't far, but the ground was uneven, and the wind pounced and roared at the lantern, forcing her to twist this way and that as she pushed on up the hill. They rounded a patch of gorse, its thorns scraping at her coat, and her feet struck a heap of something she thought at first was earth but, lowering the light, found to be tarpaulin. She pointed, raising the lantern to Nils's rain-drenched face. He nodded, expressionless, and gestured to go on. A few yards further and they reached the low stones that edged the burial mound on the south-western side. Lil followed them to a gap and strained to make sense of the shapes thrown up by the lantern. The trench they had been working on, seven feet wide and cutting eleven feet in towards the centre of the mound, was gone. She swung the light, trying to clear the shadows, but it was earth and stones rather than darkness that had smothered their efforts, caving in from the sides. The rain had been heavy for days. Several of the wooden stakes they had used to try to strengthen the walls now poked out at odd angles. One showed only its splintered end where it had somehow snapped, perhaps the sound like a shot she had heard. Lil raised her eyes, but the top of the tumulus with its central shaft, thirty feet from where she stood, was invisible in the dark.

'Come away. We can do nothing until it is light.' Nils was behind her, shouting over the wind. Lil closed her eyes, heard Madelyn's voice howl through her head: *You are nothing without me*, felt the wind take it, let it be whipped away.

She bellowed back at him. 'I have to check the cist.'

She turned, but felt his large hand grasp the back of her coat, holding her back. 'Stop!'

Spinning around, she squinted at him through the rain. He wasn't looking at her. His head was turned to a row of lights on the east side of the site, beyond where the standing stone hulked in darkness. Three lamps, and two more joining from the direction of the hamlet.

'Come away,' Nils yelled again and set off back towards the cottage without waiting. Lil lingered a moment, an awful coiling in the pit of her stomach. She knew who they were, who was leading them. The lights didn't move any nearer, but she could see others materialising out of the darkness. They were watching.

She turned and stumbled down the hill after Nils.

A grey dawn seeped into the kitchen, rinsing it in pewter. The wind had died down except for brief sallies at latches and into the chimney. They sat opposite each other, mud caking their clothes, the teapot between them. Nils's chair creaked as he shifted to lift a bottle from the side. He poured a slug into Lil's tea and then his own. The amber whisky and orange embers in the grate seemed the only spots of colour in the whole world. He knocked his back, as impervious to heat as he was to cold. 'Did you see them?'

She nodded. 'More came.'

'And the animal head?'

'Pig.'

It had been the object Nils had nearly tripped over, dumped by their door. He frowned. 'But that is an ill omen for fishermen here, I think.'

Lil choked on a laugh, comforted somehow by his ability to miss the point. 'They want to frighten us. It will be John Mudie and his like.' She said the name defiantly, hoping to rob it of its power.

Nils's frown deepened. 'I am not frightened by them. But this weather . . .' They watched the fire in silence until he shrugged. 'Perhaps they are right. Perhaps the place is cursed.'

Lil let her cup thump down. 'A storm in the middle of October this far north? Yes, surely the work of the devil.'

His expression didn't change, and she noticed how papery the skin wrinkling his neck was, the way it clung thinly to his cheekbones. He looked older, even in the few weeks they had been here, and he hadn't been young to begin with. But it wasn't just age, she knew, stealing his hair and rounding his big shoulders. With another shrug, he spoke in his precise, measured, Swedish voice. 'I do not think it is the devil they fear.'

She stood quickly and moved around the table to the window. The greyness outside was weighted: a damp, discarded blanket suffocating everything. She thought how different it was, how impossibly far removed from the crystalline light of Norway in the summer. It had been July when Effie had told her about this place, that they would be ending the season here and working into the winter if possible. Her eyes, almost the same blue as the sky, had belied her illness, an infinity of plans shining within them. It was another's death that had rekindled her own fading spark. Lil remembered how excitement had lent her voice a strangely sharp edge.

'Pitcarden's owner has finally had the goodness to stop breathing.' She was supposed to be resting, but appeared beside Lil and Nils, who were lunching on hard-boiled eggs next to a small stone circle, abruptly casting them in shadow. Lil had squinted up through the July sunshine and seen a newspaper cutting clasped in Effie's thin fingers. The name Pitcarden was familiar.

'Scotland?' She peered at Effie's face, confused.

'Three hours north of Edinburgh. We'll need permission from his son, who's in Australia, but we can aim to start in September.'

Lil rose quickly to her feet, moving so Effie had to turn into the light. The disease was taking its toll on her appearance, even then. A few months earlier, no one would have guessed she was nearing fifty. There was no need to ask why she wanted to dig into the winter – she may not see another season – but to leave Norway? Years of work lay directly under their feet, and no one else had touched it yet.

Effie's eyes glittered. 'Wait until you see it, Lily Pad; it's *pristine*. We need to move quickly or some gentleman *enthusiast* will get to it first.' She turned back to Nils. 'It's come at last.'

Lil watched the look that passed between them with a disorientating sense that she had missed something crucial in all the years she had worked for them. She glanced, alarmed, over the surrounding land. The diggers they had hired were resting in the long grass a little distance away, and beyond them between the trees were dozens of squat standing stones, circle after circle, probably Iron Age. There was so much of it, Nils would have to let her lead on some areas alone. There was room to experiment. For months they had been working in Denmark on a rotted Viking ship, connecting dots with a skeleton of rivets, and her fingers had itched to dig further into time, into prehistory. The site before her was perfect. It was *hers*.

She swung an arm. 'But we're the first here. Look at it.' Her voice had become pinched, and she recalled how she had been labelled 'Shrill Lil' simply for asking questions at public lectures. It made her snappish. 'You're not making any sense.'

Effie laughed. 'I've earned the right to do things for reasons other than sense. I'm due a little frivolity, a little glamour. Look here.'

She held out the page of newspaper and tapped a paragraph with her finger. Lil wiped her hands on her skirt and took it. The article was an obituary of a Mr Raube, owner of the Pitcarden estate. The paragraph touched on his descent into misanthropy and possible madness after his wife had died in childbirth. The first suggestion of eccentricity came with the rumour that he had buried a priceless family heirloom on that tragic night, a gold lover's brooch, laced with diamonds. He had supposedly dug the hole somewhere in a mound next to a standing stone and instructed his gamekeepers to fire over the heads of anyone who came near.

Lil raised darkening and disbelieving eyes to Effie. 'Treasure hunting?'

Effie tossed her head. 'I knew you would be scandalised. But just think, if we *did* find the brooch, the publicity it would bring. And money, I expect.'

'You don't need money.'

Effie smiled. Her love of acquiring gold had long since outstripped her need for it. She leaned in a little. 'It's probably Bronze Age.'

Lil swallowed the words she had been about to say and watched Effie's delicate fingers tracing the air. 'A large circular burial mound in a prominent position next to a standing stone – on land that has been grazed but never ploughed. We have good reason to believe it has never been looted either.' She let the picture paint itself for a moment. 'Imagine what might be inside.'

Lil's interest sharpened like a blade. If it was Bronze Age, there was likely to be a stone cist at its centre with bones, grave goods. Intact. A sweet thrill ran through her. Effie and Nils exchanged another look, and Effie's smile became feline. 'You could take the lead on it, Lily Pad. The whole thing.'

Lil remained very still, her face a mask, as her mind galloped full tilt into the future. Scotland's prehistory was mostly discovered by accident when land was ploughed or levelled and destroyed in the same instant. A clear run at an important, undisturbed site could revolutionise current knowledge. Maybe even make her name. Effie was watching her closely. Lil knew she could read her thoughts to the letter, but refused to drop the mask. 'Why are you so sure no one's opened it up before?'

'It is cursed.' Nils spoke cheerfully. He hauled his long bones upright and, flicking eggshell from his fingers, grinned suddenly. It was like a fissure jagging open in one of the stones behind him. 'We do not know how far back, but many generations have been fearful of it, too afraid to go near.'

Lil swallowed. Even this long after Madelyn, something twisted inside, as if a part of her were trapped for ever in the house of her childhood. 'Cursed?'

Effie waved a dismissive hand. 'The usual tale – a buried hoard of treasure no one must touch. The old man went digging for it when he was young and greedy and later convinced himself he had unleashed the Pitcarden hag and that was the reason all his children died in infancy. So, he buried the brooch as an offering, obeying the legend, and what do you think happened? Never mind his poor wife dying in childbirth, his final son and heir survived.'

'And moved to Australia.' Nils nodded his big head in approval. Absentee landowners caused the least trouble.

Lil tried to ignore how her heart had crouched down in her chest. 'A hag?'

Effie shrugged. 'The standing stone, of course.'

'A *Carlin* stone.' Nils's eyes shone. 'It will be older than the curse. The two stories must have merged over time. The Carlin is a hag or witch.' He smiled happily; folk tales were his hobby horse. Effie always laughed at the legends; they were asides, not even footnotes to the real work. Lil wanted it to stay that way.

'What if the son doesn't give his permission?' There was hope, almost, in her voice. 'He might feel the same as his father.'

'He's a gold miner.' Effie spoke flatly. She understood what gold did to people and what people did to get it; her own experience had taught her. Lil knew there were more powerful things in the world, but said nothing.

'Anyway,' Effie brightened, 'whether there's a hoard or not is beside the point. We *know* the brooch exists.' She took the newspaper back and flourished it. 'And that it happens to be buried in a significant prehistoric site that for the first time has become accessible to archaeologists. Plenty there to amuse a sick old woman and her friends.'

In the grey of the Pitcarden dawn, far from the warmth of that sunny afternoon, Lil shivered, thinking how Effie hadn't had the chance to be amused. The sickness had crumpled her before they'd left Norway, collapsing her world to her bed in Edinburgh and the reports Lil took back. She wouldn't join them in the field again. Nils made excuses and hadn't visited once, but he was growing thin and drawn, as if his wife's disease were destroying him too.

And the site *was* Bronze Age. Lavishly so. They had already uncovered a pit with two intact cinerary urns. Nearby were beads of jet and amber, and more bones with a bronze blade among them. The knife was so well preserved, Lil had been able to identify tiny fragments of wood and leather from its sheath. Her plan had been to record the site in detail before removing even one spadeful of earth, and then to slice it thinly, layer by layer, from the top. She didn't just want to know *what* was buried there, but how. Effie's money afforded them the time and labour for such a radical method. Her health, however, did not. She was bedridden before Lil had finished her measurements and sketches. When Nils suggested hiring more men and digging a conventional trench through the centre of the mound, Lil didn't object. Tacitly, they shared a need to bring Effie one more extraordinary thing – the lover's knot brooch if they could find it, although Lil herself gave little weight to their reason for coming to Pitcarden. The treasure had never been mentioned again. She wanted a real find, something all the way back from the Bronze Age.

When Effie's health dipped again, it was Lil herself who ordered the men to sink a square shaft into the middle of the mound in the hope of discovering a cist. It was an outdated, crude method of excavation, painfully far from her dreams for the site. She made them take up the earth in shallow layers, racing to sieve it all through before the next barrow-load arrived, trying to work both quickly and slowly at once. Their efforts were rewarded. The stony earth finally gave way to an inner mound of fine, dark soil. Scraping this away revealed one corner of a large stone cist. Effie had been right: there was no evidence treasure hunters had ever dug through the finer earth and opened the tomb. The whinstone walls and top still fitted snugly together. Lil had put her ear to the cold stone as if she might hear something within, a whisper or heartbeat. Her own heart had tapped a staccato beat with impatience. There was so much work to be done before they could open it.

In the dark evenings, she strained her eyes making detailed sketches of every potsherd and flake of flint that her sieve had caught. She sent them to Effie with fulsome notes. None of them told of a brooch. There was not a hint of a hoard anywhere, only the trouble it was causing. The stories of the curse, the lunatic reasons the old man had buried his gold, had failed to die with him. They hung in the air like an imminent thunderstorm, invisible and oppressive. People feared the hag: dig up her treasure and she would haunt every dwelling, grand hall and lowly cottage alike, until she had found the youngest and most vulnerable to prey on. If Lil had known the full extent of the story, its parallels with the Lilith myth, she would have fought harder to stay in Norway. She couldn't shake the feeling people watched her knowingly, suspecting her of something more sinister than simple archaeology.

Nils knew nothing of her deeper fears. For him, local opposition to the dig was borne of a natural distrust of strangers, especially godless foreigners. They should have shown their faces at the Free Church at least one Sunday, but a clear sky and no wind were the gods of fieldwork, and they were jealous gods. Besides, the strange symbols and animal parts left at their door and near the excavation weren't anything Christian. Nils was right: it wasn't the devil they feared.

Lil ground her knuckles against the splintered wood of the sideboard. 'Who cares what superstitions they waste their few wits upon?' Then with greater venom, 'Village idiots.'

'That is not just.' Nils spoke without emotion. 'Or true.'

Lil didn't answer. Her words had rung hollow even to herself. For hadn't she seen captains of industry weep like children at a word from her pen? Ladies of education and literary fame write breathlessly of miracles? Barristers, MPs, authors, philosophers, even men of science tremble at her touch? Credulity afflicted low and mighty, urbane and rustic, equally, without discernment. Like a disease, she thought savagely. *Like cancer.*

Enough. She glared out at the cheerless morning as if it were a desert she must cross. It would be another half hour before the diggers arrived, men hired from too far away to have grown up with the curse of the place in their bones. They were agricultural labourers forced south as farms contracted under the depression. Two were ploughmen and understood how different soils behaved at least. Nils had trained them well; the best could wield a pick like a feather. They would be camped out in one of the earth-floored bothies still, trying to warm themselves with brose and milk. She didn't want them watching anyway while she surveyed the damage. The ploughmen had grown interested in the site and trusted her, but she knew the more recent arrivals thought her an aberration, slight and female, a spinster on her knees in the dirt, telling them what to do. When she gave orders and they cast down their eyes, it wasn't out of respect. She reached again for the greatcoat. 'I'm going to see.'

As she pulled the door shut, she noticed something new: twigs crossed together and tied with red thread had been nailed to the wood. Perhaps it was the sound of it being hammered in that had woken her. Another gift from John Mudie, probably, like the pig's head. The men had seen him prowling around their quarters too. She pulled it off quickly and tossed it away, as if to touch it were to be touched by him.

At the top of the slope, the tarpaulin was still scrunched at the foot of the gorse, a corner twitching in the wind like a mighty fallen bat. Lil made herself look across the site. The burial mound was always impressive, nearly sixty feet in diameter, rising over the highest point of the ridge. Locally, it was known simply as *the brae*. The surviving stones along its edge were visible now, three-foot-long slabs laid on their sides, a prehistoric picket fence. The trench they had dug had been just as neat, cutting into the barrow with straight sides. Now it was as if a giant hand had pushed the edges, as easy as knocking over a sandcastle, and earth had folded into earth, becoming mud with the rain. It would take days to shift it all, and anything found would be out of place, its precise context lost. Lil stepped up to her ankles in dirt to peer at a supporting stake half sticking out of the mess. It too was splintered. Her finger traced gashes in the wood. It was as if someone had tried to hack through with an axe.

Snatching her hand back, she ran to where she could scramble up the mound, muttering something like a prayer. She reached the central shaft. It was the same; the tarp had blown clear away, the stakes were smashed, and the sides had slumped in on top of the cist. Yesterday, she'd been able to see all the way down to the subsoil; now there was nothing but a muddy, stony crater. She pressed the heels of her hands to her forehead and tried to calculate the time lost, how hard they would have to work before the weather stopped them completely.

She was facing the Carlin stone. It reared up a few yards from the mound, seventeen feet of mystery. The tarp had blown as far as its base and become stuck there. Lil made her way over to it and examined the ties. They were loose, all of them, either undone or cut through, the work of hands and a blade rather than wind. She bit her lip and looked into the belt of woodland beyond. It sloped down steeply to the hamlet of Balcraig and the poor soils of Pitcarden Mains. Nothing stirred. On the other side of the barrow the spoil heaps were becoming small mounds themselves. Pitcarden House, with its dark windows and burned-out stables, stood out of sight in a dip to the north. The hulk of the Highlands rose in the far distance, but here the landscape was less wild. She turned to stare across the patchy arable fields and gorse-studded hills of Pitcarden's farms. There wasn't a soul to be seen or heard anywhere, only the plaintive call of a buzzard wheeling overhead. In the quietness, she felt a deeper silence lapping at her consciousness. Effie's coming death was a cold tide rising with every moment, always present. Lil wasn't sure, when it closed over her head, how she would breathe, if she and Nils would be lifeline enough for each other.

She pressed her hand to the standing stone. There was comfort in its solidity, its permanence. She knew she could dig up every last scrap of bone, scrutinise every remnant of pot, and still know close to nothing about the people who had built the barrow. There was only the stone itself, out-existing all meaning imposed on it by its prehistoric guardians. It would no doubt still be standing there long after the frail fingers of present folklore had slipped from its sides. It maintained its own stone-lore, the truths of its formation and weathering carried silently within itself. Lil wondered if she should have thrown her lot in with geologists instead.

A gust of wind made her shiver, but there was little point in going back to the cottage before the diggers arrived. She returned to the base of the mound, stamping up and down the length of the collapsed trench and blasted stakes like a general before his defeated men. The tiredness of weeks dragged at her bones. Since the return of the night-mare, she had been putting off sleep, roaming the cold, dark hillside until the small hours in the vain hope she could exhaust herself free of it.

High above, clouds raced before a fiercer wind, and for a moment, the grey blanket of sky was rent open, allowing a length of sunlight to unfurl rapidly over the site. It was soon scooped up again, but not before it had glinted briefly off something in the dirt. Lil peered. The flash had been near the far end of the trench where the walls were higher. She walked up the side, and another slip of sunshine clipped whatever it was a few feet away. She lay on her front where the ground was still solid, but she couldn't reach far enough. Kneeling, she put one boot into the soft earth and stretched her arm out again. Her boot sank a little, and she leaned further. She was almost there, almost touching it, when she lost her balance. Her hand and knee plunged into earth as grasping as quicksand. Soil was slipping under her, but she lunged again for where the flash had been, committing her whole body.

Her fingers found it: a small, flat triangle, no bigger than a thumbnail. They pinched – hard, thin, metallic maybe – and teased out a larger triangle, the size of a small hand. Lil's heart leaped. But she was stuck. The earth cleaved to her as if it would hold her fast. She tried to raise herself onto hands and knees but slipped, squirming like something slick and newborn. A nameless fear swept over her, and instinctively, she strained her neck to look behind her. Sweat pushed through her skin. She could feel panic rising, blind and bull-headed, and looked around wildly for something to hold on to. The mound reared over her, a hulk of earth. And at the top, rising out of it and black against the light, was a shape. A dark figure.

Her hands slipped in the mud and she was face down in the dirt again. Her limbs flailed, uselessly fighting for something solid that wasn't there. She couldn't see where the shape was. A scream tried to push itself through her constricted throat, and then she was being dragged backwards, turned over on solid ground. She had kicked Nils in the chest before she could stop herself.

'Who was it? Did you see? Was it Mudie?' She scrambled to her feet, breathing heavily, and turned towards where the figure had been. There was nothing but wind in the grass and the moving sky beyond. She turned back, accusingly. Behind Nils were the diggers, stopped short by the sight of her. She counted quickly; all were present.

'Who was up there just now?' She pointed and was met with blank stares. Nils shook his head. His gaze moved to what she held in her hand. Turning on her heel, she started to run, hurrying to the top of the mound. Her eyes searched all over the slope and the surrounding land and woods. There was no sign of anyone. She made a full circuit of the site and found the diggers with spades in hand by the time she returned.

Nils strode to meet her. 'What is it? What is wrong?'

'I . . .' She looked around again. The buzzard called over the woods. 'I saw someone.' She could still feel the fear, a lingering whine in her nerves. There had been something familiar about the shape.

One of the newer diggers said something in his northern dialect and the others laughed. She turned on him. 'What did you say?' He didn't look at her, and she took a step. 'I asked what you—'

'He says you must have seen the Carlin, the hag,' Nils interrupted. He smiled gently, pursed his lips. 'It is not serious.'

Lil wanted to laugh or say pacifying words, but her throat was too tight. Nils gestured. 'You found something.'

She lifted the hand she had forgotten was holding the muddied fragment. Her voice rasped. 'I'll clean it.'

She half fell back down the hill to the cottage, discarding clothes as soon as she was through the door — coats, skirts, stockings — and letting them fall where they would. The metal object was placed on the table. Stoking the fire, she lifted the kettle onto its hook, leaving smears of mud on everything she touched, and stood shivering in her chemise and drawers, waiting for hot water. She told herself it was only the cold making her shake. Her heart still pounded, wanting to know what she had seen. She tried to push away any thought of the night-mare's dark figure, but Madelyn's voice rang in her head: *You are gifted, Lil, you have the sight, but it is warning you of great danger.* She glanced sideways at the lump of matter on the table, and realised she was reluctant to find out what it was.

Her bare toes clawed at the brick hearth. She had the sense that this was how one entered an asylum, stripped and freezing and scared. Her fists clenched and unclenched. If Dr Lachlan were here, what would he see? A woman behaving erratically, driven to impropriety by the phantoms in her mind. He must have read her letter by now, decided whether to reply or not, perhaps even written. The ghosts of her words floated back to her: *caged animal . . . I must impress . . . desperately inadequate . . . I expect you . . . I hope you . . .* She had written it in a rush, a tumbling forth of garbled fears and crossings-out, and then sent it without writing a fair copy. It was as if she had wanted him to doubt her sanity. But she knew if she had hesitated, the letter would never have left her room.

Once the water was hot enough, she scrubbed the dirt from her nails with punishing thoroughness. She was soaping her arms and throat when there came the sound of the front door opening and Nils appeared. He picked up her skirt and stockings with a pained expression.

'I'm sorry, Nils.'

He hung the clothes over a chair with care, giving a little shake of his big head. 'They already think we are godless, without morals.'

'And now without petticoats.' A small sound escaped her, nearly a laugh, and she drowned it in a splash of dirty water.

It was true. They had hired a maid to live in when they'd first arrived, for propriety's sake. She'd slept in the box-bed in the kitchen as the cottage was so small; even Nils's bedroom was only an old sty attached to the building with a doorway knocked through. But the maid had been snatched away by her family once their intent was known. No other local girl could be persuaded, so they lived scandalously alone together, shifting for themselves. It suited them, keeping what hours and meals they pleased and matching domestic requirements to ability rather than convention. Lil's education, she had discovered over the years with an ever-volatile mix of gratitude and resentment, had equipped her neither for the drawing room nor the kitchen. Fortunately, Nils had all the fastidious habits of a bachelor, despite his comfortable marriage to Effie, and enjoyed roasting meat.

Stealth, sleight of hand, and the ability to speak with authority at a moment's notice on all manner of subjects were Lil's domain. She was better marked out to be a thief or an actress. And, of course, in a manner of speaking, had been both. Shame, never far from the surface, crept up her throat and killed her smile.

Nils remained stern. 'We must not provoke them further, give them any reason to . . .'

'They don't need any reason.' Lil shook the water aggressively from her hands. 'The tarpaulins didn't untie themselves. And it wasn't the wind that took an axe to the stakes. You must have seen them.' She looked at him, and he looked at the piece of metal on the table. After a moment, he picked it up.

'You haven't washed it?' He rubbed the worst of the dirt from it, holding it over a crate, then wetted a cloth and began carefully removing the rest.

Lil dried off and wrapped a woollen blanket around herself, watching with apprehension at first and then growing disbelief. 'Gold?'

The gleam intensified as Nils worked, until it shone out like a risen sun. It was hammered flat, except – surprisingly – for a plain figure in relief. A woman, or at least female – not necessarily human. He placed it on the table, and they stared at it in silence.

Lil spoke first, her voice thin. 'A votive offering?' She released an arm from the blanket and nudged the plaque. The figure pivoted slightly towards her.

'Perhaps, but what is it doing here? It is not Bronze Age.'

'It might be Roman.'

Nils frowned. 'Romano-British, if it were further south. But they didn't settle here. This is not something that soldiers carried.'

'We don't know that for sure.' She spoke with a sort of desperation, knowing he was right. Her mind had already leaped to the most likely explanation, but she blundered on. 'Medieval?'

Nils turned his head on one side. 'That is not a saint. It is pagan, a goddess perhaps, or other entity.' He looked at her, his eyes beginning to brighten like a lamp being turned up. 'You know what it must be?'

She nodded. It was supposed to be good news, exciting. 'The rumours.' She picked the word carefully, choosing it over *myth* or *legend* or *curse*. 'The rumours about the hoard. This could be part of it. If it's true.'

He beamed like a big baby, expecting her to return his smile. 'The storm worked *for* us.'

Lil wished fiercely that she had hidden the plaque and told Nils it was only a broken trowel fallen into the trench. The brooch they could have spirited away to Effie in secret, but pieces of a larger hoard turning up were more disruptive, more exposing. She didn't like the eagerness in Nils's expression. The plaque gleamed on the table. She couldn't unknow it. Goddesses, hags; they were always bad news, or at least unpredictable. Nils's stories had shown her that. She only had to think of the Mara, the terrifying night-creature that turned up in folk tales all across Europe – Nordic, Germanic, Slavic – crushing people in their beds. The same malice could be discovered much further afield too, ribboning across cultures and centuries in different mythologies, like Lilitu in Mesopotamia, a precursor to Lilith, Lil's own namesake.

As a child, Lil had been taught the Lilith of Jewish folklore. She was Adam's first wife, his equal, who was made from the same dust and refused to be subservient. Madelyn had impressed on her how Lilith had left the Garden of Eden of her own free will, not in shame like Eve. Lil eventually stumbled across the rest of the myth in an encyclopaedia: Lilith had continued to roam the world in vengeance, killing newborns wherever she found them – a figure to inspire fear and hatred. Of course,

Madelyn denied all responsibility. *The spirits knew what they were doing when they named you.* Lil felt she had been branded, destined to carry something of the ancient venom within her. She shed the name like dead skin the moment she left Madelyn's house and reappointed herself plain Lil Vincent. No one called Lil Vincent was going to wind up a blood-curdling myth.

But now there was the Pitcarden hag, the Carlin stone, and a mysterious female figure stamped in ancient gold. She turned sharply to the window to hide her dismay. 'The men. They must be supervised. If there are more artefacts like this to come . . .'

'Yes, yes.' Nils placed his hand on the table and leaned towards her. He waited until she met his gaze. 'You must take this to her.' His eyes were bright; they didn't leave hers.

She shook her head. 'Not yet. We have lost so much time. I shall sketch it for her.'

Disappointment dulled him, but he nodded and withdrew to his full height. Lil forced a smile. 'Then we can go together and show her.' She watched for signs of resistance and found them. A muscle twitched in his face; he averted his gaze.

'Yes.' He cleared his throat. Energy and purpose returned. 'So, I shall help the men.' He paused, struck by a thought. 'Mr Haxton must not know of this.'

Lil hugged the blanket around her as if the name were a cold draught. The estate factor wanted them gone for at least two reasons, and Lil knew herself to be one of them. The other was his belief that if the hoard came to light, it would provoke Mudie and his followers to violence. 'Has he been yet?'

'No.'

She pulled the blanket tighter. 'Well, the central cist has been covered. We should begin there.'

Nils nodded noncommittally, and Lil felt her heart sink. 'While

they do that, I shall go to town as I'm washed. To the post office.'
He nodded again more cheerfully and strode to the door.

Dressing in the clothes she kept tidy for the outside world, Lil noticed her fingers had lost their deftness; they fumbled over buttons and dropped items, as if they knew something she didn't and were fearful.

2

Lil's path to town took her through the belt of trees, down the slope, and past the turning to Balcraig. The hamlet was a dismal place, run down and overgrown like the rest of the estate. Many of the younger men had left, replaced by itinerant farm labourers, who then also left for better pay and perhaps company. The low cottages looked as if they had been hammered into the ground. Even the dwellings still inhabited had an air of decay, of losing a slow battle against nature. Smoke rose and twisted from a few chimneys, the only thing that looked alive, although she could hear the biting whack of an axe somewhere, and a voice, indistinct, out of sight.

Two farms made up what remained of the estate, Eastcraig and Pitcarden Mains. The road took Lil between them, unbound by any fence except weeds and the stones that had been cast from the fields. A lone ploughman away to her left cursed at his horses and bent to grapple with something under the beam. As he straightened, Lil recognised the long, slim shape of Mudie and felt her back go cold.

He had watched her when she was first measuring the length of the barrow, weeks before. Intent on rerolling a length of twine, she hadn't realised anyone was near until a pair of hobnailed boots blocked her path. Straightening, she had stepped back quickly and watched a slow, mirthless smile deepen the lines on his face. Decades of hard work and poor diet showed in the waxy skin and the thin hair straggling from under his cap. He wasn't known to her then, but she recognised the expression – the sneer in the lip, the slightly lowered head as if he might charge, the sheer intentness of the gaze. She had seen it on streets, in train carriages, in lectures, from every kind of man, even in her own room at Madelyn's. But something about Mudie made the recognition sound deeper and darker within her. Since the return of the night-mare, she had been afraid again, scanning the world around her for a hostile figure, a manifestation of the darkness that came at night. Mudie's sudden presence robbed her of speech. She began to roll the twine as if he weren't there. Slowly, he lifted his boot and pressed it down on the cord, making it jerk to a halt in her fingers. Nothing was said. He made no other move. Lil's very bones seemed to hollow out. She was in the corner of the schoolroom again, twelve years ago, her tutor walking towards her. The reel fell from her hands and, instinctively, she ran through a gap in the stones and up the flank of the burial mound as if she would be protected by sacred ground. His laughter alone had followed.

This time, in the field at Pitcarden Mains, he was too far away for her to see his expression, but his movements slowed deliberately until he was standing square and still, arms at his sides, watching again. She turned her face to the road, gritting herself against the urge to walk faster. He wouldn't be able to tell from that distance how much her breathing had quickened. The grey sky pressed down more darkly, rain in the air. She waited until she had passed two more fields before reassuring herself there was no dark shape gaining ground behind.

One of the fields was a potato crop, already harvested. The clamp stood in a corner like a fresh burial mound heaped with earth. It seemed charged with an ancient and sinister atmosphere, rearing out of the bare fields, made more so by the clouds of smoke wreathing the hillside beyond where gorse was being burned. As she drew nearer, she heard fires crackling. Closer to the road, blackened skeletons were being smashed to dust and mattocks used to dig up the roots. Haxton was reviving the estate as best he could for Raube's heir, turning poor pasture to more profitable arable. She had heard him discussing his plans with one of her best diggers, a man who had once been a grieve – a farm bailiff – further north. Covertly, she had learned Haxton's views on the short-sightedness of wintering Irish cattle, the inadequacies of the six-shift system, his personal contempt for certain rotation crops. His vehemence against potatoes had forced her to turn away in case he saw her laughter. In the gorse field, she thought she recognised him among the labourers, sleeves rolled up, pounding iron into earth, his factorship no impediment to sweating alongside the others.

She remembered how she had reached for him, soon after they'd arrived. Out of habit, as she had reached for other men. In Norway, it had been easy as an outsider. Almost any man would do: farm workers, whalers, minor officials. She sated herself on them, aroused by their fumbling disbelief as she pushed and gripped and scratched their flesh as if intending to break before she could be broken. But Haxton was no inconsequential encounter. She had seen him notice her and simply thought – if she had thought at all – to use it to their advantage. His expression as he pushed her away was more of horror than contempt. She noticed too late how, despite his height, he gave the impression of being weighed down, hammered like the houses. His eyes saw more than was there, the trouble in them more personal than a factor's worries over a beleaguered estate. His burden seemed heaviest when he was near the brae. Nils was right: he must never know they had found the gold plaque.

The accidental find haunted Lil. Its ambivalence unsettled her – was it meant as a talisman or curse, goddess or demon? She wanted very much to speak to Effie, who wouldn't care what it meant, only that they had found it. Anything else was an amusing aside. Lil recalled her making Nils recite what he could remember of an Icelandic story about the Mara, and clapping her hands in glee when the hag is unleashed upon an errant husband. Whatever the figure in the gold plaque was, it was just a story like all the others, like Lilith. There was no reason, no reason at all, to be unsettled by it – no more than by a ploughman in a field, a figure in a landscape.

A man rounded the corner of a stone outhouse, whistling to a collie, and nodded a greeting. Lil didn't respond. Her heart had lurched halfway up her throat even though she knew it couldn't be Mudie. *The spirit that attacks you at night will follow you.* Madelyn's words. As clear as the day Lil had left. *It is warning you of great danger.* She bit down on her lip. The danger, she had once believed, had all been left behind in the schoolroom.

It was almost two hours' walk into town. As she passed the bounds of the estate, her spirits began to lift. The farms further on were well kept, the fields orderly. Ploughmen sang as they worked, the flanks of their mighty Clydesdales gleaming even in the dull light. It was as if she were walking forward in time. Even to her untrained eye, the larger ploughs, barbed-wire fences, and noisy threshing machines doing the work of God knew how many men belonged to a different age. A modern one. Haxton's frustrations with the Pitcarden estate seemed justified. Any curse on this land would surely be mown down by steam-powered efficiency and smothered under artificial fertiliser. Even the preparations for Samhain – neatly stacked bonfires and cheerful, unlit turnip faces – seemed to have had all the paganism tidied out of them.

At Gledsmuir, she let herself be soothed by the chatter of a market town. The rolling carts, darting children, and ringing shop bells lifted some of the dread weighing on her. She could smell gingerbread baking, fresh horse dung, apples dropped and bruised, spat tobacco. Her stomach growled. She had taken nothing but whisky and tea since before dawn, but food was unthinkable before she called at the post office.

She gave her borrowed name at the counter, Miss Gerrard. It had belonged to a bright young woman with sharp brown eyes and plump cheeks, who had come with her mother to Madelyn's once and never again, although the older woman returned many times. Lil, who at fourteen had never had a friend, had been unable to stop thinking of her or imagining what her life might be. She was to be a governess, according to her mother, but aside from that, the only certain thing Lil could divine about Miss Gerrard was that she was able to come and go as she pleased, and that made her fascinating enough.

The clerk smiled cheerfully and stalked into the back to look for a letter. A surge of nerves made Lil place a gloved hand on the counter as if she doubted the strength of her legs. She didn't know what she was more afraid of – seeing a real, irrevocable letter in the clerk's hands, or nothing at all, and she would have to let the paper and ink, the very hand that held the pen, dissipate again into the hazy world of possibilities for another day.

The inner door was pulled open, and the clerk appeared, a cream envelope tucked between two fingers. Lil's heart bucked. He held it up briefly, higher than his head, as if making a bid, and then placed it in front of her, so she could see the confident sweep of black ink that spelled out the name Miss Gerrard, The Post Office, Gledsmuir. She stared at it in disbelief. It had *materialised*. The thought made her want to laugh madly.

'Was there anything else?' The clerk raised his eyebrows with a hint of impatience. There were others waiting.

'No.' She smiled in a way she knew could draw blood and, taking her time, picked up the letter with both hands – gingerly, as if it were a hedgehog he had placed in front of her. Without another glance, she bore it away into the street.

The bakery had a tearoom above it. She retraced her steps to the smell of gingerbread and found a table in a corner by the window. After ordering tea and a slice of Dundee cake, she found she was gripping the envelope so tightly her thumbs had made dents. She released it, almost apologetically, as if it were the doctor himself she had taken hold of. What had he written? What had he made of her letter? *Doctors are charlatans, my darling.* Madelyn had drummed it into her so well, it beat inside her along with her pulse. *Men of great arrogance and self-conceit – they don't know even the tiniest fraction of what they think they do.* Just because Madelyn herself knew a damned sight less than the doctors didn't mean she was wrong about them. Lil touched the lettering of her false name lightly. Her fingers shook. She picked up the table knife and sliced open the envelope.

Dear Miss Gerrard,
  I read your letter with the greatest interest and, I hasten to assure you, sympathy. It is not surprising that the trials you have had to bear and – I think I am right in assuming – bear alone, have made you question how such an admission might be received by those around you, particularly, I regret to say, members of the medical profession. Whatever some quarters of the press may have the public believe (aided, it is true, by a handful of deeply distressing but extremely rare examples of criminal malpractice), it is not the habit or desire of reputable doctors to institutionalise patients without very good cause and without the corroboration of peers, as is enshrined in law. You have nothing to fear from discussing your symptoms with me. Indeed, I could only wish that more of my patients were able to approach their experiences with such lucidity and so enquiring a mind.
I am grateful that you chose to write to me after reading my article. I must say it is a very encouraging sign that you took the somewhat courageous step of consulting a medical journal at all.

So, to your symptoms. You will understand that without examining you in person, there is a limit to the degree of certainty with which I can postulate a diagnosis or suggest treatment. (For the same reason, let us set aside for now the question of remuneration, which you kindly raised, until such time as we are able, with your consent, to proceed on a more conventional footing.) What I am able to tell you immediately, is that the night-mare, as you call your experience, is not uncommon. Medical psychology is an emerging science, which means, unfortunately, that the precise cause of these hallucinations is as yet unknown. However, it is my belief, as it is your hope, that a 'physical disorder' may lie behind the otherwise frightening visions. Hallucinations are well documented among the sane. It is also my belief, although not all my colleagues agree, that this night-mare is indeed distinct from a dream or ordinary nightmare, whether the sufferer is asleep at the time or not. You allude to an instance of it occurring during the day before witnesses, a repeat of which you fear this current spate is building towards. While I fully understand your reticence, I would urge you to consider that sharing the details of this painful experience, far from threatening your freedom, may well hold the key to setting you free from the night-mares — permanently.

    I hope these initial thoughts provide you with some measure of comfort. If you feel sufficiently reassured, I would gladly arrange an appointment for you at my practice in Albany Street. However, if you are still hesitant about meeting, perhaps you would feel comfortable answering questions by letter? It is extremely helpful — imperative, in fact — for an alienist to understand the personal circumstances of a patient in order to accurately assess the nature of their complaint. At present, I know very little of your history. Perhaps we could begin at the beginning, with your childhood and the unhappy period when you first began suffering the 'attacks'? How was your health otherwise? Had you experienced any shocks or accidents?

Whichever way you choose to proceed, I remain

> *Your faithful servant,*
> *Dr J. Lachlan*

It was like being plucked out of a raging torrent — against all expectation — and left gasping for breath on the bank. Lil put a hand to her chest to try to calm its heaving, ignoring the curious glances of those nearby. His reply was more wonderful than she had dared imagine . . . *It is my belief, as it is your hope . . .* There was nothing wrong with her. Or rather, there was — something joyously, palpably mundane, a hiccup in her anatomy, a kink that threw her senses out of order, nothing more. The return of the night-mare was a simple flare-up of an old complaint, nothing to do with Mudie or the schoolroom or Madelyn, whose voice had never left her after all these years, insinuating itself into her waking thoughts. *You are gifted, Lil.* It was over. She had found a different authority; she could encounter a thousand dark figures a day without blinking an eye.

The letter lay in her lap. She read his final paragraph again, then put a hand over it. It had been her intention — her vow — never to speak of her childhood or of Madelyn, certainly never to a medical man. But, of course, Dr Lachlan would have questions. She could invent a past, something eccentric, only not as dangerous as the truth. The precise details, surely, were irrelevant. The doctor's words in their neat lines seemed to beseech her innocently through the prison bars of her fingers. What was the point in seeking his advice if she hid the greater part of her life from him?

Because I have spent so long trying to leave it behind! The words were such a howl in her head, they nearly burst from her lips. She snatched her hand from the letter and rapped the table sharply with her knuckles. The waitress, who had been lowering the tea things, jumped, making everything on the tray rattle, and gave her a wounded look. Lil glared back and didn't help make space. She turned her face to the window again as the refreshments were laid out and caught sight of her own reflection. It was the faintest outline of her features in the glass, insubstantial, almost not there at all, spectral. Disgusted, she turned back and looked at the wedge of cake under her nose. Reassuringly, it was as spectral as an oak settle.

She would tell him then, everything. But through letters and as Miss Gerrard. His offer to make an appointment hung temptingly close for a moment. To speak of the night-mare without fear in the presence of someone who considered her neither insane nor mystical would have brought untold relief. She could see him, no longer behind his desk, but in a chair close to hers, leaning towards her slightly and listening with sympathy (his word!). Remembering the cake, she picked it up and shoved it triumphantly into her mouth. A woman decked in quantities of over-starched lace, who had been watching covertly since Lil had opened the letter, gave a theatrical gasp and covered her mouth with her fingertips. Lil returned her stare levelly and chewed with her mouth open.

The walk back was more cheerful. She allowed the brightness of the rosehips and rowan berries, the wild freedom of the geese filling the skies to the north in great skeins. Her heart still leaped whenever a figure appeared, pedlars or a postboy on the road, but she thought of Dr Lachlan and several times even forced herself to return a greeting. Her mind grew busy with the letter she would write – where to begin? He had suggested the very beginning. Simple enough to answer for most, no doubt. She remembered the rages she had wasted on Madelyn when she was old enough, the tearing of hair and screaming until her throat was sore and her voice hoarse, demanding over and over that she be told. And Madelyn, always the same – the patient, sacrificial air as she toyed with the locket at her throat, the locket that contained a picture of herself as a young woman and a print of Lil as a very small child. *As I have always told you, my darling.* The misty, helpless smile. *The spirits gave you to me.*

The hamlet came into view. A woman was walking ahead of her on the road, a bundle over her shoulder. The doors of the smithy's workshop stood open, and Lil could see the glow of sparks inside and hear the clanging of metal. After the letter and the ordinary human bustle of the town, she thought less darkly of their neighbours. They were only people making the most of what they had. Many of them would live and die on this spot; who could blame them for resenting outsiders coming to dig up their legends? When she and Nils left, they would have robbed them of their stories, their collective inheritance from generations past, more precious than gold. Something faltered in Lil, an uncomfortable awareness, like catching sight of her own reflection unexpectedly and not liking it.

The woman tripped and stumbled. Her foot must have caught again in her skirt as she lurched forward and landed heavily on hands and knees. The bundle fell onto the roadside and slumped open. Lil quickened her pace reluctantly. By the time she reached her, the woman was kneeling and brushing dirt and grit from her hands. Lil saw she was young, not yet twenty, and pregnant. She stooped to gather the bundle, which was spilling fabric and old children's shoes, and turned towards her. 'Are you hurt?'

A scream tore through the countryside and seemed to split Lil's head open. A sense of threat lashed her to the spot, as fierce and immediate as when she woke to the night-mare. The girl had thrown herself to the side, shrieking again, and scrambled to stand up, not minding her skinned hands. Her condition and clothes thwarted her, and Lil, still disorientated, still not grasping that she herself was the threat, took a step towards her.

'Awa wi ye!' The girl made a crab-like movement across the track and finally stood up, breathing heavily. She wrapped both arms tightly around her belly and turned her body away, hissing over her shoulder as if Lil were a snarling dog. 'Awa!'

Lil's heart pounded so violently she thought she would be sick. She could hear it beating outside of her body and growing dementedly louder. Her hand still grasped the bundle, but the girl was hurrying away, catching up her skirt as she half ran towards the hamlet. Figures had appeared in doorways and outside the smithy. A woman burst out of one of the cottages and ran, apron flying, towards her. Lil's heart thudded to a stop. A voice spoke.

'Give that to me.'

She flinched, thinking of Mudie, and turned a face towards the speaker that must have matched the girl's for terror. It was a different man, but one she knew well enough. Haxton was holding out his hand but looking towards the hamlet. Behind him, his horse blew through its lips and shook its head, blood still high from the gallop. Haxton turned impatiently. 'Give it to me and go.'

Lil moved two paces away from him. There was no sign of the girl, but others were there, watching her. The blacksmith's hammer was still in his hand. Without looking, she lifted the bundle an unhelpful distance, and Haxton stepped forward and snatched it away.

'Now go.' He turned back to his animal. She opened her mouth to tell him the girl had tripped, but snapped it shut again. He was soothing the horse, arranging reins. She watched the grim set of his face. As he made his way past her, he met her eyes briefly, angrily. Always behind his look, she saw the memory of how she had pushed herself on him. She turned away. At the edge of the trees, she found more crossed twigs and red thread hanging in the branches.

3

In her room, Lil changed again into work clothes, her fingers as unsteady as before, all generosity of spirit towards the hamlet's inhabitants crushed. The girl's scream, the terror in it, rang in her head. It was a disaster that Haxton had witnessed it. Nils didn't trust his warnings about Mudie; he believed the factor meant to take the gold for himself. It would be easy enough with Pitcarden's new owner in Australia, but Lil wasn't so sure. She yanked the laces tight on her boot and, as she did so, remembered her fingers around Haxton's collar, pulling him towards her. Her foot fell to the ground with a thud. Regret made her lean over, hands on knees, blood thick with it. It would be simple enough for Haxton to tell Mr Raube, regardless of his letters of permission, that these so-called archaeologists were moral outlaws, already the subject of gossip: a foreigner and a whore.

And the girl was pregnant. Lil's breathing grew short, and she pressed her fingers against her forehead. The urns from the first pit were boxed up in a corner. There was a large one, nearly fifteen inches tall, everted near the top and with the intricate markings common to Bronze-Age cinerary urns. Inside, surrounded by burned remains, they had found another smaller vessel, under three inches, also decorated. It contained, among more ashes, the still-intact molar of an infant. Impossible not to think of the curse and the cruel penalty it exacted on children. Impossible, too, not to think of Lilith. The old story clung to Lil, as if to claim her. The pregnant girl's scream of terror shivered over her skin again. *Awa wi ye! Awa!* It didn't matter what Lil called herself. It had happened anyway; she had become the blood-curdling myth.

She picked up the doctor's letter from the table and held it a moment, thinking how it had come from a mind schooled in logic and rational enquiry. The ink had flowed from a pen held by fingers ruled by that mind. His hands had held this very paper, his eyes run over the same words hers were reading now. It was a physical connection, the warmth and comfort of proximity. She longed to reply, to reach back to him immediately, but more of the hoard might have been found, and she didn't trust Nils to remember it was the burial they were studying, no matter what else they unearthed.

As she walked up to the barrow, she was dismayed to see the factor's horse tied to the gnarled hawthorn tree. The diggers were standing along the collapsed trench, shovels in hand but idle. They were watching Nils and Haxton who, Lil could see by their stance and Nils's hunched shoulders, were arguing. She walked quickly towards them. Haxton was finishing a sentence. '. . . when Mr Raube's home and not before.'

Nils's face was even paler than usual, his eyes rimmed red from lack of sleep, but also, Lil recognised, anger. It roughened his voice. 'The weather will stop us by then. We have his written permission. It is not for you to change his mind for him.'

Lil felt as if the sun had suddenly gone in. The factor's face grew blacker. 'While he is at sea and out of reach, I shall act in his best interests.'

'What is the trouble?' She tried not to sound sharp, and failed. Haxton eyed her darkly.

'Mr Raube is returning to Pitcarden.'

'I thought he was settled in Australia?'

'Ay.' It was clear Haxton didn't welcome the news either. 'You're to stop digging. You can take it up with him when he's here.'

Lil frowned. 'I don't understand. He has already given his consent.'

'Only out of ignorance.' Haxton threw a look of loathing across the site. 'He wasn't much more than a boy when he left; he doesn't understand the place. But he has a duty to the people here, as have I, and that extends to you.' His expression suggested the opposite. 'I cannot guarantee your safety the longer this goes on. What happened today should give you some idea of the feelings you're stirring up.'

'*Feelings?*' Lil felt Nils turn to look at her as she spoke. 'I startled the girl, that's all.' She hoped he had kept quiet about the pig's head and sabotage.

Haxton considered her a moment. 'Jenet is near her time. I can't answer for what they will do if the child miscarries.'

'They would blame me?' She felt a thud of fear, remembered Mudie's mirthless grin, the hammer in the blacksmith's hand.

'They would blame you for raising the hag. That's why Jenet ran. She's not often given to fancies, but the old tales carry more authority here than the minister.' Haxton's shoulders seemed to sag under the weight, and Lil wondered how he came to be so well acquainted with Jenet's fancies when he had only taken up his post recently. 'All Hallows is only a week away. People are already claiming they've seen the hag on the brae at night. Samhain is not a good time, not in this place.'

'For God's sake, it's probably me they're seeing. I . . . I don't sleep well. I sometimes walk out at night.' Haxton frowned at her, and Lil hurried on. 'And I have never seen any *hag*.' She took a breath and tried to imitate Effie's unanswerable, businesslike tones. 'Mr Haxton, this site is of national importance. Properly excavated, it could further our understanding of prehistory, of mankind. *And* we have permission. But you are telling me we must pack up and go home because of a fairy tale?'

He gave her a wry look, almost a smile. 'You could call that a lesson in mankind in itself.'

She felt Nils's eyes on her, but the words were coming anyway. Her own fears made them caustic. 'I wonder what it is you are most scared of, Mr Haxton? Is it children's stories or John Mudie?'

His expression soured instantly, and Nils jumped in. 'Please tell me, when does Mr Raube arrive?'

Haxton didn't take his eyes off Lil. 'Four weeks, perhaps. He will have business in London first.'

Nils started to bluster about the weather, but the factor's patience was at an end. 'You can come back in the spring if he's fool enough to allow it. If the burial is as old as you say, a few more months won't hurt.'

'It will be too late!' Something Swedish burst from Nils, and he walked off abruptly. Haxton watched him go, baffled into silence.

'Two weeks.' Lil could feel it all slipping away from her, faster than she could catch. 'Give us that at least. We can't dismiss the men without any notice – presumably your duty extends to them too.' She saw her little dart hit home and pushed on. 'You can tell them we shall backfill everywhere we have excavated. Mr Haxton, we are so close to uncovering the cist; it could hold something extraordinary. I'm sure . . .' She hesitated, wondering if what she was about to say was true. 'I'm sure when people see how special the brae is, what it means, the curse will be seen for what it is – a recent, colourful story in a much older history.'

Haxton's face had closed off. 'And what does it *mean*?'

'Excuse me?'

'You said, when they understand what the brae *means*.'

Lil stared at him without speaking. The cist, and whatever was inside, meant that she was right and that Madelyn was wrong. The dead didn't talk; they left things behind that Lil could hold and examine and preserve. She was safe. Every inanimate object, every decaying bit of matter she dug up meant there was no spirit stalking her, no vengeful hag, no curse waiting to be unleashed. After a moment, she cleared her throat. 'It means Pitcarden is a place of importance; people will know of it, future generations. We've come this far, Mr Haxton, let us have something to show Mr Raube when he returns.'

Haxton was shaking his head. 'You don't understand, Miss Vincent, you're not from here.'

'Then help me. Please.' She was almost begging. The question faltered on her lips, but she made herself ask it. 'Why does Mr Mudie hold such a grudge?'

He shifted and looked away for long moments. Eventually, it seemed that telling her was less trouble than not. 'He and his father were tenants on Westcraig Farm. It was hard. The older Mr Raube was raising rents – he became a recluse after his wife died and let the estate fall into the ruin it is now. They managed to hold on, but then he sold the farm out from under them. A neighbouring estate wanted to absorb it into one of its own. The Mudies lost everything. They didn't have the money to go elsewhere. John's father hanged himself. To support his mother, John had to work as a labourer on Westcraig, the same farm he should have been master of. He lost his fiancée too with his fall in fortunes.'

Lil nodded slowly, aware of a strange sense of relief. 'Nothing to do with the curse at all, then?'

'Everything about Pitcarden comes back to the curse in the end. It's the reason Raube became a recluse and abandoned his responsibilities in the first place.' The muscles worked around Haxton's mouth. 'When people can't control their own destiny, they look to what little they can control and put their faith in that. Keeping cursed treasure in the ground has been important for generations here for that reason. Even to Mudie on some level.'

Lil almost said out loud that he had explained in a sentence the great lure of the séance, the reason she and Madelyn had been able to fill their coffers each week. She chewed her lip.

Haxton was slowly, grudgingly, coming to a decision. 'You can have until the end of this coming week. But it must all be put back before Samhain. That's final.'

Negligent landowners, grudges, superstitions — all commonplace difficulties, not enough by themselves to drive them away, Lil thought. She hesitated, studying Haxton's face. Perhaps it was the trouble between crofters and their landlords making more southern factors wary. She missed Norway, where prehistoric monuments were a source of national pride, coveted even. No one at Pitcarden could care less about its history. She took in the hard line of Haxton's mouth and remembered how it had kissed hers back briefly before he had shoved her away. Her eyes lifted to his, and she saw them reading her thoughts.

'And for God's sake, stop wandering about at night. Keep away from Balcraig altogether.' Without another word, he strode back to his horse. Lil watched him go, feeling the weight of every opportunity she had lost.

At the mound, Nils was barking instructions at the men, telling them, she realised as she drew closer, to dig further into the wall perpendicular to the trench. It was where the gold plaque would have lain before the collapse. He was going after the hoard. Before she could speak, he caught her by the elbow and steered her towards his greatcoat, which was draped over something on the ground.

'Look. It is true.' He lifted the coat off a crate. Inside on a bed of moss was a gold ribbon torc, still smeared with dirt but unmistakable. Lil breathed in sharply and felt her heart jump out of rhythm.

'Is it . . . Could it be part of the burial?'

'No!' Nils was dismissive. 'It is later — it was near the other gold. I think it is part of the hoard, and whatever it was all buried in has . . . *pah!*' He flung his hand out, fingers spread wide – a vanishing. 'There must be more close by.' His eyes shone with a feverish, misty light that made Lil think of will-o'-the-wisps. 'I have offered the men a bigger fee to stay silent.'

'We still have to report it.'

Nils shook his head. 'Not yet. Not yet. But you must tell *her* now.' He took hold of her arm again and put his face close to hers. 'Draw this and the plaque and go tomorrow. She will know what to do about that man.' His head jerked in the direction Haxton had gone.

'I can send her the sketches. I need to be here to help – he's given us until the end of the week.'

'No. She will want to hear of this in person.'

'Then you go; she will be desperate to see you.'

He stooped to pick up the torc and put it in Lil's hands. 'You. You found it first, with the plaque.' He was almost pushing her down the hill and grinning wildly now.

She laughed uncertainly. It was true it would be a thrill to show Effie, but finding more of the hoard – even an object like this – was a disaster for the rest of the site. Nils's excitement was too feverish. She didn't understand why he was pressing her to leave now when time was so short.

He was holding on to her still, eyes boring into hers. 'This might be a most significant find. Not just in Scotland, in Europe!'

She nodded. 'But, Nils, the burial . . .'

He had already turned away, surprising his big frame into a slow run back towards the diggers.

Lil felt ambushed. She looked down at the torc in her hands, a very deliberately crafted piece of jewellery that had been made by people living how many years ago? Many hundreds. Thousands. Humans from prehistory. A wave of vertigo made her insides sway, and she was shot through with a bolt of energy that seemed — for the tiniest, most vivid instant — to skip across the ages and seal her living hands with those that were living then. It was true this could be the find of their lives.

She watched the men gouging earth and stones from the side of the trench with little care. Her work on the burial mound would never be clean and exact now, even if she were allowed to resume it in the spring. And for what? How far would this discovery of treasure take them in knowledge? If they could learn who first buried it, that would be something, but it was unlikely. These artefacts would remain beautiful but mysterious, showpieces in a museum or private collection, floating in conjecture. They would have to wait for other finds to help anchor them one day to a particular time and people. Until then — the torc seemed to grow dull in her hands — they would be mere baubles for collectors and antiquarians to chatter over like magpies. Lil wanted to find answers, or at least to narrow down the questions, to follow the small, pale flame of what could be known carefully into the dark until it was snuffed out by the weight of time. Buried treasure like this was a box of fireworks going off in the middle of it.

She ran her fingers over the bumps of turned metal, wondering whose rightful hands had done the same. It was different from the standing stone, which could be moved or carved or broken but would remain inexorably itself, hewn by forces other than man. This neck ornament was the product of progress in technology, skill and creativity. It couldn't have existed in this form if some human or humans had not willed it so. Those unrecorded desires and lost impulses bothered Lil. While others gloried in the relics themselves, she sought the intangible things they represented. She knew only one way to draw closer to them, to reach the very edge of what she might understand, little though that was.

Half an hour later saw her at the table, the torc carefully cleaned and arranged on a stand so as much light as possible could reach it from the window. Her pencil translated curve and line, shadow and gleam onto the page, finding out the shape and feel of the object, every flaw and inconsistency. It recorded details that might not have been noted since the torc was first made. She worked quickly with no discernible beat between what her eye saw and her hand sketched.

Once she was satisfied, she moved almost reluctantly on to the strange female figure of the plaque, as if she were afraid of looking at it for too long or too intently. Despite its primitive form, it exuded presence, an impression that it was capable of looking back. The more closely she studied it, the less crude it seemed. She became aware of a sense of her pencil point moving over skin, as if the figure could feel itself being replicated in a new medium, and somehow the connection between subject, eye and hand meant Lil could feel it too. She had experienced this before, covertly sketching portraits of Madelyn's guests to use in séances, when her pencil had flown so quickly, it was as if her fingers had been touching their faces at the same time. She thought of Dr Lachlan's pen flowing over the paper.

Her pencil came to a stop. She waited, conscious of a change in the room, a thickening at her right shoulder. Her heart quickened. A moment's hesitation, a creeping nearer, and she spun around. Nothing. Of course. She kicked the table leg, swearing at herself, and stared at the plaque. It was simple rather than crude, she decided: a large head with an expressionless face framed by plain hair or a headdress, eyes that could be either open or shut, breasts and slight hips showing nothing more than sex, and arms raised from the elbow but with empty hands. It was almost a template for a female entity. Any would fit: goddess, hag, Lilith, the Mara. She threw a cloth over it, then covered the drawing.

Tomorrow was Sunday, her favourite day. The men wouldn't work on the Sabbath, which meant she and Nils had the site to themselves. If the central trench had been widened enough, she could make good progress uncovering the cist. One more day, and she would send the sketches to Edinburgh on Monday. A sense of unease still lingered in the air. She leaned forward to pick up Dr Lachlan's letter as if it were a talisman. One more day, and she would also have time to reply.

4

Sunday 24th October

Dear Dr Lachlan,
Your letter has brought me inexpressible relief. Thank you. It is a beacon of light at a time that seems particularly dark. Something happened yesterday that made me feel as distant as it's possible to be from a world of reason and lucidity (a lovely word to find applied to myself in your letter and how fitting that its original meaning is 'light'). Maybe it contributed to the intensity of the night-mare this morning and the lingering unease, I don't know. It wasn't a figure at the end of my bed this time. I could feel things — four-legged things — crawling up my body. I was expecting some sort of monstrous creature, but when they came into view it was two little boys again, tiny children, eyes squeezed shut, mouths wide as if desperately hungry — I cannot describe them, or the sensation they created in me.

But you asked me to begin at the beginning, and I shall do so here. Forgive me for declining your offer of an appointment for the time being. My history is an unusual one. I was raised by a woman I believe to be my mother, a spiritualist medium, although she has never admitted our relationship, preferring to attribute my existence to the agency of spirits, and I have long since lost any faith in her supposed powers. We have had no contact for over ten years. My earliest memories are of the séances she held, which for me meant discomfort while I waited in dark, cramped spaces for my cue to pull a rope or begin singing or make knocking noises. Punishments for fidgeting or for falling asleep and missing cues — only natural in a small child — were severe, and I quickly acquired an unnatural mastery over myself. Looking back, I realise she was at the beginning of her career and success was critical for our survival. There was no one else upon whom she could take out her fears and frustration. It became much easier as she built up a reputation for materialisations. I do not know if you are familiar with the practices of such mediums — they were very popular in the seventies, but I believe have since lost their appeal, which is hardly surprising as such an outrageous assault on the world of reason could never be sustained for long. My mother followed the convention of having herself tied up in a 'cabinet', which for us was a curtain across a corner of the room, and if the sitters waited patiently, she would go into a trance and a 'spirit' would materialise.

It is painful for me to recall these years of my life. Perhaps it is most difficult because for a time, from my later childhood until I was about fourteen, knowing no other version of the world, I was a willing participant. I devised spectacles for the show séances and believed implicitly in my mother's gifts as a clairvoyant outside of them. I also received an education that I only realised much later was unique, certainly for a girl. My mother groomed me to be precociously well informed. What money we had was spent on tutors for every kind of knowledge — the sciences, languages, philosophy, history, literature — and I was trained just as thoroughly in presenting what I had learned and defending it. Ignorant of her reasons for raising me this way, I relished these lessons; they were my window to the world outside. Window is apt — there was no door to speak of. Except for occasional errands to the post box, my life was restricted to the house, my lessons all theory. She made a game of them with surprise tests and mock debates. But there was nothing for me to fear in a wrong answer, no such thing as failure. If I could not remember a fact, I was encouraged to make something up, and the more convincing the lie, the greater my reward.

In my fifteenth year, this strange but, in its own way, happy time was interrupted by the next stage of my mother's plans for me and by the recruitment of two people to our little household. By then the modest materialisations had made us enough money to employ a live-in maid, Agnes, and my many tutors were all replaced by one, a man who had recently become a part of the circle, a Mr Lambert. He began to spend much of his time at our house, pushing me to work harder at my lessons. The joy went out of learning, and I grew to fear the way his moustache twitched whenever I disappointed him.

For myself, I was to make my debut in a new line for us as an automatic writer. I was made to sit for hours to practise. At first, I struggled to understand what was required of me. My mother never alluded directly to our deceptions — she always talked about 'helping' the spirits to join in, and so I was encouraged to write a little of whatever came to mind until an amenable spirit might decide to take over. Of course, none ever did, but my stiff limbs and great boredom from being forced to sit for so long were motivation enough to make me complicit in my mother's lies without us ever having to discuss it. I wasn't sure for a long time if it weren't in fact me deceiving her. My pen began to talk, as it were, and would answer questions put to it with just enough clarity to sound convincing, but intermittently and against a background of confused and meaningless word groupings. Different voices began to emerge, all with different opinions and areas of knowledge. My wide-ranging education began to make sense.

The first circles I performed at publicly were small gatherings of trusted sitters, all with their own reasons for playing along. As my confidence and abilities grew, others were allowed to join, and my lessons with Mr Lambert became exceptionally specialised. If a chemist were to join the circle on a Friday evening, Mondays to Thursdays were spent cramming my head with the latest papers he and his peers had written. If a man of business were to attend, I would be steeped in the latest news and concerns of his industry, my brain bursting with the movements of markets. And so on, for lawyers, novelists, doctors, educators, speculators, politicians. Mr Lambert had contacts; he and Madelyn were attempting to raise our profile from respectable mediums (who nonetheless didn't mind charging a fee) to something altogether more sought after and lucrative. If any of these new sitters had particular interests that could be found out, I became faux expert in those too. Once they were at the table and the lights lowered, our hymn singing and other rituals completed, we invited questions for the spirits. We would wait patiently – sometimes for half an hour or more – for an answer to come through my hand, and I became adept at writing with my eyes closed or staring ahead as if in a trance.

It is surprisingly easy to amaze people. Even those who, I suspect, came only to test the spirits quickly flushed or grew pale as my scrawls were read out. Perhaps if I hadn't looked so very young, a pale grub plucked from under a rock, blank and docile, they might have questioned it more. But I think not. Their own minds worked to legitimise my words and in doing so made substance out of nothing. The chemist one week excitedly reported that he had followed a spirit's advice and used nitric acid in an experiment, succeeding where he had previously failed. Reading back over those pages, I found I had *suggested no such thing, but had mentioned the acid in some garbled nonsense about explosives while pretending to be a dead German chemist. His own brain had made the connection, but he recalled the instruction as coming from the spirits directly and would have sworn so in a court of law.*

My experiences of the night-mare began around this time. To answer your question, I suffered no shock or accident, but they coincided with the beginnings of my doubts about my mother and the way she practised spiritualism. Although I took pleasure in the challenge of the séances, feelings of unease were forming wordlessly underneath. It would take many months and terrible scenes before I voiced them, and even longer before I was able to break from that life. I am sure it will come as no surprise to you that my mother interpreted my waking night-mares as supernatural. She insisted that the strange sensations and accompanying terror were to do with my 'control' — a spirit that was trying to speak to me and through me that was growing stronger through my writing. She said it was trying to warn me of great danger, and the figure I saw sometimes standing by my bed, sometimes kneeling on my chest to strangle me, was a shadow of the future. I came to believe it was Lambert.

One of his enhancements to our act was to introduce spirit photographers. The Misses Drake were monosyllabic sisters who set up their apparatus during séances and returned with images the following week that showed ghostly forms floating behind the sitters. My mother laughed at them privately, out of professional jealousy and resentment at their fee, I believe. She referred to them only as 'the sisters most sisterly', perhaps because they looked nothing alike. But she made good use of them. They were often instructed to point the camera at me, and the pictures would duly show a shadowy figure lurking by my shoulder. I remember the strange intensity in their eyes as they watched for my reaction. It was hard to dismiss what I saw at the time. The thought that the night-mare might haunt me wherever I went, even when I couldn't see it, froze my blood. My mother convinced me I would be safe only for as long as I stayed close to her, that our combined gifts would ward off the evil. It was another excuse to keep me in the house out of sight and to discourage me from walking abroad.

Forgive me for ending this letter here. I am finding the unearthing of these memories painful. Perhaps it will grow easier, but I trust I have revealed enough for the time being. I remain inexpressibly grateful for your interest and patience.

Yours sincerely,
Miss Gerrard

Lil put a hand to her chest; it was tight with rage and some writhing, nameless anxiety. The world she had been born into and embraced for most of her life overwhelmed her again like a cold wave. The *waste*. The degradation. Their séances had been a pit people willingly fell into (save those who saw them for the intellectual squalor they were and never returned). She loathed them all, the boneless dupes, who swallowed every stupefyingly obvious piece of fakery they were fed, swelling up with it like ticks, and the knowing, smiling, greasy-souled gentlemen who turned up to fondle and kiss the 'spirit', confident that none there would bat an eyelid. The spittle-gleam on Lambert's teeth as he leered towards her, his fingers pinching the curve of her waist, and the prickling of his moustache against her cheek remained as vivid to her senses as if he had only just left the room.

But her greatest contempt was reserved for Madelyn. Lil's ineffectual rages had finally blown themselves out, leaving only the arid and aching conclusion that this woman was her mother, and her father some long-gone stumble or violence. It was typical of

Madelyn's talent for self-invention that she could spin a painful past into a tale of supernatural beneficence, even if it meant disowning her own daughter. Lil had looked for evidence of kinship and found it in the narrowness of their shoulders, the shapeliness of their brows, and the surprising movement their heads made on the rare occasions either of them laughed out loud. She had caught her own reflection once when Agnes tripped head first through the cabinet curtains, and had seen something like a cormorant trying to swallow an eel.

Liar. Fraud. Hypocrite. That was her parent. She might have painted Lil's fingers with phosphorous oil, sewn secret pockets into dresses, even cut holes in the ceiling, but none of it stopped her from claiming real clairvoyance and second sight. Lil's days and nights, when she wasn't occupied with pure theatre, were filled with the relentless business of the dead, their portents and demands. Her maybe-mother wouldn't leave them alone, prodding and toying with the spirits as she did the fake jewels in her locket. Lil could have forgiven her if she had been a simple crook.

Three loud raps sounded at the front door. Lil startled. She thought instantly of the pig's head and twig symbols and leaped from her chair. Looking wildly around, she grasped an awl she had used to scrape dirt from the urns and forced herself to walk into the kitchen. She wrenched the door wide. On the other side was a woman. Young, sharp-featured, pregnant. The girl from the road. Lil almost slammed the door shut again. Behind her, the stable boy from Pitcarden stood scowling beside a pony and cart.

Lil breathed in. 'Yes?'

Something sharp was said, a statement. Lil waited for the Scots to make sense. Comprehension seemed always just within her reach if she would only wait long enough, like the use or meaning of an ancient object lifted from the earth. This time it failed her. The girl watched in remorseless silence, and Lil was reminded of a scolding she had received in Norwegian, probably from the wife or family member of a fisherman she had consorted with. Like then, she stared back, in the dark but giving no ground.

Slowly a gleam surfaced in the hazel eyes, a relenting. The girl gestured with a jerk of her head behind her and spoke slowly. 'We've brocht ye a bittie whin, frae the ferm.' The boy moved to the back of the cart and re-emerged with a huge armful of woody roots. Gorse, from the field clearing. He advanced on the door, so Lil was forced to step back, and dumped them by the coal scuttle.

'For burnin.' The girl had also stepped across the threshold. Lil flinched slightly. The 'cursed' objects were on the table only a few feet away through the open door of the bedroom. There was a silence as the boy made two more trips. Lil slid the awl onto a shelf while the girl's eyes darted hungrily all around the room. After the last load, there was a frosty exchange, and to Lil's dismay, the boy left alone, tugging the pony back towards the road. She turned questioningly. The girl only shrugged. 'I shuidna be here.'

Hairs prickled at the back of Lil's neck. 'Then perhaps you should go.'

Without answering, the girl stepped towards a box of trowels and knives. Lil moved with her and put a hand over it. 'You're Jenet, aren't you?'

Jenet looked at her sideways and lifted her chin but didn't reach for the tools.

Lil didn't move her hand. 'My name is—'

'Lilian.' The girl jumped in with it, eyes gleaming again. Lil's heart gave a frightened jolt; she had thought for a moment Jenet was going to say Lilith. She swallowed and spoke slowly.

'Miss Vincent. Lil. I frightened you on the road the other day. I meant no harm, but I would prefer it if you didn't come here.'

Jenet turned without speaking and wandered towards the fireplace, still drinking in every detail. Cursing under her breath, Lil went to the door and shut it against the possibility of prying eyes. She also closed the bedroom door.

'I thocht ye war the hag.' Jenet's nose twitched, as if assailed by a brief and unpleasant smell. 'Dunderheidit.' She didn't wait for a response, and in any case, Lil felt no need to correct her. 'Dunderheaded' seemed perfect, the word she hadn't known she was looking for. Jenet shrugged again. 'Hugh says ye're no daein ony hairm.'

'Hugh?'

A look of mild surprise was turned towards her. 'Ay.' Then with a clear sense of pride, 'The factor.'

Haxton. It was Lil's turn to raise her eyebrows. Jenet grew a little taller. 'He's ma ma's brither.'

Her uncle. A native of Balcraig. Lil's heart took the blow and promptly sank. It explained his familiarity with the people, and his stubbornness about the excavation. She looked at the door, wondering how to get Jenet back through it and quickly, but the girl was gently touching her fingers to a wall lamp – the cruisie type so common here – as if she'd never seen one before. 'He says ye're no efter the treasure.'

'We're not.' It shot from Lil's mouth like a panicked bird. She felt a stab of anger at Nils for making a liar of her. 'It's an excavation. We study . . .' she swerved the word burial, '. . . how people used to live, from what they've left behind.'

'Ye dinnae believe in the curse, than?' Jenet dropped her hand and looked straight at her. Lil didn't know if it were in judgement or awe.

'No.' She found she couldn't hold Jenet's eye and looked down. 'Do you?'

'Ma ma daes. She maks me weir this.' Jenet hooked something out from under her collar: dried red berries strung along a red thread.

'What does that do?'

'Rowan; it wards aff evil. Awbody's cairryin it. But for Hugh. An Mungo winnae weir his tae toun. Kirstie says she daesna trew in the curse but she aye weirs ane aroond her wrist, I've seen it . . .'

Jenet pulled out Nils's chair and lowered herself down, still talking about neighbours and family members. Lil couldn't follow half of it but became aware of a pang, a bruise against her heart, and after several searching moments identified it as envy. Names and events were rattling out of Jenet as if it were a given that the whole world should know whose daughter Kirstie was, or that Jenet's own father had burned his hand badly on the forge last spring. She belonged unthinkingly. Lil remembered how fascinated she had been with Miss Gerrard's freedoms, the certainties she had never known she missed before.

Jenet was growing more at ease as she talked. One arm stretched across the table, her fingertips bumping an iron arrowhead that had been Nils's first find. He took it with him everywhere. She picked it up.

'Ma ma never lat us by the brae. I wantit tae. Hugh says it's a grave unner yonder, aulder nor oor ain folk . . .' She carried on talking, and Lil let the words wash over her, some catching like light, others tumbling past in the rushing stream. She tried to imagine being so settled, enjoying sitting for a spell with a neighbour, not minding what was said so much as knowing it was listened to.

'Is this auld?' Jenet was staring at her again, holding up the arrowhead.

Lil blinked. 'Yes. But it's from Norway. An arrowhead.'

Jenet scrutinised it for a moment, turning it in her fingers. She looked up. 'Can I see something ye've howkit oot the brae?'

Lil frowned, not really wanting to understand. 'Howk . . .'

'Howkit.' Jenet stared at her stubbornly. 'Can I see whit ye *dug up*?'

There was a pricking at the back of Lil's neck again. She became painfully aware of the torc and plaque. Too close. She watched Jenet run her hand over her swollen belly.

'I can show you one thing. And then I must get back to work. Wait here.'

She hurried into the bedroom but baulked at bringing even a cinerary urn near the girl. Returning to the kitchen, she shut the door firmly behind her and placed the wrapped-up bronze blade with its remnant of sheath on the table. Carefully folding back layers of cloth, she was struck again by the sheer fact of its existence. No one but herself had touched it since it had come quite literally to light under her trowel and brush, meeting the sun again after eras had passed and the world had changed into something new. But here it was, proof of that different time, before Pitcarden or Balcraig were even words. It was a message in a lost language.

Jenet's eyes widened. 'A knife?'

'It's very fragile, don't touch.'

Lil began a stilted explanation of grave goods. She spoke naturally, it being clear Jenet understood more English than she was willing to speak. As the girl listened, Lil described more fluently how she had identified the cow hide covering the scabbard using warm turpentine and a microscope. She had been allowed to compare the hairs on her slide to those preserved on untanned shoes in the museum in Edinburgh. Jenet listened eagerly, her face hanging over the artefact as if she would pour herself into it. Eventually, she sat back.

'Div ye think thay war like us? The folk?' She ran a hand over her belly again, and for a moment, Lil thought of the baby buried in her womb rather than the prehistoric bones in the brae. The movement gave her a queer feeling, like holding the torc, a vertiginous collapsing of millennia to one point in time, all present, all within the present. She looked at Jenet with greater interest; it was a question she had often asked herself.

'I would like to find out.'

Jenet folded her arms across her chest and regarded Lil solemnly. 'An whit will ye dae if ye find the treasure?'

Lying at least came easily, if not willingly. Lil busied herself wrapping up the blade. 'The treasure is just a legend, Jenet. It doesn't exist.'

'Ay, it daes.' The girl's protest was loud enough for anyone outside the cottage to hear. Lil glanced nervously at the window as Jenet sat up straighter. 'Mr Raube – that's deid – he howkit hit up on Samhain, twa year afore I wis born. Hugh wis thare.' She glowered and said something too low to hear.

'What?' Lil squinted at her. 'The older Mr Raube . . .'

Jenet glared at her. 'He howkit hit up. The treasure.'

Lil sat back. 'Oh. And what happened?'

'Ma aulder sister *dee'd*.' Jenet spoke fiercely, almost daring Lil not to understand. 'She wis jist a bairn. And Mr Raube wisnae for pittin hit back. Sae the stables brunt doun.'

Fear crept up Lil's back. 'You mean, someone set fire to the stables on purpose?' She thought of Mudie. He would have been a young man then. 'Your sister died, and they believed it was Mr Raube's fault because he wouldn't rebury the hoard?'

Jenet looked away. 'Naebody speaks muckle aboot it. But I ken the treasure was yirdit . . .' She threw Lil a sharp look, '*buried again, wi a new thing.*'

'A new thing?'

Jenet rolled her eyes extravagantly. 'Ye dinnae ken muckle, div ye? The war fower pieces o gowd.' She held up four fingers as if she were speaking to an idiot.

The memory – her inherited memory – had upset her, and Lil realised too late she should have offered sympathy before expecting secrets. But Jenet clearly wanted to talk as much as she wanted to punish Lil, and eventually the story was told in a way Lil could understand. Every time the hoard is dug up, it must be reburied with something new, something precious to the offender, or the hag takes her revenge on the youngest children. Raube had dug up four pieces of gold many years earlier.

Jenet thrust her chin towards the brae. 'So noo the'r *five* tharawa.'

Lil remembered the sunshine in Norway, the light in Effie's eyes as she talked about old Raube's heirloom. 'A brooch. He buried the lover's knot brooch.'

Jenet frowned and then shrugged. 'Ma ma said it wis a ring. It's gowd onywey. Ye're boond tae find it afore lang.' Her eyes met Lil's again, their expression unreadable.

Lil watched her closely. 'Does that worry you? Are you frightened of the curse?' Perhaps that was why she had come to the cottage, to make sure Lil knew about her sister and how to stop the hag.

The latch on the door shot up, making them both jump. Nils appeared and stood in pale consternation at the sight of a pregnant woman in his seat. Jenet pulled herself to her feet as Lil introduced them. Before she left, her gaze lingered on the wrapped-up knife. 'Will ye shaw me mair o it? The grave guids?'

Lil hesitated. 'If your uncle agrees.' She watched Jenet's lip curl as her own would have done.

Once the girl had disappeared into the darkening afternoon, Nils fell into the chair with a grunt and a wary look. They had argued earlier. The central trench hadn't been dug out at all as Lil expected; he had kept all the diggers looking for the hoard. Her precious Sunday with the cist was ruined. He agreed to put a man to it on Monday, but they remained in bad temper with each other. Lil told him about Haxton's ties to Balcraig, how his motives for stopping the dig were personal. But Nils was more interested in the curse itself.

'Samhain again. When the veil between the living and the dead is thinnest. I wonder.' He heaved himself up to retrieve a book from a pile in the box-bed. 'Carlin is another name for the hag goddess Cailleach who arrives at Samhain to rule over winter. I wonder if the Carlin stones in this area have a special association with the festival.' He gave Lil one of his big smiles, inviting her to share his enthusiasm. 'Maybe it is the origin of our curse. The cold months are a dangerous time for sick children.'

'It's always female entities, isn't it?' Lil was dour. 'Goddesses, demons, whoever.'

The smile faded from Nils's face. 'Hm?'

'The things that hurt children. They are always female.'

'Oh. Well.' Nils frowned and then began to look interested. 'Yes, I think that is so. In most cases. The female can also be protective, or a symbol of fertility.'

'Still. Childbirth, children. A narrow role for immortal beings, you would think.' Lil was thinking of Jenet's baby, so soon to make its perilous journey into the world, but remembering the girl's proud and youthful face, her thoughts changed tack. 'And seducing men, of course.'

The girl's attitude had called to mind Rossetti's painting of Lilith. In it, she is portrayed as a sensual, self-absorbed temptress, an echo of the mythical version that preyed on men in the night as a succubus – in addition to killing newborns.

Nils cleared his throat and put his head on one side, thinking. 'Perhaps it is the interpretation that is sometimes narrow, not the myth itself. After all, a deity or demon's power lies only in what people choose to believe about them, and that can change over and over.'

Lil recalled where all her information about Lilith had come from: Madelyn, books written by men, artists' depictions. 'What we choose to believe – or what is chosen for us.'

'Yes.' Nils gave an emphatic nod.

Lil thought of the standing stone. Perhaps the original myths were as old and enduring as rock, their true nature obscured by the shadows of time and human need passing over them. Her eyes fell on the whin roots. It would have been Haxton who had sent them, an offering of fire and warmth in their last week here before Samhain. All Hallows, the night of the dead. An apology perhaps. Forgiveness wasn't to her taste, however, and she wasn't ready to make peace with Nils yet either. She picked up the bronze knife and closed the bedroom door behind her with unnecessary force.

Placing the blade safely in a crate, she thought of Jenet's question about the Bronze-Age people and realised they had something in common with the girl that Lil didn't. They belonged here. In death as in life. The ancient people's beliefs, whatever they were, bound them to this land. She glanced at the cinerary urns and for the first time questioned the decency of removing them for public display. What desecration had she so blithely committed? What gods offended?

She reached for her letter to Dr Lachlan and read it to herself. It sounded so confident, so sure, stuffed with an angry and iron-clad scepticism. She picked at her thumbnail, still rimmed with dirt from the day's work, and wished her words ran deeper than the paper they were written on. She wished they ran all the way through her like a trench of virgin earth, but if it were possible to excavate the human heart, she suspected her own would yield up all manner of ghouls and cursed objects. There had been séances where she had seemed to come to suddenly and have no memory of what she had written. Her pen had scored series of numbers, one to five, occasionally a frantic six, which could easily be dismissed, but other times there had been fragments of sentences too. One had repeated itself, which she had never been able to forget: *new bones over old*.

It had also thrummed at her nerves to write of the night-mare so dismissively. Something deep within her pulled in alarm, as if *it* were watching, its return another warning. And today, her skin had crawled in horror at Jenet's presence in her kitchen, so close to the artefacts. No, the version of herself that walked in the light, tossing her head at folk tales and Madelyn's lies, was a suit of clothes she put on, willing herself to grow into it. It had worked for a while. Before she had arrived at Pitcarden, she had almost forgotten there was anything underneath at all.

She shivered and pulled her shawl up over her nose to warm her face with her breath. After a moment's thought, she scratched out the names of the Drakes, Lambert and Agnes. She hadn't even begun to describe the insidiousness of Madelyn's maid, but that would have to wait. With the letter sealed – she knew the address by heart – she put it in her pocket, meaning to send it with the estate post from the main house. She paused, fingers still loosely holding the envelope. It would take one man most of Monday to uncover the cist, which left her free to deliver the sketches in person to Effie after all. Her heart ached at the thought. And then lifted, sharply. Edinburgh was where Dr Lachlan lived and worked.

5

Lil's eyelids prised themselves open enough to let in a dim light. A hissing sounded nearby, and there were other, confused noises, voices among them. She was waking up, but disjointedly, as if consciousness were being dug up with a shovel. Dread rose steadily. She wasn't in bed. Her body was at all the wrong angles. But she could sense the figure. It was moving. Fingers touched her arm.

'Miss.'

She jerked violently, swivelling away, and found herself pressed into the corner of a train compartment. The conductor, eyes averted, explained stiffly that they were in Edinburgh. Passengers tramped past the window; machinery hissed and clanked. Wiping the side of her mouth, Lil felt her body slowly recalibrate itself. Last night, she had put off going to bed until the small hours, letting the wind and squalls of rain outside the cottage bully her into wakefulness. She hadn't walked on the brae, mindful of being mistaken for a hag. When she did crawl into bed, she bolstered herself upright with a pillow. Her reward was a groggy head and stiff neck. But no night-mare.

The station echoed loudly with footsteps, shouts and whistles, as if the air above were as busy with folk as the ground below. She discovered she was out of kilter with city life. Her pace was too slow or too fast, her bag bumped people, her feet misstepped.

She was jostled, frowned at, and turned around before she had even made it up onto the street. It reminded her of her first real taste of London – the disorientation and crush – when she had run away from Madelyn. Then, the city had knocked her off her feet, flung her about like a rag doll between impatient bodies, farting horses, and a thousand hard and moving surfaces, before finally dumping her at the door of the Sullivans. Madelyn's dire predictions had roared in her head, sounding louder and truer than they ever had coming from Madelyn herself. For a long time, whenever Lil left the Sullivans' house, it was in full expectation of being murdered.

Beyond Princes Street, she began to recover her balance. She felt her pulse quicken with anticipation. Effie's house lay much further down the hill and to the west, but she could see the corner of Albany on the right; she must have walked past it dozens of times without a thought. It was a matter of expedience, she told herself – why post a letter when she could more conveniently deliver it by hand? But her heart was fluttering about as if it were on a quite different errand, and when she turned into the street itself, it began barrelling around her chest like a boot in a butter churn.

The neighbourhood was well-to-do, its terraced houses tall and spacious, the road wide and well swept. She eyed each man she passed with a furtive scrutiny, wondering if it could be him. In her mind he was forty or fifty, perhaps with a beard, soft skinned, attentive. But he could be this old grandfather, sunken-cheeked and bent-backed, or this large man waving his paper around as he talked to – could it be him? – a smiling young man with a sharp look. The look landed on Lil. She turned her head away and held her breath until she was past. The numbers on the doors told her she was on the right side. She was overtaken by a servant in white cap and apron and became convinced it was *his* parlour maid coming back from an errand until the girl crossed the street to a different house.

It was coming up quickly. Black door, brass knocker, plaque. She nearly walked straight past, but halted at the steps as if a hand had reached out, palm flat against her chest. Nerves, disagreeable, were taking over. She felt as if there were eyes at every window. A letter box beckoned. She took the envelope from her pocket and stepped up between the railings. Her fingers touched the flap, paused, and then swiftly, as if tricking her, reached for the knocker and rapped it three times. It sounded unnaturally loud. Her eyes became fixed on the plaque nailed to the wall. *Dr J. E. Lachlan MD, FRCPE.* She took a sudden breath in, as if just waking up. What was she thinking? Gathering her skirts, she turned quickly to retreat down the steps and immediately heard the door opening.

'Yes?'

A woman's voice. Slowly, Lil faced her. An elderly servant, so neat and stern in appearance, the very lines on her face seemed etched on purpose. She observed Lil as if mentally making a report. Lil offered her the envelope, whispered a thank you, and stepped hastily down to the street. The door shut behind her before she had reached the pavement. She hurried across the road and turned again to look at the house.

A minute or two passed. She didn't know what she was expecting — Dr Lachlan to burst out, letter in hand, looking for her? More than likely he wasn't there at all but at the hospital. Her heart thudded away anyway, expectant. A carriage rolled by; a nurse wheeled a pram; leaves were carried into the gutter by a chill wind. The door remained shut, the windows dark. She didn't want to move. A warmth had spread through her that seemed dependent on proximity. He lived here. It was from here that he had written to her. She felt the sweep of his pen again as if it were moving across her skin. If she left, she must go to Effie, to suffering and loss and the impotence of her own grief. She wanted to stay in the warmth of his strength and reassurance, as if to stand in his street facing his house were to stand in his embrace.

A cab turned the corner and rattled past. She couldn't put off Effie any longer. Or what she had become. She understood now why Nils was actively following her wishes to stay at the site; he didn't want to face her illness or watch it gnawing her body. Perhaps that was why he had lost interest in the burial, concentrating only on finding the bauble that had taken Effie's fancy, the brooch.

Another cab clattered down the street as she took a last look at the house and began walking towards the corner. The cab slowed behind her and, looking back, she watched it pull up outside Dr Lachlan's door. At the same time, she caught sight of movement in one of the windows on the ground floor. It was only a glimpse in the dim interior, but she recognised the tall figure of the woman who had taken her letter stepping back quickly from the glass. If she hadn't moved, Lil realised, she would have been nearly invisible. There was no way of knowing how long she had been watching. Lil's insides turned gelid. The driver flicked his whip, and the cab cleared her view.

Dr Lachlan. She was certain. He was standing on the pavement, one hand delving into the inside pocket of his coat, perhaps having just paid the driver, a small portmanteau at his feet. He glanced down the street before bending to retrieve his bag, and their eyes met – brushed past – the impersonal glance of strangers. Only, an incendiary thud, like a struck match, set her insides alight. She walked on a few paces, the image of him still before her eyes: about thirty-five, almost stocky in build – his upright posture lent him just enough elegance – with flaxen hair worn longer than the fashion and a beard trimmed close. She glanced back again at the corner. He was climbing the steps. In the doorway, the tall woman stood waiting. She was looking across the street, directly at Lil.

At Effie's house, the housekeeper, Bina, answered the door and beamed comfort upon her disordered soul.

'Oh, Miss Vincent! You are here!' She clasped her hands together and appeared to quiver with emotion. Lil smiled faintly up at her round face, which, though middle-aged, never failed to give the impression of girlhood. She didn't know what made her so pleased always; Lil had never been kind. In the hall, she set down her bag with relief.

'How is she?' She began peeling off layers. Bina tried to do it for her, so they were all hands and bumping fingers and Bina's apologies. She didn't answer immediately.

'This week was better.' There was an oddness to her voice that made Lil stop undoing her coat to look at her. Bina was putting her gloves on the hall stand and somehow knocked a figurine of a shepherdess on a side table as she did so. She gasped and caught it before returning in an embarrassed fluster and pouncing on Lil's coat buttons. 'She's been sitting up – oh, excuse me – in the drawing room for most of it. It will do her the world of good to see you.'

'I'll go straight up.'

'I'll put your bag in your room. Would you like tea?'

'No.' Bina's face fell. 'But wait.' Lil retrieved her leather folder from the bag before Bina took charge of it and then followed her up the first flight of stairs. The door to the drawing room was shut. Lil faltered again. Part of her wanted to turn tail and run all the way back to the station, to join Nils in his self-deception. She became aware of the scent of lilies from an arrangement on a side table, their smell of decay. A grandfather clock ticked accusingly.

With a sharp shake of her head, she reached for the door and quietly opened it.

The fire was built up high, making the room almost too warm for the healthy, certainly for one who had been rushing through the streets. It spat and snapped in the grate as if it had taken over the ticking of the grandfather clock but had abandoned its rhythm and order. Seconds and minutes behaved differently in a sickroom. Time was fraying, its ends probing the darkness for a continuing thread and finding none. Effie lay on a sofa, propped up by cushions and swathed in the Indian shawls she loved. Her eyes were closed and her mouth slightly open, the corners pulled down by slack muscle and skin, so she appeared to be grimacing. Strands of greying hair had come loose and lay on the cushions at unflattering angles. Lil made herself look. This was how Effie would appear when she was gone, when there was nothing left of her but decaying matter still masquerading for a short time as the living woman. She imagined staring at her as she was now, but in the knowledge that she would never wake up, that the shape of the bones and the yellowing flesh were all that remained. An intense loneliness ran through her like a blade. Then came a fury so wild she couldn't keep it in. She stamped her foot and coughed loudly. Effie started awake at the noise and turned her blue eyes on Lil.

Blue eyes. Mesmerising, Lil had thought on first seeing them and then was furious with herself for using the word. Mesmerism was not one of Madelyn's own practices, but she had a friend, a 'doctor', who came to the house to 'treat' her. The sessions always took place in her bedroom rather than the parlour or séance room, and even when Lil was too old to be deceived any longer, Madelyn continued to insist that mesmerism was all that took place. There seemed little that Lil could keep pure and untainted by Madelyn, even once she had left. She hadn't been far from her thoughts the day she'd met Effie in the British Museum. Lil was sketching as usual – any free time away from the Sullivans' children was spent with her pencil. That day it was a plaster cast of a grotesque with a hideous face. She didn't notice anyone on the bench beside her until a voice spoke.

'Reminds me powerfully of my sister-in-law.'

Lil turned and met the blue eyes. She had seen the upright, well-dressed figure striding about the halls before, sometimes alone and sometimes with a large, pale man, aware of them as she was of everyone on some level. It irked her to be interrupted, but the woman's gaze was so penetrating, it burned straight past gripping thoughts and seemed to illuminate her inner mind. Lil, mesmerised, was thrown off guard. 'It looks like one of my night-mares.'

Effie allowed one corner of her mouth to twitch. 'Precisely.'

Shocked at having spoken openly to this stranger, Lil took a moment to understand she had made a joke and then surprised herself further by wanting to laugh. Humour had never been made a habit in her life, not in Madelyn's suffocating company and still less in the Sullivans' household with their self-regarding earnestness. She looked at the woman as if she had suddenly doffed her tasteful hat and whipped out a rabbit. Her accent was unplaceable; refined, but with extra notes that could have come from anywhere. Effie was looking at the sketchpad on Lil's knees.

'You're very good. I've seen you here before and peeped over your shoulder once or twice. Are you a student?'

Lil blinked. 'I'm a governess.'

'Oh dear!' Effie sounded amused. 'Although I suppose if you like other people's children, that's all right. Do you?'

'No.' Lil blinked again. 'I mean . . .' She cast about for a caveat – teaching children had its rewards, centred mainly around the fact that it wasn't spiritualism – but the woman's abrupt dismissal had chimed instantly with her deepest feelings, and she repeated herself. 'No. I hate being a governess.'

'Oh, then why do you do it?'

Lil bit down on her lip. She was starting to recover from the shock of the encounter and take the measure of this mesmerist: one of those well-to-do, infinitely cushioned women who considered themselves brazen Amazons of social causes, unafraid to challenge society, and all the while unaware it was their own social position that gave them licence to be heard and indulged at all, never mind to squeeze a toe in the door of a university or pursue a profession. Madelyn's séances were full of the type, women of leisure and means and righteous fire, who were perfectly capable of asking a governess *why she did it.*

Effie snapped her fingers. 'Absurd question. What am I saying? It's only that you strike one as having an uncompromising nature. I mean that as a compliment.' She was correcting herself before Lil had even finished her thought. The older woman gazed at her again, a smile hovering about her lips. 'I won't intrude any more on your sketching. This time must be precious to you.'

'I don't mind. Thank you for the compliment.' Lil shocked herself for the third time in as many minutes. She looked at her sketch. 'For both compliments.' Her strange willingness to forgive instantly, she reflected later, was not surprising. No one had ever asked her how she felt about anything before. She wanted to yank the woman back down beside her and talk at length about how ghastly it was to be tied to children for most of the day and how terrible she was at it. She had lost one in a crowd once and another time had forgotten to feed their caged finches while they were away. Most of all, she wanted to say how much she resented them their unremarkable, comfortable upbringing.

Effie regarded her. 'If you truly don't mind, then I should have asked instead why you are sketching this.' She gestured at the grotesque. 'Or any of the artefacts I have seen you studying. I haven't been able to discover a theme, but perhaps there isn't one?'

Lil thought uneasily that she should have noticed someone taking an interest in her. She placed a palm over her sketch. 'It depends. If there's a story behind it that interests me, I want to put it on paper. Or it might remind me of something, like this one. I sketch what draws me.'

She didn't say it was the only way she knew to ground the fear, that she sketched anything reminiscent of the night-mare to try to keep it at bay. Nor did she say that she used her pencil like a knife, slicing and cutting at the relics of human superstition and religion, so that she might find nothing there after all but matter and shape – no meaning, no genie, no auguring. It was obsessive; she couldn't do it enough; she wanted to sketch the whole world into submission until there was no place left, not even a hairline crack for ghosts.

Effie raised her eyebrows. 'You draw what *draws you*?' She laughed. 'What a lovely idea.'

Lil's accidental pun asserted itself. 'Oh, yes.' She smiled faintly, unpractised at word play, but it occurred to her that, yes, that was it. By studying these objects, she was learning her own shape, distinct from Madelyn and her own early beliefs, the invisible roles she was forced to play. The artefacts were giving her an outline, definition at last. Effie watched her as if she were enjoying following the play of thoughts across her face. She held out her hand.

'Mrs Jensen. But call me Effie for heaven's sake.'

Lil saw her again several times over the following weeks. Sometimes they merely nodded and smiled at each other, at others Effie asked to see her work and Lil invited her to sit. They discussed whatever Lil was drawing, and Effie told her about the work she did with her husband, an archaeologist – the large, pale man Lil had sometimes seen. They studied burial sites throughout Europe, particularly in Scandinavia. Much of the research, planning and writing up before and after their trips was done by Effie herself. She came to the museum to work in the reading rooms. The fifth time they met, Lil was ready with previous sketches she had made of stone tools and votive offerings in the museum, and the stone circle at Avebury she had drawn while on a holiday with the Sullivans. Effie pored over them and then gave her a sharp look, as if Lil had spoken and said something odd. 'May I borrow these? I'll return them any day you like.'

A quickening had licked about under Lil's ribcage, a sense of something approaching that was still out of sight. She nodded, not daring to risk flattening the feeling by asking why. When Effie returned as promised a few days later, she brought Nils with her, her husband. They had a proposal for her.

In the over-warm drawing room in the New Town, Effie recovered from the shock of being woken and smiled at Lil like a cat. Lil let out a laugh of relief and fell heavily into the nearest armchair. 'Bina says you're having a better week.'

'Yes, the doctor is very pleased with me. He was quite cheerful this morning.' Effie began pushing herself up into a straighter sitting position. Lil didn't try to help. It was one of the first things they had discovered about each other, their mutual loathing of interference. Once she had arranged herself to her satisfaction, Effie fixed Lil again with her blue eyes. Her illness had done nothing to diminish their intensity. 'Something has rattled you.'

Lil laughed again; it came easily around Effie. She sometimes thought fiercely of what Madelyn would think if she could see her enjoying herself so readily, taking life lightly. Effie frowned.

'Are you going to tell me, or did you come here simply to deprive an invalid of her rest?'

Lil leaned forward. 'The nightmares I told you about. They have come back. But I think I have found someone who can help me.'

'Who?'

'A doctor. An alienist.'

There was a moment's silence while Lil floundered, unable to begin. A churning had started up inside that was both pleasurable and painful and interfered with her thoughts. Effie continued to regard her with the patience of stone, and Lil finally gave up and let herself slide off the chair to her knees. Abandoning the leather folder on the floor, she began crawling towards the sofa, a difficult feat in skirt and petticoat. She giggled when a knee trapped too much material and pitched her forward towards the rug.

Effie tutted. 'What have you done, Lily Pad? What are you on your way to tell me?'

Lil finally reached the sofa and laid her head in Effie's lap. 'I have made a fool of myself.'

Effie stroked her hair and waited.

'I have been writing to him, the doctor, and today I went to his house to deliver a letter. I didn't mean to show myself, but his servant saw me standing outside for – oh, for ever – and then he arrived in a cab, and I ran away.' She turned her face into the Indian shawls until she could barely breathe. The memory of Dr Lachlan's handsome form – she could admit to herself, miserably, that she had found him handsome – and the thought of what his servant might say mortified her.

'Why did you run away?'

'Because . . .' She turned her face. 'Because I haven't told him who I am. I read a few papers he wrote – he seems sensible – but I'm scared he'll think me mad or hysterical.' It sounded weak, saying it aloud, but then she had never told Effie the exact nature of her visions; she had let her think they were merely bad dreams. Whenever Lil spoke about the 'night-mare', the hyphen stayed silent in her head.

'I think that was wise.' Effie stopped stroking her hair, and Lil raised her head to look at her. She had been expecting a peremptory dressing-down for being silly and over-sensitive, but Effie was matter-of-fact. 'It is best not to put too much faith in professional men. Not before we have looked into their hearts.'

'How do I do that?'

'Time and observation.'

Lil was disappointed. She found herself wanting to defend him. 'His letter was reassuring.'

'Good.' Effie smiled. 'See what he has to say about you turning up on his doorstep.' She gave a small laugh finally. 'I imagine that in itself will have poked a hole in his professional armour. You might be able to peek through.'

Lil nodded and sat back on her heels. 'I shall do as you say, sage.'

'I have never seen you suffer fools. If he fails to live up to your expectations, I rather pity the man. Now . . .' Effie's gaze moved beyond Lil. Without the smile, her face appeared much older suddenly. 'Tell me about the excavation.'

Lil looked back at the leather folder and scrambled to her feet. She retrieved it and sat on the edge of the sofa, clutching it to her chest. For all her reservations about the compromised burial site, the thought of sharing the finds with Effie was delicious. 'We think we've found the Pitcarden hoard, some of it.'

Effie instantly started forward. 'The brooch?' The question was too abrupt, too eager.

'No . . . but some of the hoard. Perhaps. You didn't think it existed.'

'Oh.' Effie nodded, her eyes unfocused. 'Good.' She brought

her gaze back to the folder, and Lil offered it mutely. Opening it, Effie leaned over the sketches of the female figure. Lil waited, not breathing, but Effie simply laid them aside and scrutinised the torc drawings. Only after she had shuffled them back together and closed the folder did she look up at Lil with light in her eyes. 'You clever things.'

Lil laughed weakly. 'Nils thinks there's more, but he wanted you to see these as soon as possible. They don't belong to the burial; they could have come from different countries for all we know.' She scratched her arm and looked a little sharply at Effie. 'He's abandoned the plan.'

Effie returned her gaze. 'You don't approve.'

'I know these are unusual, but Effie,' Lil heard her voice rise, 'the factor has ordered us to stop digging by the end of the week.' She waited for the news to sink in. 'Nils is in a rush to go after the hoard, but we're losing all the detail of the burial.'

'Why?'

'Some of the local people are causing trouble, sabotaging the site. Haxton is blaming the curse, but of course it's not really about that; it's old grievances, and the owner is coming back soon. Haxton wants us to wait.'

A jolt of electricity seemed to pass through Effie. 'The owner is coming back from Australia?'

'Already sailed.'

Effie nodded slowly and placed a hand on the folder. 'This find could mean great things for you.' There was a familiar fire in her expression as she turned her eyes to Lil. 'You must think what it will cost you if you let it get away from you.'

'But the burial . . .'

'Lil . . .' Effie put her hand on hers. It was cold. 'Women like us need to know when to be ruthless.' She gripped Lil's fingers. 'Pitcarden's owner returning will leave you with no dig at all.'

'Why? You have his letters – he already gave you permission.'

Effie shook her head and eyed her steadily. 'No, my dear, we forged the letters.'

Lil thought she must have misheard. 'What?' She took her hand from Effie's. 'What did you say?'

Effie leaned back against her cushions. 'We knew the Pitcarden site was a golden opportunity – so prominent and untouched; we've been eyeing it for years. But the older Mr Raube refused every request. Aggressively so; he even threatened us. He believed in the curse.'

Lil gave an impatient jerk of her head. 'I know this; all his sons died except one.'

'Children die.' Effie waved her hand. 'An hereditary weakness. His wife's nephews all died in infancy too. I don't know why believing in a curse makes it easier.'

'Because if there's a curse, there's someone else to blame,' Lil snapped. She couldn't seem ever to shake free of Madelyn's séances. There she had repeatedly seen people ready to turn to anything, even the supernatural, to relieve themselves of responsibility. 'So, his surviving son believes in it too?'

Effie looked sideways. 'I honestly don't know. He was sent away for most of his childhood to try to protect his health. He rarely came back and eventually settled abroad. He wasn't expected to return again, even after inheriting the estate – the factor you met was appointed to manage it in his absence.' Her voice turned matter-of-fact again. 'We couldn't risk it. We knew we would be finished before we were found out. And Lil . . .' She softened, looked vulnerable for the first time. 'I don't have time.'

A wave of panic nearly swept Lil to the floor again. She shook her head, wanting to plead with Effie to forget the dig and allow the people who loved her to be with her for the time that was left, but she knew Effie would never agree. She would push forward until the end, especially now she had crossed the line with the law.

Effie patted her hand, remorseless. 'I wasn't going to tell you about the forged letters. I have confessed formally – the document is with the solicitor and attests your innocence, should there be trouble. You will have to act a little now.'

Lil felt sick. Acting innocent belonged to her old life. 'What about Nils?'

'I have cleared him too, stating the letters are all my own work. It's plausible that knowing my time is short has made me desperate. He is willing to carry the blame if it comes to it, though I don't see how they can prove that he knew. And it will be difficult for Mr Raube to profit from these,' she ran her fingers over the folder, 'and at the same time demand too harsh a penalty.'

'It will ruin Nils's reputation in the field.'

'Good grief! It will shoot his reputation *higher*.' Effie raised a hand weakly towards the ceiling. 'A little public mauling for appearances' sake will be eclipsed entirely in private by what you and he have achieved. He will be forgiven, have no doubt.' Her eyes shone with triumph, and Lil thought she had never looked more alive.

'Now.' Effie sat up straighter and pointed to a desk in the window. 'Bring me pen and paper and fetch Evans off the shelf – and the Anderson. I shall fend off your Haxton and then I shall start making discreet enquiries about these.' She opened the folder again. 'Tell me your theories, wild and wonderful.'

For the next hour and a half they discussed the artefacts, searched for comparative examples, pondered the hoard's origin and time of burial. Bina brought in a light lunch and they ate while they worked, as if they were in the field rather than a drawing room. It was like the old days, bent for hours over axe heads, sword blades, gouges, potsherds, sifting through dirt and their combined knowledge for connections, for a deeper understanding. The work worked on Lil, smoothing her ruffled edges. Effie was reassuringly incurious about the figure's meaning, it being too ancient to know. She shrugged it off as a goddess of some sort. But from where? Not Britain. They agreed it had more in common with finds from Mesopotamia, reaching further back in time. Lil's unease receded until she noticed the tiredness leaching the interest from Effie's face. She put the folder to one side, insisting she rest again, and to her private dismay, Effie agreed.

In her own room, Lil sat on the bed and felt the restlessness of a visitor obliged to entertain themselves for a while. Effie's decision not to tell her about the forged letters lodged in her chest like an arrow. They didn't usually keep secrets from her – that she knew of. She chewed her lip until it hurt. The brooch bothered her too; it kept slipping in and out of view, and she no longer trusted Effie's light-hearted speech in Norway about frivolity. Questions hovered, tiny biting insects.

She searched herself for a sense of guilt about deceiving Haxton and Mr Raube and found she could summon very little. The weeks spent surveying and exploring the site had given her a sense of ownership that transcended title deeds. From the very first scrape of her trowel in Norway, she had discovered that the deeper she excavated a piece of land, the deeper it dug into her. A part of herself was exposed with every buried thing she brought to light. And somehow finding the goddess, as she was beginning to think of the plaque, had given her a greater sense of ownership, as if the figure itself had transferred it to her. Whatever rules had been broken, her bond to Pitcarden and its history was now irrevocable.

With that, her thoughts returned to Dr Lachlan. He wanted to dig into her past, to expose her secrets. A shiver ran through her that was almost desire, almost repulsion. The doctor–patient relationship was perilously one-sided. Perhaps Effie was right and there were ways to see into the heart of J. E. Lachlan, to unearth whatever lay under his professional words. The churning began in her middle again. What if she gave him more? What if that brought him out? She remembered wondering if part of her wanted to show him the worst. Was that why she had turned up at his door? She remembered the strange burn of his presence, even though she was a stranger to him, and realised how much she wanted – needed – to make contact again.

6

Monday 25th October

Dear Dr Lachlan,

Business has brought me to Edinburgh, and I took the opportunity to deliver a letter to your house this morning. I think you arrived as I was leaving. Please excuse me for not speaking; I was unprepared to see you.

In my last letter, I wrote about the spirit writing and how my tutor schooled me in whatever field of knowledge would be most useful for each week's séance. He also sat in on the materialisations, which were becoming bolder. I would already be installed in our newly built cabinet or would emerge in another part of the room as if from a pool of light, perhaps with some spirit substance billowing out of my mouth (an unpleasant pairing of muslin and egg whites). Our theatricality was almost at its height at that point. Dulcimers played without being touched, the air grew cold, flowers tumbled into the laps of sitters — the fact that they were real and not some sort of ephemeral spirit flower seemed only to inspire greater awe, which always astounded me. Certain participants were allowed into the cabinet sometimes to see my mother in her trance, and would come out gagging from the smell of decay, swearing she had physically shrunk and was already in a state of decomposition.

As with any theatrical spectacle, we couldn't afford to become complacent; our audience was always hungry for something novel. It was no longer enough simply to see the spirit glowing in a dark corner; other mediums were making their materialisations walk about among the sitters, even touching and talking to them, and we had to do the same.

My tutor, who remained stern and exacting in our lessons, showed another side of himself in these sessions, taking full advantage of the licence these 'meetings' allowed. Because we were all silently complicit in the games we played, never speaking to each other openly of deception, I could not complain. He would have feigned confusion and insisted it was the spirit — a being beyond human and therefore social restrictions — inviting him to experience briefly the physical junction between two worlds. I did try to tell my mother, using our ridiculous code, and pretended concern that he was too rough with such a delicate spirit and might frighten her off. My mother dismissed it, reassuring me obliquely that the spirit was safe from any real harm in a room full of well-wishers. But I think she must have said something, as for a while afterwards, I noticed his straying hands kept themselves to the outside of the drapery I wore.

The girl my mother had hired was working for us during this time as maid and cook. I believe she had been recruited for something other than her domestic services, however, as they were wanting in the extreme. She adored my mother, and for a while I thought it was sheer flattery that had won her the position — they had met at a meeting of one of the spiritualist societies where my mother, uncharacteristically, had given a talk. She usually kept aloof from such circles, reluctant to involve herself in the politics or publicity of the movement. Investigators were never invited into our house. I think she went out purposely on that occasion to find an assistant. The maid's enthusiasm for spiritualism was sickening. She treated me with an exaggerated, wide-eyed reverence I found insincere and profoundly irritating. My mother used her at the séances, at first simply to greet the sitters and provide refreshments, but later as an aide to the performances. I was kept in the dark about the extent of her involvement, but over the months, the air became thick with their whisperings and sudden silences when I entered a room. I was jealous.

I find myself surprised to have written that word. But of course I was jealous. My mother was the one stable fact of my life, and the maid's ambition was clear. She lurked around me, as if wanting to befriend me, until I couldn't open a door without finding her simpering behind it, pretending she hadn't been spying. I always assumed, because it hurt less, that she was following her own wicked agenda and not my mother's instructions.

I was growing increasingly sceptical of the world my mother had spun around me. I began to rebel against it. My spirit writings became purposely bland and unexceptional, and as the spirit, I avoided going near the gentlemen. The materialisations grew shorter, until my mother finally received complaints and we lost a few regulars to a rival. While this was happening, the terror of the night-mare intensified. My sleep was suffering because of my fear of waking up to the figure at the end of the bed. I fought off oblivion each night for as long as possible, which made me dull and snappish during the day and even less effective as a medium. The sensations while hallucinating were becoming increasingly physical. As well as the suffocation when it sat on my chest, I was experiencing dreadful pain. I felt fingernails sink into my flesh; insects swarmed over me and burrowed into my skin, crawling and boring between sinew and tissue; my limbs were pulled apart as if I were on a rack. I felt all of it, as real as day.

My mother blamed it on my resistance to the séances, of course, saying I was paying the penalty for blocking the spirits, that I was bringing harm to myself, as if I were a locked door that the spirits were throwing themselves against. I resolved to stop telling her what happened each night, even as it worsened. The pain lingered beyond the hallucinations, and one morning when I was able to move again, I found bruises on my arm and neck where the figure had held me down. Scratch marks were scored down the length of my legs, locks of hair pulled from my head. This continued until I was convinced the night would come when it would kill me. The marks weren't confined to my body either. Rips appeared in the sheets. Sometimes blood stained my nightgown, but I could find no wound. A full glass of water by my bed was empty in the morning; only, a little later, I would find the contents of my underwear drawer soaked. I mentioned none of this to my mother, but the activity spread like a dark stain and grew more violent until its presence was felt throughout the house. Strange writing appeared on the walls and ceilings, at first right over my head when I woke up, but soon in other rooms. It was gibberish mostly, written in charcoal or a viscous substance that looked like congealed blood. Objects began to disappear or move about, ornaments fell from shelves; once, we heard a dreadful screeching from the kitchen and rushed downstairs to find the heavy dresser had moved six feet across the flags, nearly blocking the door and our way in. Often, coming down in the morning, we discovered all the candles and lamps had been lit and the fires roaring in their grates. It was this phenomenon that nearly cost the maid her life.

My mother had called a meeting between the three of us. We were to attempt a private séance, asking for protection from the poltergeist I had unleashed in the house. Her eyes never lost their look of reproach when turned on me in those days. She had tried everything to make me less stubborn, from confiscating my favourite books to promising a holiday. She had even begged me on her knees tearfully. That afternoon, her anger was brimming over. None of us had sat down yet, and she was pacing up and down, making one of her speeches. She asked if it were my intention to ruin us all. The maid was standing with her back to the fire – it had been swept and re-laid since that morning – and kept interjecting with conciliatory, mewing noises. For days she had been trying to position herself as my confidante, offering fake sympathy, but I had ignored her. Neither my mother nor I took any notice of her then as we spat accusations and counter-accusations at each other. The first I knew of what was happening was hearing the whump of dry wood bursting alight. We all jumped, and the maid darted away from the fireplace. But the fire came with her. The back of her skirt was already blazing, and flames rapidly climbed one sleeve. She didn't scream at first; her body made frantic, silent movements, and she whirled in a circle, which made it worse. My mother and I tried to pull her to the floor, but in her panic, she fought us off and ran about trying to slap her own back. I remember the singed hoof smell of a blacksmith's as her hair caught alight. It was then she started screaming. Finally, my mother ran at her with the chenille rug that usually covered the séance table and, wrapping it around her, brought them both to the floor.

It seems obvious now, writing it down, that the maid's clothes could only have caught so quickly if there had been an incendiary liquid on them, accidentally dropped as she primed and lit the fire at her back while my mother drew my attention away with the argument. She wasn't yet proficient enough in such tricks. It also seems odd now that I never *seriously considered the possibility my mother would use the same deceptions we practised on paying sitters against me. She and the maid must have contrived most things while I slept or struggled with the night-mare, and it would have been easy enough to pay a boy or two from the street to slip in through the area door and push the dresser while we were all upstairs. The poltergeist's manifestations grew so naturally out of my night-mares, I was blinded by my deepest fear that the figure, and therefore myself, was the source. It worked, is all that matters. We needed money for the maid's doctor's bills, and I could no longer jeopardise our income with my recalcitrance. I felt too guilty anyway. However much I hated the maid, I never wanted her disfigurement on my conscience.*

My mother saw her moment and pushed me to study more quickly to lead as a medium, to be the one tied into the cabinet (the 'study' being how to escape undetected and appear as the spirit). She wanted my first truly public performance, when anyone could volunteer to tie me up, to be on my sixteenth birthday, a few months away. My supposed powers would be at their strongest then, and word spread that it would be a particularly special event with a full materialisation. She had already recovered some of her popularity by turning the maid's accident to her advantage – people came just for the thrill of standing near the fireplace that the spirits had used so violently. The maid herself was given a new role, which she seized on readily, of recounting the experience, greatly embellished, whilst wearing a veil over her face. The climax was the slow reveal of her still-raw flesh. My job was to hold pieces of offal over a flame, out of sight, the hideous smell allowing punters to revel more sensorially in their own disgust. I obeyed my mother in everything without complaint. The house stopped throwing itself about and we could live without fear of it burning down or crushing us with furniture.

Only the night-mares didn't abate. There was no longer writing on the walls or blood on my clothes, but almost every night now the figure, the hallucination, didn't keep to the shadows but invaded my body, leaving me sweating and shaking and in pain. Nor was I free from molestation in my waking life. My tutor abandoned all restraint during the materialisations, knowing that after the fire, I was powerless to protest. It was around then that I began to wonder if the night-mare was truly a premonition as my mother insisted, and it was the tutor himself it represented. Even in lessons he began sitting too close, or he would stand behind my chair, leaning over while I completed some task. I can still feel his thumb under my collar and his breath warm against my neck. It was clear that very soon he would go further, that the excuse of non-human communion with the spirit world would be dropped completely. I was living between two nightmares.

The hour tells me I must stop there. I shall write again when I return to Gledsmuir and have perhaps had the pleasure of your reply.

*Yours sincerely,
Miss Gerrard*

Lil sat quietly for several minutes, rattled by the memories. She wondered if she was, after all, revealing too much. The burned maid story had been notorious at the time; a little digging would quickly lead anyone to the famous Madelyn de Vallon. But perhaps that didn't matter. Madelyn didn't know where Lil was now, nor did the Sullivans. She considered leaving the letter until morning and deciding then, but remembered how she had scurried away from Dr Lachlan like a frightened rabbit while his housekeeper watched. The same compulsion and sense of urgency that had made her knock on his door in the first place made her send Bina off to the post with the letter at once. That done, she returned to her room as Effie was still asleep. Tiredness was pulling at her too. She sat on the bed. A few moments' rest, just to clear her mind, and she would return to the books to continue working on the artefacts.

When she opened her eyes, the light had changed. Late afternoon hung mellow and evening-like in the room as it sometimes did at that time of year. She had woken suddenly, annoyed at herself for drifting off but relieved to be alone. Something pressed lightly against the top of her head – a pillow; she must have moved down the bed in her sleep. She tried to sit up.

A shouting, instantly, right next to her ear. Every muscle in her body strained as if the ceiling were falling in. She tried to open her mouth to scream, but her jaws were jammed shut. No air could reach her lungs. Her eyes, barn-door wide, were the only part of her not locked down. They searched frantically, sideways where the shouting came from, then wainscoting–door–window. What was it? Where was it? Fireplace–corner–wardrobe. The shouting stopped abruptly to be replaced by a hissing noise. It filled the room and seemed to crackle in her skin. Washstand–bookcase–chair. *Chair. Sitting in the chair.*

A shape. It rose slowly, floated upright, a dark silhouette with hints of flesh, teeth, breast, hair. The upper half continued to rise, stretching taller and taller above Lil, until its head was bent against the ceiling. It was a female thing. Human-shaped, almost, but not human. Tilting towards her, head still bent, it began to move across the room. The closer it came, the greater the pressure on Lil's head and chest. Her neck was being crushed into her shoulders. Something pressed on her sternum to the point of cracking. Unable to escape, her screams burned in her throat.

Insanity: it was right next to her. Her brain heaved like every other muscle, fighting at the limits of its strength not to give in.

Closer. The thing's arms grew longer. Its face rolled forward onto its chest, and then the neck began extending as its body and arms had, longer and longer. Swinging on the end of it, its head was an outline of matted hair, level with its chest, then its waist. Lil waited for the face to lift towards her, knowing that when it did, her mind would snap. It swung lower again, and lower, out of sight. It didn't come back up, and she realised with a fresh crest of horror that it was moving beneath her, under the bed. A scream pushed its way through her throat, the sound that escaped as thin as paper. The rest of the body still came on, its grotesque neck arching down from its shoulders, its arms still lengthening. One hand followed the head under the bed; the other moved up the front of Lil's body. She thought this was how she would die. Its fingers reached her face and grasped her jaw. Cold and damp, the flesh squirmed loosely around the iron-like bones beneath. It forced her to look to the side. Something was emerging above the blankets – hair and forehead, the face rising again on the other side of the bed from its body. The moving shadows showed more – rotting flesh and sunken cheeks. Closed eyes. The hand held the jaw, like the other one grasped Lil's face, as if it were keeping the head up, as if the head itself were dead while the body moved and grew. The eyes flicked open.

Lil came to with a jerk of her whole body. Her chest heaved. Her gaze was still fixed on the spot, but the thing had gone. She brought her hand up to her face and found her cheek slimed with dribble. Wiping it on her sleeve, she pushed herself upright. She glanced cautiously around the room. The afternoon light gave the same muted glow, the hour sagging with the day. A soft knock came from the door.

'Yes?' Her voice was a croak. She cleared her throat and tried to pull herself together. The door opened and Effie appeared, festooned in shawls. She smiled questioningly.

'I thought you might be resting, but I heard a squeak.' She studied Lil's face and raised her eyebrows. 'Another bad dream?'

Lil scrambled off the bed. 'Yes, but what are you doing up here? Sit down at once.' She drew Effie over to a chair and helped her lower herself. Even through the shawls, she could feel the slightness of her. 'Why aren't you on the sofa?'

'Dying can be boring.' Effie's tone was light, but exhaustion showed in her face. Climbing the stairs must have been like climbing a mountain. 'I recommend you adopt a swifter method when the time comes.'

'I recommend you stop being in such a hurry. Bina will throw a fit.'

Effie laughed weakly, and Lil retreated to sit on the bed. She felt more angry than she wanted to show. Her friend and employer regarded her for a few moments. She spoke softly. 'What was the dream?'

Lil looked down at her hands. The night-mare always left a residue of dread, which, if she let herself dwell on it, would begin gathering itself again like a slow swarm, threatening to reform, to replay the horror.

'There was a sort of demon . . . a demon crone.' She avoided saying *hag*. 'Its body . . . its arms and . . .' She raised hers, then let them drop. 'Utterly ridiculous really.' Her mouth tried to twist itself into a smile but made a grimace. 'It made me think of the Mara. You remember the stories Nils told us?' She began to say it was unusual for her to see a female figure, but Effie suddenly shouted.

'AND WILL YOU TELL THE DOCTOR, *LILITH*?'

Lil jumped and looked up. Effie was sitting as she had been, but above her shoulders was nothing but neck. It swayed, elongated, high above the body, reaching up to the ceiling where it was forced to bend. Effie's face stared down at her from ten feet above, mouth grinning, eyes ablaze.

'WILL YOU, *LILITH*?'

The shouting sounded point-blank in Lil's ear. Crying out, she threw herself away from it and fell. Her forehead scraped down the little chest of drawers by the bed, and she landed heavily on her arm. Pushing herself over, she kicked her legs until her back was against the chest. Sweat slid into every crease of her skin. Her eyes stared wildly while her lungs laboured. She didn't need to search the room to know there was no one there, that the chair was empty. Only the late-afternoon light remained as it had been throughout, soft and fading. Lil put a hand to her forehead. It stung from the graze, and she felt tears squeezing up. She had a memory of being a small child, sitting cramped and frightened in the box Madelyn had hidden her in to pull strings on cue, and wanted to cry like she had then. A sob choked out of her. And then a furious shriek through gritted teeth. She stamped a foot and pounded the rug with her fist. Yanking herself to her feet, she glared around the room, but there was nothing to accuse or lash out at. Nothing to do but straighten her collar, tidy her hair and wash her face. She examined the graze in the dressing-table mirror; it was an uneven streak of red in her pale skin, as if she had been caught by a nearly spent paintbrush. No matter; she would be back among the stones and dirt soon where no one cared.

She grasped the door handle and paused. There was a sense of something in the room behind her still, but it didn't worry her. She knew she was too far out of its clutches now. It was just the residue, an echo in her head. But it was strange that it had appeared as female, and then as Effie. A female voice had spoken to her once, indistinctly, on a fateful night at Madelyn's, but it had never taken that form before. She thought inevitably of the plaque with the ancient goddess hammered into the metal, and her heart skipped a little. But perhaps her mind had simply weaved it in, and dredging up old memories in her letters to

Dr Lachlan was the reason that awful name had reared up. Even the real Effie didn't know what 'Lil' was short for. No one did.

Effie was awake, leaning over the drawing of the plaque in her lap. Lil watched her from the doorway. Her heart had juddered to see her face again, coming so soon after the night-mare version, and she waited until reality established itself before speaking. 'We haven't told the factor we found some of the hoard.'

Effie started at the voice and placed her hands over the sketch, an instinctive movement. When she saw it was Lil, she smiled, then frowned. 'Your face.'

'I fell. It's nothing.' Lil made a dismissive gesture, and Effie didn't pursue it. Instead, she placed a hand more deliberately on the drawing.

'Good. People can behave strangely when they know there are riches underfoot.'

'The diggers know. They won't keep it to themselves whatever Nils pays them.' Lil resumed her seat in the chair across from the sofa.

'But they are outsiders. The news may not spread so fast. Haxton grew up in Balcraig. He went away, but that doesn't mean he doesn't believe in the curse. Better not to provoke him before it's necessary.'

'How do you know so much about him?'

Effie gave a look of contrition that was somehow all mischief. 'We were planning to hoodwink the man. We needed to know whom we were dealing with, how well he knew the Raubes. Which was rather too well. He even worked under the old factor for a time before a landowner further south saw his worth and fattened him up with schooling and manners. But for some reason, Haxton decided to return to Pitcarden, despite the state it was in, once the old factor retired – that was soon after Raube's death. Which was not in our favour.'

Lil shook her head as if at the transgressions of a child, but felt unease billowing under her ribcage. Hoodwinking people was Madelyn's game. No, she corrected herself, Effie lied too – she had once faked a find to gain full access to a site – but it was never personal, always for the sake of a dig, and she had never shut Lil out before. It was cold and bitter being outside of that 'we'. She swallowed down the hurt and became purposeful. 'What will you write to stop him from throwing us off the site?'

'Oh . . .' Effie stuck her chin out. 'I shall be terribly polite and understanding. And at the same time pinch him where all men are tender – his pride in front of a woman. I shall make him question his own authority. After all, Mr Raube needs a factor willing to carry out his orders without fail and who isn't afraid of local gossip. I might . . .' She pursed her lips. 'I might include a letter from Mr Raube to Nils that says how much he is looking forward to returning home and seeing all the work himself.'

She paused, mulling it over in her mind, as if she were doing no more than deciding whom to invite for dinner. Lil had done the very same thing to Haxton, goading him for being a coward, but something baulked in her that Effie should do it too. 'What if he's too stubborn?' She recalled the grim line of his mouth.

'Well, in that case . . .' Effie peered at her, as if curious to see how she might react. 'Thanks to you and, apparently, those troublesome villagers interfering with the excavation, we are now in a position to negotiate. Haxton doesn't know what or how much we have found.' She lifted up the sketch of the gold plaque.

Lil stared at her. Effie had always been willing to sidestep the law for the sake of a dig, but this ruthlessness was new. 'That's . . . extortion?'

Effie winced and put her head on one side, as if considering.

She smiled conclusively. 'Expedience.' Her eyes fixed Lil like two blue arrow points, and she leaned forward. 'It's all a game, Lily Pad. A game no one wants or expects you to play, never mind win. That's your trump card. Learn how to use it.'

A simple crook. Lil remembered wishing Madelyn had made no greater claims for herself. She opened her mouth to say something, but found she had no words. Effie's eyes, burning through to Lil's heart, had brought her back in from the cold. Laughter peeled out of her instead, and she let it take hold of her until she was shaking in her seat, throwing her head back like a cormorant swallowing an eel.

There were pressing reasons to return to Pitcarden – to deliver Effie's letter to Haxton, to work on the cist, and to try to curb Nils's wanton destruction of the burial mound in his pursuit of the hoard. And, even greater than these, although Lil wouldn't admit it to herself, to visit the post office at Gledsmuir. Would *he* have written? Did she still have his sympathy? The nightmare had returned that morning, the grinning head rising from the side of the bed on its grotesque neck, inches from Lil's own. She hadn't been able to shake the residue off. It lingered at the edge of sight, threatening to gather itself into being.

But then there was Effie. She had said she was feeling stronger that morning and insisted on rising to sit at the breakfast table. She ate so little, the effort hardly seemed worth it to Lil, but she made no comment. As she hurried to retrieve a dropped napkin before Effie could attempt to herself, she understood the unwelcome distance that had opened in their relationship since they had last met. The illness had forced itself between them, so Lil now had to navigate *it* before she could meet with Effie on their usual terms. Their paths were diverging on either side of this intrusion: Effie towards death, and Lil towards a future without her. The distance between them was short for the time being. To cross it meant only tactfully ignoring Effie's lack of appetite or saving her the effort of leaning down to the floor. But the distance would grow with time, Lil suddenly saw, unstoppably, until it became impassable. Soon, there would be more illness than Effie; she would grow smaller on the other side of it, more unreachable, until there was nothing left at all. Except — and the thought was unbearable — except for the night-mare version of Effie. Lil's own appetite vanished as she returned to her seat. All her hunger seemed to centre on the woman opposite, for what too short a time there was left. 'I'll stay today. I want to go to the museum.'

Effie gave her a surprised look. 'I thought you would be staying longer than that to research.'

'Did you?' It was Lil's turn to be surprised. 'I must speak to Haxton and—'

'I have already sent the letter. Let it do its work. Your presence will only irritate him.'

The comment stung Lil. She felt its shadow pass across her face, but Effie regarded her without remorse. 'Well, do tell me. What kind of impression have you made on him so far? Will the sight of you inspire friendly thoughts and willing cooperation in the man?'

After a moment, Lil spoke simply. 'I disgust him.'

'*Disgust?*' Effie raised her eyebrows. 'What did you do? Oh.' Understanding dawned before she had finished her question. For the first time, disapproval hardened her face. 'That wasn't sensible.'

'No.'

'Could you not have found someone less involved? Another sailor or something?'

Lil ground her teeth. She didn't know how Effie had found out about her encounters. Her only comment in Norway had been to wonder how Lil could stand the smell.

'I thought it would help us. I misread the situation.'

'Clearly. Well,' Effie sighed the matter away, 'all the more reason for you to stay here.'

'I still have to help with the dig.'

'You will be helping. If you can discover anything about the torc and our mystery plaque.'

Lil hesitated. Effie would usually be pushing her out of the door by now, anxious about lost time at the site. Watching the thin face, Lil wondered if she was as reluctant to part as Lil was herself. If underneath it all, she was scared. She leaned a little towards Effie, aware of words she had never said to anyone trying to form themselves on her tongue, when Bina bustled in with the post.

Effie became all smiles, but Lil couldn't disguise her irritation. She preferred the privacy she and Nils shared in the cottage, even if the grime was starting to show from their half-hearted house-keeping. Every time Bina appeared, uncalled for, it reminded Lil of Agnes and her constant lurking. She didn't understand how people could bear to install strangers in their home and let them move about at will. When Bina started fussing over refreshing the teapot, Lil remained silent and kept her gaze averted until she was gone. Effie laughed at her while she slit open an envelope with the paper knife. 'You look as bad-tempered as a cat.'

'I like cats.'

'Cats don't like cats.'

'They respect each other's space.'

'Respect? I remember meeting you in the British Museum and forming the distinct impression I was about to be scratched. Your . . .' She stopped, looking down at the letter. Lil sipped her tea, restraining the urge to ask immediately what it was about. She looked for the envelope, but it was out of sight in Effie's lap. Staring out of the window at the grey day instead, she didn't relish the thought of the museum. It was unlikely to hold any answers, being mostly, in her view, a depository of coins and flint heads that could have come from anywhere in Scotland, and foreign antiquities that she knew by heart. Nor could she enlist anyone's help by telling them what had been found. Besides, as a female, without an estate full of Roman remains or a large fortune to spend on her interests, she was merely an irritant to most Society fellows. Her work with Nils was welcome, just so long as her name didn't come with it. It was perhaps the one thing she had been surprised to find in favour of spiritualist circles, once she was outside of them, that the concept of human equality was taken seriously. They applied it logically to gender, race, class and even sexuality in some circles, even religion. Certainly, women were allowed to be experts and respected as such. Lil begrudgingly gave them credit for it. That and their discarding of corsets.

She had turned away only for a moment, but when she looked back, there was a change come over Effie. Her face was stone, hard and grey. She was still looking down at the letter.

'What is it?'

Effie didn't move. She didn't seem to have heard.

'Effie?'

There was a longer pause, during which even the clock seemed to stop ticking.

'Excuse me.' Effie took a deep breath and lowered the letter to her lap, putting it back into the envelope.

'What's wrong?'

'Nothing. It's probably for the best. Only, unexpected.' She paused, and an emotion Lil couldn't name but would describe only as awful changed her face almost beyond recognition.

'Effie?'

Effie's attention returned slowly to the breakfast room. She blinked. 'It's . . . An acquaintance has died, but I believe she was quite unwell; clearly more so than I had thought.'

Lil hadn't been schooled in social graces – the spirits weren't expected to be polite, certainly not about death – and she didn't offer condolences. She squinted across the table, worried. 'Shall I stay with you today?' The offer came out gruffly, but Effie barely seemed to notice it. She shook her head distractedly.

'No, go to the museum.' She turned in her seat to get up, but was halted by another thought. 'And you're right, you should go back and help Nils tomorrow if the weather is good. In case the factor still manages to stall us.' She rose with effort, leaning heavily on the table, and gathered up the rest of the post. 'I'll lie down.'

Lil watched her make her slow way to the door, relieved that the awful expression had passed. She sensed the sudden reversal about her leaving was bound up with the news of the acquaintance dying. She pushed her plate away and leaned her elbows on the table. Perhaps it had brought home how little time remained. When Lil returned to the site, she decided, she would throw herself into searching for the hoard with Nils, if that's what Effie wanted. She placed her napkin on the table and surveyed the detritus of breakfast. It was a welcome change, not to have to clear up after herself. She would try to be more appreciative of Bina too, also for Effie's sake.

The museum had its usual effect on her. Excitement mixed with dread. The glass-fronted cabinets rose up to the ceiling, shelves groaning with artefacts, pot after pot after pot in one direction, and in another, acres of arrowheads in serried rows. They had at least been rescued from the threat of collectors or vandals, but for most of it there would be no record of the position they had been found in or how they related to anything else recovered from the same area. Axes, swords, brooches; objects of daily use, war, adornment, ceremony, burial, that had lain for centuries in or near the place where the last human hands had touched them, moved only by the slow shifting elements, had in a moment been snatched from the earth by modern fingers, too hasty for knowledge, and at once stripped of their significance. All context lost.

Lil felt a familiar gnawing in her gut. She preferred the field to the archives, to inhabit bodily the places people had been before. That way she felt she could learn far more than studying an isolated specimen in a museum. But perhaps that was fanciful. Time had swept so much away. It was still a mistake, she thought, to lose all that knowledge. Improvements had been made to recording in the Edinburgh museum, but they didn't go nearly as far as Lil would have liked (she had written a letter, which, to her surprise, had received a sympathetic reply), and the practice hadn't reached the regional museums at all. They were robbing the future, which would certainly have advanced techniques, the opportunity of learning more.

Archaeology was at the mercy of amateurs and enthusiasts. They couldn't even agree on what it was all for. Such scorn and disgust had been heaped on it during the passing of the Ancient Monuments Protection Act, such derisive contempt for its advocates, Lil had privately thought it might as well have been spiritualism under discussion. Some people didn't want to be confronted with the dead, either in spirit form or through the evidence of the things they left behind, at least not before the reassurance of written histories. Looking at the thousands of artefacts lined up all around her, Lil felt herself surrounded by a legion of resentful ghosts. They had been forced to 'materialise' from the past, their stories incommunicable. Their true owners had once handled them, thought about them, attached emotions to them. The objects themselves had lived, in a sense, and when that existence was over, they were buried. Only to be dug up now like corpses.

Lil shivered despite the warmth of the room. She didn't know if people of prehistory experienced the same emotions as she did, or if they would even recognise each other as kin. Perhaps evolution had refashioned humanity's inner landscape in the ages since, in the same way it had moulded physical characteristics. It was tempting to read love and affection into the child's urn being buried within the adult's. Some mooted that the very presence of precious grave goods, the fact they had not been stolen in an earlier time, was evidence of collective respect. But respect can be born of fear as much as of love. Why should objects and remains come to be seen as cursed? Out of some atavistic fear of the unknown people who had left them behind, the fear that they had not really gone? One objector to the parliamentary act had argued that people from prehistory were to be thought of only as our predecessors, not our ancestors. The distinction had made Lil laugh until she choked on her tea, the insistence on it. Predecessors, not ancestors. Beneath the arrogance and condescension, she could smell the fear, sharp as sweat. They were familiar, too familiar, but they *weren't us*.

Lil cast her eyes over the rows of artefacts. She had embraced archaeology as an antidote to the sickness of spiritualism. The dead were still very much her business, but whereas before she had taken what was unprovable and presented it as fact, she now uncovered real evidence and refused to draw conclusions. After two years working as Effie and Nils's sketch artist, observing the hired diggers and their finds, she'd wanted to feel the earth under her own hands. She'd spent months studying the techniques of past and current archaeologists, most of them hobbyists. She scoured libraries, wrote dozens of letters to local societies, and attended any public lecture she could get to. Eventually, Effie and Nils had been forced to admit she had more to offer than her drawing skills alone. They wouldn't let her excavate as she wished – by herself with only a handful of well-trained helpers. Time and Effie's patience wouldn't allow it. But they let her work alongside the men, and Nils began to join her in the trenches himself.

What a relief it had been to work with physical things. Her knife, trowel and brushes became extensions of her pencil, cutting away to the heart of the matter. She would have liked to dig up the whole world, to scrape, sift and record every last nub of bone and fragment of potsherd until she had proved there was nothing else there. The desire, the work, was urgent and unending. Her eye fell on the flint arrowheads. Not so long ago, they had been called elf bolts. It was inconceivable to people that so perfect and delicate a thing could ever have been made by human hand. Lil tried to imagine living with the certainty that elves existed. Was it thrilling, or terrifying, or too ordinary to think about? She wondered what they might yet dig up to confuse and consternate the age. Anything inexplicable would eventually be attributed to supernatural agency by some person or other. She was only ever one step ahead; she couldn't rest.

It was too cramped in the museum, so many fragments of so many lives and eras all rammed in together; it felt more like a mausoleum. There was nothing that could help with the goddess. A need to be among the living pushed her back out the way she had come, but she wasn't ready to sit in a sickroom yet. The Old Town beckoned.

She walked quickly despite the steepness of the streets and steps, a pale moth flitting through the shadows. The city swiftly closed in on her, impossibly tall and quickly dirty, until she felt like an insect indeed, crawling between stony stems among the other grubs and creatures of that underworld. She liked it. Fears of the night-mare manifesting itself were neutralised by the sheer number of possibilities. There were too many figures in doorways or on corners or suddenly leaning out of casements for her to watch them all. Children ran past in sudden bursts of noise, possessed with an energy that seemed at odds with their malnourished bodies. They vanished, as if they had never been. She thought of all the lives gone before, all the layers beneath her feet. Edinburgh had been cascading down the sides of the old volcano like fresh flows of lava for centuries, repeatedly burying and renewing itself. Was all that energy still stored somewhere, packed into the rock and rubble? As she reached the top of the hill, a fight broke out between some boys, a game gone wrong. A marble bounced and skittered past her into the gutter and disappeared. She wondered where it would end up, if it would be recovered or left to be scabbed over eventually by the city. Perhaps it had just that moment known the last of human warmth for this epoch. Perhaps in some far, far future time it would be dug up again by an unimaginable archaeologist. One of the boys was shaking a smaller one as if he were no more than a rag. Finally, he threw him to the ground and turned to run headlong after the marble. Lil stuck her foot out as he passed. There was a grunt, a muffled thud. She crossed over towards the bridge as howls of pain and rage bounced off the buildings behind her. She didn't look back.

In her head, she was sharing her thoughts with Dr Lachlan. She would like to talk to him about archaeology. His own branch of science was not fully established either, although its asylums outshone most museums of antiquities in size and grandeur. It was exciting to be at the beginning of something, when real discoveries could be made, the ground prepared for future work. The thought of it, and how they would discuss it, carried her all the way along the bridge and almost to the edge of the Old Town. She turned left down Chambers Street past the medical school with an idea of making a loop down South Bridge. Dr Lachlan's work at the asylum in Edinburgh must be like having dozens of field sites all in one place to delve into. She wanted to know if studying the dissected brain, post-mortem, held all the answers, or if it only yielded results when read in tandem with the symptoms of the living patient, much as she preferred to study an artefact in the context of its excavation. How much did culture and personal history and experience play a part? He might have a theory about whether ancient humans had felt the same emotions as present-day people. She could perhaps ask him this in their correspondence.

Her head was so full of him and their imaginary conversations that her mind didn't at first check itself at the sight of his name; it seemed a natural reflection of her thoughts. Only for an instant, and then she had doubled back on herself, heart galloping. A handbill, fallen askew on the inside of a window, advertised the current lectures and fees of the Royal Colleges. And there he was, Dr J. E. Lachlan, next to his subject, Insanity. The next lecture was in three days' time at Surgeons' Hall.

She walked on, barely taking a breath. Did she dare go? The thought of being able to sit and observe him while he talked seemed to rob her of all normal function. She would have to be invisible herself, though, and how would that be possible in a room full of medical students?

'But don't they take women students now? Or there's a women's school opened or something? I thought the great cause was won.'

Effie waved the problem away while battling feebly to pull out a cushion from behind her. Lil had swept across Edinburgh in a state of agitated mental suspension until she could pour out what she had seen and thought. She helped move the cushion and pounded it with her fist, quite needlessly.

'No . . . not really. Anyway, there can't be such hoards of women students that I would go unnoticed.' She caught herself echoing Effie's dismissive tone and wondered silently at her mentor's lack of enthusiasm for the rights of women in general. It seemed strange for one who had made her own wealth against the odds. As a stockbroker, of all things – a door not so much closed to women as bricked up and trip-wired for a thousand miles around. But Effie had found a niche among women of independent means — wealthy widows, opera singers, high-class prostitutes — and quietly grown her business through word of mouth, all the while posing as a young, well-to-do widow herself, whose charms won her insider knowledge from unsuspecting men of business. Nils and archaeology had come later.

Lil paced. 'I don't see how I can do it. Women probably have separate lectures, and even if not, I would attract attention like a female . . . duck.' She recalled seeing one drowned beneath a frenzy of males in a pond. The screams of the Sullivan children.

'Then you will have to go as a drake.' The faintest colour came into Effie's face as she thought about it. 'Yes, with your form, we could dress you up very nicely as a young student, barely out of boyhood. With binding, and you'd have to lose the hair. But your walk is already manly enough.'

Lil stopped in the middle of the room and stared, open-mouthed. Effie licked her dry lips. 'I mean that as a compliment. You don't tiptoe about; you stride as nature intended.'

'That's not the . . . I'm not . . .' Lil tossed her head, almost laughing. 'Are you in earnest? You think I should dress up as a *man* to go to the lecture? This isn't an operetta.'

'No. Well, it would make for a dull operetta, wouldn't it? But you wouldn't be the first to do it, and if it achieves what you want, why not? Even if people suspect you, do you think they would do anything more than stare?'

Lil blew air through her lips. The idea was preposterous. And delicious. It set something alight in her. Effie remained matter-of-fact. 'You wanted to see into him more, gather what sort of an alienist — and man — he is. A closed lecture that he believes he is delivering exclusively to medical students sounds a perfect window to me.'

Lil looked for objections but found she was already playing along. 'I don't have the clothes.'

'Leave that to me. Bina has your measurements. I can find a tailor and a barber.'

'They won't let me in anyway. I'm not a student; I don't have a ticket or whatever they need.'

'Oh, I'm sure I can ferret one out for you.'

'How?'

'Lily Pad!' Effie's eyes lit up. The thought of this mischief clearly filled her with glee. 'We're not trying to get you an audience with the Queen. I'll get you in, don't worry.'

Lil pressed her lips together. Maybe this was why Effie showed so little interest in women's rights. It was the breaking of rules, the winning in spite of them, that she loved most. Equality would ruin all of that.

'Well?' She was looking at Lil now, expectantly. Lil reasoned to herself that anything that kept the blood in Effie's haggard cheeks was worth attempting. She nodded.

'Very well.' She stood to attention and gave a stiff bow. '. . . Eustace . . . Wylie. At your service, ma'am.'

Effie made a little whimpering noise, which might once have been a shriek, and clasped her hands together. 'Oh, we *do* have work to do.'

7

Tuesday 26th October

Dear Dr Lachlan,

    Forgive me if these letters are unwelcome. My business in Edinburgh keeps me here, and I do not know if you have written to the post office in Gledsmuir or not. The letter I sent yesterday broke off in the middle of my story. I shall continue in the hope that you would still like to learn it, and if not, then only for the satisfaction of completing it myself. There is a power in writing, I believe. It may not summon spirits, but it can throw a light on the shadows of the mind.

    After the maid was burned so badly, quelling my rebellious spirit and leaving me open to the advances of my tutor, life became very bleak. I could see no way out of my troubles and I had no friend to turn to. Eventually, the glimmer of an idea began to form – to escape, not merely from my mother's and tutor's demands, but from the house itself. It was an indistinct thought at first, barely even articulated. I had hardly ever left home and knew no one on the outside. I had no money. My mother had cocooned me in a world of her own making. Although I didn't know it at the time, I was far more conversant with the realities of life than most girls my age, but she and the tutor had controlled every sliver of that knowledge.

The simple practicalities of navigating the world, even the city, remained a mystery. Escape was an impossible idea, but one I returned to every night, tracing all around its edges, as if it were a door with no handle that I couldn't leave alone.

Then one day, a sitter dropped the newspaper he had brought with him. I saw it while I was prancing around ridiculously as the spirit, and managed to nudge it with my foot underneath an armchair. To distract him, I clasped the small snuffbox that was filled with crushed ice and concealed in a pocket, and then paddled my cold fingers over his face. His absurd bellows of awe, as if he'd been transported, distracted everyone else. I retrieved the newspaper later the same night and laid it out on the séance table by candlelight. My hands trembled like the sitters' always did when flames started flickering. Evidence of the beyond. But for me 'beyond' meant the pulsing, solid, real world, a place I yearned for and couldn't inhabit. In that way, I really was a ghost.

I studied the paper like a treasure map, and when I reached the advertisements, I knew I had found the spot. A resident governess was wanted for three children under ten years of age, capable of instructing in writing, arithmetic, drawing and various other subjects. A daughter of one of our sitters had gone off to be a governess, and it had always sounded to me like a dream of sophistication and freedom. But poring over the stolen paper, a realisation hit me so forcefully, I cried out like the bellowing gentleman and had to stand for long moments, hand clapped over my mouth, staring at the ceiling. I knew writing, arithmetic, drawing and the rest, enough to bamboozle professional men, so surely enough to teach children under ten. All my learning had been driven for so long by the needs of the séances, I had seen it in no other light. It had been as much a tool as the rigged cabinet and sleights of hand, useless tricks outside of the sittings. That night, for the first time in months, the night-mare didn't come.

I applied for the position, waiting until the others were asleep before creeping out of the kitchen door and posting the letter. Needless to say, I fabricated the details of my experience. I was sure to be first in the hallway when the post arrived, so if a reply came, I could squirrel it into my pocket without detection. To my near disbelief, one did. My excitement was soon quelled, however. The letter invited me to be interviewed, but insisted I bring references that would bear scrutiny. I considered forging a testimonial myself, but I would have had to use our address, and even a brief enquiry about the house would have exposed me at once. There was no one to ask. The faint spark of hope, the promise of a way out, had served only to illuminate the thickness of the walls around me. There was no door.

The blackness that descended on me then was terrible, as if the building had fallen in on me; I could barely move my limbs. When my tutor leaned over my chair, a hand on my neck and his thumb sliding further under my collar, I didn't even shrink from him. He smiled approvingly as if he thought I were beginning to bend to him, ground won, and he praised my work with an air of self-congratulation. In the séance that evening, I felt as if I were outside my body, watching numbly from some no-place while it went through the motions like a manipulated corpse. I knew I would not be able to continue the charade. It came to me as I lay in bed that there was another way to escape, a much simpler one, and I wouldn't even need to leave the house. The thought brought with it instant relief — the first sensation of uplift after the relentless crushing weight. And curiosity. My mind finally spied a chink of light through the rubble, towards which it could pick its way.

There was carbolic acid in the house, but I knew that would be painful. A knife would be better, or rope; from the first-floor bannister down into the hallway offered enough height. I went to sleep almost happily, and when the night-mare arrived, I didn't fight it. How easy it would be, I thought, if I could simply die in my bed. But, strangely, it was as if it knew my plans and that hurting me was therefore pointless. There was still the same hissing in the air and clutch of dread, but when I put up no resistance, physically or mentally, allowing it to do what it would, it changed its approach. I felt the bed dip as it climbed on. It leaned over me, but rather than crushing the air from my lungs, it hovered close to my face. Its own face was indistinct, the features blurred. I didn't recognise it, and at the same time I knew it was familiar, that I had always known it. A woman spoke. I couldn't hear the words, but it was the voice itself that shook me. Like hearing a lost loved one speak, someone long gone and inexplicably forgotten until that moment. It seemed a lifetime of tears streamed from my eyes, drenching my hair and pillow. I was overwhelmed by an emotion that felt both as remote and rediscovered as the voice. I thought I would dissolve into it. I think it was love.

When it was past, and the paralysis lifted, I lay for a long time, trying to understand the change that had been wrought in me. My resolve remained undiminished; I meant to end my life, but I felt as if something had been left behind from the night, some essence hiding within me. As I washed and dressed, I watched my body perform its familiar tasks and felt I was not quite alone in watching. I don't mean to suggest that I felt I was possessed. Perhaps some part of me, long dormant, had been awakened by the night-mare, and its very strangeness made it feel like a foreign presence. It was this other thing, this alien within, I believe, that was still desirous of life and made me act the way I did.

I decided I would do it that night, and I would use some of the rope provided for the sitters to tie up the medium in the cabinet. My skill was improving in escaping all the knots and binds my mother tested me with. It would be fitting, I thought, to tie the final knot myself, the one I could not escape from in this world but that would, ironically, release me from all that held me fast. The final escape. I say 'in this world' as if I believe in another. Do you, Dr Lachlan? We use such expressions mindlessly — the human 'soul', the 'spirit' of a thing, 'mesmerising' — but are they anything more than the linguistic residue of wishful thinking, a sort of slime caught between other words? Or perhaps there is room for the soul in your study of the mind? I would be interested to know.

With the decision made, I went about the day free of my usual inner wrangling. There were only the final, meaningless pantomimes to get through, which I did barely consciously, and was surprised when my mother remarked on how cheerful I sounded. It was the same with the tutor. I parroted information to impress a civil engineer at a Friday séance I believed would never come. Emboldened by my apparent acquiescence the day before, he was less restrained in his treatment of me, pinching my cheek and kissing my hand wetly when I incorporated details of the Stirling engine in a practice spirit writing. It was nothing to me — merely the final, petty incursions on matter already as good as dead. I didn't react, not until he took up his usual place behind me and leaned down to plant another kiss on my neck. He let his lips and moustache linger there, a prickly limpet. I was impassive. My eyes rested on the heavy paperweight that sat on the table. I remember wondering, almost idly, if I might not end his life too that day as I was already destined for the noose when, without registering a single further thought in my head, I turned swiftly and placed my hand between his legs.

I think I need not go on. I don't know where the idea or impulse came from, but I made a deal with him. I would do what he wanted, and he would write me a reference to take to *the interview. I thought I had found my way out. But I was naïve, and of course he did not keep his side of the agreement.*

Lil's pen hovered over the paper. She would never write the details of it to Dr Lachlan, but she remembered how Lambert's whole body had jolted at her touch; his sudden, wide stare fixed on a point over her head – as if he were seeing a ghost; his eyes turning to hers with a look of near horror; the low, involuntary sound that had escaped his throat. She felt the lump under her hand, like tightly bundled yarn at first, become harder, more defined, astonishingly warm. Her fingers squeezed slightly, and he took in three staccato breaths, one after another, as if in pain. A small smile, which didn't feel like hers, crept over her lips. Without removing her hand, she stood up, stood close. He blinked at her stupidly. One of his hands grasped the back of the chair; the other was flung wide, fingers spread stiffly, as if revealing a magic trick. For the first time outside of a séance, Lil felt in control. 'I want something from you in return.'

She watched him take this in, take the entire situation in. The muscles in his face flexed and quivered as he tried to master himself, to recover a look of authority. His mouth broke into an unstable grin that was both lascivious and lined with contempt. He drew his head back, trying to look down on her when they were really the same height. His voice came as a stage whisper. 'What?'

His legs were trembling violently. She opened her lips slightly and let her chest rise towards him, some part of her marvelling that her body was so sure of what to do. 'A reference. I need a character to apply for a governess position.' His eyes widened. 'It must be your address and bear scrutiny; you can say I am a private student of yours.'

His eyes moved to her lips. She let her thumb snake down the front of his lump, which made him breathe in again, filling already full lungs, and almost put him on tiptoe. 'Yes?' He gave the slightest of nods, his mouth falling open. She hesitated, only for a second. 'It's agreed then.'

She began to do what seemed logical and expected. He made noises like a distressed squirrel and urgently clawed at the buttons of his trousers. His nails caught and scratched her fingers. She was afraid suddenly. Something powerful had entered the room, something blind and full of chaos, beyond her control. Everything in her recoiled, but she forced herself to stay, to make her bones heavy.

The theory of a man's anatomy was known to her. In automatic writing, she was supposed to be channelling all the worldliness of dead men, and the lessons designed for her had not fought shy of what lay beneath everyone's clothes and the functions of different parts, especially when a physician began attending the séances. To master the fear, she recalled what she knew from diagrams and tried to apply the knowledge dispassionately to the physical reality, which was right then springing out from under both their hands in a shock of hair and flesh, like a strange and robust toadstool emerging from leaf litter. She clamped her hand around it, surprised and revolted by the softness of the skin, and made it her grim project to understand its contours, as if it were merely another exercise in acquiring knowledge. The rest of Lambert was as taut and vibrating as a plucked bow string. His breath came heavily, punctuated by guttural sounds, and he grasped at parts of her body, pinching painfully – her arm, her breast, her hair – as if he were falling from a cliff and desperately seeking a handhold. She tried to shake him off, loosening her hold on him as she did so, and he cursed at her, lip curled. 'Tighter, you little bitch.'

His hand grabbed hers and positioned it as he wanted, showing her how hard, how fast. A kind of horror began breaking through her edges, the lines she had thought defined her. It warped her insides, the dark and chaotic presence taking control and pushing her out. She felt herself beginning to drift, felt the pull to abandon her body, to own it no longer. Lambert let go, allowing her to continue alone, which came as a relief of sorts. She sensed, from a distance, it would be over soon. But his fingers reached for her face next, trying to push themselves into her mouth. She pulled her head away and, grasping him more tightly, brought her other hand up to his throat and squeezed. His eyes grew round, but he didn't resist. She pushed her thumb into the soft space beside his Adam's apple, pushed hard. He convulsed, mouth wide. The toadstool bulged, and then spewed.

Looking down at how it pumped and streamed over her hand and onto Lambert's shirt and trousers, Lil found herself thinking unemotionally about the spirit substance that was believed to issue from a medium's orifices. She had been conditioned to look continually for ways to improve the séances, and this whitish substance would surely be more convincing, gushing from someone's mouth, she thought, than muslin and egg whites.

Lambert pushed her away and bent over himself. 'Leave.'

She obeyed, wiping her hand with her handkerchief. In her bedroom, she scrubbed her fingers in the wash bowl until they were red, then her face and neck, everywhere he had touched. Afterwards, she sat on the bed for a long time, staring at nothing. The feeling of being pushed outside of herself persisted, and eventually she lay down without taking her shoes off and waited without expectation like an empty vase in an unused room.

Lil read over what she had written to Dr Lachlan. What had happened the next day was even more difficult to relate. The doctor might change his mind about the asylum when he knew what she had done: the violence, the strangeness of it. People had been locked away for much less.

There was a knock on the bedroom door. Lil jumped, for a moment barely remembering where she was, then swore under her breath. It could only be Bina. Pulling blank sheets over the letter, she barked a command to enter. Bina slipped in and, irritatingly, closed the door behind her. She clasped her hands together, face eager. 'I wonder if I might have a word with you, Miss Vincent?'

'What about?'

'Mrs Jensen.' She dropped her voice as if Effie could possibly hear from the sofa downstairs. Lil sighed and leaned back in her chair.

'Go on.'

'Well, I mean rather Mr Jensen.' Bina paused as if this made everything clear. 'I wondered if you knew his intentions . . . about coming back . . . to visit?'

Lil watched her face, hoping to decipher where the question was coming from without having to prolong the conversation, but Bina's expression showed nothing but need and expectation. 'Why are you asking?'

Bina wrung her hands for a moment and stepped closer. 'She is not well, miss.'

'I know that.' Lil spoke harshly, suddenly fearful. 'But the doctor is pleased—'

'The doctor said what she wanted to hear.' They both blinked at her interruption. Bina rushed on. 'To tell the truth, she as good as told him what to say and he repeated it back to her. But when I was showing him out, he shook his head at me and said it couldn't . . .' She caught her breath. 'He said it couldn't be very long. A matter of weeks. And I don't know what he expects me to do about that when he's just told her herself she's doing so well.' The muscles in Bina's face jumped about.

Lil regarded her with unconcealed resentment. She didn't want to hear her own suspicions spilling from Bina's lips. She looked away. 'I'll tell Mr Jensen.' Quickly, she looked back. 'Has she been asking for him?'

'No, miss, that's the other thing I wanted to say.' Bina had regained her composure. 'She speaks of nothing but finding the lover's knot brooch.'

'What?'

'The brooch. The one they say is buried there. It's become an obsession. She's ignoring the truth about her health, and I fear she will leave it too late, and if Mr Jensen is unaware . . .'

Lil nodded rapidly to hide her shock, and waved her away. 'I'll talk to him as soon as I return. Wait . . .'

She sat up to the desk again. The letter to Dr Lachlan was poking out from under the blank sheets. She couldn't return to it now; her head was too full. Hurriedly signing off, she stuffed it into an envelope and wrote the address. 'Post this for me. Please.'

When Bina had gone, Lil remained seated and motionless. The cowardice of the doctor didn't surprise her. Talk of death to a female patient was probably considered impolite, and Effie would have made it difficult for him. Lil didn't doubt that she knew all the same. Grief gripped like a fist. She wasn't ready. There was too much she didn't understand. A wave of dread that felt like a sickness passed through her. What if Nils's refusal to come to Edinburgh was less about his reluctance to watch Effie dying and more about finding the brooch at any cost? They had both lied to her about it. She faced the fact almost more in awe than in pain – it was a mountain range rearing up between them. Effie would reveal nothing she didn't want to, but Nils had neither her talent for deception nor her iron will. The train timetable was on the desk. Lil reached for it.

Rain pelted the train window so relentlessly the outside world was reduced to dim shapes and colours, trapping the passengers within in a twilight state, as if between sleeping and waking. Lil fidgeted, pulling at the fingers of her gloves and tapping her feet, until a man opposite with whiskery jowls stared over his paper at her in undisguised irritation. She stared back, grateful for the distraction and hoping he would say something. An argument would eat up the miles more effectively than this unending clatter of rain and train tracks. He clearly sensed the futility of complaint, however, for with a ferocious clearing of his throat, which startled an elderly lady out of her doze, he disappeared behind his paper again.

'Coward.' Lil said it loudly enough to be heard, but it provoked no response. She let the timidity of people enrage her. Effie was right; as long as she did just enough to appear outwardly as a man at the lecture, no one would challenge her. After some séances, she had accepted plaudits from sitters who, she could see as clear as day, hadn't believed a moment of it. There were times she longed for someone to have the courage to yank the curtain down on the whole thing. It would come as a relief, she had thought. And it did in the end, like a purifying fire.

Her thoughts kept returning to what Bina had said about the brooch, circling endlessly as if caught in the lover's knot itself. She tried to compose what she would say to Nils. Anger kept surging in her chest, but she knew shouting wouldn't help. If Effie's letter to Haxton failed, there would be no brooch and no central trench, and what then? To distract herself she thought of Dr Lachlan. Any letter from him at Gledsmuir would only be in reply to her first two about her life with Madelyn up until the fire that had burned Agnes. *If* there was a reply at all, after she had turned up on his doorstep. She recalled the moment he had glanced at her, a stranger across the street. What if their eyes met at the lecture? What if he somehow recognised her? She brought her palm down sharply on her thigh and let out a growl. The newspaper shook twice.

There was an hour left of this journey. Sleep was unthinkable, despite another restless night. A passenger stood and slid a small suitcase off the rack. As it dragged past the bag beneath, it made a *shush*ing noise that instantly set Lil's heart beating faster. Any hissing sound was the same – Bina using the bellows, the rasp of someone's skirt, even a sniff. She had to reassure herself that she could move, that it wasn't *it*. That morning, she had opened her eyes to the crone-like figure standing at the bottom of her mattress, its back to her. The hissing had come in distorted waves, each one seeming to lift her sanity a little further from its moorings. Then, almost imperceptibly, the figure began to tilt backwards. She watched helplessly as it lowered itself over her, the back of its head drawing closer to her face. There were sparse tufts of hair on its scalp, the skin in between scabbed and bleeding. Something moved beneath, protruding at points. It was the skull, she realised. The skull itself was turning independently of the flesh and face that covered it. The ridges of the eye sockets slid slowly around towards her through the back of its head. As the jaw turned, the skin was stretched too tightly across the teeth. Unable to look away, she had watched as the flesh began to tear.

On the train, Lil breathed in sharply, and then again. She stooped quickly and pulled her bag onto her knees. The letter she had given Bina to post stopped short of what had happened after Lambert had reneged on their agreement. Dr Lachlan still wouldn't know the worst of it. Taking another, purposeful breath, she took out her folder and a fountain pen.

The movement of the train made writing difficult. Her letters jumped as she headed the paper. She paused, ink pooling on the page, and closed her eyes to recall what had happened the next day. The lesson before the incident. Arriving early, she had positioned herself on the far side of the table. Lambert had entered and greeted her cheerfully, placing an armful of books in front of her usual seat. He had gestured to it. 'Shall we begin?'

A terrible sinking feeling had prevented her from answering at first. Did he mean to pretend nothing had happened? Her voice was thin. 'The reference, Mr Lambert?'

He beamed at her as if she had brought up a subject of mutual delight. 'Ah yes, of course.' He flipped open his folder and lifted out an envelope. Lil could scarcely believe it and held out her hand eagerly. Immediately, he drew back a few inches, putting it out of her reach. Still smiling, he lowered his voice. 'I was thinking. You rather . . . *ambushed* me yesterday.' He gave her a libidinous look, which turned her stomach. 'You really didn't give me a fair chance to consider my terms.'

Lil had felt as if she were being pushed out of her body again. She could only watch him in silence.

'You have to think of what you are asking. I give you this reference,' he waved it at her, 'and then off you go. Vanished.' He snapped the fingers of his other hand. 'I lose my pupil. Madelyn loses her protégé. After all the time and effort, the sacrifices we have made.'

He dropped the envelope back into the folder. There was a crushing sensation in Lil's chest, not unlike the night-mare's weight. Lambert began walking around the table towards her.

'It would take years to train someone else, and how could we find the heart for it when you are so gifted, my dear? A medium with your potential can only be met with once in a lifetime. And you must remember you have not even reached the height of your powers yet. You are still developing. It would be dangerous for you to leave the protection of your friends now.'

She began moving away from him, but it was as if someone else were manipulating her limbs while she watched. He raised a hand, smiling in repellent sympathy. 'But I understand. Of course I do. Madelyn, for the best of reasons, wanting to protect you, has kept you too close. She has forgotten you are also flesh and blood and, to thrive, must be allowed to experience the . . . corporeal side of life.'

There was a hissing in the air. Lil felt herself starting to drift. He was going to pretend that she wanted him, that she wanted what had happened yesterday.

'I can persuade her if you'll let me. I'll help you spread your wings a little, to see some of the world. There are places in London I can take you: restaurants, theatres, salons. Wouldn't you like that?'

She backed further away. The hissing was growing louder.

'And in return, you can from time to time . . .' his nostrils flickered, 'show your appreciation as you did yesterday. I think that is an altogether fairer and more mutually beneficial arrangement than the one you so precipitously sprung on me before.'

'No.' Lil shook her head. Her voice sounded far away. He lifted his chin, still smiling, and studied her as if she'd presented him with a puzzle he was entirely confident of solving.

'The alternative, you realise, is to return to things as they were? A life that, of course, could be made harder for you?' He was briefly the exacting tutor he had been when he'd first arrived. Lil took another step back. Her heel hit the bottom of the bookcase; she was cornered.

'Well.' He dropped his head. 'What about a compromise?' He peered coyly at her from under his brows. 'You will be sixteen in a few weeks. I say we follow my arrangement until then, and after you have successfully completed your debut as the medium, we can return to the question of the reference. If you still want to.'

It would never end; she could see that. There was nothing she could use against him to force him to give her the reference; there probably wasn't anything in the envelope at all. And after yesterday, it was impossible he would be content to go back to kissing her neck. Madelyn was her only hope, but she had proven how willing she was to turn a blind eye for the sake of the séances, and the sixteenth birthday tickets were already sold; she needed both Lil and Lambert there. The night-mare had taken its real shape finally. There was the sound of shallow breathing, panting almost. For several moments, Lil didn't realise it was her own body, her own breath. She seemed to be switching in and out of her senses. Lambert watched until she fully understood there was no way out. He smiled and stepped towards her.

And then? The rhythmic clattering of the train to Gledsmuir reasserted itself in her awareness. Lil looked down at her hand. She hadn't written a word, and the nib had made a great mess of ink on the page. She lifted it off and took a breath, tried to imagine Dr Lachlan was there in the carriage with her, only inches away on the opposite seat, waiting to hear her story.

8

Dear Dr Lachlan,

At my lesson the next day, my tutor reneged on our agreement and sought only to take further advantage of me. We both knew I was powerless. Strangely, my thoughts did not turn again to taking my life. As he walked towards me, I was aware only of a hissing in the air as I had experienced with the night-mare, and a sense of being outside of my body. Somewhere close by, I knew, there was unbearable panic and desperation. Mental agony. But I was disconnected from it, my eyes fixed to a patch of white wax on the rug that the maid had missed. It had melted into the pile, blurring with the paler threads and distorting the pattern. I stared at this while I waited for the tutor. Only, he never reached me that I was aware of. I could hear him though, very close. There were choking noises and fragments of words pinched through his throat. The last thing I remember clearly is raising my head to see what had happened.

Dr Lachlan, I cannot tell you what I saw; my mind has drawn a veil over it. I have only flashes and impressions where the veil wears thin. There was screaming, but I cannot say for sure if it was my own voice. Images rattled by in quick succession, seemingly out of sequence and with impossible jumps in perspective. I saw the side of his head very close to my face; the button of a waistcoat; then the whole room with a chair knocked over and a lamp on its side. Reaching hands blurred past; I looked down from above at legs kicking the carpet; I was close enough to see the tiny jump of his pulse under his skin. I felt no emotion. I was not aware of making any decisions. I barely felt anything at all until the heat. It came with a roaring noise and more than one person screaming. The first physical sensation I became conscious of was a fierce burning on the side of my face, then fingers clutching at me, trying to pull me somewhere. My own hands were clamped around the tutor's neck. I could feel the muscles all the way up my arms and down my back clenched tight with the effort. Sweat dripped down my face. In another moment I had jolted, with what felt like great violence, back into the rest of my body. I was kneeling on the tutor's chest, strangling him — just like the Mara of folklore. My mother was shrieking and trying to prise me away. I could feel the strength seeping out of my limbs, like water draining out of an old bucket, and let go. The musty smell of carpet filled my nose, then a caustic wave of burning matter. I saw the maid using a throw to beat at flames that were rippling up the wall by the fireplace.

And that was all. When I woke up, I was in my own bed. The events in the schoolroom seemed faint, distant. When the memory of it first returned to me as I lay trying to make sense of consciousness, I thought it must be the disjointed fragments of a night-mare. But two days had passed since the fight in the schoolroom. My body was feeble, as if from a long illness, and remained so for nearly a week. It was my mother who took care of me; no one else was allowed in the room. That week was the only time in my life I felt truly mothered. She was kind and gentle, stroking my hair and feeding me with a spoon until I could sit up and serve myself. Most of her posturing fell away, and I found that, after all, she was capable of carrying out mundane and practical tasks without fuss: helping me change my clothing, brushing my hair, carrying a chamber pot. I was tempted to ask again for confirmation that she was my mother – to hear it from her own lips – but feared breaking the spell.

Of course, I asked about the tutor and that day. I wondered if he had told her of my plan to escape as a way of muddying any accusation I levelled at him. Part of me suspected that that was why she had changed her behaviour towards me, simply employing a different tactic, but I pushed the thought away. It was too painful to let it ruin the sweetness of those days. She certainly never said so if she knew. His account, apparently, was that I had spontaneously manifested a spirit that had attacked him, and she believed it. It is a question that still troubles me – did they ever drop the charade and speak frankly to each other or was the fraud of the spirits maintained even while they plotted in private? I don't know the true extent of my mother's faith in her powers, how deep her delusion ran. Perhaps the tutor was clever enough never to challenge it.

I think now that I had experienced some version of the nightmare, brought on by the extreme agitation caused by my situation. Paralysing my will, it used my body to act out its violence on the tutor. Nothing like it has ever happened since. My mother claimed the fire also started spontaneously due to the spirit activity as before, but I remember the lamp on its side. We must have knocked it over during the struggle; perhaps it smashed.

When she told me how the tutor had explained it, I burst into tears and poured out how he had handled and kissed me during our lessons. I didn't breathe a word about my attempt to bargain with him. Shame prevented me from confiding that. 'Shame' – what right, really, did such a feeling have to darken my heart? Perhaps you can tell me, Dr Lachlan, why the simple instinct to survive should bring with it such a burden of self-loathing. As if self-destruction would have been the nobler course when flight was denied. Or perhaps the reason is simpler. I held my tongue through fear, also instinctive, that if my mother knew what I had done, she would use it to blame me for the tutor's behaviour and tighten her own grip on me. I suppose I shall never know. After comforting me with kisses of her own and declaring she would chop him into little pieces, she shook her head and took my hand.

'Mr— is a very silly man. However,' her fingers squeezed mine, 'he can be useful to us, my darling. For just a short while longer, until your birthday. Could you bear it if I promise he will never touch you ever again? Very soon – oh very soon – we won't need him at all. We won't need anyone, no one but ourselves.' She whispered it with such a glorious, conspiratorial relish, as if it were her dearest wish, that an answering smile bloomed from me in spite of myself.

'But, of course,' she looked at me solemnly, 'if you want me to, I shall banish him immediately. It is your decision. And we shall find another way.' It was only on the last few words that she allowed a light dusting of doubt to settle.

I think I remember what she said so perfectly because it was one of the few times I was able to believe her. I still do. Even beneath the games. Her powers of manipulation were muscular and habitual, writhing through everything she said and did. But even as the coils tightened around me, I could tell she was speaking the truth, that her plan was always for us to be together, a spiritualist double act, mother and daughter. After the months of alienation and jealousy and then her sudden attentive kindness towards me, it was irresistible. I was all that mattered to her, after all, not the tutor or the maid. In my weakened state, I agreed. There would be only one more time that she spoke to me with such honesty and perhaps even love, but by then it was too—

―――――

Lil lurched forward as the train braked, scoring a line of ink across the page. They were at Gledsmuir. She stuffed the pages and folder back into her bag and hurried out of the compartment, forgetting even to kick the jowly man's ankle as she passed.

At the post office, she waited, shivering and dripping after her run from the station. The fear that he hadn't replied, that she was to lose this frail hope after opening herself up, gave her the grotesque sense that she was disappearing, dissolving away beneath her clothes. But a cream envelope appeared as before, and she snatched it out of the clerk's hands, quickly retreating with it to a corner of the room like something feral and starving. Even her gloves were saturated. She tried ineffectually to dry her hands on the sodden wool of her coat before prising the envelope open with unsteady fingers. *My dear Miss Gerrard*. Dear God, how her heart leaped at that 'my'.

My dear Miss Gerrard,

I sat down to write to you as soon as I read the letter you delivered but have begun afresh, here, since receiving your second by post. Miss Gerrard, I am honoured that you have chosen to share your remarkable story with me, and I completely understand why you chose not to introduce yourself on Monday. Please be assured, however, that there can be no question of either yourself or your letters receiving anything but the most sincere welcome here.

Given the circumstances of your upbringing, your caution in confiding in a physician does not surprise me. I have come across spiritualists before in my work and have witnessed the contempt for the medical profession that is often expressed in those quarters. No doubt you were exposed to the same suspicions and prejudices. My view of your night-mares is much clearer when I can see the pressures that were working upon you, the unhealthy sequestering in the house, the rigorous schooling, the advances of your tutor. All this before we even begin to consider the malign influence of a childhood immersed in spiritualist beliefs and practice. What strength of mind, Miss

Gerrard, if I may say so, what lucidity indeed in one so young, to question the words and actions of those around her without the support and example of one other single dissenting voice.

You evidently found a way out of that household and away from your mother and tutor, escaping at least one of the nightmares. I would be very interested to learn how, and to know the circumstances in which you now find yourself where the night-mares have returned. From your account, it seems your sixteenth birthday and the special séance that occasioned, was a highly significant, if not decisive, event. The more detail you can give me about what happened, the better understanding I shall have. So far, you have rather listed the spiritualist practices you were forced to take part in than described them or their effect on you at the time. I realise this is because the memory is painful to you, but if you will keep your courage for just a little longer, Miss Gerrard, I am sure you will be glad of it. Anything you write to me will be kept in the strictest confidence, of course.

My invitation to discuss your case at my office remains open. I believe I can help you far more swiftly if we meet in person. However, I have no desire to persuade you into a course of action that you are not yet ready to take. That you felt able to deliver a letter by hand encourages me, but if it is too soon, I would only urge that you continue to write to me with the same candour as you have shown in your last letter. Above all, Miss Gerrard, please do not allow any doubt to undermine the trust you have placed in me, not for one moment.

Yours sincerely,
    Dr Jonathan E. Lachlan

Lil poked about herself for a handkerchief and read the letter from start to finish again while wiping her nose. She was seized by the desire to run back to the station, board the next train to Edinburgh and fling herself at his door. Perhaps he would not judge her too harshly for what had happened with Lambert. He would understand, as he had about the nature of spiritualist circles. To have the core of her experience recognised and repeated back to her with sympathy, even admiration, undid her. Not even Effie knew the full details of her history; Lil had locked it all away in a box in her mind so there could be no risk of it spilling out and poisoning her present. Even writing it down was terrifying. Madelyn's voice scored through her head. All the distrust about doctors that Dr Lachlan himself had witnessed. Dr *Jonathan* Lachlan. The inclusion of his Christian name caused a sweet buckling of her defences, even while Madelyn's voice insisted loudly it was designed on purpose, cynically, to do just that. He was taking advantage of her loneliness, fishing for a patient, a case study to submit to journals perhaps.

Her wet fingers were threatening the integrity of the paper. She drank in his handwriting once more, giddy in spite of herself that he had touched this very sheet. It was like holding the torc, that sense of a leaping spark between living hands, which, for an instant, she could persuade herself, placed them outside of space and time. She tucked it away into her carpetbag and, before she could change her mind, retrieved the crumpled letter she had written on the train for posting. She was halfway to Pitcarden before she realised she had sent it unfinished and unsigned.

The rain intensified and then lightened to a fine mist by turns while she walked the long road back to Balcraig, as if she were being breathed upon by an elemental. She didn't mind bad weather on her own account, only how it affected the excavation. For a long while after her hothouse existence with Madelyn, the outdoors had felt uncomfortable and intimidating. She had resented the Sullivans' insistence on twice-daily walks for the children, finding the changing weather as intrusive and peace-robbing as their squabbles and demands. Aside from miserable days in the cold and wet, there was the endless inconvenience of puddles and runny noses, insects and dirt, sunburn and wind-blown everything. She failed to see how her closeted upbringing had been any less healthy. But then long days in the field with Effie and Nils, reading the landscape and immersing herself in it while the skies shifted eternally above, had awakened her senses. She discovered she was a body and that bodies are alive to their environment, that they can sing with the whirl of sensations passing over and through them, like a wind chime. She became attuned to subtle changes in the air until she could feel what was coming; the scent of the earth told her what rain there had been in the night; different plants told her different stories of what lay beneath, of what had come before; her own tongue distinguished between bone and rock, wood and clay. Being indoors became numbing, a diminishing. She began to see colour – to experience it – as she never had in the dim light of Madelyn's spiritualism. When sleet whipped and cold pinched, she surrendered. Real physical discomfort became evidence of escape, a triumphant denial of the disembodied spirits and her mother's netherworld of the imagined dead. It was different from the violence of the night-mare. This was the place she belonged as a living being; it owned her, and she would have chosen to die by its storms a thousand times over than by the sickness that preyed on her in her bed.

But the rain and wind had not been her friends at the burial site. She dropped her bag behind a hawthorn and ran up the slope towards the dig, excited to see how much of the central trench had been cleared. The deluge had stopped, but only just. Rivulets of water streamed down the path under her feet, and anything with a stem had been bent and cowed. The air was busy with a thousand fresh scents released by the battering of raindrops. No one was there; Nils must have abandoned work because of the weather. She could see they had made good progress, digging perpendicular to the original trench, biting into the site for the treasure. A large amount of timbering held back the walls against the sagging earth, and tarpaulins had been pegged down over parts. She strode up the mound to the centre.

And stopped. A few planks for timbering had been stacked at the side, but the central trench was more filled in now than before. It was as if the earth had risen up from below like lava, smothering the cist. For a moment, Dr Lachlan, the lecture, even Effie, were all forgotten. Lil ground her teeth down on her lip until she tasted blood. She believed in curses in that moment.

At the cottage, she wrenched the door open and didn't bother to shut it. Nils was sitting at the table in the kitchen.

'You didn't even touch the central trench. It's ruined.' She stood dripping and vengeful on the threshold. Nils turned his head towards her but didn't meet her eyes.

'Nils?' She ripped her sodden gloves off and slapped them down on the table. 'There's not a hope of saving it. We would have to start all over again, but that's never going to happen now, is it? Effie told me you forged the letters of permission.' She felt as if she had been buried alive with the cist.

Nils still didn't answer, and something in his silence made her look at him more closely. His shoulders were stooped, and there was a greyness in his face. She might have been away for years rather than days. He shifted a little and placed a hand on the table, feebly evasive. There was a candlestick, dazzlingly crafted out of gold: medieval loot. She had nearly thrown her gloves on top of it.

Lil scoffed, as if it were nothing more than some old coins. 'You haven't found the brooch then?' Her words landed like the back of a shovel. 'Bina says it's all Effie talks about, but I've barely heard either of you mention it since we came here. *What are you keeping from me?*' The question tore at her as it was forced into the open, as if something of herself were coming away with it. Her throat pinched shut. Whispers and laughter mocked her from some place in the past. *Shrill Lil.*

Nils blinked and glanced to the side as if hearing something in the distance. He wasn't really listening. She became aware of how cold it was in the room. Her body was cooling down after the walk, and she was starting to shiver. She glanced at the hearth and directed her fury at that. 'Why have you not lit the fire?'

'Enough!' His fist slammed down against the table, making her and the candlestick jump. He glared at her, a sort of desperation in his eyes, and then faltered, something shifting his attention. He lifted his fingers to his mouth, looking horrified. 'You are bleeding.'

Lil tasted it as he spoke. Her lips were almost numb from the wind and rain, but she could feel the burn where she had bitten herself. 'It's nothing.' She wiped her mouth, and Nils leaned forward, strangely eager again.

'What did she say about Haxton?'

Lil moved her tongue slowly over her lip, watching him. It was as if he couldn't see her properly. 'She's written to him. Have you seen him?'

He stared at her a moment longer, then shook his head. 'We have lost men. More animal remains and human filth placed outside their quarters. I paid the rest more to stay.'

'What is it, Nils?' Lil spoke sharply. 'What's wrong with you?'

She waited, even after it was clear he wasn't going to answer. Finally, she retraced her steps to shove the door shut. She was on her knees in front of the fire, blowing life into the reluctant flames, when he spoke again.

'How is she?'

The question hung between them like a shred of flesh torn from his side. She didn't spare him. 'Worse. She's eating less and sleeping more. The doctor told Bina she doesn't have long. You should go to her while she still has the energy to talk. Before the pain is too much.'

The anger rose again. He was leaving her to witness Effie's decline alone, to bear it all by herself. And when that was over, she would have the burden of his regret.

'I must change.' She stood up, brushing bits of kindling from her skirt, and left him to suffer her bruising words alone.

The cold didn't leave her even after she had dressed herself in dry clothes and wrapped a shawl around her head. As she moved about the room, she became aware of the artefacts shrouded in their cloth wrappers or, more truthfully, she became aware of the goddess and a growing desire to look at it again. It was like wanting to look over a steep drop or stare directly at the sun. Sitting at the table, she reached out and turned back the folds of cloth. The goddess gleamed in the light from the window. It both drew Lil in and unnerved her. *Who made you and for what purpose?* She shivered suddenly, and the old superstition whispered in her head about someone walking over her grave. With it came the words she had written unwittingly in séances: *new bones over old, one two three four five, new bones over old.*

She slapped her hand on the table and took out the letter from Dr Lachlan, hoping to warm herself with his words. She succeeded a little.

I am honoured . . . the most sincere welcome . . . what strength of mind . . . do not allow any doubt . . .

Words to fight words. Madelyn's were always there, of course, at war with the doctor's. But Lil remembered she had the power to write her own, too. It was true what she had told Dr Lachlan, that writing illuminated the shadows. She longed to talk to him, this man who had been honest with her, who was able to see her clearly even through her letters. After a moment's hesitation, her hands reached for paper, pen and ink. She would finish her story.

Dear Dr Lachlan,

You will have read my last letter by now. You know how far my ordeal with the tutor went, the dark thoughts that nearly made me take my own life and the violence that occurred. I can only trust, as you ask, that these frank admissions find a safe haven with you and that they do not alter your belief in my sanity. I trust also that if you revise your opinion, you will tell me. After a lifetime ensnared in the lies of others, I would far rather be told the truth, however bleak it may be.

Your own last letter, of course, was most comforting and reassuring. It is a relief to know that you have some knowledge of spiritualist circles and their beliefs. That world is difficult to explain to outsiders without sounding mad merely by association. It is true that describing it in any detail makes my stomach revolt and my pen shake – to put down on paper what I subjected myself and others to! But I shall do as you ask as fully and honestly as possible.

You rightly surmise that my sixteenth birthday was decisive in the break from my mother's house. As I described, her affection towards me during my illness almost made me reconsider. I felt a life of deception would be bearable if it were just the two of us, without the tutor and maid. And there was always the lingering fear that the night-mare would pursue me into the world and my mother's prediction would come true. Better the devil you know etc. How true that old saying is; how timid the human heart at the very moment it might free itself.

There were only a few days left before the birthday séance. My mother came to some agreement with the tutor – he had threatened to leave and take his high-placed patrons with him, but I doubt he was ever truly serious; the promise of a larger share would have been persuasive. In our lessons, he was once more the aloof tutor I had first known. Aloof and careful – I think my presence made him anxious, and with good reason. I took pleasure in how he flinched when I reached suddenly for my blotter or turned to ask a question. My triumph over him was a pyrrhic victory really, but it was the only taste of winning I had ever had. It was also arranged that the maid would sit in, so I was never alone with him. We were, I believe, both grateful for that. She was a better student than I – I could see her in the corner of my eye making notes and practising spirit writing in a notebook she held on her knees.

We rehearsed all the sleights of hand for escaping the knots and appearing dressed as the spirit until I felt capable of slipping out of any bind or constriction I could ever find myself in. I was nervous though, especially now I had all but decided to accept this as my life. For the first time it was important to me that the séance be a success. My mother continued to treat me with loving gentleness, winking at me behind the tutor's back and whispering, 'Not much longer'. Perhaps she really did mean to drop him once we had more powerful friends and my 'education' was complete.

The evening was to begin with automatic writing but only for a select group of sitters, old friends and, of course, two more lofty patrons we were hoping to ensnare. It took place in the smaller séance room that doubled as the schoolroom, where the marks of the recent fire had been left on purpose to unsettle and enthral our audience. An effective move; it was difficult not to think of them as the lights were dimmed and they were lost in shadow. I include myself in that. I was still puzzled as to how the lamp on a sideboard had caused scorch marks up the side of the fireplace, but as I have said, my memory of that day is fragmented and incomplete. Much was made of my turning sixteen – the spirits sent their congratulations, if you will believe it, and messages of advice for me about the great surge in my abilities, warnings to be careful as I was not yet mistress of my own power. This, as you will no doubt realise, was to set up the theatrics planned for later in the evening.

The spirits' attention then turned to the sitters. Lord Randall was known to have a special interest in algae, particularly diatoms, and much of my study that week had been in microscopy. I remember he had an enormous moustache, like a stuffed vole draped across his upper lip, and an unconscious habit of pursing his lips suddenly, the only external sign he ever gave of excitement. As the 'spirit' filled pages with plausible nonsense and my pencil traced the face of an eminent dead phycologist, the vole was thrust forward with increasing frequency. I noticed my tutor smiling to himself for the first time since I had tried to strangle him. There was also a Mrs Andrews present, a recent widow — wealthy, of course — who rattled me with her kindness. She smiled at me with an expression of great pity as well as curiosity, and observed proceedings with a look of quiet intelligence in her face that made me worry she would see through our tricks and reject us, perhaps publicly. But the need to believe can twist the wisest of minds, and this lady was in a raw state of grief for her late husband. (Can grief be described as a type of madness, Dr Lachlan? The things it makes us do.)

Mr Andrews had been a manufacturer of decorative tiles, so I was ready with allusions to glazes, encaustics, kilns and so on. My tutor had discovered his favourite flower was the tulip and that his wife had included a single stem in the usual funeral bouquets. He had also managed to procure an example of his handwriting — a letter written to a business associate — and I had laboured for hours to copy it until it felt as natural as my own. When Mrs Andrews recognised her beloved's lavish scrawl, clear among the spirit gibberish, thanking her for the flower, her face became contorted with the most appalling expression of hope.

The lights were raised, and a photograph was taken of the group. There was to be a follow-up meeting the next week when the developed image would be produced. Examples of the Drake sisters' other work had been shown, and hopes were kindled that, due to my heightened magnetic presence, the results would be remarkable. No doubt they would have been, too, if the sisters had seen it through. The sitters whispered excitedly to each other and glanced around as if Mr Andrews might be hovering in shadowy form behind them. It was the most successful automatic writing session we ever held. I hated every second of it.

There was then a short break so I could rest and recover my powers before attempting the spirit manifestation. More people were in attendance than usual. My mother and tutor were determined to extract every last penny from the unique event of my birthday séance and debut. I was worried the chairs at the front were too close to the cabinet, that they would hear me struggling out of the ties and changing my clothes. A larger space had been left around the fireplace. My mother and the maid had planned something. She had told me not to flinch if I heard a blaze, that they had taken precautions in the event of another spontaneous burst of flame. The maid looked fitting in her black veil. I think she enjoyed how the finely dressed ladies and gentlemen stared at her with an awe tinged with fear and obeyed as meekly as lambs as she directed them to their seats. There is surely no other house or situation on earth where her injuries would have raised her value or earned her so much respect as they did at my mother's.

The scene was set. Another photograph was taken before the lights were dimmed, and it was time for my entrance. It was our practice that my mother did all the talking. I, as a medium, was always to be the pale and silent vessel, feeble and defenceless, the very model of female receptivity. (I do not know if you have ever considered, Dr Lachlan, how spiritualists have turned the so-called natural virtues of respectable women into a powerful commercial asset. It is perhaps the one area of business, outside of a brothel, where women have the professional advantage purely by conforming to society's expectations.)

My mother played her role perfectly, displaying great anxiety *for me, her precious child — she was happy to admit our relationship for the sake of the séances — but humbled by and subservient to my great gift. She claimed she allowed these evenings reluctantly, only out of respect for the world beyond. My spirit control demanded it. She actually trembled as she led me to the cabinet. My steps were slow and uncertain. I wore a plain, loose dress and a draped turban — I looked a sort of exotic invalid — and I never smiled. All the greater contrast with the sociable souls who would emerge to commune with the living. But first I was to be tied up by volunteers to prove it couldn't possibly be me wafting around in gauze. Lord Randall was allowed in and another stranger, but they were accompanied by two regulars who had been part of our practice sessions. When it comes to it, most gentlemen fight shy of hurting the medium, I think, but Mr Randall, for all his love of microscopic organisms, was not a subtle man by nature. I gasped when he yanked the rope tying my wrists to the chair legs. One of the regulars, probably paid by my tutor, leaned in, muttering, 'A little tighter, to be sure,' and I felt him discreetly loosen it instead. Once all were satisfied, a veil was draped over my face. They retreated, and my mother led them in hymn singing to cover my breathless contortions and preparations inside the cabinet.*

I was quickly out of the ropes and divesting myself of dress and petticoat. No corset — I was bound tightly with strips of linen so spirits could be of either sex or any age. It also served as a welcome defence against prying fingers. My hands moved mechanically, trained to land just so on the necessary items in the darkness. There was a chest that the rope was kept in, which had a false bottom. Beneath that was everything I needed. The first spirit was both the easiest and most uncomfortable. I was already wearing a short wig underneath the turban, and I donned a small, phosphorus-coated mask, which pinched, and a bizarre sort of front-wearing jacket with arms only the length of my forearms. I heard the light plucking of a mandolin, controlled by the maid to signal the arrival of the spirit (it would end up miraculously in the lap of one of the sitters). Kneeling and thus awkwardly attired, I opened the door of the cabinet a fraction with a wooden, painted child's hand. It was attached to a stick I held in the sleeve. Gasps came from the sitters as the little glowing fingers appeared, and one of the regulars cried out breathlessly, 'Oh, it's little Willie!'

Little Willie was a shy boy, peeping out at the audience and giggling before retiring again. Sometimes he advanced a few short steps in front of the cabinet if a sitter was particularly cajoling, but he never came within reach, and it was mostly a game of peek-a-boo until I could feel the audience tiring and ready for something new. Back inside the cabinet, I returned wig, mask and jacket to the hidden compartment. After a short while, I heard exclamations and the creaking of seats. It was the maid's moment, dressed and masked as a man, Mr Morelli, standing on a camouflaged block and faintly illuminated in the doorway behind the audience. No musical signal for that one; we waited until one of the sitters became distracted by the light and, discovering the vision for themselves, alerted the others. I imagine the effect was quite unnerving, even for sceptics. Meanwhile, I was stuffing my ordinary dress with cushions and propping it up in the chair, the turban draped over a sizeable pincushion for the head. Then I slipped into a loose tunic, let my hair down and applied a little phosphorus oil to the back of my hands and feet. This was for my 'control', a girl named Beth, who had died most heartrendingly of consumption on her sixteenth birthday but seemed to have no regrets. She was the main event, and as it was my birthday, she was to be in a particularly gay mood, summoning flowers from the ceiling to wear in her hair.

I took a moment inside the cabinet to try to will myself into the right mood. Already, the thought of doing this week after week was like lead in my bones, and I couldn't banish Mrs Andrews' dreadful, hope-filled face from my mind. But it had to be got through. I took three deep breaths, chilled my palms in a bowl of icy water, dried them and pushed open the cabinet door. It was almost as dark as inside the box. Bells and chimes were tinkling. As I emerged, I could sense the tension in the room after Mr Morelli and felt more than saw people's eyes on me. There were sounds of delight and relief from sitters who had met Beth before, even greetings. I posed, smiling and a little coy, until a woman near the back begged me to come closer.

'Yes!' A man near the front whispered it loudly, patting his lap. 'Come and take a seat, my dear.' Some tutted, some laughed quietly. I tittered.

'Good evening, my friends.' I kept my voice low and breathy, so they always had to strain to hear me. They all returned the greeting either in murmurs or hearty voices. I shook hands with several on the front row, including Lord Randall, and began moving about the room, smiling like a debutante. They began asking standard questions: what was it like to materialise? Was it painful? Did I have a message for anyone there? I explained that materialising was strange and tiring but not painful, and it was thrilling to walk among the living. And, of course, I had messages. There were the usual bones thrown to the regular sitters. Tails wagged. A spirit aunt was concerned about her niece's recent cold, a late coal merchant urged his business partner to expand into aggregates, a dead child wanted his grandmother to sing his favourite lullaby once again. She did so with tears streaming down her cheeks. Next, I laughed at the persistence with which the dead phycologist had urged me to thank Lord Randall for the stimulating conversation in the first part of the evening and how much he hoped the discussion would be continued next week. I was supposed to give a follow-up message to Mrs Andrews from her husband, but I shrank from it. She was watching me with

that same intelligent scrutiny, laced with a desperate need, and I felt keenly how I was degrading us both.

Someone asked if the whole body had materialised under the drapes. I was grateful no one had yet demanded an explanation for the clothes themselves — how we had to squirm around that subject with talk of electrical substances. As far as the whole body was concerned, that depended on the conditions and the powers of the medium. To materialise, spirits borrowed from the physicality of the medium while she was in a trance. I explained that as it was her sixteenth birthday and I, Beth, had died on my sixteenth birthday, there was a powerful sympathy between us. The materialisation was complete. With that, I threw my arms in the air and raised my voice. 'Let us celebrate!'

On cue, thanks to the maid upstairs, crowns of flowers started apporting and falling onto the sitters. I darted about, laughing and heaping them on heads. Cries of delight filled the room.

'So does that mean the medium is no longer visible in the cabinet?'

The voice cut through the merriment of the others. It was dry and serious and came from a man I didn't recognise. I had barely noticed him in the gloom on the end of a row near the back.

'Oh, she is there still, but diminished, temporarily. There is as yet no language on earth to express what is happening, but in a way, we are sharing the same body.'

I paused. This was a stranger, not the loyal regular primed for this part of the evening, but something prompted me to take a risk, and I held out my hand. 'Would you like to see?'

His head moved as if in surprise. 'I would.' He reached with his own hand, and I let only the tips of our fingers touch. A murmuring started up among the others. They had been taught to respect the medium's vulnerability in her trance state; any harsh light or force inflicted upon her or the spirit could be harmful, possibly fatal. The tutor stood up. I could feel his alarm at my departure from the script.

'Please be careful, Beth. You know how dangerous opening the cabinet can be for a medium.'

I smiled. 'We shall merely peek in at her.' An unstable feeling was growing in me, an impulse to act recklessly. I held his eye a beat longer than necessary. We both knew I could do anything I pleased as Beth. Anything at all.

It was warm in the room, and the man's fingers were clammy. I led him to the front and pulled open the door. My tutor had also come forward. He was glaring at me – a silent, furious warning. The shape of the stuffed dress was visible in the cabinet, plausibly from that distance a person sitting in a trance. Others were standing up to try to see, when the man snatched his hand from mine and lurched past as if to charge right into the cabinet. There was a sudden roaring noise and an orange blast lit up half the room. The fire had exploded alight, apparently by itself. There were yelps and gasps as the audience turned as one. The flames didn't keep to the grate but licked around the front, hurrying across the tiles and up towards the mantelshelf in ropes of fire like a plant flinging out tendrils. It was, I have to say, ingeniously designed.

The man paused, halted on the threshold of the cabinet. I had instinctively grasped his arm as he darted forward. The stuffed dress was a little more visible with the light spilling in from the fire, a little less convincing. For those who wanted it to, it would still have passed as a person sitting there, but this man, it was clear, had come looking for fraud and would find it. The sceptics, the investigators, had finally caught up with my mother.

Since the maid's accident, buckets of water had become a standard feature in the house and at séances, and my mother now flung one at the fire, dousing most of it and plunging us back into gloom. But not before the man had turned to look at my face. I could see him more clearly too; mid-years, brown hair only just on the respectable side of unkempt, slightly bulging eyes. It was not so much his features that impressed me as his expression. A precise sort of loathing, professional almost, as if the feeling were impersonal. The fire had startled me, for all my mother's warnings, and I met his gaze very much as myself and not as Beth. We saw each other quite clearly in that moment — the false spirit and the false believer. Panic leaped up in me, as fierce as the fire, but immediately died away. What came in its place was relief. A great wave of it, flooding my body and washing away all the lies that had sprung to my lips. His eyes widened as he read my face, and I watched his chest expand with the words that would strike us all down. I felt giddy, as if a die had been thrown and my fortune with it. The reckless feeling returned in force — let the die fall as it would. I let go of his arm.

'Lights!'

Despite my lack of resistance, he grasped my tunic at the neckline and yanked until it ripped, then shoved me away and flung himself into the cabinet. I was thrown backwards, stepping onto the hem of my tunic and falling full-length into the sitters who had gathered behind. They were too taken by surprise to catch me, and I landed awkwardly, bashing my shoulder on the edge of a chair. The room brightened so quickly at the man's shout that I think there must have been several sitters in league with him. Him and the Drake sisters. At first, all I could see through arms and legs was the tutor grappling with him as he tried to pull my dress into the room. As hands hauled me upright, I saw one of the sisters had brought the camera forward and was pointing it at them. When she saw me, she turned the tripod my way.

I have seen that photograph. For all I know, Dr Lachlan, you have too; it was striking enough to be taken up by papers beyond the spiritualist press. It catches me just as I've reached a relatively static standing position, so the image is not too blurred. My ripped tunic exposes an indecent amount of flesh, hands are gripping my arms on both sides, a blur of hair hides much of my face, but it is clear that I am looking directly, wildly at the camera. In short, I appear insane. The image was used to support entirely conflicting arguments against spiritualism. To some I was the madwoman, either driven out of my mind by spiritual practices or drawn to them because I was already unstable, and at the same time, to others, I was the cold-blooded charlatan, furious at being unmasked. A feat of double possession to rival the claims of most mediums.

The room was in uproar. The next thing I knew, my mother had her arms around me with a hand over my face, and was bustling me towards the door, shrieking that they had killed me. The only person not on her feet and shouting was Mrs Andrews. I caught a glimpse of her as I was hurried away. She was looking at the floor, oblivious to the carnage around her. There was no anger in her expression, no disappointment; nothing but the most desolate sadness.

It was Mrs Andrews I was still thinking of as my mother pushed me up the stairs. Her face goaded me all the more for the lack of accusation in it. It is difficult — perhaps impossible, do you think, Dr Lachlan? — to like people whom one has harmed. Feelings of contempt rushed to my defence; she was a fool for coming in the first place, for ever letting herself think she could talk to the dead. If she were in pain, if she felt newly bereaved all over again, it was no one's fault but her own.

My mother was talking in urgent and consoling tones. I wasn't really listening, too preoccupied with Mrs Andrews while I tore off the tunic and bindings and threw them on the floor. Looking at the crumpled heap at my feet, I realised with a fresh blaze of anger that I intended never to wear them again. I stamped on them as I crossed the room for my dressing gown and then began scrubbing the phosphorus oil off my hands at the washstand. My mother's words finally filtered through, and when I understood what she was saying, I stopped abruptly to stare at her. She was still talking as if the spirits were real.

'I promise you, my darling, we shall survive this. People who know the truth, they understand that the spirits manifest through the body of the medium. They will come back.'

I felt a scream tearing up my throat. My hands reached out, sending water droplets flying into the air. 'He was pulling <u>cushions</u> out of my <u>dress</u>.'

She turned her head to one side as if I had struck her. I think my mother could stick a knife into someone's back and still pass herself off as the victim. The silence was broken by the tutor crashing into the room. He was sweating. His lips were pressed together into a thin line and, at the sight of me, he lowered his head, like a bull.

'You've finished us.' Hatred licked around his lips. 'You did it on purpose, didn't you?' My mother spoke his name, but he ignored her and took a step towards me. 'Are you working for them? Is that why you invited him to look in the cabinet?'

'Of course she isn't.' There was a low and sinister warning in my mother's voice, but he shook his head, still glowering at me.

'I saw the way you looked at each other. You didn't try to stop him, did you, you little slut?'

I thought he was going to lunge at me. His fists clenched and his upper lip pulled back, but before either of us could move, a candlestick had hit him hard in the side of the head. He flinched and stared around at my mother in disbelief, a hand raised to his temple. Fury followed. I thought he might fly at her instead, but she was already advancing, a pair of sewing scissors from my dressing table in her hand. She stopped within striking distance. 'Get out.' He glanced at me, *but she gave him no quarter.* 'Take another step in her direction, and I shall put this through your neck.'

I believed her; I'd never heard her sound so deadly serious before. It was different from the earnest voice she used in séances and about the spirits. A thrill of fear ran up my spine, a sense of chaos bending itself across the threshold. The tutor must have felt it too. He started nodding, as if to himself, and slowly backed away. At the safety of the door, he narrowed his eyes at her. 'You won't come back from this.' It was a threat. He left without another look my way.

Outside, the sitters were spilling into the street, still chattering excitedly. I thought of rats deserting a sinking ship. My mother was regarding me steadily. 'He won't expose us further. He has nothing to gain by it.'

I let out a sort of laugh, due in part to the complete irrelevance of anything the tutor might do, but mostly because of the odd tilting in my heart that my mother had defended me with such unthinking force. It was the most maternal thing she had ever done, and I didn't know what to do with it. We stared at each other for several moments, both unsure of which way the evening would topple. I felt my breath coming faster. Something was rising in me, though I didn't know what until I said it.

'Stop pretending. Stop pretending to me. And to them.' I gestured out at the dispersing sitters. Tears, unexpected, welled up and spilled from my eyes. I ran forward to take her hands. She blinked, unsettled, and I felt her resisting the urge to pull away. I gripped harder. 'Admit it. Admit it's all spectacle and clever tricks.'

The answer revealed itself to me, suddenly shining and clear. 'They will still come!' I laughed, a proper laugh. It was so simple. 'We shall carry on doing everything we do so well, amazing everyone with the impossible.' She was looking at me in horror but didn't interrupt. 'We can talk of spirits and give them the experience of a séance — they will have no idea what is going to happen. But it will be theatre, and we won't pretend otherwise.'

She started shaking her head as if she couldn't accept what she was hearing, and she tried to release her hands. I held on. 'We can work on the act, take it even further since it's for entertainment. Like magicians.'

With a cry, she wrenched herself free and staggered backwards. 'The act?' She hissed it. 'Magicians?'

But my mind was racing ahead with possibilities, ideas blooming like flowers beneath my feet. I stretched out my arms towards her. 'And perhaps we can still help people who are grieving. It might be good for them to say everything they want to say to a loved one and receive a loving answer, to act it out, even if they know underneath it's only make-believe. We could—'

'How dare you?' She had backed against the wall, bristling. 'How dare you say these things to me?'

Her outrage was as real as the threat to the tutor had been. I felt a misgiving briefly, as if the backs of my knees had been shoved. But I recovered.

'Say these things to you? To *you*?' I glared back at her. 'To the person who has schooled me my whole life to dissemble and deceive, whose entire livelihood depends on trapdoors and hidden levers and stolen information and the credulity of fools?'

She threw her arms up and looked to the ceiling. 'You know very well what all that is for. But darling,' her eyes burned at me, 'they are not fools. I will not have them called so in this house.'

I brushed that aside. 'You can't actually have thought I would continue to believe you — that it's all about creating the right atmosphere for the spirits to appear for real. I am not a child any more. You must think I'm feeble-minded.'

'I have never thought that. But what are you, my darling, without the spirits? I readily admit there is the question of *income — but that's not something you've ever had to concern yourself with, is it?'* Her voice dropped into a pit of bitterness I hadn't heard before. *'You simply accept the food on your plate and clothes on your back. How do you think we would survive if we were dependent on patronage that was only forthcoming when the spirits spoke?'*

I was silent.

'No answer? Nothing to say? Of course not. You <u>are</u> still a child — an ungrateful, spoiled little girl. You are nothing without me.'

She shouted it in an ugly, guttural voice that seemed to shock even her. I felt punched, incapable of speech. After a few moments, she regained control and spoke levelly.

'Like it or not, this is how the world forces spiritualism to work. If we are to do any good at all, it is how we have to proceed. And it serves; it draws people in, and it most certainly does create the best conditions. The spirits themselves have never objected.'

It was my turn to toss my head, but the violence of her outburst, the truth of how she saw me, had robbed me of strength. My voice was thin. *'Well, of course they haven't. They don't exist.'*

She looked at me as if I had said door handles don't exist. Rather than angrier, her expression became thoughtful. I tried to summon back my own rage.

'I have been playing along with you my whole life, obediently, as I've been taught, but I won't do it any more. I have never seen or heard or . . . communed with any one of your damned spirits.'

There was no trace of hostility left in my mother's face. It was filled with curiosity. And worse: pity.

'But my darling, you have already seen more of the world beyond than I have. And felt it.' She took a small step forward. *'The figure that comes to you at night . . .'*

I flinched. It was as if I had forgotten all about the nightmare, and the memory of it was visceral. I shook my head violently. 'It isn't real. It's in my mind.'

She put her head on one side and took her time, watching me, before speaking gently. 'Is that how it feels? Not real?'

I couldn't look at her. She had gone straight to where I was weakest, where all my doubts were born and flourished. Tears threatened to overwhelm me again. Nothing in my life was more real than the dark figure at the end of the bed. She didn't speak, leaving room for my fears to grow, to cast their shadows across the silence. I did not have the words then to cut through the confusion and misery in my mind. There was only the knowledge, deep within me, that the night-mare, whether it was supernatural or not, had nothing to do with the theatrics of my mother's séances. And those, I had to escape from. Mrs Andrews' grief-hollowed face grew sharp in my mind, and I turned suddenly, reaching for the armoire. As I never went anywhere, I didn't own a travelling bag, but there was an old carpetbag stuffed with offcuts from the spirit costumes and hidden pockets I sewed into our skirts. I emptied this onto the floor and, throwing it on the bed, began pulling garments blindly from the shelves.

My mother watched. I could feel her calculating her next move, how best to handle me, but my only thought was to get away. I don't think she was worried. It must have been clear I had no plan.

'My love, where are you going at this hour? Go to bed. We can talk about this in the morning.'

I finished stuffing an old blouse into the bag and then turned to face her. 'Goodnight, then.'

All I could think was to get her out of the room. She looked uncertain; my abrupt acquiescence must have seemed suspicious. But it was true that the night was cold and I had nowhere to go.

What she had said was also true: without her, I was nothing. She lingered, perhaps regretting how far she had gone. 'You will feel differently in the morning. You are right; you are not a child any more. We shall talk properly.'

I nodded quickly, not looking at her and, after another moment, she left. I didn't move for a long time, but my mind was already ransacking the paltry stores of my experience as chaotically as I had just pulled articles from the armoire. There had to be a way out; there had to be, some thread to catch hold of that would lead me to safety. I don't know how long I was standing there before I found it. It flashed suddenly, as if catching the light, and I seized on it, pulling it out until I could see it clearly. I turned it over, amazed at what I was contemplating. It was far from assured, and it wouldn't be the clean break from spiritualism and from her that I wanted. But it was the only possibility I could see of putting a roof over my head.

I upended the carpetbag for a second time and then repacked it sensibly, only with what was necessary: a shawl, items for my toilet, hairbrush and pins, nightgown, spare gloves and handkerchiefs. There was no money and nothing of value to take with me. I put out my wool dress and cloak for the morning and, as there was nothing more I could do, lay down on the bed. I didn't expect to sleep, but exhaustion must have overwhelmed me at some point because the next thing I knew, morning had come, a grey light suffusing the darkness. My dress and cloak looked like a corpse slumped in the chair. I was exhausted still, but I took the failure of the night-mare to materialise as a good sign. Come nightfall I would either be in an unknown bed or the gutter, but I would be far from my mother's house. Washed and dressed, I crept down to the kitchen to find what food I could. After packing bread rolls and a hunk of cheese into my bag, I tiptoed up to the hallway.

When I turned towards the door, my mother was standing in front of it in her dressing gown. She took in my clothes and the carpetbag. 'Won't you have some tea first? We said we'd talk.'

'You said that, not me.' I gripped the carpetbag more tightly. Every nerve was taut. I was terrified she would say something or give me a look to pull at my sympathy, to make me doubt myself.

'Where will you go?'

I didn't answer, and her expression shifted for an instant into a deep, anguished look — private, as if she didn't mean for me to see it. It achieved its purpose, making me feel I had witnessed true pain, pain that I was the cause of and could relieve if I chose. I bit my lip, thinking of what I intended to do and how it would destroy her. She was so much a part of me, I surely risked destroying myself too. I tried to summon Mrs Andrews' face, but it didn't help. The woman in front of me was all I knew, my only source of warmth and safety, all I knew of love, or what passed for it in that house. I didn't know any other kind. She could always smell weakness in me like the blood of a wounded animal.

'If I have pushed you too hard, asked for too much, it is only to give you the independence that I had to struggle for years to win. You don't know what it means to be a woman alone without money. It is to be nothing.'

'I don't want to make money this way.' I knew it was a mistake to answer her, but I couldn't stop myself. My poor heart needed so desperately to be heard, and there was no one else.

'Oh, my darling.' She seemed close to tears. 'What choices do you think you have? How much money do you think you can earn? Enough to be independent?' She shook her head. 'It is only a form of bondage. You are not free.'

'I am not free here.'

'But you will be.' She made to move towards me and stopped herself. 'You are so close. If you only stop fighting your gift, it will give you everything, mastery over your own life. Think of it — freedom.'

I nodded. 'Freedom to fool other people. Freedom to fool myself. I can pretend every night that it's really the spirits being pawed by the gentlemen, not my own body. A whore's life is more honest.'

Anger showed in her face for the first time. 'You are so naïve, so ignorant. You think you suffered at the hands of Mr—?' She named the tutor. 'You were never in danger. Who do you think will protect you out there? Or are you stupid enough to imagine governesses are untouchable?'

Her eyes widened as mine did, aware she had misstepped. Nausea broke over me, making me hot, but I smiled through it. She knew about the advert in the paper. Of course she did. I was stupid indeed to believe I could keep a single secret from her. My very thoughts weren't my own. Her mistake was enough — the reminder of the control, the manipulation at work behind everything she said. I stood taller, adjusted my grip on the handle of the carpetbag. 'I am leaving now.'

She looked at me squarely for a moment and then reached into the pocket of her dressing gown. Pulling out an envelope, she held it out. 'Your reference.'

I stared, waiting for the trick, my footing lost again. She flapped the letter at me. 'I looked through his folder after you nearly strangled him to death. I knew there had to be a reason. I suppose you made some kind of agreement with him, and he thought he could cheat you. The fool. He won't help you now. I have rewritten it. I lied a little.' She raised an eyebrow. 'I won't stand in your way.'

I approached cautiously, and slowly took it from her hand, as if from the jaws of a wolf. She turned and unlocked the *front door.* Pausing with her fingers on the handle, she looked at me again. 'Go and see for yourself. You have that right. And when you are ready, come home. I shall be here. Your true path will still be here, waiting for you.'

She pulled open the door. The cold air rushed in and seized me in a cruel, gleeful embrace. There was the pavement, the road, the houses opposite, all the same hard grey in the begrudging light. My freedom was an inhospitable wasteland. I stepped towards it, but my mother clutched my arm suddenly.

'Wait.' With her other hand she scrabbled to catch something from under the neckline of her nightgown and lifted the locket over her head. She pressed it into my hand. 'Keep this with you. The spirit that attacks you at night will follow you; it will be stronger away from your home. Be careful.' She looked at me with such unfeigned love and fear in her face, I thought I would fall into her, surrender. 'Your efforts not to believe are no defence against it. They only make you more vulnerable.'

I didn't fall. I took the locket from her and walked out of the house. I could feel her eyes burning into my back all the way down the street. It wasn't until I heard the door being shut, like a cord snapping, that I truly felt myself safe in my own body, outside, free. I don't think I have ever felt so alone in all my life.

Geography had figured largely in my lessons. The men of the world whose spirits I impersonated knew their way around, and a map of London was sufficiently lodged in my head to know roughly how to get from my mother's house to Camden. Which direction to take. The Drakes' studio address had long been in my possession. It was a flat and papery knowledge, this internal map, a bird's-eye view of an idea, as I had never been in the real streets alone before. I remember how they seemed too full of happenings, noise and movement and the smell of dung and smoke coming from all angles. My lack of *experience meant I didn't trust the space around me or know what to anticipate. There seemed no reason why the hansom cab trotting at speed around the corner shouldn't veer onto the pavement, or the driver's long whip miss its mark and cut me instead. The sudden, hacking cough of a man mending a cane chair on some area steps nearly frightened me into the road. As the pavements grew busier, I found myself out of rhythm with other pedestrians and progressed in jerks, tripping over myself. Crossing the street was an ordeal of stamping hooves, implacable wheels rattling down, and shouting men. And eyes, eyes everywhere. My mother's warning kept step with me. There was no certainty that I had left the night-mare behind with the tutor.*

It wasn't all terrifying. I glimpsed little islands of wonder when I was able to surface from the maelstrom. Flowers are always beautiful, especially so when their improbability is due to the season rather than them being apported from the spirit world. I eyed the hothouse displays in their baskets and the bunches in the hands of street sellers, women whose own faces were fast withering above the blooms. The morning found its stride just as I found mine. I was unaccustomed to walking any distance and became aware of the weakness of my body but also the stirring effect of exercise. The creamy smell from a milk cart made me realise, to my surprise, that I was hungry, and that hunger felt different when the body had worked hard. Catching the scent of ginger cakes on a tray around a girl's neck, I considered how hunger must be a different thing again when one had money.

I had to ask directions and was half amazed when my words were met without suspicion. The Drakes' studio had a substantial awning and a large front window, displaying pictures of severe-looking families. I watched from the other side of the street. The shining idea that I had pulled from the wreckage the night before seemed a fairy tale on the hard pavement with horse muck soiling my hem. Supposing the Drakes and their friends believed me and were willing to accept my help in exposing spiritualist fraud, it didn't mean they would take responsibility, offer shelter or employment. In my mind, I had been an unmissable opportunity for them, their trump card; they would want to keep me close. More likely, they would despise me. Take my testimony and use it to shame me publicly, as well as my mother and the tutor.

The air was still chilly, and I set down my bag so I could put my hands in my pockets. My fingers closed on the locket my mother had thrust at me, and I felt a pang that pressed the breath from my lungs. She had worn it for as long as I could remember. As a child, I had played with it, running my fingers over the fake ruby and diamonds. Perhaps she had given it to me for this very purpose, to remind me of the bond between us. Its value was trifling otherwise; all her jewellery was glass and paste, false glitter like everything else. I pulled it from my pocket and opened the case. She was there as usual, perhaps twenty years old, but the image of myself as a small child that had always graced the other side was gone. In its place was a much more recent picture of me taken by the Drakes. My mother and I face each other, and we look more like sisters, barely a few years apart. Its effect on me was exactly as she must have planned. If it weren't for this vivid reminder of our entwined lives, of how much she had made me in her own image, would I have knocked on the Drakes' door anyway? Offered to demolish her reputation for good and humiliate her? Where would I be now? Performing fake séances, probably, to disprove the mediums and provide entertainment in one lucrative hit. Or perhaps I was wrong that people would still pay for that. That morning, I chose a different path. I hooked the necklace around my neck, tucking the locket under my collar.

And there it remains, Dr Lachlan, although there have been many times over the years when I have thought to throw it out. Some half-sentiment always stays my hand.

I joined the ordinary, rational world and was able to provide for myself. The position I had missed the interview for was still open, and the family accepted my made-up excuses. Mrs Sullivan took the envelope with the reference inside and placed it on her writing table. It wasn't touched for weeks — I don't believe she ever did open it in the end. I think about that often. I knew my mother could still find me if she wanted to — she would have gone through my things as she had the tutor's and found the letter with their address. Sometimes I thought I felt her watching me in the street or when I took the children to the park, but I never saw her again, however quickly I turned around.

The night-mare didn't return as she predicted. I felt triumphant. With time, I came to believe it had simply been a symptom of my unnatural upbringing and strange adolescence. Fresh air, an honest occupation, tedium: they were the cure. And I would believe that still; only, as I have said, it returned a few weeks ago, far worse. No longer an occasional event, it comes almost nightly. Its forms are more varied and horrifying than they ever were at my mother's house. It is sometimes a woman, someone close to me. I don't know why it should return with such force when my life is as quiet and secure as it has ever been. My health is otherwise good, my appetite strong. I am well loved and am conscious of a purpose in the world — I do not feel the lack of a husband or children.

~~*I long to meet you*~~ *You have been kind and patient enough to sympathise with my reluctance to meet you — please believe me, your assurances have found in me a receptive heart. I hope it is clear that my hesitation owes nothing to you yourself —* ~~*I would dearly love*~~ *it is simply an unwillingness to risk disturbing the even tenor of my life, of exposing my weakness to the eyes of the world. Now I have committed my story to paper and to your safe-keeping, perhaps the next step does not seem so hard. I shall not run away! Meanwhile, I await ~~with impatient heart~~ your reply to these last two letters.*

 Yours ~~most kindly~~ sincerely,
  Miss Gerrard

Lil leaned over the letter, one hand pressed against her mouth. She ploughed her pen into the phrases already crossed out. Was she mad? What was Dr Lachlan to her but a handful of letters and a glimpse on the street? Had she confused the cure with the physician? And she had lied to him. She never truly believed the night-mare had been cured by fresh air and honest work. Her heart continued to insist it was the danger of Lambert that had summoned it – a terrible warning, as Madelyn had repeatedly urged. It was in his presence that it had taken control of her, and it was only after she had escaped him that it had left her alone. No one else had inspired such dread since, not until Mudie.

 She sat back again. Her younger self on that first full day of her seventeenth year didn't yet know that the night-mare would leave her alone for twelve happy years. Lil hovered by her side like one of Madelyn's spirits. She wondered if she would have been able to sense it then, her older self looking back, if she had thought to consider it. Perhaps it would have been a comfort. If memory were a form of haunting her own past, if she were able to act as a ghost from the future, it would be better if she had kinder thoughts to offer, but she failed to conjure any. A fog of shame and impatience with the person she had been prevented her.

 And what of herself now? What would she think, looking

back, some day in the future after Lachlan's reply, the younger Raube's return, Effie's – a cold breath on the back of her neck – Effie's death? Lil lifted her head and listened. Would she think more kindly of herself in the future? She waited as she had hundreds of times in séances, aware of the quality of silence in her own body, how it shifted almost imperceptibly like curtains in a breath of air. If she decided for herself now, to look back at this moment once she had all the answers, would she be able to feel her own future thoughts, be reassured that she would escape the night-mare again? She strained to hear something in her mind that was not of the present. Nothing, at first. She lowered her eyes to the table and they fell on the goddess, the strange presence lurking in its ancient, blank stare. And then it came, a sense of dread so sudden and powerful, it stopped her breath. She lifted her hands to her throat as if to prise away invisible fingers and stood up quickly. Her skin shivered as if all the doors and windows had been thrown open, and the room was ice-cold again.

9

It was completely dark by the time Lil slid and stumbled down the path towards Pitcarden House. The clouds had gathered low but were keeping their own counsel for the time being. Her letter to the doctor was safe in her pocket, a pregnant wad of paper. She couldn't stop herself now from sending it, whatever grim issue it might bring forth. An invisible twig scratched her cheek, and she corrected her course. A light would have made her feel exposed. Mudie might be just beyond it in the darkness, watching.

Pitcarden House crouched at one end of the valley as if it were trying to hide from more than just the elements. Only a few rooms on the ground floor were lit, so the rest of its bulk was more sensed than seen as Lil dropped down onto the drive. It was unkempt underfoot, with grass and moss reclaiming the road. She was aware of the ruined stable block across the way, also overgrown and still scorched black from the fire Jenet had mentioned. It was said that the older Mr Raube had closed off most of the house and lived in one room with few servants.

She turned off to the side to a humble door – the pillared main entrance hadn't been used for decades – and pounded the heavy knocker as if to test its limits. The household had been scaled back even further since Raube's death; just an ancient housekeeper and a maid remained to keep the mice and cobwebs at bay. She waited for one of them to answer the door, but when it was finally heaved open, Jenet stared back at her. Lil was surprised into a smile and even more surprised that she meant it. 'Hello.'

Jenet looked her up and down coolly, but Lil had seen the little start of recognition, the warmth in it. She thought of how she had felt when Miss Gerrard had appeared at one of Madelyn's séances, how much she had wanted to know this girl who was so unlike herself. Tiring of her own pose, Jenet put on an amused look and stepped back. 'Come ben.'

Lil followed her along the stone-flagged passageway, past the estate office where she usually left the post, and into a warm, brightly lit kitchen. Brass objects were laid out on a table, some of them gleaming like gold, with cloths and pieces of leather neatly piled. Her knock had interrupted the cleaning. Jenet didn't take her seat again but headed towards the range where a kettle was whistling. Lil pulled the letter from her pocket. 'I've come to put this with the post.'

'Ay.' The girl nodded to put it on a sideboard. 'Sit.'

Lil hesitated before putting the letter down. She pulled out another chair but didn't remove her coat. Haxton lived at the Mains but might be working in the office even now. Jenet brought down a large earthenware teapot from a shelf, humming to herself. Lil cleared her throat. 'Are you employed here?'

'I'm helpin, for whan Mr Raube wins hame. 'Til the bairn comes onywey.'

Lil watched her back as she moved slowly about, organising tea things. 'Are you looking forward to it? The baby?'

Jenet threw a spoon at a basin of water rather than make the journey and turned to sit heavily in her chair. 'I'll be gled whan I can pit him doun and dinnae hae this gettin in the road.' She rested her hands on her belly.

'Him?'

'Sae thay say.' Jenet seemed uncomfortable suddenly and looked to the side. Lil wanted to ask more but stopped herself. Folklore predictions of gender extended to where and how conception took place and which side of marriage. Nils knew a dozen such old wives' tales. Begetting a child was beset with weird agency the world over.

'You never answered my question the other day.' Jenet looked up. 'About the curse. If it frightens you.'

'Ower late tae worry noo, is it no?' Jenet shrugged. 'Ye've howkit up the treasure.'

Lil started in her seat. Nils had said nothing about word getting out. Surely that would have brought Haxton to their door immediately. She spoke sharply. 'Why do you say that?'

'Kirstie asked ane o the howkers this morning. A gowd caunnle stick?'

Lil tutted. Of course a find like the candlestick would be talked about. 'Does your uncle know?'

Jenet looked coy. 'No frae me.'

Only a matter of time then. Lil bit her lip and glanced at Jenet's middle. 'We've dug up supposedly cursed objects before and nothing bad has ever happened.'

'Sae faur as ye ken.' Jenet's voice was as flat as the look she gave her. She seemed to swing between mischief and cynicism. If Lil had been spirit writing for a doubting sitter, reassuring words would have poured out of her automatically. She felt them piling up on her tongue, as easy as nursery rhymes, but pressed her lips shut. There was something about Jenet that told her flummery wouldn't do. Or perhaps it was just harder to talk someone out of superstitious beliefs than into them. But also, despite her efforts to ignore it, there was that voice deep and distant within her, echoing back her own doubt. Everything she believed was only so far as she knew, and what she knew seemed to be in retreat. As she didn't respond, Jenet rose to pour the tea. 'Can I see it?'

'What?'

'The treasure. The gowd, I mean?'

Lil stared at her. 'Your family wouldn't approve.'

Jenet rolled her eyes. 'I've ne'er seen onything I'd caw treasure afore. An the'r nae hairm really, are the?'

Lil paused. She picked up her cup and warmed her hands around it before throwing a sideways look. 'So far as I know.'

Jenet's face broke into a smile, and she let out a laugh. Almost immediately after, her cup and saucer thumped onto the table, slopping tea, and she was bending forward, hands on her belly.

'What is it?' Fear shot through Lil's guts. She stood up. Jenet winced and looked towards her, then past her to the door. Her eyes widened. Lil felt it at once, the thing behind. She turned around so quickly, her chair slammed onto its back.

Haxton was on the threshold. Water dripping from his coat hem told of the rain's return. He passed a cold look over Lil and then narrowed his eyes at Jenet. 'Kicking again?'

She nodded, crinkled her nose, and then sat back with a sigh. 'He's got a haimmer blaw like a smiddy's.' She smiled. 'I reckon he'll be a boxer.'

'Girls can fight too' – Haxton shifted his eyes back to Lil – 'and not always fairly. Fortunate you're here, Miss Vincent. I was going to come to the cottage.'

He stepped backwards into the passageway to wait for her. After a moment's hesitation in which she resisted the urge to refuse him, Lil righted the chair. She doubted Jenet could reach down so far. 'Thank you for the tea.'

The girl looked at her almost sullenly. Lil wondered if she was simply bored and annoyed to be left alone again. As she left, she swiped the letter to Jonathan Lachlan from the sideboard.

Haxton stalked off before she reached him and opened the

door of the estate office. While he shook off his coat, despite the cold, and lit a lamp, Lil took in the two big desks, laden with papers, and the floor-to-ceiling bookcases filled with bound records. The lamp wasn't bright and struggled to push back the shadows.

'You'll stop digging immediately and backfill the trenches tomorrow.'

'I beg your pardon.' She turned towards him. 'You agreed until Sunday.'

'And you agreed to tell me if you found anything from the hoard. Also . . .' With two fingers, he plucked a letter from the desk and flicked it at her. It floated a moment, twisted in the air and plummeted to the floor. 'I don't know what sort of people you're used to dealing with, but I'm not going to be told my duties by a woman who's never even set foot on the estate.'

He was angrier than Lil had realised. She picked up the letter. Effie, usually so astute, must have hit the wrong note. 'Mr Raube . . .'

'Isn't here. Until he is, you'll hand over what you've found and send your workers home. I want you out of the cottage too.'

'Mr Haxton . . .' Lil faltered. The end of the dig came sharply, cuttingly into focus. Raube's return would banish them entirely. There would be nothing left except to wait for Effie to die – the thought was a needle pushing into her heart – and for the nightmare to grow worse. She considered telling him about Effie's illness, that it was the last wish of a dying woman to complete the dig. She considered theatrics: sobbing, cloth-rending.

He had dropped heavily into the chair across the desk from her and pulled a ledger towards him, as if he didn't intend to give her another word or look. Tears would not move him. Effie had said they should use the hoard if all else failed through bribes or threats, but Lil could see such sallies would be paper darts against Haxton's hide. She stared at him as she had at the gold plaque when Nils had removed the dirt from it – an anomaly, a puzzling find in an unexpected place that she didn't know how to categorise. Effie got around people by sniffing out their weak spots and leading them from there like a bull by the nose. But she had failed. Madelyn had worked the other way, offering tantalising glimpses of what they desired most until they followed as eagerly as kittens. What did Haxton want? It wasn't gold torcs or wealth. She glanced around her. The estate factorship. His niece. All things he had already.

He let her stand there, ignoring the awkwardness with a commitment Lil recalled she was equal to. She stepped forward and, perching on the edge of the desk, read Effie's letter. It surprised her. Respectful, reasoned, and with only one reference to the permission granted by Raube. The only sort of approach she imagined Haxton would listen to. It wasn't the letter that was the problem. She looked at him. 'Why don't you want us here really?'

'Don't ask me to repeat myself, Miss Vincent.'

'You've been against us from the start.'

He gave a shake of his head. 'My duty is to the people—'

'—who live here, I know. And they are afraid of the curse. But it's already too late, isn't it? We tried to keep the so-called treasure quiet, but the damage is done. Even Jenet is resigned.'

He looked up at her darkly, a warning to watch where she stepped. She raised her eyebrows. 'So, if the worst has already happened – gold has been dug up – and they did nothing more than break the stakes and loosen the tarps to prevent us in the first place, I don't see that we are in any real danger. You needn't be concerned.'

Haxton sat back in his seat. 'Someone broke the stakes?'

'It's the reason the walls fell in.' Lil dropped Effie's letter onto the desk and moved a heavy inkwell so it was parallel with the ledger. 'That was how we discovered the gold. You could say they brought it on themselves.'

He continued staring at her, eyes narrowing. 'You think it was people from Balcraig?'

'Who else would it be? We saw them watching us that night. It must have been John Mudie.'

Haxton observed her a moment longer and then heaved forward to put the inkwell back in its place. 'It wouldn't have been the villagers, Miss Vincent. Not one of them would have dared set foot on the place. Not even John Mudie. They might attack you and the cottage, but they would never touch the ground on the brae.' He drew back enough to lean a forearm on the desk. 'It seems there's someone else who would like you to leave.'

'What bloody nonsense.' It came out more vehemently than she intended. He winced slightly, and she despised him for it. 'They can't all be that scared.'

But it was true she had never seen Mudie on the mound. The day he trod on her twine, he hadn't followed her as she'd run up the bank, and she had never strayed far from it in her night-time wanderings, half aware of it as a place of safety. She set her jaw. 'Jenet isn't frightened.'

He pointed a finger. 'You'll keep away from her.'

'Tell her that.'

'You don't know these people.'

'They are just people, Mr Haxton.' Her hand was straying towards the inkwell again, but he lurched forward, grasping her fingers. The movement was sudden enough to make her flinch. She had come out without gloves, and there was intimacy in being held, even at the edges. In séances, she believed half the allure of materialisations for sitters was the touch, even the thought of it, of the spirit – the thrill, ironically, of living flesh. She made to pull back, but he held her fast, leaning towards her as if he meant to speak. Finally, he released her and stood up. 'Wait.'

He strode around the desk to the door. There was a skittering in the passageway, Jenet fleeing as fast as she was able back to the kitchen. With the door firmly shut, he turned. 'Jenet wasn't alive the last time the hoard was dug up. It's not something that's talked about. But they are all thinking it. And waiting.'

'Waiting for what? Death?'

'For all the pieces of the treasure. There are five.'

'She told me.'

'They have an order, according to legend.'

Lil didn't know if she wanted to laugh or spit. Haxton watched her a moment as if expecting to catch her out. He blew air through his lips and folded his arms.

'The oldest piece carried the original curse. No one knows where it started, but once it was dug up, the legend goes, it caused misery and the death of any child under a year or a few days, depending on which version you listen to. The only way to stop it was to rebury it with something else, something priceless to the one that dug it up – in that case, the gold torc you found. When someone eventually dug up those two pieces, the curse struck again until they were reburied with a third, the candlestick, and so on. It's believed that that's when it was first buried here. Whoever owned the candlestick brought the treasure from somewhere else, perhaps during the crusades. The curse grows stronger with each object added. People here believe when you have found all five, it will be back. Worse than before. Some of them aren't going to wait that long. I persuaded them you were only interested in the Bronze-Age burial, but now they know you've found bits of the hoard, then yes, Miss Vincent, I do have reason to be concerned.'

'I see.' Lil nodded and pressed her lips together. 'And it was the late Mr Raube who dug it up last time?'

'He did it twice. First when he was a young man, newly in charge of the estate. He didn't believe in curses, but he liked money and wasn't going to ignore the rumours of treasure on his land, so he went looking. A while later his firstborn died within hours. He wouldn't let go of the hoard, though, despite his wife's pleading, not even when his second son also died before he was three weeks old. It wasn't until his wife herself died giving birth to the current Mr Raube that he acted. The baby wasn't expected to live either. They say the moment he was told, he went straight out in a storm and reburied the treasure himself along with a Raube heirloom, a gold and diamond brooch.' Haxton gave Lil an odd look. 'The boy lived.'

She grimaced. 'Proof, then.'

'Yes, for him. He wasn't the same man after. He became a recluse and let the estate decline, although he never lost his love of money. He sent his son south to protect his health — the boy was never strong — and I think also to keep him away from the brae. He wouldn't let anyone near it.'

'But you said he dug it up twice?'

Haxton rubbed his chin. He seemed reluctant to continue. 'It was a long while later.'

'What changed his mind?'

'A woman. His fiancée.'

Lil frowned. 'I thought he was a recluse.'

'She sought him out. She came from America or somewhere and wheedled her way in. Everyone knew she was after his money, everyone except himself, of course. He summoned his son back — wanting to be head of a family again, I suppose. She either already knew about the brooch or he told her, and she convinced him to dig it back up.'

'She must have been very persuasive.'

'There was something dark going on. They say she had uncanny powers.'

Lil laughed. 'What were they? Youth and beauty and a clever mind?'

Haxton tipped his head but carried on. 'She was said to be . . .' He searched for the word, '. . . clairvoyant, something like that.'

Lil's smile vanished. If spiritualism had added to the misery of these people, she didn't want to hear about it. The old shame burgeoned in the pit of her stomach.

Haxton walked to a cupboard by the window and brought out a whisky bottle. He tilted it at her, uncertainly. She nodded, surprised. She had assumed a man who flinched at coarse language in women wouldn't approve of them drinking liquor either. Perhaps she had lost all feminine credibility in his eyes. He poured for them both and sat down again at the desk, opposite her. She could tell by the way he took a slug and then stared at the glass, turning it between his fingers, that he was about to unburden himself. She had seen it a thousand times before in private sittings. Wait long enough in a dark room and people cracked open by themselves.

'I was ten years old at the time. My oldest sister had a baby, her first, another girl before she had Jenet.'

'And the baby died when the hoard was dug up.'

'Yes. Suddenly. A delegation went to the house that night to demand the hoard be reburied, but he wouldn't see them. Most of the village turned out then, determined to bury it themselves if they had to. The house was attacked, windows smashed, and . . .' He paused, gripped the glass harder. 'A fire was started. You'll have seen the damage it did. The east side caught, but the wind was blowing too strongly from the west. There was a lot of confusion. Some were trying to put out the fire and others tried to stop them. Fights broke out. The rest were trying to get into the house and recover the hoard. No one noticed hot ash and sparks landing on the roof of the stables.'

Haxton cleared his throat and shook his head slightly. The movement was a sort of tic, Lil realised, signalling dismissal, as if he could shake away thoughts too ugly or too stupid to bear. He was still staring at his glass.

'I heard the horses.' His fingers stopped fidgeting, and Lil could see he was hearing them then.

'Oh.' A shiver lifted the hairs on her arms. She remembered the sounds Agnes had made, the smell of scorched skin and hair. Haxton continued.

'No one would listen to me. I did my best, saved two. But nobody realised . . .' He took in a deep breath, leaned back and looked at Lil for the first time. 'It was Samhain.' He paused as if the weight of that fact might crush her with its significance. 'People had been building fires and celebrating all day, including the stable lads, or there would have been someone to act sooner. My brother drank too much in the afternoon with friends. He must have wandered into the yard and been so addled he decided to lie down on the hay. The drink meant he didn't wake up in time.' Haxton's voice had been gradually growing quieter until it was barely more than a rasp, rough wind in the grass. 'We heard him above the horses, above the stalls we couldn't save.'

Lil watched the muscles in his face flicker. Niece and brother in one day, and it was Samhain again this Sunday. Her fingers itched to seize the inkwell and throw it at whatever would suffer most damage.

Later, she was arrested by a stab of shame that she had neither felt nor displayed any pity for Haxton in that moment. She was too familiar with such stories. The only people she had met regularly for half her life were mourners, people like Haxton, trailing personal tragedy around with them. They had all wanted the impossible from her – and it was never her pity.

When she looked at him again, still seeking a target for the inkwell that would bring most relief, he was so deep in memories, she could probably have murdered him before he even recalled where he was.

'Was anyone held to account for the fire?'

After an age, his fingers twitched around the glass. His voice was thick. 'No.'

'Mr Raube just accepted it?'

Haxton came a little more to life with a cough and a deeper frown. 'He didn't care. They found him in his sitting room with the hoard at his feet, holding the wedding ring he had bought for his fiancée. He could hear the crowd and the fire but he hadn't moved. The woman had abandoned him. I don't know why. Some said she ran off with the son, though he was no more than eighteen. The next we knew he had gone to Australia and though he never returned, he and his father wrote to each other. He was left the estate.'

'Did the son ever marry?'

'If he did, I never heard of it. He's coming back alone.'

'*You* must blame someone. For the fire.'

He nodded slowly. 'For a long time, I blamed everyone, the whole village, the Raubes. I couldn't get away from here fast enough, did everything I could to make sure I wouldn't have to live the rest of my life in Balcraig.'

'But you came back.'

He nodded again, even more slowly. 'I came back.' His eyes turned on her like a wounded dog's. It was her own fault she had made an enemy of him, but it was too late now; his jaw was rigid. 'I should never have let you come here. I shouldn't have let you anywhere near the brae.' He threw back the rest of his whisky.

Lil jumped up, speaking quickly.

'All I want is the chance to uncover the cist. I don't care about the hoard. What if we rebury everything we've already found?' Her voice went higher. 'Or if we fail to find it? On purpose, I mean. What is it, anyway. What did they add to the hoard?'

'The wedding ring. He handed it over himself.'

'A *ring*? It's only a few days; we'd probably never find that or the brooch anyway.'

'They don't trust you. And nor do I.'

Lil returned his gaze and was amazed she hadn't seen the loneliness in it before. There was a hurt child in there, a young boy she almost recognised. She looked down at her hands. The letter to Dr Lachlan was creased. 'What was the first piece of the hoard? The original curse?'

'An ancient bit of gold with a female figure stamped on it. Why? Do you have it?'

She shook her head, not looking at him. 'Nils thinks the myth of the hag originated with the Carlin stone.'

Haxton let out a sigh. 'It doesn't matter where it came from. People expect to see it, so they have.' After a moment, he stood and reached for his coat. 'I'll walk you back. You can hand over the gold from the hoard now and start packing. I'll have the other artefacts picked up tomorrow. You can still put that with the post.' He nodded at the envelope. Lil handed it to him and watched it disappear into a basket by the door. Something caught Haxton's eye in the row of pigeonholes above. 'A telegram for you. Must have come this afternoon.'

She took it and opened it in one breathless movement, heart jumping like a spring wound tightly for news of Effie.

Mr Wylie's suit and barber ready fri am.

Haxton took the lamp with him into the passageway, so the words vanished in the gloom as soon as she had seen them. Her heart subsided in her chest and silently rewound itself. Effie was alive and scheming still. Lil really would be going to Dr Lachlan's lecture dressed as a man. She put the telegram in her pocket.

Jenet was standing in the kitchen doorway when Lil entered the passage. She called a question to Haxton. He gave her a short reply and then emphasised his point with a finger that she was to stay in the house. When he had turned, she gave Lil a small wave. Lil gave a quick nod back and hurried away from her. She felt as if the curse had merged with the night-mare, that its evil polluted the air every time she moved, trailing off her like vapour. She wanted to be in the cold air, away from people.

It was mizzling outside. Threads of moisture landed on her face like a fine net. Haxton stalked ahead into the darkness, lamp swinging. He was speaking again.

'I brought her to the house so she'd be further away from the brae than in the hamlet. Her mother's wish.'

Lil broke into a jog to keep close enough to hear him. 'Your sister?'

'Ay, Margaret.'

'What about Jenet's husband?'

'Mungo wouldn't cross Margaret even if he wanted to. She called a meeting about the gold being found. That's where I just came from. I persuaded them you would leave. Or tried to.' He stopped suddenly and turned on her. She nearly ran into him. 'I'm telling you all of this so you understand that you must go; you are not safe here. There will be other meetings now, you can be sure, that I'm not invited to. Mudie will be taking advantage of the unrest.'

Lil shivered. Haxton held the lamp so he could see her face, lower than his as he was a step ahead where the ground rose. The shadows reached over his own features like fingers, half obscuring his eyes and hiding his brow. Only the lower half was clearly visible, parted lips, tense jaw, dark stubble. The fine rain had lacquered him; his mouth gleamed in the light, but he was watching her from the shadows. A thrill of fear leaped through Lil; his face was as close and weird as some of the night-mares. But there was something else in the thrill, unexpected. She grasped the bottom of the lantern and forced it up so she could see his eyes – but quickly, like a child might yank open the wardrobe door to face hidden monsters.

The movement took him by surprise. He had been waiting for acquiescence, a sign that she understood, but her half-fearful stare startled him out of his frown. They met each other anew for a moment in the unevenness of light and dark. Being alone together outdoors in the little circle thrown by the lamp felt more intimate than when they had been closeted between four walls. It was the first trick of the séance, the rationing of light, but Lil wasn't thinking about that then. She was remembering her last Norwegian fisherman and how strange and close his face had seemed when she first went to him. Their meeting had been the negative of this one — seeking out a small space of darkness for themselves within the unrelenting northern light. The memory triggered a feeling that ricocheted back to the more recent past and the street in Edinburgh where Dr Lachlan had briefly met her eyes. She remembered the telegram in her pocket. On Friday she would see him. She dropped her gaze, and Haxton turned to continue up the hill.

She had expected a scene at the cottage: angry men too big for the space. But Nils listened expressionlessly to Haxton's demands. He didn't appear to have moved from his chair and had let the fire die down to embers. Lil built it up again, stealing glances at him as Haxton talked. Finally, he nodded, and Lil thought she saw something like relief pass across his face.

'Tomorrow then. We finish.'

'It's for your own safety.' Haxton seemed thrown by the lack of opposition too. He frowned at Nils and rubbed his chin. 'I'll take the torc and candlestick now for Mr Raube.'

'You have to declare them.' Lil stood up quickly.

Haxton nodded. 'Mr Raube will do everything properly. And you don't need to tell me,' Lil had opened her mouth again, 'your names will be included.'

Lil fetched the torc from her room. She wrapped the candlestick too, thinking how in other circumstances it would have been an astonishing find. They disappeared inside Haxton's coat. To her mind, each time they changed hands, their connection to the past grew weaker. She could feel Nils's eyes on her and knew he was thinking about the plaque. Neither of them spoke of it. When Haxton left, she brought it out from her room and placed it on the table. They sat with it between them as they had the morning she had found it. Their argument, at least for the moment, was set aside.

'Why did you not give it to him?'

'Better if no one knows it's been dug up. They can rebury the other things and believe they are protected from the curse if it suits them. That way everyone wins.'

A pale light gleamed in Nils's eyes. 'You think like her.'

Lil shrugged. 'How could I not? I've worked with you both for long enough.' She held his gaze for a beat. 'You didn't need to keep secrets from me.' His eyes grew blank again, and he looked away. Lil bit down on her lip. 'Why didn't you fight him about cutting us short?'

Still without looking at her, he cleared his throat. 'His mind is made up. If her letter didn't work . . . And perhaps he is right, about the danger to us.'

Lil frowned at him much as Haxton had done. He seemed cloaked in defeat. She thrust her chin towards the plaque. 'Well, they are not having this. It's not even from here. And she deserves . . . I want to be able to give her something from this dig. Something to hold.' There was a silence as the brooch hovered between them, unspeakable.

Lil stared at the gold figure. The truth was that although it frightened her, she couldn't give it up. It wouldn't let her. She had come to think of it as a goddess, but what evidence did she have? There were amulets still in use in some places that protected women in labour from demons, from Lilith.

'I've dreamed about it – the female figure. I think.' Her admission surprised her. She had never told Nils about the night-mare. 'I've been having bad dreams. It was terrifying.'

Nils seemed to take a moment to hear her. He surfaced slowly from his own thoughts. 'Tell me.'

She described the shape in the chair at Effie's, how it had lengthened so horribly and clutched her paralysed face. The version it had taken of Effie herself she left out. When she had finished, Nils gave a slight nod. 'It sounds like the Mara.'

'Yes, I have thought that.'

'It comes at night and crushes people in their beds. My grandmother always put her shoes next to her bed before sleeping with the toes pointing out to stop it coming.' His brow creased. 'Or was it toes pointing in?'

'Did it work?'

'I don't know.'

'Is it always a succubus?'

'There are different stories, different kinds of demon.'

Lil tried not to ask the question kicking in her head. It broke away from her anyway. 'And it kills people?'

'Oh yes.' Nils nodded again and then said something almost under his breath that didn't quite sound Swedish.

'What's that?'

'A Norse saga. The Swedish king, Vanlande, is killed by the Mara. He had promised to return to his wife in Finland after three years but stayed away. In revenge, she asked a witch to persuade him to go back or . . .'

'Or kill him, I remember now. He wanted to return, but his counsellors convinced him not to, and the witch sent the Mara that night. Effie loves that story.' She recalled her laughing and applauding as Nils recited the Old Norse.

'It is very sad.' Nils stared into nothing. 'They burned his body and marked the place with a standing stone.'

Lil thought of the Carlin stone positioned yards away up the hill and felt cold. She tutted. 'If only Vanlande had pointed his shoes the right way.'

After a moment, Nils turned his eyes towards her. There was no change in his expression, but she recognised the nature of the pause; it was his way of acknowledging humour. 'There are many other ways to banish the Mara. In some places, you only have to tell it what it is. Tell it, "You are the Mara", three times, and it will leave you.'

'Is that all? I thought she was supposed to be terrifying?'

'Not always.' Nils sounded defensive, as if she had criticised a favourite aunt. 'Crones often have wise and benign versions. And sometimes the Mara is a real person who does not even know that their spirit tramples people at night. Calling them the Mara three times frees them from it too.'

'I'll bear that in mind.'

Nils looked at the plaque again. 'I wish it were so easy with people.'

'Yes. Imagine telling Haxton he's a meddling bastard three times, and he let us do as we pleased.'

Nils paused again, and Lil began laughing, the gasping, helpless sort of laughter that comes from a body trying to weep.

10

Lil woke to a whispering in her ear, urgent and pleading, but couldn't make out the words. They merged with the hissing. Her eyes strained left. It was next to her, crouched by the bed. The whispering grew louder, angry. She shut her eyes, and it stopped. Silence. After a moment, she opened them again. Inches away was the face of the old man. She had seen him before, his eyes bloodshot, bulging with rage and pain. His mouth opened as if to scream, but air rushed into her own lungs, and she jerked upright. She was halfway out of bed before remembering there was nowhere to rush to.

The night-mare left her clammy with sweat, and an aching fog filled her head, a legacy of the whisky the night before. She rubbed her eyes. Their last supper had been strange and quiet, punctuated mostly by the refilling of glasses. They toasted the strange deity or demon where it shimmered, golden and ancient, in the candlelight. Now Lil was grey inside and out. She laboured into her clothes without lighting the lamp, looking around dully at the shapes of books, tools and crates she would have to pack. The plaque was wrapped up again on the table and, on impulse, without knowing why, she slipped it into her pocket, overcoming the spike of unease it cost her. Nils had apparently not bothered to get up either. In the kitchen, she regarded the dead fire with contempt.

Outside there was just enough light to see by. Too early still for the diggers, if any remained after Mudie's attacks. Nils would compensate them for the lost days, but they would still grumble. She wanted to be with the burial site alone one more time, and wrapped herself up in the greatcoat. As she shut the door, something clattered against it. Nils had buried the pig's head and wooden symbol days ago, but a new arrangement of twigs tied with red thread hung from a nail. She was lifting a hand to rip it away when she remembered Jenet's necklace of berries and hesitated. Perhaps it wasn't from Mudie. If the twigs were rowan, it might be a gesture of protection, not a threat. She let it be.

Trudging up the hill, she was surprised by the freshness of the air, as if she had expected the new day to care what it held for them. A mist was clearing. It peeled away from the wet grass and half-stripped branches, leaving tiny jewels strung along spiders' webs and caught in twigs, relentlessly beautiful in spite of her sorrow. It was so quiet, she felt as if she were the only person alive. The standing stone stood like an ancient guardian, its presence amplified in the stillness. Awe turned her gut. She wondered if it was because it was upright, making her mind read it as a person on some level. Or if it was knowing that people had put it there, people so long dead that the earth had forgotten them and everything they meant by it, but the stone itself remained. Mortality, then, simply. The extraordinary brevity of human existence. The terror that outside of our own skulls everything is meaningless.

A sound came from inside the barrow. Very faint, but she wasn't alone. She stepped forward cautiously into the trench. The bulk of the mound rose around her. She skirted the pit where the urns had been found and peered around the corner into the new trench where the hoard might lie. It was wider and longer. A man on his knees mostly with his back to her was gouging earth out of one wall with a trowel. The heaps of dirt on the floor and haphazard craters in the sides showed where else he had been digging, apparently at random. Nils. Two lamps were still burning next to his coat, several feet behind him — abandoned, Lil guessed, as the light grew stronger. It was possible he had not even been to bed.

She watched him, reluctant to call out in the quietness, and unwilling, she realised, to see his face. In the end, it was unnecessary. He dropped the trowel and dug his hands into the earth, pulling it out to one side. She must have been caught in his peripheral vision as he froze suddenly and looked up. Terror flashed in his face, a wide-open, primitive expression, and he jerked backwards. It was over in a moment. He lowered his head, cowed and exhausted. Mud covered him so completely it was impossible to make out the buttons on his shirt.

Lil stepped fully into view. 'It would be better if Haxton and the men didn't find you like this.'

He rubbed mud-clogged hands against caked trousers and nodded without looking at her. She glanced around. 'Did you find anything else?' His head hung down further. She spoke gently. 'What are you doing, Nils? What are you not telling me?'

He didn't answer at first. Some emotion was lifting his shoulders and crushing his throat. 'She wants . . .' He looked up. The whites of his eyes were startling, peering out of the dark trench. 'She wants the brooch. That's all she wanted.'

The tears shocked Lil, the *aliveness* of them. His eyes were crevices in the dull morning, bloodshot, and dripping like the mist. She understood she had been lied to even more than she realised. The knowledge spread through her core, cold and leaden, but Nils was sobbing like a child now, his frozen sorrow finally undone by this failure. She knelt in front of him and put her hands on his shoulders. He pitched forward, leaning against her, until she felt his grief would crush them both.

By ten o'clock, the three remaining diggers had almost filled the new trench and two of them had begun on the main one. Nils's erratic digging had already looked a part of the backfill when Haxton had arrived an hour earlier to check on them. Lil had been aware of him looking at her, but had turned away. He left again when he had assured himself the work was in earnest. Nils, though washed and changed, hadn't reappeared to supervise. He had ignored the porridge and tea she made him, reaching for the whisky bottle instead. His grim, determined movements told her there was no use bringing up the brooch or asking why Effie wanted it.

The mist had cleared away completely. As she wasn't needed for filling in holes, Lil walked up to the central trench, now so thoroughly collapsed that backfilling was unnecessary. She wanted the time she had been denied earlier, and breathed in the scents of wet earth, dead leaves, decay. The storms had acted like a hinge to the year, swinging autumn to the fore. A glow of orange swept across woods that had still been green even two weeks earlier, and an underlying coolness permeated everything, as if the earth had begun to inhale, retracting its warmth and pulling matter to the ground. It was the season of dying – for all natural things, for Effie. She thought of the cist under her feet and what it might contain. Even the dead were being reburied.

'Fine morning.'

She turned quickly at the voice. It was a man at the base of the tumulus, dressed for walking with stick in hand and binoculars around his neck. Of middle years, she thought, under average height. His face was weathered, but he had the look of a gentleman at leisure. He smiled up at her while she calculated. Remembering what was expected, she called out a half-hearted agreement. His smile widened, and he raised his stick, pointing it at the burial mound. 'An interesting place. Looks like they're digging around the other side.'

She couldn't place the accent. An English speaker, not Scottish. She sighed, wanting to be rid of him. 'They're filling it in.'

He nodded. 'End of season, I suppose. Do you know if they found anything?'

'Nothing.' She half turned from him, hunching, aware of the plaque in her pocket.

'That's surprising. It's Bronze Age, isn't it? One would expect a few bits of pot at least. If not actual treasure.'

She looked back sharply, but he was still smiling pleasantly, an idler passing the time. Her shoulders lowered a little. There was something attractive in his open face and relaxed stance, his easy ownership of the scene. She pointed at the ground. 'There is a stone cist under there, quite large. It's an unusual site. I'm sure it contains grave goods. But the walls caved in during a storm, before I could open it . . .' She stopped, not trusting her voice. She hadn't spoken of it before, beyond sniping at Nils and Haxton. There hadn't even been time to sketch what had been uncovered.

The man considered her and then the ground. 'Could it not be dug out again?'

She swallowed and took a breath. 'Of course. But now we can't.'

'Because of the weather.'

'Because of the estate. The factor.' It snarled out of her, the sudden bitterness jarring the morning. She laughed, mirthlessly, trying to cover it and tossed her head. 'But also the weather. It's been so wet.' She didn't look at him.

'Well, there is always the spring.'

She nodded, cranked a smile his way. 'Yes, thank you, good morning.' She was moving away as he spoke again.

'Perhaps you'll have permission then.'

She had walked another two paces before the remark brought her to a stop. The humour in his voice sounded like a private joke. She turned to look back at him, but he was already heading towards the path that led down the hill to the house. His light hair and burnished skin spoke of days under a fiercer sun. The accent could be colonial. Australian. 'Mr Raube?'

He stopped and turned. They were at a distance from each other now, but she saw his smile, and in it, the kick of his joke. She had only a few seconds, as he walked back towards her and onto the brae, to wonder at his sanguine attitude and decide on her story. He couldn't know about the forged letters yet. It was only a matter of time, a very short time, but she was supposed to be as innocent as he was. That was how she must appear. She stepped towards him and stuck out her hand. 'Miss Vincent. I beg your pardon. Mr Haxton said he was expecting you weeks from now.'

'So he is, so he is.' Raube climbed the mound and clasped her hand firmly. 'I'm the swine who should be begging pardons. I wanted to arrive early without the fanfare, you see? Take a proper look around before all the forelock tugging gets in the way. I'm looking forward to meeting my factor.' He gave her a quizzical look. 'Gave you permission and then took it away, did he?'

Lil bit her lip. 'He's worried about the strength of local feeling around the legends. He thought it best to wait until you were here in person before doing more.'

Raube looked over the burial site, his smile fading. 'The Pitcarden curse.' He nodded faintly. 'Mr Haxton was right to wait.'

Lil watched his eyes narrow and waited for him to ask more about why the dig had been allowed in the first place. Before she could head him off with a banal question about his journey, he grimaced and sniffed. 'I would have the place flattened and the stone pulverised if it weren't for the archaeological interest. But the history . . .' He looked beyond her and struck out towards the top of the mound, talking over his shoulder. 'It is important. I didn't use to think so. Not when I was a boy here.' She joined him next to the collapsed trench, and he smiled at her. 'Mining in Australia has taught me a few things about this earth we scuttle around on top of.' His boot nudged the pile of wooden planks. 'Reminds me of my early attempts, digging for alluvial gold. We sank shafts straight down – one hundred and fifty, two hundred feet – and tried to keep the walls up with timber slabs. We never knew if there was anything to be found though, digging straight down for months in blind faith, risking life and limb.' He squinted at her. 'At least you know something's there.'

Lil's eyes widened. She felt the sad little ghost of a flame leap in her breast. Raube would have given his permission. The forged letters had never been necessary. And now they would turn on them, banishing Lil and Nils from the burial when they might have completed the dig in Effie's memory, if not in her sight. She became conscious that she had Raube's good will and his willingness to listen only for as long as she kept him from the house. A tiny island of opportunity to share what they had found, to convince him of the purity of their intent. Her intent. She cleared her throat.

'There is so much to find here. We've already excavated unusual cinerary urns in a separate pit from the cist and a bronze knife with a scrap of scabbard still intact. It's extraordinary. We don't know how it relates to the standing stone.' They both looked at the huge monolith. 'We've barely begun really.'

'I see. So there is more than one burial; this is more of a cemetery?'

'Yes, and I think it must have been important. The position of it. We've found jet beads too and a few of amber on their own, too few to know what they were a part of; it's almost as if they were dropped by accident.' She laughed at the strangeness of it.

'Well,' he laughed too, 'I've always been sceptical of ancestor worship – I'm sure they blundered about just as carelessly as we do.'

A feeling of defensiveness surprised Lil. 'We wouldn't be here without them.'

He smiled at her. 'Of course. All I mean is we might not be so different. People can seem terribly distant from each other in terms of custom and belief.' He thumped the ground with his stick. 'But whoever's under here could no doubt teach us something we've lost, given the chance.'

Lil stared at him. 'I suppose I'm trying to give them that chance.'

They held each other's gaze for a moment, recognition dawning. She had not experienced it before, this sweet journeying of fellow spirits towards each other, where each tentative step on the bridge between them proved joyfully solid. Meeting Effie and Nils had felt like a homecoming, but she'd had everything to learn about archaeology back then and had yet to establish her independence of thought. Raube betrayed no hint of surprise or judgement that she was a woman holding forth. Knowing his respect for her would be flattened within half an hour nearly choked her. He also seemed reluctant to leave, but finally tapped his stick on the ground again and adjusted the bag on his shoulders.

'I had better go and confess my arrival. It was a pleasure to meet you, Miss Vincent.' Lil made a noise, incoherent. He paused. 'Would you and . . .?'

'Mr Jensen.'

'. . . care to come down to the house this afternoon, and we can discuss your work? Give me a few hours to settle in and discover what refreshment I can offer you. Say, four o'clock?'

Lil had a vision of the estate office at Pitcarden with the fire lit, Jenet bringing in tea things, and herself and this astonishing man talking prehistory and making plans for the spring. It was a flash of what might have been, dazzlingly lovely, already dead. He would be back long before four with Haxton and probably a constable. She nodded pretend enthusiasm. 'I shall bring the sketches.'

'Excellent.' He started to turn but hesitated again. 'And tell your men to stop. The drier weather is supposed to hold for another week. We might as well do a little more.'

She nodded in answer, feeling sick, and he gave a wide smile before setting off. He walked slowly, as if tired, and Lil opened her mouth to call him back, to tell the truth. The thought of the scene about to play out at the house made the blood revolt in her body. It surged to the surface as if yearning after Raube, trying to warn him. But Effie was in there also, pulsing through her veins. She had gone to great lengths to make sure Lil came out of this clean. Admitting complicity would be a betrayal of sorts. Lil shut her mouth. She would act out her part then, but when it came to it, she would not say one word of criticism about Effie in front of Raube and Haxton.

The men stared at her disbelievingly as she told them the owner of Pitcarden had returned and countered Haxton's instructions, that they could take the rest of the day for themselves. She didn't want witnesses to Raube's angry return. In the kitchen, Nils's haggard face betrayed something more complicated. He was still in his chair, nursing another whisky. Lil's heart sank. When Raube returned, he'd find a drunk squatting in his property. When she had finished speaking, a dim light appeared in Nils's bloodshot eyes. 'He'll let us work another week? We can widen the trench for the brooch.'

Lil banged her fist on the table. '*Sober up.* He's finding out right this minute that you and Effie forged letters *from him.* They'll be coming back — do you hear me, Nils? — and you have to pretend you didn't know. It's what Effie wants you to do.'

Nils's face dropped as if she'd slapped him. He searched the empty tabletop. 'She would make him see. If she were here.'

Lil ran her hands over her face and walked to the window. There was nothing to do except wait. But she couldn't bear to be near Nils's liquor-soaked misery. She slammed the door on her way out. At the mound, the men had finally gone, and there was no sign as yet of Raube or Haxton. She picked up a spade and climbed the barrow. It didn't matter that her efforts would be useless. If these were her last moments on the site, she would spend them as she had the first, half buried in dirt, in the company of the vanished. In Edinburgh, she had promised herself she would look for the brooch for Effie's sake, but the subterfuge, the pointlessness of it, hardened her. Their lies had robbed her of her best chance of making her name. Let Nils chase baubles if he wanted to.

She rammed the spade hard into the dirt. The work warmed her, and gradually she forgot to expect approaching figures, angry voices demanding explanations. There was only the ache in her back, the scent of earth, and her slow progress into the trench. Dumping another load onto the spoil heap, she paused to stretch. She couldn't be certain how much time had passed. The only movement was where wind tugged the grass, sudden bursts of starlings overhead. She would surely have heard Raube if he had skirted the mound on his way to the cottage. Perhaps he didn't know yet. Haxton might have business elsewhere on the estate, still unaware of his employer's return. She walked back to the cottage for food. Nils dozed at the table, head resting on his arms. Sleep had failed to smooth the tension from his face. She studied him a moment, the deep lines in his cheeks and forehead, the thin scalp through thinner hair, as if she might draw him. When she left, she closed the door softly.

The day wore on. She dug deeper than she expected, down to only a foot or so from the corner of the cist, she guessed. Her muscles ached from repeatedly lifting buckets of earth and stones to the surface. It was time to stop. She placed her hands against the floor of the trench for a moment, a farewell or a promise, and clambered back out. Returning to the cottage, she was relieved to see that Nils had left the kitchen. Muffled snores came from his room next door. She looked down at herself. Mud streaked her skirt and was lodged under her nails. If Raube didn't return, she would have to go down to the house at four. She washed and changed, expecting the front door to be thrown open at any moment, and then sat where Nils had, too perplexed to do more than keep glancing at the clock and wonder what had happened. At a quarter to, she rose and with a sense of disbelief started making her way in the dying light towards Pitcarden House. She didn't bother taking the sketches.

It was Jenet who opened the door again. She was clearly expecting her and talked rapidly under her breath as she ushered her in. 'He's in the office wi Hugh. Gie me your coat. I heard them argiein. I think it wis anent you. I howp ye can keep howkin. Hugh shawed me the gowd neck cheil.' She put her hand to her throat briefly, and her eyes flashed. 'It daesnae look aw that auld, daes it?'

Lil straightened her collar, pulled down her cuffs, and tried to gauge what lay in wait for her from Jenet's words. The girl hadn't stopped.

'He's no like the auld ane; he's freenly. Smiles muckle, but he's wee, is he no? I think Hugh is crabbit he didnae send a telegram first.'

She fell silent as they neared the door. Lil felt as if she were on the lip of a waterfall, riding a smooth wave before the plunge into chaos. Jenet knocked for her and gave her a meaningful look. A voice called to come in.

'Miss Vincent.' Raube smiled at her warmly. He looked wearier than he had a few hours previously. Both men were standing in front of the desk, Haxton looking darker than usual next to the smaller man's sandy cheerfulness. He nodded. A fire was roaring in the grate. Raube looked beyond her, expectantly. She shut the door but didn't move further into the room.

'Mr Jensen sends his apologies. He's not feeling well. Only a cold, but he's in bed.'

'I'm sorry to hear that.' Raube murmured further platitudes, while Haxton peered at her more intently. She held his gaze. Raube spoke again, changing his tone. 'Miss Vincent, you lied to me.'

She didn't flinch. Coolly, she turned back to him. He was looking at her with an inscrutable expression, one eyebrow raised. She determined not to speak first. Massaging his left palm with the thumb of his other hand, he observed her a moment longer before abruptly leaning forward and whispering, 'You told me there was no treasure.' His eyes flashed with humour, and he stepped to one side. Behind him, on the desk, were the torc and candlestick, carefully placed on lengths of velvet. Both men waited for her to speak. Lil allowed herself several seconds. She knew from séances that people would tolerate silence, trusted it more than bluster. Her heart steadied a little. She kept her eyes on the torc.

'Well, yes. When you asked, I didn't know who you were. You could have been anybody. We never discuss important finds with idle onlookers.'

Raube laughed and clapped his hands. 'I thank you for your discretion. However, I have a feeling there's another reason you forgot to mention it. I think you are more interested in the burial itself. Is that true, Miss Vincent? Bones and urns captivate you more than gold?'

'No.' Lil didn't return his levity. 'But these artefacts,' she gestured at them, 'they have no provenance. We don't know who made them or where. There is little they can tell us by themselves. I came here to study the burial site, all of it, so we can learn something. What we don't find might be as important as what we do. It's an excavation,' her voice hardened slightly, and she threw a sharp look at Haxton, 'not a treasure hunt.'

Raube bowed his head. 'It seems I am fortunate you chose Pitcarden. The old place is evidently in the best hands.' He said the last to Haxton, who inhaled deeply and placed his cap on his head, as if to mark an end to it.

'I have said what I think.'

'And I have heard you and appreciate your position keenly.' Raube put a hand on his heart. 'You already have my lasting gratitude. I shall go to Balcraig first thing and speak with them. If there is any further trouble, the responsibility will be mine.'

Haxton nodded, satisfied but not happy. Lil could see him thinking it would still be his lot to take the brunt of the villagers' anger. His look as he passed her was not hostile, as she had expected. There was deep worry in it. And for her part, she felt no sense of victory. Raube was acting as if nothing untoward had happened; he hadn't told Haxton his letters of permission had been forged. A cold draught ran down her spine in spite of the fire. She was almost sorry Haxton was leaving. Was Raube waiting to be alone with her? It struck her that no one had laid eyes on him in nearly thirty years. No one knew anything about him.

Haxton left the door open, and she didn't shut it. Raube had moved to the other side of the desk. As he sat down, he raised an eyebrow at her again. 'You didn't mention the sabotage and intimidation either.'

Lil folded her arms. 'I'm not as worried about local opinion as Mr Haxton.'

'Brave or foolhardy, do you think?'

Lil didn't answer, and he suddenly stuck out an arm, waving her forward. 'Please, have a seat, let's talk about this week. Assuming we have, say, five clear days, what would your plan be?'

Lil took the offered chair but sat on the edge of it. 'I'd like to dig out the cist again. We could do with more men.'

'Ah yes, Hugh told me some had absconded.' He leaned his elbows on the desk, fingers interlacing. There wasn't much room, as papers had been pushed aside to make space for the artefacts. Lil noticed the pile nearest his right arm. At the top was an envelope, the type used for personal letters rather than business correspondence. The handwriting was difficult to see from that angle, but she was sure she recognised the slant of the first few letters. Effie had said she would enclose a letter from Raube with the one she wrote to Haxton. But this envelope was addressed *to* Raube. He was still talking.

'I can see if there are any volunteers in the morning. If I offer to boost their wages, it might loosen the hold of the curse a little in their minds. The more local people involved, the better.'

Lil felt breathless. 'I have an appointment in Edinburgh tomorrow, but I shall be back on Saturday morning.'

Raube flexed his hands. 'Our paths may cross. I also have business in Edinburgh, once I've settled matters here. But what am I thinking?' He placed his hands on the desk. 'I promised you refreshments.' He looked around for a bell and, finding none, rose to his feet. 'One moment. I'll have the redoubtable Jenet bring us some tea.'

He left the room, whistling. Lil lunged for the envelope. She stayed in that position, leaning across the desk with the torc digging into her arm, as she slipped out the single sheet of paper and unfolded it.

Dear Alec,

You will know by now the liberty I have taken. I doubt you are very surprised. This letter is merely to state that the subterfuge, both in idea and execution, was mine and mine alone. My colleagues and family, Nils Jensen and Lil Vincent, have no knowledge of it and will no doubt suffer a greater shock than yourself.

Ill health prevents me from moving, but if you care to learn something of importance that I shall not trust to a letter, you may call on me at the above address. My doctors would urge you not to delay too long.

Yours,
  eUphemia Jensen

Footsteps sounded in the corridor. Lil swiftly returned the letter to the envelope, the envelope to the pile, and fell back in her chair as Raube entered the room. Her heart was racing as quickly as her thoughts. It was as if Effie's secret had burst into being, flailing monstrous limbs. And Raube, the owner of Pitcarden, knew more about it than Lil did; he was a part of it.

'We have been promised bannocks.' He sounded as innocent and carefree as a child. 'It's a long time since I tasted one of those.'

She made herself look at him as he retook his seat, her smile a little fierce. His gaze landed on the torc. 'Astonishing.' He touched it gently with his fingertips. She noticed his hand shook slightly. 'Decades struggling to scratch out gold on the other side of the world, and this is what awaits me at home.'

'You must have seen it before.' Lil felt as if every nerve and tissue in her body had woken up. He wasn't going to throw them off the site, whatever the history between himself and Effie.

'No. I knew it existed, of course, but my father wouldn't let me see it. He remained superstitious to the end.'

'You were here when he dug—' She was cut off by a loud knocking at the side door.

Raube stood again. 'I'll get that if you'll excuse me. Jenet isn't in any condition to move quickly.'

Lil rose to her feet also. The knocking came again, forceful and urgent. She heard the bolt draw back and then voices. Nils. She glanced at the envelope, wondering if even he knew the full story of Effie and Pitcarden. Raube was leading him towards the office, calling to Jenet to bring a third teacup. He dragged a chair over from the other desk and cleared some papers out of Nils's way. As he resumed his own seat, he placed them on the stack with the letter, covering it.

'We were just discussing my father's obsession with these.' He gestured at the torc and the candlestick. Lil lowered herself back into her chair, watching Nils. He looked ill enough not to make an obvious liar of her about the cold. His face was puffy and his eyes red. He seemed as wary and nonplussed by the friendly reception as she had been, but he only nodded and cleared his throat.

'My condolences on the loss of your father.'

Lil felt the jolt of her own omission. She would never get used to speaking of the dead as irretrievably gone. The idea had been drummed into her as heresy.

'Thank you.' Raube smiled. 'In Australia, it was easy to believe his letters had simply miscarried. Coming back has brought it home to me.' He gave a breathy laugh. 'Or, I suppose, has brought me home to it.' He blinked, overwhelmed by some thought. To Lil, he looked less grief-stricken than amazed, as if he had received a shock, the import of which he couldn't yet grasp.

'I understand.' Nils stared at him, unblinking. Lil bit her lip, thinking of how he had never gone home to Effie. Raube refocused his attention and gave an elegant little bow of his head.

'So, to the burial mound. Miss Vincent was explaining where you will focus your efforts before the weather closes in again.'

Lil and Nils spoke at the same time, contradicting each other. She turned to look at him, but he kept his eyes on Raube.

'The south trench is half open still; we can do more in the time.' His shoulders had hunched as they did when he refused to move on a subject. It was the brooch he was after still, for Effie, but neither of them could say that in front of Raube. He was watching them with interest. Lil hesitated. Did he already know what they were really fighting about? Effie had written that he wouldn't be surprised. She raised her hands.

'You can continue with it, of course. But the cist is the central burial; it will tell us more about the site, and I've been digging all day – I'm nearly there.'

Nils turned sharply. He was furious suddenly and thundered at her. 'Why would you do that? No.' He turned back to Raube. 'We will put all our efforts into the south trench.'

There was a short, uncomfortable silence. Lil bit her lip and also looked at Raube. She didn't dare appeal to him. He was no longer the amiable and fascinating stranger she had met on the mound. His private thoughts and motives were as unknowable as one of her night-mares. For a moment, Madelyn's parting warning rang deafeningly in her head, making her catch her breath. She gathered herself and spoke calmly.

'I'm going to look inside the cist. I'll continue digging it when I return from Edinburgh. You can keep the men.'

She felt rather than saw Nils's expression and looked at Raube. He shook his head. 'I had not appreciated digging for bones could excite the same passions as digging for gold but, of course, it must. Why wouldn't it? It's gold to you. Here is the tea . . .'

Jenet had appeared in the doorway, moving cautiously. The effort of keeping the tray aloft showed in her face. Lil stood to help her, noticing Nils had turned pale. Jenet's eyes latched onto the torc that Raube was lifting out of the way with the candlestick. She lingered, straining to keep it in sight until it was folded into velvet, and only retreated when Raube made a point of thanking her.

It was a disjointed tea party. They spoke of excavations in Norway, the state of British museums, the sudden mania in London for investing in Queensland's gold mines, but the topics floated like unmanned boats on the surface, bumping and drifting, while their pilots grappled monsters beneath. No one mentioned Effie.

It was as if they had agreed to pretend she didn't exist. The conversation returned eventually to practical matters. Nils declared he would go to Gledsmuir in the morning to try to recruit more diggers, and Raube offered the use of his trap and the stable boy to drive them in time for Lil's train. As they were taking their leave, he plucked a small parcel of mail from the pigeonholes and handed it to Nils.

'I am very pleased to have met you, Mr Jensen. I hope the next few days will prove fruitful.' He clasped Nils's arm, and Lil formed the impression he was holding on to the bigger man for support. 'Let's see if, between us, we cannot drum up a few more men to help.'

Nils nodded, looking a little wild, and moments later he was walking with Lil in the darkness past the burned-out stables. Once they reached the drive, they both began speaking at once again, Nils asking if Raube had said anything at all about the forgeries. Lil seized the material of his coat and brought them both to a halt. She didn't want to tell him about the contents of Effie's letter in case he didn't know. However angry she was with Effie herself, her loyalty was stronger.

'The brooch is the only reason we're here, isn't it? It was never about the mound. You both lied to me.' She couldn't see his expression in the gloom, but his silence was answer enough. 'Tell me now. Why is it so important to her?'

He remained mute and motionless as a standing stone. She shoved him, which served more to propel herself backwards, and turned, a cry of anger and impatience in her throat, to stomp towards the path up the hill.

'I promised her.' Nils's voice was a whisper on the night air. Lil stopped, took a step back towards him.

'Promised her what?'

'That when the older Mr Raube died, whenever that might be, we would come here and excavate. She knew about the hoard, and the brooch. She wants it very much. It's how we met. She was looking for an archaeologist who would be interested in the site and would provide a cover. It was the only thing she made me promise.'

'Why? What does it mean to her? She doesn't chase after treasure.' Even as she said it, Lil wondered if that was true. Effie's pursuit of wealth had never been so blatant or crude as digging for buried loot, but the obsessive effort she put into watching and researching the markets was as exhausting and intensive as any spade work. Nils's career – and Lil's – were largely financed by her dogged eye for a windfall. His voice was hoarse.

'It's hers. It was given to her.'

Lil strained uselessly to make out his face. 'What do you mean? By whom?'

He didn't answer for a moment, and then his dim shape shifted, and she realised he was moving past her in the darkness, more presence than person. He dropped the hushed tones. 'I promised, that is enough. It was not so much to ask in return for what she has done for me. And you, yes?'

Lil listened to the receding sound of his boots grappling against mud and stones, and tried to make sense of what he had said. Was the brooch from Raube somehow? Haxton had told her there was a woman, the fiancée of Raube's father, and the older man had dug up the hoard a second time for her. She peered back towards the house and the ruined stable block. It was in almost total darkness and seemed deserted. The only sound now was a light tapping and scraping of dried leaves falling one at a time onto those gone before. Each one, for an instant, sounded like a footstep. The accumulation of faint pats and rustlings, coming from different directions, gave the sense of something closing in on her, something she couldn't see. Another leaf dropped a few feet away, sounding almost like a twig snapping, and she set off for the path, heart thumping in spite of herself.

At the cottage, Nils had disappeared again. The table was

strewn with the mail Raube had given him: correspondence, reports and bills. And ripped envelopes. He hadn't bothered with a paper knife. Propped up against the whisky bottle was an unopened letter with so many scrawls and crossings-out on it, she didn't immediately see it was her own name at the top. She picked it up to decipher the mess of addresses and then sat down quickly, almost missing the chair. She threw the letter among the rest of the post as if it had burned her, and gripped the edge of the table. Black ink obscured most of the original address, but she could make out 'Care of Sullivan' beneath her own name. Another pen – Mrs Sullivan's – had written Effie's London address, and that in turn had been crossed out in favour of Cumberland Street in Edinburgh. Finally, Lil recognised Bina's hand redirecting the letter to Pitcarden House.

Her instinct was to throw it straight into the fire, unopened. It had been weak and foolish of her to give the Sullivans a forwarding address. She should have disappeared without trace. There was only one place a letter could have come from, but the handwriting wasn't Madelyn's.

She picked it up again and went to stand in front of the fire, holding the envelope over the smouldering embers so she could be rid of it for ever just by letting go. Slicing it open, she found two different types of paper inside, folded separately. She opened the first, a letter. The address at the top was indeed Madelyn's, but again the handwriting was not hers. Relief swept through her, followed by the vertiginous thought that this could only, therefore, be from Agnes with news of her death.

Dear Miss Vincent,

I write to you in desperation, praying fervently that this will reach you and find you safe and well. Please believe that I would not impose on you if it weren't of the greatest importance. There is no one else left I can try.

Madame de Vallon has disappeared. Something upset her dreadfully at our Wednesday séance, and I am terribly afraid for her safety. She wouldn't say what was wrong, but I believe it was something I wrote during an episode of spirit writing, and it made her very afraid. When I read it out, she appeared shocked and asked me to repeat a few sentences. She then fixed me with a look of such fury and accusation that I was quite frightened. She demanded to know what I meant by it. What could I say? I never know what I have written until it is done. She continued to berate me in front of the sitters — not all of them regulars — and then stormed out of the room. I have included the page of spirit writing in the hope that it will lead you to a better understanding of her state of mind and where she might be.

She refused to open her door for the rest of the evening or to answer questions from me or anyone else. I could hear her moving about and talking to herself. In the morning, she was gone. Her room had been ransacked, with clothes pulled out of drawers and a box of papers upturned. Among the papers I found a letter that had been sent before you left about a governess position. When Madame de Vallon didn't return, I went to the address, hoping to find you. A Mrs Sullivan told me you had left her employ a long time before and that no one had enquired about you since. She wouldn't tell me where you had gone, but said if I sent a letter, she would forward it.

Our regular sitters have expressed great concern, but none of them is willing to do more than that. Their ingratitude breaks my heart. I have even spoken to the police, but they refuse to take her disappearance seriously.

If I am honest, Madame de Vallon has not been herself for several months. Something is preying on her mind, distracting her, and her professionalism has suffered because of it. I have often heard her muttering to herself, and her behaviour has become erratic, asking peculiar things of the spirits. To be *frank, I was half expecting a scene like the one we had last Wednesday. My fear is that her mind is weakening and that great harm may come to her.*

You are the only family she has, Lilith. I pray that the circumstances of your leaving have not entirely hardened your heart against her. I beg of you, if it is at all within your power, come back, <u>please</u>. Help me find her before something awful happens.

Desperately and with the love of the spirits,
  Agnes

Lil wished fervently that she had thrown the letter into the fire unread. The suffocating atmosphere of Madelyn's house returned like feverish fingers closing over her face. She stood for a long time, on the point of dropping it all into the grate. Even if she owed Madelyn anything, which she didn't, there was nothing she could do to help find her after all this time. There was no need to read whatever nonsense Agnes had written in a séance. Her fingers relaxed a fraction. But then, in spite of herself, she was slipping the page out of the envelope. It was folded double, and she recognised one of the thick sheets they had always used for spirit writing, oversized so her pen could roam around the paper. The messier and more chaotic the spirits, the more convinced the sitters.

She opened it up. Writing covered most of it, but the first words she saw, much larger than the others and in the middle of the sheet, read:

NEW BONES OVER OLD

The page slipped from her fingers and dropped straight onto the flickering embers. For a moment, she was paralysed. A flake of ash floated upward and, with a cry, she fell to her knees, hands darting at the paper, which had rapidly turned brown, then black at points, before a glowing shoreline ate it away into widening pools of nothingness. She snatched it out and onto the hearth, halting further damage with her sleeve.

Some part of her, far distant, was trying to reason, to draw her back to the present, but she was a child again, hounded by spirits that could set anything alight, that could write on walls, and draw blood from her body. She wiped her eyes and nose roughly with the back of her hand and bent over the page. There was gibberish and meaningless scratchings at the top. A few lines about a translation of Cicero; no doubt a classicist or historian had been present. And then, before the worst of the damage, words written as if by a different hand.

one two buried buried beneath NEW BONES OVER OLD

Her breath came in short gasps; there didn't seem to be enough air in the room. Beneath the words, the paper was badly singed, but some writing was visible, guessable.

__ur five bur__
    __ew bones over o__
        __ive six__
__x six six six SIX SI__
Run run run run run run run run run run

She recognised it. Memories she had tried to bury filled her mind, surging upwards like an underground flood. She remembered the first time she had lost control of the pen, coming to from an unrehearsed trance to find her hand had moved anyway, Lambert's warning glare.

one two three four five one two three four five
one two three new bones over old
four five new bones over old
one two three four five SIX

She clutched the front of her dress, trying to breathe, aware of a keening noise filling the kitchen. Strong hands grasped her arms, pulled her around. Nils shook her. 'Stop it. What is it? What is wrong?'

She fought to speak. 'It's coming. It's coming for me.'

He looked down at the scorched paper and Agnes's letter, then pulled her to him. Even through her panic, she could feel how tightly, too tightly, he gripped her, as if he too were terrified.

On the ride to Gledsmuir the next morning, they were both silent. The air was clear and still, the sky a disorientating summer blue. A good day for excavating, but Lil barely noticed the world around her. Nils had dosed her with whisky the night before and when she'd eventually grown calm, had sent her to bed. Too scared to sleep, she had lit an extravagant number of candles and watched them burn down, a cup of water in hand to wake her if she dozed off and dropped it. It made no difference. She still woke to her ribs straining under the impossible weight, her skin fizzing. Faces appeared above her, melting rapidly into each other. Old man, crone, Effie, child. Sickeningly fast. And others she didn't know: burned, weeping, angry, frightened. They changed and changed and collapsed suddenly into one. Twice the size of life, monstrous eyes pinning hers: Madelyn.

At breakfast, Nils had waited for her to explain Agnes's letter and the spirit writing, which he must have read. She'd found them neatly stacked on the table and weighted with the iron arrowhead. He and Effie knew little of her past life; she had hinted at the strangeness of Madelyn's household, but was too ashamed to admit the extent of her own involvement. Finally, it was Nils who'd spoken. 'Will you do what this Agnes asks of you?'

'I believe that my mothe— that Madame de Vallon's mind is weakening, as she says. But there is nothing I can do. It caught me off guard yesterday, that's all.'

He nodded. His lips moved as if words were fighting to be let out. 'These people . . .' He looked at Lil and away again. Finally, he surprised her by reaching over and laying a heavy hand on her shoulder. 'I know you are angry at us. But . . . we are your family.' He seemed about to say more, but only nodded again and released her.

Lil didn't speak or move, scared she might somehow break this delicate offering. *Family.* It was the word Effie had used in her letter to Alec Raube. Her gaze fell on Agnes's letter and the spirit writing. She had, she believed, freed herself of the need for familial bonds after Madelyn. But now a yearning swelled in her heart. And even Madelyn herself wouldn't stay gone. It was true, Lil told herself, what she had said to Nils. Madelyn's mental faculties must be failing. Agnes herself believed it. Perhaps the medical men were halfway right about spiritualistic madness. And the spirit writing could be a simple ploy by Agnes to lure her down. Lil had moved suddenly, snatching up the papers from under the arrowhead and, in answer to Nils, she thrust them into the fire.

But now, in the cart on the way to Gledsmuir, she could feel the worm turning within her, a knowing that cleaved to the dark spaces of her body, as much a part of her as bone and blood and tissue. If everything else were stripped away, dissolved to nothing, this dark knowing would still stand, and its shape would be hers. She slipped a hand into her pocket to hold the plaque. Perhaps she really was mad. Mad like Madelyn, her brain prematurely disintegrating. The thought had returned steadily throughout her near-sleepless night, like the beam of a lighthouse. And with it, the image of Dr Lachlan, brilliantly lit — a figure of hope, salvation, her redeemer. She clung to the idea of seeing him before the writhing shadows of her past could envelop her again. To fill herself up with the sight of him, the sound of his voice, which she had not yet heard, his clarifying words, would fortify her, like a blessing.

The boy dropped them outside the post office, and they faced each other. Nils's look was searching. Lil put a hand on his arm. 'I understand you searching for the brooch, Nils. I hope you find it.' He looked startled but didn't speak. Her voice grew firm. 'But if the weather holds, I shall do as I said and dig the cist.' She withdrew her hand. 'You both chose not to share with me your real reasons for coming to Pitcarden. I won't now be stopped from doing what *I* came here to do.'

She left him still wordless on the pavement and entered the post office. There was nothing from Dr Lachlan. Too soon, she told herself, and anyway, it hardly mattered. In a few hours, they would be in the same room, breathing the same air. She hurried to catch her train.

11

There was colour in Effie's cheeks, brought on both by the suit of clothes laid out on an armchair like a gentleman so overcome with ennui he had deflated, and by the barber in the kitchen, who was at that moment taking his revenge for being made to wait downstairs like a servant by helping himself to another of Bina's scones. Lil stood in the centre of the drawing room, as rigid as a post. The words she wanted to say were wedged tightly inside, like splinters. Effie saw how it was. She patted the sofa beside her.

'Nils sent a telegram. You know I have an ulterior motive in digging up Pitcarden.' She paused. Lil didn't sit. 'And a letter has come from London. It upset you.'

'Why didn't you tell me about the brooch?'

'I did.'

'You didn't tell me how important it was to you.'

'Why should I?' Effie's tone was straightforward, without anger. Lil's, however, rose with emotion.

'Because you lied to me. You let me believe what wasn't true.' Her words rebounded on her as soon as they had left her mouth, like the lash of a whip. The same could be levelled at her by a thousand different voices.

Effie remained calm. 'I did no such thing. The site holds special archaeological interest. I employed you to investigate it. The other does not concern you.'

'The *other* has compromised the entire site.'

'You exaggerate.'

'Nils is butchering it this minute. You should have told me. I could have helped you do both. I'm not . . .' Her throat closed on a spring of misery that was welling up. She imagined Nils's hand on her shoulder again and had the impulse to shake it off. 'I *thought* I was something more than your employee.'

'Oh, for heaven's sake, you know you are.' Effie leaned back against the cushions, tiredness suddenly showing in her face. 'But Lily Pad, you must allow me to keep some things private. There are elements of my past I choose not to share.' She held Lil's gaze and raised her eyebrows a little. 'You do the same, do you not?'

A sound that was almost a sob, almost a groan, escaped Lil. She half fell towards the sofa, sitting down heavily and taking Effie's hands. 'Won't you tell me anything? What is it about the brooch? You knew the older Mr Raube?'

'A very long time ago.'

'You were engaged to him?'

Effie shook her head, but it was a refusal to discuss it further rather than an answer to the question. Lil pressed on anyway. 'I saw the letter you sent to Alec Raube. You know him too; you have some secret between you, or you have something over him, which is why he hasn't made a fuss about you forging his signature.'

For the briefest moment, Effie seemed to freeze. She then gave a slight smile, as if caught out in some mischief. 'Ah.'

'You know he's letting us continue the dig? Did Nils put that in his telegram? He would have given his permission. I told him about the cist.'

Effie rearranged their hands so hers were now on top, holding Lil's wrists. 'I am so sorry, Lily Pad, that you have been tangled up in all this and it's turned into such a mess. We were supposed to be back in Norway before Alec Raube even knew we had been. I didn't anticipate the factor being quite so troublesome. And I apologise for keeping things from you. Though I must tell you that I would do the same again. I was right, but it pains me deeply to have hurt you. Especially as there is so little time left.' Her grip tightened. 'I wanted to ask you. Will you stay with me now?' Lil looked up at her in sudden fear. There was a vulnerability in the blue eyes. 'I think the time is near, and I would like that. Pitcarden can wait until the spring, can it not? Now you have the backing of Raube.'

'But can't the doctors . . .' Everything seemed to fall away from Lil in an instant: the room, the sofa, even Effie. She could still see and hear, but felt suspended in a horrible emptiness. Effie gave a small scoffing noise.

'Doctors are all well and good, but they are not clairvoyant.' The word was an unfortunate one. Lil looked down. Effie freed one hand and raised it to her face, gently touching her cheek. 'What I would like to see again, is a smile, just here.' She tapped her fingers softly on Lil's lips. 'And I think I know of a different doctor for that.' She turned her eyes towards the chair with the suit on it. Lil looked too and gasped a laugh.

'Do you really think I'll get away with it?'

'Of course. I'd say you are in greater danger of starting a fight and ending up bloodied and bruised in a cell. In which case I promise to pay bail.'

Lil raised Effie's fingers to her lips and held them there a moment. Then she wiped her eyes, thudded her fist against her own leg, and set off towards the deflated gentleman.

The clothes were well made but worn, the Oxford boots both polished and down at heel, all to mitigate the appearance of dressing up. Bina was summoned. As she bound Lil's chest, Lil had to push away memories of Madelyn and Agnes doing the same, preparing her for materialisations. She remembered tearing the material off on that awful final night and vowing never to be wrapped up and hemmed in again. It was the only painful intrusion on an otherwise giddy few hours. There couldn't have been more fussing and exclaiming if it had been a fitting for a wedding dress. Lil was already light-headed from lack of sleep. Shrieks of laughter accompanied each article and were only temporarily stifled for the sake of the barber. His simmering indignation was almost, but not quite, as great as the fee Effie must have paid him.

Excusing herself to have a moment alone with the full-length mirror in the bedroom, Lil took the stairs two at a time, marvelling at the freedom granted to her legs. She had expected male attire to inspire a sense of gravity, but felt more inclined to climb a tree or play hopscotch in the street. Had she, she asked herself, discovered the key to the gender paradox? How men wielded immeasurable power while behaving like oversized schoolboys, and women remained near immobile, their life force stalled beneath layers of fabric until physical freedom survived not even as a memory. Lil amused herself with the thought as she skipped into the bedroom. Perhaps the burden of moral duty and obedience, upheld as the feminine ideal by many a woman, was simply a ghastly misinterpretation of the severe weight of her crinolines.

She came to a halt in front of the mirror, in mind as well as body. The jacket and trousers were fashionably narrow; lucky, as Effie said, that Lil had no hips to speak of. Her hair was short and slick, showing off the real shape of her skull, her features unsoftened by stray wisps. It was a strong face. The prettiness that caught men's stares like flies in syrup had given way to a starker beauty, more elemental. Like denuded rock. She enjoyed the sharper definition of her whole figure, as if she had come more into focus. Several minutes went by. The longer she stared at her face, the more unfamiliar it seemed. It flickered almost, shifting indefinably from her own to not her own and back again so quickly that she blinked. A trick of the eye, the result of almost no sleep. But as she continued to watch, the flashes grew more vivid, staying put in the mirror for seconds at a time. Fascination locked her eye to eye with her reflection. Someone else was looking out at her, or some thing. A strange smile teased the corners of her lips, dropped them, returned again. And then it was there. Sudden, inhuman, conscious. The goddess or demon of the plaque. Its awful presence resided in her own face, its awareness blazing through the glass.

Lil wrenched her whole body away and flew to the door. Her breathing short, she looked back at the mirror, which at that angle reflected the bed, as if expecting a figure to lurch out of it. She pressed her hands to her face, reassuring herself it was hers. The illusion was gone, but the residue remained, as if it were the night-mare she had escaped. Its presence crowded the air. The furniture, through its very stillness, seemed possessed of a sinister awareness. She moved swiftly and furtively back down the stairs, avoiding glancing at mirrors, windows, glass-fronted cabinets, anything that might show her reflection. In the cheerful warmth and chaos of the drawing room, she tried to summon the same light mood as before, but her eye kept straying to her skirt, which was thrown over a chair, as if she expected to see a hole burned in the pocket by the plaque.

Effie's instructions were military. Lil was marched up and down the room until her gait and bearing screamed cigars and sporting fixtures. She wasn't allowed out of character for a moment. If she took a seat or lifted a fork, Effie was watching like a hawk and barked corrections. If she spoke, it was to be in monosyllables and hoarse. A muffler and brutal rubbing of the nose and eyes suggested a head cold and helped obscure the face a little.

'But whatever you do, you must not look as if you're trying to hide. It will draw all eyes to you. If you have to speak, you're a student from the university, taking an extramural lecture.' Effie spoke with effort, her voice losing strength. Lil had insisted she rest often and try to sleep, but her initial healthy colour had now withered to grey, the sickness calling in its debt. Her eyelids were already closing. Lil exchanged a look with Bina.

'I shall walk there and accustom myself to being in public.' She took the ticket from Bina that had somehow been procured and that she had decided not to ask about.

Kissing Effie gently on the cheek, she whispered, 'Thank you.' She could smell the disease on her, sharp and alien. Pausing, with their faces still almost touching, she whispered again even more quietly, 'I love you.' They were so close, all she could see was skin and lashes, the shape of bone and cartilage, a blurred landscape that couldn't see her in return but held everything of importance. Effie made a sound in her throat, either replying in kind or more likely groaning: straightforward expressions of love were not indulged between them, and encroaching death had brought with it no softening of Effie's view. Nothing had been left unsaid; it had all been reiterated countless times over in how they lived and worked together. The words themselves were superfluous, self-seeking even, an admission of doubt.

Lil sat up again and needlessly smoothed the hair above Effie's brow. She would be back in a matter of hours, at her side and full of stories about the lecture and her fortunes as a man. One last look at that face – more dear to her, if anything, for the signs of its wasting – and she turned away. Bina handed her the hat. Now Effie was asleep or as good as, all trace of laughter and playfulness had vanished from the housekeeper's face as surely as if the woman had found no reason to smile in months. Lil eyed her askance. She had paid little attention to Bina during the day, but thinking back, her displays of jollity had sounded forced. She didn't want to read the gravity of Effie's illness in the face of her servant. Bina looked as if she might say something, ask something, and it was more than Lil was willing to hear. She rammed the hat on her head and swirled the overcoat around her, shrugging off Bina's attempts to help. 'Make sure she's comfortable. I'll see myself out.'

She fled. Her feet carried her out of the front door and halfway down the street before she remembered she was not herself running from a sickroom but a medical student strolling towards a lecture. She unfolded her arms and recalled Effie's instructions to lead from her upper body, to let her hands swing further forward, to hold her pelvis still. Embodying different people, be they man, woman, or child, was something she had excelled at in materialisations and at round-table séances. At the latter, with no recourse to props, disguises or even freedom of movement, the transformation had to come from within. She discovered that if she could conjure a feeling of a person and dwell within it while spirit writing or in a trance, it somehow communicated itself to the sitters. At least, something emanated from her that successfully met expectations and desires, even if only halfway. Halfway was enough.

She went inwards now, searching for the medical student. It was easy to feel his weariness. After hours of poring over textbooks with a head cold, diagrams flickered in front of his eyes. His circumstances demanded a profession, a reckoning of his worth, and he had sisters. Men like him always had sisters. He also had good boots, and a beautiful late afternoon cooling the back of his neck. He paid little attention to others on the pavement. If faces turned too intently his way, he swept past them with indifference, as if he were pulling a veil across.

By the time Lil reached the Old Town, she was as comfortable being Eustace as if she had never worn a petticoat. Walking in trousers had lost the odd sensation of nakedness, and she delighted in the feeling of being a free, forked animal. No one had spoken to her. Two groups of boys, who might have seen a chance for sport, let her pass by without a glance. Her confidence grew. She was Eustace, and Eustace, for all his worries and obligations, was happy. Lucky Eustace.

She strolled back and forth along Nicolson Street to avoid waiting outside the lecture room and risking interrogation. With a few minutes to spare, she strode through the courtyard of Surgeons' Hall in a loose band of other hurrying young men and into the building. Following blindly, she showed her ticket when asked, and moments later, was miraculously sitting near the end of a bench, looking down over a sea of heads at a lectern and magic lantern on a platform. She was in. Her heart, already beating fast with nerves, doubled its efforts with a boom at the thought that Dr Lachlan was nearby. The hall was humming with men's voices, the sound punctuated by bursts of overloud laughing or a hollered greeting. Her neighbour on the right was talking animatedly to someone the other side of him, his large hands flipping a notebook on the desk, his elbow repeatedly knocking her arm. She wished she'd brought something to occupy her hands. Someone took a seat to her left. He cleared his throat, as if about to speak, and Lil immediately faked a sneeze and then a cough into her muffler. She felt a slight but definite shift at her side and watched a slim hand dip into a pocket for a handkerchief, which was lifted to the face and remained there. Praise be for medical students, she thought; everyone in the room would be familiar with how germs were spread. She remembered playing a pioneering epidemiologist for a curious physician and felt the familiar wave of shame.

A door next to the platform opened and immediately a hush fell over the room. Dr Lachlan was clearly a popular lecturer. But none there was keener than Lil. Every inch of her was centred on that door. He appeared, and she felt as if she herself had ceased to be real. The fact of his presence filled her consciousness to the exclusion of all else. She was out of her body, existing only in the minute and vivid detail of his appearance: the wave in his hair, the angle between jaw and neck, the direction of his gaze. Her senses seemed preternaturally powerful and entwined with each other. She heard in the sound of his step the weight of his body, but she could also feel it, as if it were her own. Her eyes saw him cough quietly into his fist, but her own skin felt the warmth of the breath. So forceful was the illusion, she was paralysed in her own body, unable even to join in the applause that welcomed him.

He took his position at the lectern and ordered his papers, a small frown of concentration on his brow. Lil felt the creasing in her own forehead. Without hurry, he looked up and ran his gaze over the packed benches. Smiled. He didn't look directly at her, although he might have done. She felt the sweep of his attention pass over her like a flush of goose pimples raised by a touch.

'Good afternoon.'

His voice. Warm. She felt the vibration of it in her core. He began his introduction, entirely at ease and often breaking free of the lectern, as if to facilitate a more direct transference of knowledge from himself to the students. Immersed as she was in the reality of him, rising and falling with the movement of his voice, she had to catch up with the sense of what he was saying. He was explaining definitions, tracing the muddied history of terms such as illusion and delusion to illustrate the importance of their distinction for modern physicians and patients. She felt a smile blooming inside. The promise of his letters, his faith in her sanity, the assurance, almost, of effective treatment was embodied in him. The very gestures he made with his hands helped her feel calmer.

He talked for over an hour, and she slipped in and out of listening to his words and simply dwelling in his presence, the caress of his speech. The audience laughed suddenly, and she laughed too, turning to share it with the student next to her. It was the first time their eyes had met, and from the curious expression on his face she realised she had forgotten her disguise. That laugh had not come from Eustace. She faced forward again but felt the other's eyes resting on her still. It hardly mattered; she was confident now that no one would confront her. A sensation stole over her, so novel she couldn't place it at first. It spread through her like the warmth of spring sunshine: safety. She would meet Dr Lachlan properly as his patient, in person. The thought sent the blood surging through her body.

'Now.' His voice changed. He was standing beside the lectern and let his hand fall lightly on top of it, glancing sideways at the notes there. 'I'd like to end by sharing an ongoing case study.' He gave his audience an almost coy look. 'I think it will interest you, and it should serve to illustrate some of the arguments that have no doubt wreaked havoc on your unsuspecting minds, if not unsettle them further.

'An unmarried woman, aged twenty-eight, wrote to me, complaining of disturbing visions during the night. She reports the sensation of being fully awake but unable to move and vividly hallucinating that she is being physically held down and strangled by a shadowy male figure.'

Lil felt everything in her body fall into stillness; her very heart seemed to stop.

'Miss G, as we'll call her, expresses herself articulately and is very aware of the improbability of her statements. She claims to live an otherwise normal and healthy life and is only troubled after several hours of sleep. She puts much stress on her sanity . . .' A laugh rippled around the room; he waited for it to pass. 'And hopes the visions are a symptom of some treatable physical disorder. A problem with digestion perhaps – her own joke.' He opened his hands. 'What is going on here? What do you think?'

Lil's heart began pounding again, so fast and hard, she thought her neighbours would hear it. After a pause, a voice from the front rose faintly. 'She's only dreaming but thinks she's awake.'

'Possibly.' Dr Lachlan gave a nod.

Another voice came from the middle. 'If she's dreaming of being attacked by a man, it could be a disorder of the uterus.'

Lil's neighbour tutted, and on the platform, Dr Lachlan pursed his lips. 'A form of hysteria, you mean? I'll come back to the subject of the dream or hallucination in a minute, but yes, I would certainly like to know much more about her sexual and reproductive history.'

As he said it, his gaze lifted over the lower rows of seats, towards Lil. She felt the same bolt of electricity as she had outside his house, the sharp thrill of fear. It was happening; his eyes met hers. For a moment, she was convinced he had recognised her. But as she stared back, transfixed, she realised it wasn't her he was looking at. Her neighbour had raised his hand. The student cleared his throat, his voice loud and close.

'I would not dismiss out of hand her claim to be awake. Might not congestion of the cerebral capillaries result in the sort of sleep disorder she describes?'

'Good!' Dr Lachlan wagged a finger in the air. 'That is certainly one avenue to be explored. These are all sound ideas.' He had moved back to the lectern and grasped both sides. 'However,' his expression became conspiratorial, and he paused to look meaningfully around, 'what if I were to tell you that this patient had worked as a spiritualist medium from childhood until the age of sixteen?'

A rustling and murmuring started up in the audience as if it were a huge bird shaking out its feathers. Dr Lachlan tapped the top of his lectern for emphasis.

'I have never met this patient; I do not know her real name. She concealed her identity, more than aware that her history might call into question her sanity. She claims to have rejected all belief in spiritualism and not practised it for more than ten years. What then? Well, let me show you a page from one of her letters.'

He went to the magic lantern placed near the lectern, and Lil watched her first letter rear up onto the wall at a horrible scale.

'Even before reading it, what do you see?'

Crossings-out, underscoring, messy script. Lil saw it all as the students began calling them out. Dr Lachlan nodded along.

'Precisely. She is inadvertently telling me a huge amount about herself through her handwriting and punctuation alone. We know that this sort of chaotic and emphatic writing can indicate a hysterical condition. And just to show you how her writing has developed during our correspondence, this is from a recent letter that she sent to me unfinished, without a signature even.' He swapped the slide, and a page that she had tried to write on the train was flung up. The jerky, uneven letters, magnified enormously, looked deranged.

'In it, she is describing physically attacking – indeed, strangling – her male tutor when she was fifteen years old, a man she had engaged with sexually.' He glanced towards the student who had talked about uterine disorders. 'Interesting when one considers her recurring dream – or hallucination – of being strangled by a man.' The students were left to ponder this as he returned to the lectern.

'As to her disavowal of spiritualism, doubts emerge when one reads the letters more closely. She deliberately calls these experiences night-mares, with a hyphen, meaning evil spirits or demons – in order to differentiate them, she says, from the ordinary nightmares of sleep. She even references a demonic figure from folklore, the Mara. But why not call them something entirely different – visions or waking dreams? She reports a sense of *knowing* that the night-mare has always been near her, and I quote, "even before I was born". She is preoccupied with metaphysical questions, asking for my opinion on the soul and the afterlife. It would seem, then, whether she is aware of it or not, that she is still very much influenced by spiritualism. And we know that patients with hysterical personalities are capable of conjuring up visions of spirits for themselves at will.

'Has anyone read Maudsley?' A few hands went up. 'I encourage you to do so. His studies have shown that spiritualism can not only *cause* derangement but that it also *attracts* the incipiently insane. Which is interesting when we consider Miss G's probable mother, the medium who raised her. If this woman already suffered from a mental disease that first drew her to spiritualism, there is the question of hereditary illness. Miss G may have been born with a disorder that would only have been exacerbated by her upbringing.' He walked back to the magic lantern and manipulated it as he continued talking.

'Her mother apparently was able to maintain the genuine belief that she could communicate with the dead while simultaneously stage-managing fake séances. Her faith was unshaken even when Miss G was publicly exposed as a fraud.'

He brought up the next slide and there were gasps and laughs from the students. Lil's image was projected mountainously against the screen. She stared out like a cornered animal. It was the photograph from her sixteenth birthday séance: mad eyes, torn garments, hair wild across her face.

'Added to all of this is her young age when the episodes began and the unhealthy environment in which she was sequestered during those transitional years. Almost the first thing she wrote to me was that she admired my questioning of a colleague's views on women's education during adolescence. In a later letter she describes being driven relentlessly by her tutor to study a multitude of subjects for the purpose of automatic writing. It is as if she were trying to flatter me out of a conclusion she doesn't want to hear, but I am afraid I have to concede that in this case Dr Clouston really does seem to have a point.' More laughter.

'We are nearly out of time, but to sum up: possible hereditary illness, an overworked adolescence, immersion in spiritualism, lack of self-awareness, chaotic handwriting, and I haven't had time to go into the relationship with her tutor or the subtle and, frankly, less than subtle behaviours she has exhibited towards myself — impassioned language, ah, imagining touching me, not to mention lurking outside my house. A truly fascinating case.

'So,' he clapped his hands, 'can we reassure Miss G that her night-time hallucinations are a case of bad digestion?' A chorus of laughs and negatives rose to the rafters.

He held out his hands and smiled around the room. 'The truth is we don't know. Welcome to the edge.' Turning, he considered the photograph a moment, then cocked his head comically at the audience, as if to say, of course we all know. They laughed. Relaxing his face, he joined in and returned to the lectern. 'No, we *don't* know. Not until I can persuade her to undergo treatment. I need to borrow some tricks from the spiritualists and learn how to *summon* her, to make her *materialise*.' More mocking laughter. 'Questions.'

Lil snatched at her hat and turned sharply. 'Excuse me.' She kept her eyes fixed on her neighbour's lap but rose from her seat as if she intended to clamber over him. Perhaps she would have, but the student moved quickly, slipping from the bench into the aisle. He put a hand on her arm. The grip was firm. 'Are you quite well?'

Lil ignored him and pushed out of his grasp, taking the steps two at a time. She could feel bodies shifting, turning towards the disturbance, the room quiet, and climbed faster. Once through the door, she ran like something hunted, pell-mell through the building, across the courtyard and into the street, coat flapping behind. Eustace had disappeared. There was just a forked creature bolting through the city, looking for a crack to fall into and disappear. Lungs burned, dragging air, until the headlong rush was finally exhausted. Feet clattered unevenly to a walk; shoulders wrenched high with the effort of breathing. Sobs came then:

painful, wild cries that heaved their way out like escaping bats, winged and clawed.

Still, she kept moving, blundering her way across the bridge and over Princes Street. Faces passed by in a blur, unheeded. She climbed the hill and all but fell down the other side. Reaching the house, she threw herself against the door and pounded the knocker. Bina answered, but Lil barged past her and up the stairs in a blind race to the only source of comfort she knew. She threw the door wide. Effie was still on the sofa, sitting up with a cup of Bina's medicinal tea in her hands; its perfume filled the room. Her eyes widened. 'What happened?'

'He . . .' Lil swayed back and forth as if rocked by the memory. 'He lied. Used me as a case study in his lecture for his students to pick apart. They all think . . .' A wave of nausea nearly bent her double. She tried to swallow, but tears mangled her throat. 'He thinks I'm mad. He is trying to trap me.'

'Come here.' Effie beckoned, both hands reaching out. The tears flowed suddenly from Lil with a ferocity that in a dulled and distant part of her mind amazed her. She went to Effie, but sat on the edge of the sofa, elbows resting on her knees.

'Am I mad?'

Effie was unmoved. 'If you are, I would rather have your madness than what passes for sanity in most people. It is the world we live in that is lunatic.'

Lil rose suddenly and went to her skirt that was still hanging over the back of a chair. She pulled out the plaque, unwrapped it and threw it on Effie's lap. 'This thing. It is in my head. It comes in my dreams and when I am awake. I feel cursed by it or blessed, maybe, I don't know, but I can't let go of it. That's madness, isn't it? You can hear how that's madness? I can.'

Effie was looking at the plaque, her eyes glittering. She gently placed her fingers on it, and Lil felt a kick of alarm and revulsion, as if a strange hand had touched her. She darted forward and snatched it back, covered it again with the cloth. 'I must go to London. Now.'

Effie's composure was knocked askew, like a hat. She opened her mouth, but it was Bina who spoke. She had slipped into the room unnoticed. 'Oh no, Miss Vincent. You mustn't.'

Lil ignored her. 'I have to find out what's happened to my . . . to the woman who raised me. If I don't . . .' She didn't know how to say it. Lachlan's deception had skinned her; she was flayed by his words: *hereditary illness, overworked adolescence, immersion in spiritualism*. Madelyn was the only person who could tell her the truth about herself. She looked pleadingly at Effie. 'I will never have peace.'

Bina was too close. 'You cannot leave now.'

Lil didn't shift her gaze. 'Two, three days at most, and I shall never leave your side again.'

Effie had retreated into her private thoughts, but Bina couldn't keep still. She huffed and kept starting to speak, her words cutting off before she allowed them the liberty.

'It's all right, Bina.' Effie put a hand out and caught her wrist.

Bina shook her head vigorously. 'It is not. You know it is not . . .'

'Yes, it is.' Effie smiled up at her. 'Let her go. She will be back soon enough.' Her eyes turned to Lil. 'Sometimes there are things we have to do, even if it hurts us. Even if it hurts others. You are not mad, Lily Pad. But if you must go, you must go.'

Bina whimpered and retreated to the fireplace. Lil stood. 'A few days. I promise.'

'A few days.' Effie's hand, which had been left hanging, clutched Lil's arm instead. Lil pressed her own hand to it and, as she pulled away, had the cruel impression it was the grasp of a dying woman losing her hold on the people she loved.

12

There was no sleeper carriage on the 10.40 train from Waverley Station. Lil was too on edge to lie down anyway. Effie had insisted that she rest for a couple of hours first, and she had dozed fitfully in front of the fire, the lecture repeating in her head. It continued on the train, new details recalled with every pass, while her eyes, wide open, stared sightlessly at the dark window. She heard Lachlan telling the students how she had lurked outside his house, and groaned audibly. Eventually, inevitably, she dozed again in brief snatches, but her dreams blurred the line between waking and sleeping. Her only certainty that she had crossed from one to the other came when her head cracked against the window, or the passenger opposite kicked her shin in his own half-awake state.

She reread Agnes's letter. The earnestness and insistence on the love of the spirits, even now, recalled the woman's cloying attempts to befriend her, her wide, innocent-seeming eyes as she talked poison. She had achieved all she wanted, becoming Madelyn's close second, and she had remained loyal, Lil could admit that. There was no doubting her concern. Unless it was all an elaborate plot of Madelyn's to lure Lil back. But why now? For what reason? She felt the ground had given way beneath her. Lachlan's betrayal, Effie's secrets, Madelyn's disappearance. She was plummeting unchecked through a void, like the black nothingness beyond her own reflection as the train hurtled her towards London.

It was foggy at King's Cross. Her memories of the city were mostly from working at the Sullivans. Madelyn's house had been a place apart, its own fevered and claustrophobic country. She was travelling back through time as she walked the pavements. The smoke-heavy air and odorous crush of humanity wrapped around her like a familiar shawl. It had always felt like a holiday, when she wasn't encumbered with the children, to be able to walk at her own swift pace. She had weaved and darted between people, following her own course, on a different footing with the world.

Her route took her north, and without thinking about it, she diverted to walk further into Camden. The Drakes' photography studio had disappeared, transformed into a confectioner's. Her stride slowed. She had hoped perhaps to soften the discomfort of seeing her old home by first approaching a place associated with it. But the sisters had moved on or died. It would be possible, she supposed, to search for their work in the anti-spiritualist press, to find out if they were still debunking mediums. But she wouldn't. She didn't want to see where her life might have led if she had knocked on their door that day. Because, she realised with sudden, fierce clarity, she regretted the choice she had made. If they had let her join them, she would have confronted Madelyn and Lambert and all the injury they had done her. Their lingering hold over her would have been smashed years ago, and perhaps working with the Drakes would have rid her of the night-mare for good. She might even have helped, saved others from the worst violations of the spiritualist movement. Spiritualism was Lil's business one way or the other, whether she liked it or not. The circumstances of her birth, or at least her childhood, dictated it. Madelyn herself had made it so, and Lil had thought she could walk away.

She resumed her journey in bitterness. How foolish to believe she had escaped into a world of truth and fact. She was drowning in lies and deceptions, myth and superstition. Her own mind was diseased. And here she was after everything, returning to the very place she had run from, searching for the woman she wished never to see again. It was the locket that had stopped her from joining the Drakes on that far-off morning, the cheap bit of paste and glass with their images inside that Madelyn had put in her hands as if she knew it would pull her back. And Lil had continued to wear it; she was wearing it still. *You are nothing without me.* It was the truest thing Madelyn had ever said.

She stood in front of the house as if facing a foe for the final, long-postponed encounter. It was shabbier than before, the colours dingy, cracks showing. Business must have suffered. Perhaps it had never fully recovered after her own final performance and exposure. The curtains were drawn as if someone had died. She stalked up to the door and pounded the knocker. Immediately, the bolt was drawn back. No footsteps, no delay, as if someone had been waiting on the other side. Lil took an involuntary step backwards as the door slowly swung away.

Agnes. Agnes after twelve years. Older, of course, more mature. The burn scar still lapped around the right side of her face; it had cooled like lava, leaving a sinewy landscape of ridges and shiny plateaus. She had made no attempt to hide it with veil or hair. Her right eyelid was pulled permanently to the side, which obscured her expression. Lil, still half panicked, turned to the left eye and caught a look of recognition but no surprise. Agnes's voice was a hoarse whisper, as if she hadn't used it for a long time. 'You came.'

They stared at each other, locked in private scrutiny. Finally, as if coming to her senses, Agnes jerked backwards and opened the door wider. Lil stepped over the threshold and stopped. 'Why did you answer so quickly? Were you about to go out?'

'No . . .' It was spoken with a small burst of energy, as if she meant to explain, but then she stopped abruptly. They watched each other again. This time, it was Lil who broke away. She needed answers to only a handful of questions. Everything else could remain in shadow. She faced the hallway and the last twelve years collapsed and folded themselves away as she'd known they would. She was standing exactly where she had stood when Madelyn had pressed the locket into her hands. Her eyes automatically searched the room, as if her mother might suddenly appear. The wallpaper was different and already old, but everything else was in place; hat and umbrella stand, side table with flowers, the crucifix above it. And most of all, the smell: faint lavender and lilac, fainter beeswax and paraffin, all mixing with the indefinable personal scents of Madelyn and Agnes. She was home.

'Please come in.' It was more entreaty than invitation. Lil walked forward and stopped again in the middle of the hall, unsure where to go. She put down her bag. Agnes slipped past her and opened the sitting-room door. 'Take a seat in here. I'll bring us some tea.'

An ancient flicker rose up in Lil. Even now, it scandalised her that Agnes dared to play the hostess in this house. She didn't want tea. 'You've heard nothing?'

Agnes shook her head, then paused. Her shoulders dropped a fraction. 'So you haven't . . .?'

'No.'

'No.' Nodding faintly, Agnes gestured towards the sitting room. 'I won't be a minute.' She backed away uncertainly as if nervous that Lil would flee. Lil glimpsed the stifling velvets and stuffed cushions through the doorway and turned her back on them.

'Let's talk in the kitchen.' She marched past Agnes and down the stairs. The lower level was not a place she had spent much time in; memories were thinner there. She couldn't tell if it had changed, or what was new. The sense that Madelyn must be nearby diminished.

They made the tea in silence. Lil searched for cups and saucers while Agnes warmed the pot. Once everything was assembled, they sat down opposite each other. Lil untied her bonnet and then changed her mind. She kept her coat on too. The silence grew leaden. She had expected Agnes to speak first and was surprised that she kept her gaze down and to one side, as if she were too timid to look Lil in the eye. It wasn't consistent with the desperate tone of her letter. Two nights of poor sleep brushed the situation up the wrong way. Nothing sat right. Even the familiar pattern on the teacups seemed uncanny. She cleared her throat. 'You wrote that you were worried about her state of mind.' Agnes nodded. 'And you have no idea at all where she might be?'

'If she's not with you . . .' Agnes's habit of trailing off was starting to irritate Lil.

'Does she know where I live?' There was no answer. 'Agnes?'

'It was hard, you know, after you left? After what happened.' Agnes spoke so quietly, Lil had to lean forward. She shook her head, remembering. 'So many regulars abandoned her. We had to go anywhere that would pay.'

'That wasn't my fault—' Lil stopped. She would not justify herself to anyone, least of all Agnes, but her old foe's lapse into silence and the way she studied the sugar bowl expressed a whole world of accusation. Lil couldn't help herself. 'I didn't pick that man on purpose. I didn't know he was there to expose me.'

'I know.' Agnes spoke quietly, still looking down.

'Well then. It's not my fault the whole house of cards came down – we *were* tricking people, and we were caught out. That's all.'

A look of pain crossed Agnes's face; she almost winced. 'You know that's . . .'

'What? I can't hear you.'

'You know that is only a part of it. You know it prepares the ground for the real work.'

Lil dug her nails into her palms. It was nauseating to be back in this argument. She reminded herself that she needed Agnes, at least for a short time, and spoke meaninglessly. 'It's done now.'

'The work we had to do afterwards was everything you hated, cheap tricks.' There was more heat in Agnes's voice. 'We were hired for music halls, private parties — but by people who mostly only wanted sport, something to jeer at. And then even that became impossible. The law . . .' The corners of her mouth pulled down as if she had tasted something bitter.

Lil remembered the law; a few years after she had left, it had become illegal for mediums to charge for their services. She had read about it in the Sullivans' newspaper and stole a bottle of their champagne to celebrate. Drinking and laughing to herself on the floor of her bedroom, she had toasted the government and lobbying medical establishment until her stomach revolted. The kitchen maid was blamed for the theft. Lil had smuggled the empty bottle out of the house in the children's basket and said nothing.

'You got by, it seems.' She spoke brightly, wanting to rouse Agnes to something more to the point, but Agnes continued doggedly.

'It's what made them come back, some of the old regulars. They liked the secrecy, the pretence. Some used it as an excuse not to pay cash, but gave gifts instead. You can't eat or pay bills with cast-off furniture though. It's never been easy. We should have left, started again somewhere new. We could have done so easily.'

'Why didn't you?' Lil regretted the question immediately, seeing the trap too late.

Agnes paused before speaking. 'You.' She said it to the side still, swallowing her words. Lil tried again.

'She was looking for me, do you mean? Did she try to find me?'

A deep frown gathered itself in Agnes's brow. 'No . . . Not by herself . . .'

'With whom then?'

She looked up. Lil sat back in her seat, startled. It wasn't nerves that had made Agnes turn to the side and keep her voice low and controlled; it was anger. Her expression was a loaded gun. 'She was willing to let you go, even though it nearly killed her. Even though you nearly ruined her.'

'I see.' Lil scratched her temple and then slapped her hand down on the table. She gave a smile that was all jackal. 'But what do you mean she wasn't trying to find me by herself? Was someone helping her? Lambert?'

Saying his name out loud felt ugly and threatening, as if it had the power to bring him physically into the room. It was like the residue after the night-mare, a dangerous kind of memory that could take form and grow. Agnes was shaking with quiet laughter, or perhaps inner weeping, Lil wasn't sure, and spoke into the space between them.

'Mr Lambert dropped us. We never saw him again. We had no one except you, don't you see? But she said we had to let you find out for yourself. There was no point continuing as long as you fought your gift. She was convinced you would come back. So, she waited, every year, determined not to interfere with you. But it cost her.' She fixed Lil with her gaze again. 'I saw how it cost her.'

Lil didn't know if she was going to burst into laughter or reach out and slap Agnes hard across the face. She recalled the bruises and scratches she had found on her own body that could only have been Agnes's doing – the whole campaign of terror that she and Madelyn had waged against her. This woman, so eager to please Lil's mother, had happily watched Lil herself descend into such darkness and confusion, she had nearly taken her own life.

Lil bit down on her lip until her eyes watered. Showed her teeth again. 'So, you're saying she did know where I was? Someone told her?'

Agnes leaned across the table suddenly, very close. 'You know who I mean. They told me you were coming today. I knew when to expect your knock. And they wouldn't leave *her* alone about you. *The spirits.*'

Lil stood up, pushing her chair away. She made straight for the door, speaking without looking back. 'You wrote there was a box of papers in her room.'

She ran up the stairs to the hallway and then to the first floor. Pausing at the landing, she looked down. Agnes hadn't followed. She stood for a moment, waiting to catch her breath, but the door to the séance room was yards away, as solid and real as the day she had left. Everything that had happened within it came back to her as if it were all still playing out: Mrs Andrews' dreadful expression of doubt and need; the pen writing beyond Lil's control; Lambert's suffocating scent, his body pulsing in her hand. She hurried away from it and up to the top floor, where she stopped again.

There was a marked difference in this private part of the house. Her memory of it fell away like a dropped photograph, and she took in the peeling paint, worn rug, tarnished mirror. The air was chilly and unwelcoming. What money there had been had gone only to the rooms the sitters would see. One more illusion.

She walked unsteadily to the door of Madelyn's room and pushed it open. It was clean and neatly ordered. Agnes had tidied up. Like the kitchen, it wasn't a place Lil had ever spent much time in; Madelyn wouldn't tolerate her looking through her personal items. But her presence was there; it roiled the air, lifting off the richly patterned wallpaper, the velvet- and silk-covered cushions, the apothecary of bottles and powders on the dressing table. Candelabra were everywhere, dripping solidified wax. Her writing table was heaped with books on mesmerism, hypnosis and the biographies of mediums. And a large rosewood box Lil had never seen before. She crossed the threshold and was enveloped in Madelyn's scent despite the cold. Lavender and darker spices. A wave of emotion rolled through her. She couldn't name it – grief? Sadness? Homesickness? In all the years away from Madelyn, she had reduced her to the bleached bones of her egomania, tied the dried pieces of her together like a stark and evil symbol of all she was running from. But standing among her things, she was confronted again by the flesh and blood woman who had also held her when she hurt herself, brought her treats for her birthday, played games of hide-and-seek. Her mother existed in so many parts, and they would not be reconciled. A sob rose in Lil's throat. She had tried to forget there was also love, packed it away in the locket that she wore around her neck. Another symbol to hold, not the feeling itself. She could not let herself love the angel and at the same time survive the devil.

She crossed to the box and lifted the lid. Papers, as Agnes had said. The letter from the Sullivans inviting her to interview was placed on top. The box was more like a small trunk, scuffed and marked. And heavy. She hauled it over to the bed, heaving it onto its side so the contents spilled and slipped over each other across the counterpane. Documents, letters, newspaper clippings: loose, or in envelopes, or rolled and tied with ribbon. Plucking a sheet out at random, she found it was the first page of a letter, dated twenty-five years earlier, from a hotel in Paris and addressed to Darling Maddie. Lil skimmed the contents, which ranged from scolding to apology to passion.

I have made my peace with you – without you – whether you like it or not. There is no need to blame each other. I shall return home. This is simply how things are . . .

I know you think I should be begging for your forgiveness, even though this is about your choice as much as mine. Well, I could never refuse you. Forgive me, for all my sins against Maddie . . .

Oh! Maddie, I do NOT want your forgiveness. How can I? I hope you rage at me for eternity if it keeps me in your mind and seething in your blood. We were like two parts of a glorious, faultless machine, together; apart, let us be for ever out of kilter and misfiring . . .

I forgive you. May we never be at peace . . .

WTLOTS,
Utica

Lil had never heard of a Utica, a woman enveloped in the mists of Madelyn's past with everything else. But Madelyn had kept the letter. In private, at least, she had allowed what had been to exist. This proof of a larger life weighed heavily in Lil's hands. She herself would have been nearly three years old when it was written. Had Utica known her? Could she be found? Twenty-five years; too long ago, perhaps, to matter.

Lil floated her hand over the heap of papers and pulled another towards her. An ancient newspaper clipping, yellowed and soft. It was an article about a disturbance in an orphanage, a case of hysteria; the children had fled as one, breaking through locked doors and out of windows. Because of spirits, they said. The article had been clipped too close to show the name of the paper or the date.

If Madelyn was an orphan, it would explain the contradictory stories she had told about herself. Could she have been the cause of the hysteria? Or was this where her interest in spiritualism had begun? Lil let it drop. The papers were raising more questions than they answered. She swept a hand through them impatiently, looking for something more recent. A crisper sheet emerged – an admiring account of Madelyn's talk at a spiritualist meeting, perhaps the one where she had met Agnes. Lil placed it at the far end of the bed and started sorting papers into piles of likely years or decades. There were many letters and cuttings from the spiritualist press. Leafing through a wad, Lil came face to face with her own picture. It was the photograph taken by the Drake sisters at the moment she was exposed, the image used by Dr Lachlan. The article poured vitriol on herself and Madelyn. A wave of shame and humiliation swept over her.

Fatigued suddenly with the hopeless task, she threw the wad carelessly towards the far pile. The pages landed on their edges; some flattened out, others folded and flipped chaotically. One spun clear towards her, upside down. Her eyes rested on it. She blinked. Leaned forward. Her hand shot out and dragged it around.

Death of Mr Andrew Raube

Raube. Old Raube. His obituary. She picked it up, incredulous. It was all there: Pitcarden House; the death of his first two sons and his wife; his later life as a recluse and the rumours he had buried the priceless lover's knot brooch; his remaining heir, Alec Raube, an émigré in Australia. Lil's heartbeat was the loudest thing in the house.

'Have you found something?' Agnes was standing in the doorway. Lurking again as always. Lil grasped the paper, creasing it, and held it up.

'Did you read these? Do you know about this?' She lowered her hand. 'Of course you do.' Her lip curled. 'What game are you playing?'

Agnes no longer seemed angry. She wasn't nervous either. 'You sound like her.' She moved into the room and sat on the other side of the bed, moving piles out of the way. 'She thought I was up to something with the spirit writing. The page I sent you.'

Lil stared at her wildly, still clutching the obituary. Agnes looked at a letter she had picked up. 'I couldn't make sense of most of it, so I gave up. I thought they might mean something to you, though, maybe tell us where to look for her.'

Lil studied her, looking for signs of performance or trickery. The scarring made her face more difficult to read. She had also had many years with Madelyn to hone her skills in dissimulation. Lil's mind raced to bring the different ends together, to see the connection between Pitcarden and Madelyn, to reveal a plot with Agnes to draw Lil back or to send her mad. But how and why would she have Raube's obituary? He had died before Lil had even heard of Pitcarden.

Agnes was reading the letter. She turned it towards Lil. 'Did you ever meet Utica?'

'Who is she?' Lil growled it, suspicious of any path Agnes led her down but unable to keep herself from following. Agnes looked at her curiously for a moment and then cast her eyes over the disorder on the bed. She picked out another newspaper clipping and held it out.

'Her sister. I assumed you knew. Another medium. They were partners. I thought of trying to contact her but I didn't know where to start.'

Lil hesitated — *sister* — before taking the page mutely.

The Leake Sisters in Brooklyn

The Leake sisters gave a very interesting séance to a party of eight ladies and gentlemen on Friday last. The sitters were placed around a table, with their hands interlocked, including the mediums, who sat opposite each other and whose hands were

> *never released during the whole time of the séance. After sitting more than half an hour in vain, the first manifestation took place. Raps were given and in obedience to requests, three notes were played on a piano in the corner of the room. Presently the table lifted and lowered again, after which more raps were heard, and beautiful messages were transmitted through Miss Madelyn Leake for those present. The communications were all of an elevating character, full of love and wisdom. I must remark that the mediums do not let anything be counted for a rap that is not genuine; they prefer total failure, rather than that we should deceive ourselves by mistaking other sounds for rappings . . .*

Table turning, spirit rapping. The whole tawdry display of early spiritualism. So, this was where Madelyn had begun. Agnes handed her another article celebrating the sisters' miraculously accurate predictions on horse racing and markets. 'They were just like the Fox sisters but even more talented!'

'Talented charlatans.' Lil spoke automatically. When Agnes didn't respond, she glanced up and found she was being judged again. She welcomed it. Anything to sink her teeth into so she didn't have to think of Madelyn having a sister, herself having an aunt. Anything to convince herself she was still in her right mind. She folded her arms, crushing the paper. 'So, death is a mystery to the living for millennia, and then one day,' she lightened her voice, 'two little girls start chatting with a murder victim, using one tap for no, two for yes—'

'*Three* for yes.'

'And suddenly everyone is able to talk to their dear departed grandpappy and poor consumptive little Flossie, if only they let fall a few coins into the medium's pocket.'

Agnes was unmoved. 'I don't know why you persist in this, Lil. Of course spiritualism didn't start with the Fox sisters. But they showed that ordinary people can do it too; they brought it into drawing rooms and respectable houses. They started a *movement*. It's a new dawn.' She laughed, bright-eyed and happy for a moment. 'Keep reading, Lil. The Leake sisters were part of it; they were pioneers. And then Madame de Vallon found you.'

'*Found?*' Lil concentrated so hard on Agnes's face, she felt she was straining at the end of a leash.

'I mean she found the talent in you.' Agnes stumbled for the first time.

'What did she tell you about me?'

'Nothing. Only that the spirits sent you to her. I thought . . .'

'What?'

'Well, I didn't know. If you were . . . if she had . . .' She shook her head, then meeting Lil's eye, became calmer, serious. 'I promise,' her gaze didn't flicker, 'she didn't tell me anything more than that.' After a pause, she pointed at the article. 'She didn't tell me she had a sister either, or that her name was really Leake.'

Leake. It caught on something in Lil's head, and she looked down quickly at the mass of papers, searching. She found it, the old news snippet about the incident at the orphanage. *The Leake and Watts orphan house.* She stared at it for several seconds and then turned suddenly to look at the top of the chest of drawers. It was there. A photo Madelyn had once smacked her for touching and put out of reach. She flew to pick it up. It was heavy, a daguerreotype. Rows of girls in smocks; a school picture, she had thought. She turned it over and tried to cut the back with her nail, cast about the room until she saw Madelyn's scissors on the dressing table. Agnes asked what she was doing, but she ignored her. Released from the frame, the name of the orphanage was visible, scratched into a corner. Lil stared at Madelyn's image; she was unmistakable, clearer than some of the others, who were blurred or blanched out. The girl next to her had moved very slightly, her features smudged, and yet there was something about the shape of her face that made Lil pause. On the back was the daguerreotypist's label; an address in New York city.

Something was coming for Lil; she could feel it. Something that would fill the horizon when it came into view, cover the sky and blot out the sun. She carried the plate to the bed and cleared a space among all the papers. The orphanage article, the portrait, the clippings about the Leake sisters, Utica's letter, Raube's obituary; she placed them all in a row and stood back. After a long moment, she leaned over the obituary. She had been in Norway when he had died and Effie had announced the Pitcarden burial mound was finally available for excavation. Lil ran her finger along the lines of the letter from Utica. The handwriting seemed to tremble. She turned to the daguerreotype again and studied it for a long time.

'Is there a photograph of the Leake sisters?' She looked at Agnes, who had been watching silently.

'Yes, at least I think it is them.' Agnes began searching through the heap, finally pulling out a stiff-backed envelope and handing it to Lil. 'In there.'

Barely teenaged, the girls stared out of the picture, dressed in white, clasping each other's hands, their expressions solemn.

'What have you seen, Lil? Are you unwell?' Agnes was hurrying around the bed as Lil stumbled backwards, her legs giving way. She made it to the chair of Madelyn's dressing table and leaned over her knees. Her hands and face were greased with sweat. She heard Agnes scrabbling about in one of Madelyn's cupboards and then a glass of brown liquid was pushed into her hands. A roughened sweetness in her nose. Brandy. Agnes gently pushed her up a little. 'Sip it.'

Lil obeyed. She sat like that for a long time. The photograph had fallen to the floor. Every now and then, she turned her eyes towards it, but it was like putting her hand into a fire. Agnes brought her water and biscuits, which she ignored, and held a damp cloth to her brow until Lil brushed her off.

She stood up and gathered the different clippings together with the photograph and daguerreotype. Unsteadily, she made her way back down the stairs to the hall, Agnes hard on her heels. She wrapped the pictures in a shawl and placed everything in her bag.

'What will you do? What did you see?' Agnes sounded frightened. Lil didn't answer. She picked up her bag and reached to open the front door.

'Don't leave me alone here!'

It was a wild shriek, full of panic. Lil stopped. She looked behind her and saw the Agnes that had written the letter. Terrified, desperate, abandoned. Her face was a mask of misery. Lil observed her with an almost detached interest. She became aware of the empty house looming behind and above Agnes, and the word mausoleum sounded in her head. If Madelyn didn't return, who and what was she? The unburned side of her face trembled, the eye wide with distress. The other side was paved over by the scar. It shut her in, as if trying to bury her in her own flesh. For the first time, it occurred to Lil how painful it must have been, how much agony Agnes must have suffered while it healed. She had never complained. There had been no bitterness. She had simply put it to use to help Madelyn. And now Madelyn had left her without explanation. The cold sense of triumph that had been gathering in Lil to see her enemy brought low shrivelled away. What was Agnes really, but a flipped version of herself? The other side of the coin. Madelyn's willing, believing assistant, whose pen had written the same words anyway. Who, like Lil, was nothing without Madelyn. She turned and walked up to her. How closely they had watched each other in the short time Lil had been in the house. Two faces ransacked for secrets.

'I shall tell you what I find out. If anything.'

'I know you've always hated me.' Agnes was fighting tears. 'I don't know what I did to you.'

'Oh, Agnes. Why pretend now? You nearly sent me out of my mind writing things on the walls, making me believe there was a poltergeist. You were so eager to collude with her against me, this happened.' Lil placed her hand against the side of Agnes's face and ran her thumb between soft skin and hardened scar. Agnes swayed, almost as if she might faint, and Lil wondered if she had ever been touched gently by anyone in her whole life. The tears glistened.

'The fire was my fault. Yes. But we were just trying to bring you back to the spirits. She said it would help you.' Agnes's eyes widened. 'But nothing else was us. The writing upset her terribly. I was as frightened by what was happening as you.'

Lil felt a wave of tiredness surge through her, so heavy she thought she would sink to her knees. What did it matter, Agnes's lies? They were wisps of smoke compared to the inferno raging towards her. She kissed her, first on her good cheek, which was wet with tears, and then on the other. 'I shall write.'

Agnes didn't say another word, and Lil found herself on the street again, not an hour since she had knocked on the door.

When she reached the station, she walked straight past it. Her mind was too full with what she had learned to bear being hemmed in by strangers for hours. The obituary of Raube, the photographs of the Leake sisters, Madelyn's letter and disappearance. There was too much of it. At times she had to stop, lean against a lamp post or sit down on a bench. The third time she pushed herself on, she found she had walked herself to the British Museum. She peered through the railings at the massive columns and felt she was at the entrance to a land of giants, a place big enough perhaps to hold the monsters in her head. An overwhelming wave of nostalgia washed over her for her days as a governess when she had run here for solace, to lose herself in drawing and crowds and history. Her first true taste of independence, her choice and hers alone which way to turn, which object to sketch.

And out of all of that had stepped Effie; a chance encounter, a curious passerby. Had Lil come here to try to convince herself of that – to linger a moment longer before the truth blistered it? She delved into her bag and brought out the letter and the photograph of the Leake sisters. Madelyn, achingly young, even more so than in the locket. And Utica. Lil stared at her and then at the letter. The handwriting was recognisable now. She hadn't seen it at first, when it was just a fragment from Madelyn's past. The older hand that she was familiar with was larger and more confident of taking up space, as it was in the letter to Alec Raube. Effie had signed that 'eUphemia', with the u not the e capitalised. She knew he would understand what it stood for. Utica.

When Agnes opened the door again, Lil didn't give her time to speak or exclaim. She thrust the parcels of cake, fruit and cordial she had bought into her hands and pushed past her. 'I need to read all of it, every letter.'

13

The train finally clanked into Edinburgh in a squall of rain, steam and dirt just before six o'clock on Sunday morning. Darkness still pressed down on the city, seemingly trapping the grime and soot that clung to Lil's clothes and caught in her throat as she toiled out of the station. The rain scored diagonal lines across the gas lamps, half blinding her. She turned out of the wind into the New Town.

Bina looked as if she hadn't been to bed. There were no smiles this time. She seemed more agitated than pleased to see her, and took her coat almost reluctantly. Lil bit her lip to keep from speaking. She knew Bina had been with Effie for years, but the letters had shown just how long. Her name cropped up from the beginning of the correspondence that had started in Paris, along with references to herself, 'little Lilith'. Whatever the truth was, Bina had always known it. But Lil didn't want to hear it from her. She marched up the stairs. Bina hurried after her and took her arm as she turned towards the drawing room. 'Leave her, miss, she's sleeping now. We've had a terrible night.'

Lil tugged herself free and entered the room. It was lit dimly and, behind the scents of soap and polish, lingered a faint smell of vomit. She turned up the lamp nearest to Effie and sat beside her. 'Effie, wake up.'

Effie's face was tinged with grey, the lines in it more deeply etched. She didn't look peaceful sleeping. Bina was close by. 'Please don't do this now.'

Lil said Effie's name louder. She put her hands on her shoulders and leaned closer. 'Effie. Effie. *Utica.*'

Effie came to with a start. She blinked and looked vaguely around, not quite seeing and not at all understanding.

'Look at me.' Lil's voice brought her further into the room and her expression cleared a little.

'Lily Pad.' Her hand fumbled to free itself from under the blanket, but Lil moved her own before Effie could take it. She opened her bag and, without a word, laid out on Effie's blanket the photograph of the two girls, the orphanage daguerreotype, a letter from Utica, and a gossipy article she had found about the Pitcarden curse and the lost lover's knot brooch. Effie looked at them without expression. Eventually, her hand reached for the orphanage image and drew it towards her. 'I had forgotten about this. We stole it. I'm surprised I allowed her to be the one to keep it.' She glanced at the other image and the letter before turning to Lil.

In the moment before their eyes met, Lil felt dread seize her. She longed to see distress, regret, even shame in those eyes, but knew Effie would never concede so much. The lie was out; she had snatched away the mask, but now she didn't know whose face it was turning towards her, what she would see in it. She wasn't ready.

Effie looked at her. Curiosity. That was all. And, perhaps, God help her, pity. 'What do you know?'

Lil breathed in and battled the muscles in her face. She would not cry in front of her. 'You are sisters. You were mediums together. You came here from America. For some reason, you parted. Twenty-five years ago. When I was three years old. You didn't . . . you didn't meet me by chance in the museum.' She stopped rather than lose control of her voice.

Effie continued to watch her. 'Still in the dark, then. Poor Lillith.'

Lil stood abruptly, knocking into Bina. That name on Effie's lips – it was as if the night-mare Effie had returned. Bina scuttled backwards out of her path, and Lil went to lean against the mantelshelf, unable to look at her own reflection in the mirror still. 'Tell me then. At last.'

'Are you sure you want to know?'

'My God.' Lil turned. 'What are you, Effie? What have you done to me?'

'You should be asking what I have done *for* you.'

Bina stepped forward. 'Enough. Now is not the time. You must rest first.' She turned to Lil. 'Surely you can see that. *I* can tell you . . .'

'No.' Effie shook her head and tried to sit up more. 'I am not dead yet. If the truth must be told, this is the time. Come.' She patted the sofa beside her. Lil hesitated. The truth was what she had come for, but now it was offered, she faltered. The few yards back to the sofa seemed the hardest journey she had ever taken, more perilous even than leaving Madelyn's house for the first time. By the time she sat down, she felt as grey as the face in front of her. Effie's eyes were bloodshot from fatigue and illness. Lil saw her summon the strength to begin.

'We grew up together in the orphanage, but we were not sisters. Blood is not so strong, whatever people say. Our bond was greater. Spiritualism was sweeping the country at that time; the Fox sisters were talked about everywhere; we could hardly escape hearing about them – the rapping and so on. Neither of us believed in it to begin with, but we thought it would be amusing to pretend. We played tricks on our fellow orphans.' She laughed weakly, eyes gleaming. 'It was so easy, it shocked us. We became braver, more daring. In the end, we caused so much havoc that we were in the papers. It caught the attention of New York society. Ladies visited. The orphanage authorities, who had seen us as a nuisance before, now saw us as an asset. They scented money at the same time that I did. It wasn't just mischief any more; I saw a future for me and Maddie. At first, I hoped someone would take us in and adopt us, one of the ladies dripping in jewels and furs — I had wild fantasies of what their homes might be like, and then I found out. We were taken to perform in grand drawing rooms at private parties; they must have offered the orphanage hefty donations. I began to understand our power in those circles — we could never be one of them, accepted as equals, but they were hungry for us, for what we represented. I became more ambitious. I wanted us to have our own money, our own house and jewels. The Fox sisters and others had shown it was possible. We only had to find something that set us apart. That came by sheer chance in the end.'

She coughed and was quiet for a few moments, resting or remembering. It helped that she didn't look at Lil while she spoke. Her words seemed almost for herself, landing at a safe distance.

'One evening, a gentleman jokingly asked if we could tell him the winning horse at a race in Lexington in Kentucky. Such predictions were not a part of our act, so we let his friends laugh it away. But later, while pretending to be in a trance, Maddie started saying the word Lexington. We did that sometimes, picking up any word at random to buy time. I assumed she had plucked it from the gentleman's comment earlier. But she wouldn't stop. She became more insistent and started shouting out, 'Lexington wins', sometimes with another word that sounded like 'darling'. Lexington wins, darling wins. It exhausted our audience's humour and nearly ruined the evening. I was angry with her after, but she was evasive; she said she was trying something new. Then we learned the results of the race. The winning horse was itself called Lexington. It had recently changed hands and been renamed after the race; the previous owner had called it Darley.'

Effie picked up the daguerreotype and studied it as she continued. 'It changed things for us; our reputation and fame shot higher than we could have dreamed. Our wealthy patrons paid for an apartment, and we left the orphanage in triumph, exchanging chores and dull lessons for comfort and real tutors.

'I saw that predictions could be our special gift. But we had work to do. Horse racing was too difficult to carry off consistently, though I spent many hours studying the words of racing men and watching odds. We dabbled with other sports, international events, even the weather. Once people had faith in us, it didn't seem to matter how often we were wrong. We could always explain it away as confused signals from the spirits.

'And then I discovered capitalism.' A laugh broke out of her, which might have been born in that distant time, a hoot of triumph. 'Although that wasn't the word then. But markets and profits, trade and fortune, all waiting to be exploited. And the best part of it was that we didn't need our own capital to invest; we didn't need any money at all, only the ear of the wealthy and the would-be wealthier.' She laughed again. 'It was all there in the papers that we had delivered to our apartment. We only had to pay attention, do the research, use the wits we were born with. I was better at it; Maddie didn't have the patience, and she was starting to change by that point. She succumbed to the devotion and praise heaped upon us, began to believe it. The Lexington episode lodged in her mind as something real; she claimed she really had been guided by a presence outside of herself. She started to talk as if the spirits were real.' Effie placed a finger gently against Madelyn's image. 'I let her believe it. It only made her the more convincing in séances.

'We had been styling ourselves as sisters since the orphanage. It was a game at first, but then I saw how it was to our advantage. People thought of the Fox sisters, which was in our favour, and it also made us more palatable as women who were essentially running a business. Sisters clinging to each other to survive in the absence of other family make pathetic figures; they inspire pity, pose no threat. But two women choosing each other as partners in an enterprise unnerves people. It suggests calculation, agency, ambition. No one wants such creatures in their drawing rooms.' She paused again, still looking at Madelyn's image. 'Sisterhood can hide a multitude of sins.'

Something in her voice made Lil look at her sharply. She remembered the Drake sisters and Madelyn's jealousy of them, how she had called them 'sisters most *sisterly*' in mocking tones, and a comment she had once made about sisters sharing beds. The letters from Utica that she had read were full of passion and longing; she had wanted to seethe in Madelyn's blood for goodness' sake. 'You were lovers?'

Effie glanced at her as if the question had intruded on private thoughts. 'We were everything to each other. For a long time, there was no one else. The world rejected us from birth, so we had to carve out a new path for ourselves through rock. We didn't have peers; there were no mentors; no rules bound us. Spiritualism saved us because it lent a kind of respectability to oddities such as ourselves. It was a disguise. You must know that, having lived with Maddie for so long.'

A wave of vertigo made Lil feel queasy. Effie had always known everything about her, could talk of her past as if it were her own.

'Mediums must appear as passive and feeble as ladies to be taken seriously – it is the spirit that has the authority. To our patrons, we were lesser Virgin Marys, revered but replaceable. A Virgin Jane or Florence or Kitty would do just as well if she could deliver the goods. Imagine if I had tried to offer investment advice to people as myself. I'd have been ignored or locked up. But a dead man, a name they respected, speaking through me?' Effie's face suddenly opened like sunshine breaking through; she appeared much younger. '*Thousands* they invested. *Thousands.*' The laughter returned, irresistible, shaking her frail frame. 'On the word of a penniless orphan . . . not yet eighteen years old,' she gasped for breath, barely able to speak, 'because they believed . . . they believed *Adam Smith* was talking through her.' Tears streamed down her face, and she leaned forward, trying to recover. Bina fretted to one side.

Somewhere in the beat of her blood, Lil laughed too, felt the glee, the audacity, the winning of it. But she let her face show no sign. She offered a glass of water from the side table. Effie drank and wiped her eyes. 'I think it is possible I might die from laughing. It would be fitting, don't you think?'

'Not before you've finished telling me.'

'Of course.' A willing nod. Effie was enjoying her own story now she had started. This wasn't a confession. 'We had our own money for the first time. We weren't performing to the sort of people who *paid* for things, but we were given gifts of cash or we sold the lavish trinkets they presented us with. I was able to take my own advice.' She waved a limp hand at the room. 'Some of this is paid for with one of those original investments.

'We toured around the country, again playing to private parties by recommendation. But I always had Britain in mind.'

'Why?'

'The challenge. It was still catching up with the spiritualist movement. I wanted to make an entrance. See if the aristocracy had more money than sense like the American elite. Maddie didn't need convincing; she thought Europe must be teeming with ghosts. We began in London. It was a mixed beginning, but our fame grew again.' She sounded weary suddenly, remembering it. After a moment, she continued, but seemed to be laying down her words with more care. 'We had read about the Pitcarden curse while still in the orphanage and the story that Raube had buried the lover's knot brooch. It surfaced every few years in certain types of magazines. It became a symbol of sorts for us, a goal – to have the wealth to be able to bury something like that, and a lover's knot as well. I made a promise to Maddie that I would get the brooch for her; it was a half-serious joke between us. But once we were in Britain, it seemed possible suddenly, within reach. Raube was said to be a recluse and a miser. I thought if he was credulous enough to believe in curses, and also greedy, he would be easy to control. And I wanted to test my power, to see if I could make him dig it up. They said he was so superstitious he had armed men guarding the site. But Maddie changed; she didn't want to go to Scotland. Begged me not to. She said she was being warned about it in dreams and during séances. She refused to come any further north than Edinburgh. It was the first time we ever parted.'

She fell silent, her eyes on the photograph. Lil could tell her thoughts were unquiet by the way her fingers fidgeted. The clock on the mantelshelf struck seven. It was so early still, and the curtains were closed; if dawn were struggling to break through outside, there was no hint of it in the room. Lil felt light-headed. 'You succeeded. He dug it up. But only once you were engaged. Is that why you agreed to marry him? Is that what it took?'

Effie closed her eyes for a moment before blinking them open. Her voice was slowing. 'I would have married him. I was tired of spiritualism. I wanted to study the world of finance without the frippery and absurdity of mediumship. A good marriage would have been a less degrading and more secure cover, and by that point he would have done whatever I said with his money, spirits or no. I saw myself living with Maddie in London for most of the year, attending to business. As long as I made him a good return and didn't cause a scandal, I believe he would have let me do as I liked.'

'So why didn't you?'

'I was twenty years old. I thought myself invincible. I was careless.'

Lil remembered what Haxton had said about a rumour. 'Alec Raube? His son. He was home when you were there.'

Effie lay back against the cushion. 'Alec Raube.' The energy from talking was leaving her, taking with it another bite of her vitality. The grey colour returned, more alarming than before.

'Effie, what were you going to tell him? In the letter, you said there was something important he should know.' Bina tried to step in, but Lil shoved her away with both hands and held Effie's shoulders again. 'Effie, talk to me. Tell me, please. Am I going mad? Is it about me? Am I the thing he should know about?'

There was a small smile on Effie's face. She seemed to be making an effort to raise her eyelids, and one hand groped for Lil. But the attempt was abandoned. She turned her head to the side.

'Effie!' Lil almost shouted. 'Is it me? Am I your daughter?'

Bina took hold of her arm and with surprising force wrenched her from the sofa. 'That's enough. Leave at once.'

Lil slipped from Bina's grasp. The shock of finding herself on the floor silenced her for a beat, but then she began clawing her way past Bina's skirts, back towards Effie's lap. She didn't know when she had started crying.

'Just tell me. Effie! One word.' She repeated it over and over, pleading. Bina was struggling between holding Lil off and tending to Effie. Another moment and she had twisted around like a skirt in the wind and clapped both hands either side of Lil's face.

'Yes. She is your mother.'

Lil stared into Bina's brown eyes. The only thought fluttering in the suddenly vast and empty chamber of her mind was that she had never suspected them of being capable of such fierceness.

'Now, if you ever loved her, let me look after her. There will be time for talking later, but you both need to sleep. Her most dearly. Go to bed, Miss Vincent.'

Still on the floor, Lil walked herself backwards with her hands before pushing herself up to standing. Bina held her eye for a final moment and then returned to Effie, to bustle and efficiency and concern. Wide-eyed, Lil stepped back, as if retreating from a fire that had blazed out of control. Her heel eventually hit the leg of a chair. She fumbled for the door and made it out of the room.

Bina woke her. Lil's limbs were so heavy she thought for a moment the night-mare was upon her and that Bina's face was the hag-like form that had terrified her the last time she had slept in that bed.

'Miss Vincent? It's time to wake up.' Bina was whispering urgently. Her face came slowly into focus, more agitated than when she had first opened the door to Lil, although she was trying to force a smile. Lil squinted and raised her head. Someone – Bina – had put a blanket over her while she slept. She sat up.

'What time is it?'

'Eleven o'clock.' Bina startled her by taking her hand again. 'Why don't you wash and go for a walk? Find a teashop? She's sleeping now.'

She. The scene earlier moved into Lil and filled her up like too much heavy furniture. She pulled back the blanket and swung her legs off the bed. Bina continued talking about fresh air and food, but Lil barely heard her. She moved to the washstand and doused her face with water. Once she was dry and properly awake, she gave Bina a quizzical glance. 'I'll find something for myself in the kitchen.'

'I thought it would do you good to leave the house for a while.' Bina followed her down to the next floor. 'You've had a shock. A change of scene will help your nerves.'

Lil ignored her. She stopped at the drawing-room door, and Bina's voice fell to a whisper. 'She's sleeping still. Leave her.'

Lil put her ear to the door and slowly turned the handle while

Bina hissed and sparked behind. Effie was awake and rubbing cream into her hands. With a look back at Bina's stricken face, Lil walked into the room.

Effie lifted her chin, considering her. A few hours' rest had restored her somewhat, but the needle of her health was flickering narrowly now. That she had strength enough to sit up and talk belied how quickly it would be spent and push the needle back. Lil realised that time was short; she could not afford the luxury of anger and remonstrance if she wanted to understand. She dragged a chair across from the window and sat facing Effie. 'I believed Madelyn was my mother, all these years.'

Effie swallowed. 'She let you think that. I never asked her to.'

'Have you heard from her? You know she's missing.'

There was a pause while Effie looked down and continued rubbing her hands. 'She wouldn't come to me for help. If she *needs* help; more likely she's taken off on some whim and neglected to tell her poor assistant.'

'What if she's coming for you? What if she found out you're digging up the hoard again?'

Effie spread her fingers like a cat extending its claws. 'She knows where I am. She didn't stop me last time.'

'Tell me more about what happened. You ran away with Alec Raube.'

'No.' Effie smiled faintly, looking up. 'Not quite. I was careless, as I said. The old man followed me around like a duckling, and he caught us eventually. He was merciless – weak men always are. He threw me out, of course. It might not have mattered, but Alec was as weak as his father. He came with me, vowing the usual things, until his father threatened to cut him off completely if he didn't renounce me. Given time, I believe Raube would have relented. His sole surviving heir? It meant too much to him to pass the estate on to his own flesh and blood even if he couldn't bear the sight of the boy. But Alec panicked. I woke one day to a letter on my pillow. He was on his way to Australia.' Effie's voice lost all emotion as she told the tale; it became almost a monotone, but Lil saw how tightly her fists were clenched. Nearly thirty years, and the cut was still fresh.

'Did he know about me?'

'No. It wouldn't have made any difference.'

Lil bit down on her lip. Difference to what? To whom? She held herself back until she could speak calmly. 'What about Madelyn? You were more than friends.'

Effie hummed a laugh. 'Jealous. Terribly so. But we would have settled down.' She became pensive. 'The brooch was for her.' Her expression deepened into something darker. 'I was so close; I even held it in my hand, but he wanted to lock it away for safety. I thought it didn't matter, that I had all the time in the world to retrieve it.'

'But Madelyn didn't want it.' Lil felt the words rising hard and bitter in her throat. 'She didn't want you to dig it up once she knew about the curse. Don't say it was for her.'

The darkness in Effie's expression turned bullish. 'She'd have changed her mind if she'd seen it. Maddie changed like the weather.'

It wasn't true. Effie, Lil realised, had always decided *for* other people, choosing to believe she did so out of love and not simply to please herself.

'Why . . .' Her voice quavered, and she paused to harden it. 'Why didn't you tell me, Effie?'

'Oh, Lily Pad.' Effie shut her eyes, tiredness masking her face. 'Does it really matter?' She opened them again and turned their blue gaze on Lil. 'Blood – look at the misery it causes; the expectations and obligations. I kept you as free from that as I was. Maddie and I had no one; we made our own family, and later I had Nils.'

'Is that why you left me with her? Because I didn't matter to you?'

'Don't be melodramatic. I went to Europe to start again. Maddie was looking after you in London and was to follow when I was settled. But she changed her mind. She wanted to stay and build her reputation as a medium, working alone, as I had given it up. I couldn't bear to go back to that life. Earning a living was far more difficult without it, and I had reinvested most of my share of our money. But I was determined. I passed myself off as a lady fallen on hard times. I had seen enough of them to know their ways by then. I wanted to be a women's broker, but it turned out Europe was even less tolerant of women in business than America. I knew I had a greater chance back home, but it wasn't going to be easy, and impossible with a young child. By the time I was on my feet and in a position to have you, you were older and settled with Madelyn. She needed you.'

'She used me. I was her prisoner.'

Effie sank back against the cushion. 'More melodrama. I notice she was good enough to give you some of your inheritance.' She pointed straight at Lil. Confused, Lil lifted her hand to the spot and felt the lump of the locket under her collar.

'What?'

'My engagement ring. The only thing I salvaged from Pitcarden and the old man. I hated it for reminding me, so had it made into a locket and put pictures of me and Maddie inside. I left it for you. Though I suppose she must have fiddled with the miniatures.'

'You mean . . . it's *real*?' Lil recalled the times she had nearly thrown it away.

'The diamonds are very old. Valuable.'

Lil scrabbled to unhook the necklace and opened the case of the locket. There was a thin bezel around her picture. She picked at it with a fingernail until it came loose. The paper photograph that the Drakes had made peeled away easily, and behind it in the recess, mirroring Madelyn's older print, was Effie. Young, ambitious, a new mother. She had always been there, lying next to Lil's heart, ever since Lil was sixteen years old. Lil flung the locket away from her, as if it were red hot. It bounced off the rug and slid under the sofa.

Effie sighed. 'This is what happens to people when blood relations crawl out of the woodwork.' She directed it past Lil's shoulder. Lil turned and saw Bina just inside the door, hands clasped together and the same look of desperate trouble on her face. Finally finding an outlet for her rage that wasn't her dying mother, Lil shifted around in her chair.

'And what do you think, Bina? It can't have mattered to you much, all these years, can it, knowing more about me than I do myself. Or is that what all the cakes and simpering were for – did you think you could make up for it with treats and petting?'

'Lil . . .' Effie had leaned forward to touch her, but Lil shook her off and stood, still glaring at Bina, whose whole face trembled, no single emotion gaining a hold for long enough to form an expression. Lil yelled at her. 'Do you think it makes you any less complicit?'

'Lil, stop it.'

The front door knocker sounded. It was pounded so loudly against the plate, the noise seemed to originate in the drawing room itself. Bina jumped violently. For a moment, her features surrendered themselves to one single expression of terror.

'Stop savaging Bina so she can open the door. And sit back down, Lil.' Effie's voice was as calm and cool as snowfall.

'Lilith.' Lil turned on her. 'You mean Lilith. Who names a baby after a mythical figure famous for murdering children?'

'She was also Adam's wife who marvellously left the little toad. No need to take it personally. High time her reputation was restored, especially since Rossetti got his grubby hands on her. Bina?' Effie peered around Lil. 'The door?'

Bina groped for the door handle and left the room.

'Now. Listen to me.' Effie gestured as firmly as she could to the chair, her face serious. Lil sat. 'You have been kept in the dark about many things, I admit. You may never fully understand all the reasons why, and you may never forgive me, but I need you to hear me now.' Her eyes burned, shedding for a moment the ravages of illness. Lil thought of kingfishers, how they seared the air blue. 'Nothing is as terrible as you think. Sometimes you have to pay the price before you know what you're buying – sometimes you never learn even that much.'

Lil shook her head. 'Riddles . . .'

'Hear me.'

Bina had opened the front door, and there was the sound of footsteps – more than one man – in the hallway and on the stairs. Effie clutched her arm. 'You are dearer to me than anyone alive. If you believe nothing else, believe that.'

Lil looked towards the door as the footsteps drew closer; they were hurrying. 'What is—'

'Believe me, Lilith.' Effie's face was alight and flickering with something awful. 'Courage, dear one.'

The door burst open as she said it, and Lil leaped to her feet, turning. Three men crossed the threshold. Two she didn't know. They waited by the door in their overcoats and caps. Striding a few paces further into the room, as if swept along by his own vitality – like a prize stallion – was Dr Lachlan. He removed his hat, turning it into a respectful doffing, and smiled with the reserve of one who understands the gravity of his own presence. He addressed himself rapidly to Effie.

'Mrs Jensen, forgive the abruptness of my appearance. Your message led me to believe it was necessary.' His gaze immediately shifted to Lil and softened into kindness and interest, lingering with an intensity that would have better suited a lover. 'Miss Gerrard. Or perhaps you would now permit me to call you Miss Vincent? Or Lilith?'

Lil drew herself up so rigidly she felt as tall as the ceiling. She had been trained to handle the unexpected, to cut off all expression and physical tells before her reactions could breach the surface. Her thoughts were corralled into a subterranean holding chamber; she could hear them screaming through the floor. Effie's betrayal, so cruel, so shocking, so unfathomable, eclipsed even her twenty-eight-year-old deception. But the fact Lil kept before her now, holding it with a steadfastness that would admit no emotion, was that her great fear was about to break into reality. She was to be locked up as insane. The men blocking the door were walking restraints, Lachlan's portable asylum. She must not let them take her. She held his gaze. 'I have nothing to say to you.'

He smiled with understanding. 'You are upset with me because of the lecture.'

'Insightful.'

'That is natural. It is unfortunate that you heard it, but I would like to discuss with you how and why you came to be there.'

'I'm sure, but I'm afraid our discussions are at an end.' She smiled at him.

'I'm sorry to hear that. I thought we were making progress, and I am confident – *very* confident, Lilith – that I can help you eradicate the night-mare. That is what you want. Isn't it?' He spoke quietly, confidentially, as if they were the only two people in the room. Lil felt the ghost of herself melting towards him, a phantom urge to surrender responsibility, to give in to this burnished saviour. He was watching her intently. 'It is the reason you wrote to me in the first place. It would be tragic indeed if a misunderstanding, if pride and distrust, prevented you from trying a simple cure. Imagine it – undisturbed sleep, no fear of ever waking to monsters. If you come with me now . . .'

'To be clear,' Lil smiled again, 'the only monster I am sure of and that I wish to be rid of is standing in front of me. I do not wish to go anywhere with you or your friends. It is entirely against my will, and it would be unlawful to force me.'

Dr Lachlan seemed to relax at this, as if a question had been answered and the way forward illuminated. 'I believe in a very short time you will smile at your words and be glad you came with me.'

'You can't make me. You said so yourself; you can't lock people up without corroboration from another doctor.'

'I have no desire to lock you up, as you put it. I do have a colleague who is very interested in your trouble and keen to meet you. An internationally recognised alienist. Together, we will find the cause of your affliction and then you can return home and put all this behind you.'

'No, thank you.'

'It would be by far the best solution if you agreed to come and meet him. When people have reason to be very concerned for their loved ones – for their safety,' he glanced at Effie, 'that does give me the power, however unpleasant I find it personally, to act alone initially. I don't want to, especially not with a patient who is as capable of such lucidity as yourself. But what I do want – what is, in fact, imperative here – is to help you get better.'

Lucidity. She had given so much away in those letters; he knew exactly the words to use. Effie was behind her. Lil found she couldn't look. Her head simply would not turn. She wondered if she would ever lay eyes on her again.

'I see.' She lifted her chin. 'This minute?'

'We have everything at our disposal to make your stay as comfortable as your home. Be assured, you can come simply as you are and want for nothing.'

Lil took a step towards him. He smiled in approval and moved a little to the side to let her pass. The two at the door shifted but remained vigilant. She saw she was to be sandwiched between them on the stairs, one slightly ahead, the other behind.

The hissing started. A sense of weightlessness as she walked through the door. It was as if she were leaving her body, like mist burning off a lake. Apart from the hissing, there was silence, everything moving in a bubble of profound peace. She was scared she would disappear again, block everything out, as she had with Lambert, but her mind remained present and alert. At the top of the stairs, she lifted her skirts to step down, hitching them a little higher than necessary. The man in front was half turned towards her as he went ahead, braced for anything. She watched his legs. And then she watched her own foot, swift and pointed, meeting the back of his right knee. If he made a sound, she didn't hear it. The silence continued for the length of the fall, which was shockingly swift. He had no time to catch himself on the bannister. She fell with him, lunging forward until he hit the stairs, and her foot pushed off the top of his back, one glancing step that stamped him against the boards and sent her flying again towards the bottom. She was too headlong to right herself. Her feet scrabbled for the final steps as the hallway floor slammed up to meet her.

Sound returned with the impact. Bina screaming. Shouts from above. The dull clatter as the man behind her completed his tumble to the bottom, his partner running down and climbing past him. She was hauled off the floor, arms wrenched back. Blood streamed and dripped from her cheek. There seemed such a lot of it, running off her like spilled claret. Lachlan was hollering instructions. They weren't addressed to her now; she was all object, a *her* to be done to and dealt with. A leather strap was lowered over her head and shoulders. She instinctively breathed in fully, expanding her ribcage as she would have done as the trussed medium in the cabinet, and steeled her arms a discreet distance away from her body before the strap was cinched tight. The man she had kicked down the stairs was crawling to one side, cursing and checking himself over. He stood again, bruised and breathing heavily, a wall of packed meat blocking the front door. She flailed one way and then the other as if helplessly trapped and weakening. Behind her, she could feel her captor straightening, ready to pull her upright. She guessed the moment, feeling his grip on the strap, and, as he yanked, she dropped and turned, arms clamped to her sides, air rushing out of her lungs. It worked, almost. She slipped through the strap to her throat. Swivelling onto her backside, she launched her left arm blindly at his face. He caught it, holding her by the wrist, and she used his grip to lever herself around further and swing her boot at the side of his head. It was a weak kick in the circumstances, and she missed, but it made him jerk backwards and release the strap if not her wrist. The movement created enough space. She nearly bloodied her own nose with her knee as she cranked it back, and then struck again with her boot, nearly full force in the groin. He folded like a newspaper and fell back against the bottom of the stairs. She lunged forward but couldn't get up fast enough; the other one was on her. Using his own arms instead of a strap, he pinned her from behind and simply held her there. No part of her could reach him. Feet, hands, teeth; she was caught fast.

Dr Lachlan was standing halfway up the stairs, watching. She saw relief sweep across his face, followed by a considering look that wasn't meant for her even as their eyes met. He was looking *at* her, as if she were an animal unable to respond, the pretence of social niceties no longer necessary now she was pinned to the floor. It was playing into his hands, she knew, compounding her new, bestial status, but she couldn't contain it; she opened her mouth and screamed, renewing her efforts to break free. The calm expression on his face didn't change. Not until he saw something above and beyond her. Shock blasted his features, and he shouted, reaching out his hand. But too late. There was the dull, truncated ring of breaking crockery close by Lil's ear, the arms around her turned slack and a dead weight pushed against her; she was forced forward and down.

'Get up!'

A hand seized her arm, pulling her sideways. Lil scrambled to find her feet, crabbing out from under the unconscious man, her hands landing on pieces of white china. Before her lay the head and torso of the shepherdess from the hall table. The front door opened, and she was bathed at once in a thin, chill air. Bina's hand reappeared, and she grasped it.

'*Run.*'

She could sense teeth bared behind her, claws scratching the wooden boards and snagging the rug in haste. Her eyes met Bina's for the briefest of moments — no time even to wonder — and she threw herself towards the pavement. The door slammed shut on Lachlan's furious roar. She turned, already past the railings and down the step, and collided forcefully with another body. Hands grasped her arms, and she nearly screamed again in sheer rage, certain this was another of Lachlan's men left on the street to head off an escape.

'Miss Vincent!'

Her eyes found his face. Anyone else and she would have pushed straight past and fled, but Alec Raube's presence hooked her, just. She trembled on a thread. A hansom cab waited behind him.

'They are trying to put me in an asylum. She did this.' She spoke rapidly and without expectation, watching for the first hint of what he might do. His face was still wide at the sight of her bloodied cheek, her chopped hair. She saw her words sinking in as the door behind was wrenched open again. Bina shrieking. Lachlan's footsteps.

'Thank God! Hold her, sir, she's my patient. Hold her!'

Nothing to chance: she made to pull away, but Raube found her hand, whispered *wait*. He manoeuvred them so he was facing Lachlan. 'What is the meaning of this?'

Lachlan pulled up short, irritation flashing in eyes and teeth. 'That is my patient. My name is Dr Lachlan. Sir, the woman is violent, I beg you to be careful . . .'

'This "woman", *sir*, is my daughter.' Raube didn't raise his voice, but the word seemed to fill the street, to rattle windows and lift cobbles. Lil couldn't have moved in that moment if her life had depended on it. The irritation was blanched from Lachlan's face. In its stead grew suspicion.

'Your daughter?' He flicked his gaze to Lil and kept his eyes on her as he spoke. 'Sir, I was given to understand the identity of this woman's father was unknown.'

'Ah!' Raube cannoned it across the pavement. 'That, sir, is your problem. Not mine.' He began to turn.

'Can anyone vouch for your claim?'

Lil watched anger paint Raube's face crimson, but before he could reply, Bina spoke up from the doorway. 'I can.' Her hair was torn from its pins; she must have physically grappled with Lachlan, trying to keep him from the door. The fierceness Lil had seen earlier was still evident in her straight back and shining eyes.

As Lachlan looked around at her, Raube moved quickly, ushering Lil into the cab. He followed, pausing on the step and turning his head. 'Lachlan, was it? My name is Alec Raube. I will get to the bottom of this. Expect to hear from my lawyer.' With that, he barked a word at the driver and dropped into the seat beside Lil, shutting them in.

The cab lurched forward, and Lil felt the growing ache in her head roll back and forth. Raube didn't look at her immediately, and even when he turned, they simply mirrored each other silently, both compelled to seek something of their own reflection in the other's features. Lil broke first. Aware suddenly of the heavy strap still hanging around her neck, she grabbed at it and flung it clear of the cab and into the road. The driver reined in the horse, but Raube called up to continue. He shrugged off his overcoat and wrapped it around her, then folded a handkerchief into a square. He held it against her cheek until she pressed her own hand to it. The touch of their fingers seemed to trigger a shyness in him. He sat back and looked down to the side, hands resting loosely on his thighs. Lil also did not know how to begin. He cleared his throat and started with where they had just left.

'You say "she" did this?' Their eyes met again.

'Effie. I only discovered yesterday that her real name is Utica. And today that she is my . . .' She tried to swallow and failed. 'And you.'

Emotion was working his face, pulling at muscles. Pain, pity, anger. He bit his lip, gathered himself, and made a gesture with his hand, as though pushing it all away. 'What happened? Today? Why the doctor?'

Lil shook her head, eyes widening. The shock of it returned. 'She tried to lock me away. I don't know why. I don't know why.'

'You found out about her past?'

'Yes. We spoke about it. I was angry, but there was no reason . . . I don't understand . . .' The words jammed in her throat. She fell silent. After a moment, Raube shouted up to the driver to take them to a physician.

Stitched, bandaged, and clasping a bottle of laudanum, Lil watched the familiar countryside between Gledsmuir and Pitcarden jolt and waver past the carriage window, the colours deepening to black in the dying light. Only the orange flare of bonfires, already lit for Samhain, burned at intervals along their way, and the odd flicker of turnip lanterns outside cottage doors. She was suspended in comfort. A cloud of feathers, deliciously soft, cocooned her from events, past, present and future. The drug had killed so much more than the pain in her head and cheek.

On the train, they had spoken little. Raube took advantage of other passengers leaving to ask her if Nils knew of Effie's plan. She had been wondering the same and shook her head. 'I don't know. She's kept other things from him.' The question made her look at him more closely. 'Do you believe her? About me?'

Raube rubbed his chin. 'Yes. Don't you?'

Lil heard Madelyn's voice drifting down the years. *The spirits gave you to me.* She remembered how Effie had looked at her in the British Museum.

'Yes, but I have more reason to believe her. To you, she reappears after twenty-eight years with a bold and unprovable claim . . .'

'Twenty-eight years in which she has never forgiven me for abandoning her. Even after her marriage and success, her anger . . . I cannot – do not – blame her for that; your existence only makes more sense of it.' He turned his head to the window. 'Even so, I think it is not me she came to Pitcarden for.'

'She wants the lover's knot brooch. The one your father promised her. She has never forgotten. Perhaps it is him she wants vengeance on most.'

He didn't answer for a moment or turn from the window. 'She offered me a deal when I saw her yesterday. She couldn't be sure how I would take the news of having a child. So, she said she would do as I wished. Either sign a statement saying the father was someone else, so you could never make a claim on me, or, if I were paternally inclined, as she suspected, encourage you to accept me. She promised to give her blessing. She gave me to understand that she could turn you whichever way she chose, depending on whether I agreed.'

Lil felt something tear at her centre, even through the first effects of the laudanum, as if the meat of her heart had given way a little. 'Agreed to what?'

'To allow Jensen to find the brooch and bring it to her. As you say.'

Lil's voice seemed to come from somewhere outside of herself. 'And your answer?'

He turned to look at her. It was the eyes, perhaps, that showed their connection. She studied the colour, similar to hers.

'I don't make deals like that.' His voice was gruff and hard suddenly. It suggested anger near the surface, a simmering will that made Lil think of his years in the gold mines of Australia. Not a place, she imagined, for the timid. He eyed her almost accusingly. 'If you're kin, you're kin. If that brings trouble, I'll deal with it on my own terms. I came back today to look for you or find out where you'd gone.' His gaze moved around her face, his thoughts apparently veering off track. 'She knows I have no heir. She wouldn't have handed you over willingly.'

'I'm not stolen goods.'

'You are to her. As good as.' He sat back and put a hand up. 'Forgive me. I've learned to speak bluntly. It's possible this business with the doctor is part of her plan to force my hand.'

Lil felt anger rising to the surface. It met with a foamy tide of laudanum and dissolved away. As the wave streamed back, it left behind a single word, an unusual shell catching her eye. *Heir.* She picked it up. It was heavier than she'd expected, but she couldn't at that moment understand why.

The effects of the laudanum began to fade as the hired carriage neared Balcraig. A dullness throbbed in one half of Lil's face. There was a small group of people on the road outside the hamlet. Raube opened the window and leaned forward to greet them as they passed, calling names. His words were met with grim silence, the men's faces made stark by the light of the lamps. He sat back. 'Something is wrong.'

'They've lost trust in the estate since we started digging.'

'No, I spoke to those men yesterday morning. They aren't the troublemakers. I was able to reassure them; some even agreed to help you with the dig. The women offered me bannocks, and babies to hold.' He looked somewhat mystified for a moment before turning to Lil. 'We shall go straight to Pitcarden House. You'll stay there.' His eyes made it a question. She nodded.

As he helped her out of the carriage by the stables, a lone figure ran around the corner of the house and past them towards the road, a young man. It was too dark to see more than that. He didn't respond to Raube's shout. They entered the house through the side door, Raube holding her arm as if she needed support. Perhaps she did. She was acutely aware of him physically, the pressure of his hand, his proximity, the smell of tweed and something else to do with his person, perhaps soap. *Father*, she thought with each discovery, trying to tether a doubtful concept to a collection of sensations.

The place seemed deserted although lamps were lit and there were signs of a dinner being prepared in the kitchen: half-chopped vegetables abandoned on the table and large pans of water coming to a boil on the range. They stood for a moment on the threshold, listening, and were rewarded with muffled voices further down the corridor. A door flew open, and a girl Lil didn't recognise ran towards them carrying a jug and an air of emergency. She was dressed like one of the local girls, but her clothes were stained. As she drew near, Lil saw the smears on her sleeves and apron were blood. The girl's eyes took them in, but she didn't stop or speak, slipping past them into the kitchen to fill the jug with hot water and ransack drawers and cupboards for, it became clear, any cloths or linen she could find.

Raube began to question her, but Lil understood. She ran down the corridor, her face seeming to shatter with each step, and turned into the room, a storeroom. A violent smell of blood, newly discharged, thickened the air. Three women busied themselves around a makeshift bed fashioned out of a pallet and blankets. Between their movements, Lil saw Jenet's face, white and sweat-sheened, her eyes shut.

No. Her heart lurched in her chest. The plaque in her pocket seemed to burn against her leg. 'What happened?'

A woman looked around sharply, and then beyond Lil, ignoring her question. 'Whaur is she?'

'Coming.' Lil moved further into the room. The housekeeper was holding Jenet's hand and talking to her, apparently trying to keep her awake. At the other end, the woman who had spoken — the village midwife, judging by her tone and assurance — dumped a red-soaked cloth on an already sodden pile at the side. Next to her, another woman was assisting. The girl from the kitchen returned, arms laden, and they silently absorbed the things she had brought into their urgent business.

Lil had never felt such helplessness in the face of another's struggle, not even with Effie. That this could be happening now, at Samhain, was cruel and unthinkable. A coincidence, her mind said; of course a coincidence. *As far as you know.* Jenet's own words repeated back to her. The plaque was growing in her consciousness, as if its weird presence were reaching beyond its material form. Curse or amulet? She pushed the thought away. There was nothing she could do, and she turned to leave. But on a sudden impulse, the same that had first made her put the plaque in her pocket, she pulled it out and dropped it between an old washboard and the wall.

Raube was in the passageway. He spoke quietly. 'She said it happened suddenly a few hours ago; they tried to take her upstairs, but she only made it this far. Everything was fine at first.' He frowned. 'The man who passed us outside was her husband.'

'Running for a doctor?'

'Haxton has already gone for him. She said he left straight away.' They looked at each other. He lowered his voice further. 'If the child dies . . .'

'I know.' Lil matched his whisper. 'The men on the road.' A cold hand suddenly on the back of her neck. 'Nils.' Her head turned quickly, instinctively, in the direction of the cottage. 'I have to warn him; he won't know.'

'Wait.' Raube put out his hand, but she was already striding back towards the door. She stopped as it flew open, half expecting an angry mob to burst through. Haxton appeared, his face flushed from hard riding. His eyes locked onto hers. 'What news?'

The doctor hurried behind him, hauling his bag with a look that was both pained and glum. Lil didn't know what to say. She had never seen so much blood. Haxton read his answer in her face and silently took in her own injury and strange appearance. 'I need to speak with you and Mr Raube, now.'

They passed her in a tight storm of haste and purpose. She drifted back towards the storeroom to wait with Raube. After a short while, Haxton reappeared looking even grimmer, and ushered them further out of earshot. 'There'll be a delegation from the village; it won't be peaceful.'

'What can we do?' Raube was calm, alert.

'They will want the hoard reburied, but I doubt that will be enough.' He looked at Lil. 'They found the brooch this afternoon.'

She cursed under her breath.

'There was already trouble that some of the men were helping you. Those you spoke to yesterday,' he turned back to Raube, 'so word spread as soon as it was found. When news came that Jenet's time had come early, they went to take it from him.'

'My God, is he all right? Where is he?' Lil felt panic moving up her body.

'I had to go for the doctor, but they won't have harmed him.' He said it quickly. 'Not if he gave them the brooch.'

'If.' Lil felt her heart thudding. All Nils's grief for Effie was centred on that brooch, on getting it to her; it had eroded his reason. Without another word, she turned and ran down the passageway. She reached the door and swung it open, ran out into the dark. Turning the corner of the house, she felt more than saw the bodies in front of her. A few carried lamps, but most were folded into night, only parts of them outlined: the edge of a cloak, glint of a buckle, head of a hammer. Lil couldn't breathe properly.

'Where is Nils Jensen?' Her voice was high and thin. Haxton and Raube arrived beside her, Raube speaking. Haxton took her elbow, drawing her back inside. Two of the night figures were coming too. The delegation. They stood squinting in the passageway, a thickset youth and an older man she recognised as the blacksmith. Jenet's father and husband. Lil was amazed it wasn't Mudie. His presence seemed inevitable. She looked into the men's faces and saw fear, as if it were her own reflected back. But theirs was not the fear that paralysed. It tightened the fingers' grip on the hammer, set fire to the blood. Haxton bolted the door behind them.

The father held something up. The lover's knot brooch. It flashed briefly in his hand. Lil was shocked by how small it was. She had imagined it an improbable size, too large to wear, fattened and made garish through the lens of Effie's need for it. But this trinket, for all its great value, seemed surely too scant a thing to have driven her to such lengths for so long. The father was not offering it. 'It shuid ne'er'a been touched. The brae haes been left weel alane for years.'

There was a strange resignation in his manner, and Lil sensed he was in some part embarrassed, that in a less distressed state, he did not believe in curses that threatened the life of his grandchild. Haxton saw it too. 'You ken better nor this, Ross. An ye, Mungo. The doctor's wi them; awthing that can be done is in hauns wi.'

Jenet's husband stood taller. 'Gie's the treasure, or we'll tak it.'

'Och, that's aw she wants,' Haxton raised his voice and stared down the younger man, 'a fecht at her door.'

'We'll no lea it tae chance, Haxton.' The father stepped

forward. 'The hag's been seen affen sen ye lat thae folk in.' He thrust his chin at Lil.

Raube spoke up. 'I let them in, Mr Henderson. It's my decision. As I told you yesterday. There's no doubt some poor vagrant passing through, trying not to draw attention to herself.'

Lil wanted to say it was herself they had seen pacing the brae, but realised she was as bad luck for them as the hag itself, that it wouldn't help. Jenet's father had paused, being confronted by the owner of the estate, and he softened his voice slightly. 'Wi respect, sir, yer faither wad never'a lat a body come by the brae.'

'I'm afraid my father and I were not in unison on many things. We didn't enjoy the common view of the world that you clearly share with your son.'

Voices from outside. Shouts. The crowd seemed to be swelling and had moved closer to the door. Raube appeared unhurried. 'But I understand. I shall respect your wishes at a time like this. Better for us all to keep occupied. Haxton, please bring out the artefacts; we shall rebury them.' Both Haxton and Lil looked at him. He kept his eyes on the visitors. 'Sooner would be better I think.'

There was the sound of glass shattering, quite distant, at the front of the house, and a lone howl. Haxton stalked into the office as pounding started up on the side door. Raube gestured towards it. 'Perhaps we should share our intentions before anything else is broken.'

Jenet's father nodded and exchanged a look with his son-in-law. They both turned doubtfully towards the door, which was being made to rattle continuously. Demands were hollered through the wood. Jenet's husband looked back, his eyes sliding to Lil. Something inside her recoiled, but then he was looking beyond her. His mouth opened, lips drawing back, and his eyes grew wide. 'Hech!'

Lil turned to look. The blood-smeared girl had come back out of the storeroom cradling a bundle in the crook of her arm. It dripped crimson. She stopped on seeing them. Lil looked back to the boy's stricken face and reached out for him. 'No! It's not the child.'

But he yelled again, staggering backwards and then turned to run to the door and pull the bolt open. 'Thay've murdert it. They've murdert ma bairn!'

Lil backed up, her legs obeying an instinct beyond her will, pushing past Haxton, who was holding a leather bag. Bodies coursed into the passageway, a tide of clenched muscles and flaming faces. Mudie was at the front as she knew he would be. He was holding an old-fashioned sickle up, higher than his head. The dark energy pulsing through the group seemed to crackle around it. His quick eyes dismissed Jenet's husband, who was still shouting, and took in everyone present. The light in them changed as they rested on Lil: a settling, an anticipation of violence. But something else was happening, forcing him to look past her. Raube had moved quickly, running to snatch the bloody cloths from the terrified girl and was advancing on the rabble, calling on them to look in a voice that rebounded off the stone walls. Rags were flung this way and that until there was nothing in his hands but blood. He held them out to Jenet's husband.

'No infant. Do you see, lad? You're getting ahead of yourself.' He took the leather bag from Haxton and held it up. 'You want the hoard buried?' Shouts went up, a host of ays. 'Then take it.' He held it out to Jenet's father. 'Take it and bury it, but leave the girl in peace. God knows what she's suffering without her friends and neighbours doing violence over her head.'

Mudie snatched the bag off him before Jenet's father could take it. 'That's no aw.' His eyes were brimming with triumph and an awful hunger. 'Something maun be yirdit wi it, something o value tae the man that howkit hit up.' He looked at Lil. 'The auld man haed naething tae offer, but for her. She's as muckle tae blame. The wumman's comin wi us.'

There was another roar of assent, although it was doubtful how many truly heard what they were calling for. For Lil, Mudie's words, his intention, were a blast of searing heat, clarifying, excoriating. Jenet, her baby, the curse: she saw that none of it mattered. Grievances that had been building for decades, smouldering out of sight like the innards of a muck heap, had finally caught light. Useless to point out the hoard was incomplete, that a piece remained buried, the curse unfulfilled. Worse than useless to speak at all: her voice alone would provoke him. The thing coming for her now was beyond justice or reason; it was as blind and raging as the fire that had killed Haxton's brother nearly thirty years before. Mudie lifted his sickle higher.

Lil, you have the sight, but it is warning you of great danger.

Was this it, then? Against all reason, the night-mare finally come for her. The embittered son of a tenant farmer, robbed of his land by her own grandfather. He wouldn't even know it was blood vengeance he had exacted. Not until later.

Burial. She could feel it: the weight of earth, mud clogging her nose and mouth, her body robbed of breath until it merged with the soil, becoming dark material, artefact. She had lived it a thousand times.

New bones over old.

A premonition. Was that the truth? The night-mare's crushing weight only a fore-echo of the suffocation to come.

Run run run run run.

Raube was demanding that they leave, roaring at them to hear what they were saying, to see what it would mean. There was a moment of precarious balance. Mudie had taken a step, and the others followed. Raube stood firm, but Haxton was easing backwards. She remembered he had been part of this before; he had been on the other side and knew what happened once the scales tipped from self-preservation to abandonment, from calculation to chaos. He had known the same violence in himself.

New bones over old.

Her bones. She waited for the hissing in the air, longed for the thing she had dreaded – for control to be taken from her. It didn't come. She was trapped in her own frail and breakable flesh. Hands clasped, she prayed to the goddess, or demon, she no longer cared which, if it would only come to her now in all its blazing terror. Nothing. She thought of the plaque, hidden in Jenet's room. What if this was how the amulet worked? What if she herself were the threat, the summation of her parents' and her grandfather's sins, of the excavation, of Mudie's rage: what if everything were unfolding as it was meant to, and she had always been moving towards this moment of sacrifice? She bit down on her lip, aware that her thoughts were spiralling into lunacy. Time was running out. Raube had now taken a step back. The moment was coming to turn and become prey.

'Haun her ower, Haxton. Ye ken whit this means. It's yer niece in thare. Or haes yer maidenheid gane tae yer harns?' Mudie's eyes shone. 'I'll no gie ye anither chance.'

'Ye'll no tak anither step, John. Pit that heuk doun.' Haxton continued to talk, shifting his body in front of Lil.

Raube, very softly, without turning, spoke under his breath. '*Run.*'

And she was moving, turning, already fleet, already seeing herself past the storeroom, already through the door at the end of the passageway. Safety, freedom: they were reachable; she only had to run.

Her hands and knees landed hard on the flags. The blood-soaked rags had tripped her, twisting where they were thrown, a sling for her toe. Claustrophobia closed in. She couldn't breathe. A brawl above, a flash of the sickle, Haxton shouting. Her mouth opened to scream, and it was then that it happened. A sound, not hers, distinct over the fight. It undulated along the passageway, past where she cowered on the floor, over Raube and Haxton grappling with Mudie, swirling around Jenet's father and husband. They were all hooked by it, drawn in by its primitive insistence.

A baby. Crying.

The world changed in an instant. No one moved for long seconds, fixed like a tableau, listening silently. The wail died down and returned again, louder. Its meaning billowed around them. A child: alive, healthy.

Jenet's husband was the first to move, pushing past without a word. Lil found her feet, as if released from a spell. Haxton was next, running down the passageway to his niece. Lil followed. She halted again just inside the door and saw the child, slathered in pre-birth, a blind and squirming creature newly risen from the dark. The midwife was placing it on a clean petticoat laid out on the top of a barrel and a girl brought over a basin of water. Their faces were intent still, but released of the great fear. Lil turned her Lilith eyes away. Jenet's husband was at a standstill halfway into the room, staring in amazement. He looked towards Jenet, but was drawn back by the sight of his own offspring, materialised from a world of reeking blood and suffering in a dusty storeroom. Lil made herself look at Jenet but could see little past Haxton and the women attending with the doctor. Turned backs meant there was a life still to be saved. A body pushed past her, Jenet's father. He made for his daughter and hovered at a distance, twisting his cap in his hands. Words were being spoken along the passageway, but Lil couldn't hear them clearly. Haxton began pacing. He ran his hands through his hair. The midwife beckoned Jenet's husband over and put the swaddled, screaming baby into his disbelieving arms.

'Are you hurt?'

Lil turned. Raube's lip was split, his face full of worry. *If you're kin, you're kin,* he had said in the hansom. Were paternal affections formed so quickly, like the thunderbolt that had just hit

Jenet's husband? But there was Effie's voice too, her real mother: *Blood — look at the misery it causes.*

Lil blinked. She could not think what it all meant. Her thoughts turned to the one man she had ever dared think of as a father. She looked quickly down the passageway. Mudie and his followers had vanished, as if they had never been. She had heard nothing of their leaving. 'Where are they?'

'I told them if they went home immediately and let Jenet's family decide what to do with the hoard, I wouldn't bring the law down on them.'

Lil saw he was holding the bag of artefacts in his hand. 'But you're bleeding.'

'Just a lick in the lug. They had a point to make, and I know who they are now. There will be a reckoning for Mudie, don't doubt it. He stirs up the others. But we'll keep it within Balcraig. If I can't make peace with him, I'll keep him close and in my debt.' He met Lil's eye. 'Once they know who you are, it will be easier to manage.'

Lil brushed that aside. 'What about Nils? What if they haven't gone home at all?'

'I'll go with you to find him.' Haxton was behind her. The skin around his eyes had become white and puckered. 'We'll start with the cottage.' His gaze shifted from nothing to nothing until it settled on Lil. 'I can't do anything for Jenet here.'

Lil turned back to Raube. The passageway was still wet with blood and ringing with violence. 'What will you do if they return?'

'I shall thank God that they are not with you.' They regarded each other a moment. He nodded. 'Be careful. Bring him here if it is safe to do so.'

The gathering had truly dispersed, from outside of the house at least. Rain was turning to sleet: kinder against her face but soaking her bandage and slipping past her collar. The cold bit into her neck. She toiled with sliding steps up the path that skirted the mound, finding her way without a lamp and trusting that Haxton followed. When she rounded the hill, she saw there was a light in the cottage kitchen and the front door was open. She peered through the window first but could see no one. They entered into the sudden calm and dryness of the room. There were signs of a struggle: a chair on its side, the whisky bottle broken, a workbox overturned and tools spewed across the floor. She picked up one of the lamps and moved quickly through the other rooms. When she returned, Haxton had righted the chair and was lifting loops of thick twine that she had used to mark out the site. 'They tied him up. Looks as if he managed to free himself.'

Lil could see it unfolding before her. Nils's rage that they had taken the brooch from him. A few hurried knots would not have held him for long. She looked towards the door. The wind swiped at her through it like a mad thing reaching through bars.

An indistinct shout came from outside. Before either of them could move, Nils had charged into the kitchen. He was coatless, his soaked shirt clinging to his body and hair plastered to his head. The wildness in his eyes was unlike anything Lil had seen in him before.

'I thought she had come back.' He seemed to recognise Lil suddenly and spoke eagerly. 'Did you see her? Did you see where she went?'

'Who?'

He ran to the window, straining to see into the darkness outside. Lil took his coat from the hook. 'Who are you looking for, Nils?'

He turned to her, startled, as if she had materialised out of thin air. A dreadful smile filled his face, and he grasped hold of her. 'She was here. I saw her. Just there, in the doorway.' He pointed. 'I was . . . they tied me up . . .' He turned to the chair. Lil tried to throw his coat over his shoulders, but he was moving too much. 'They took it . . . they took her brooch from me.'

The words froze Lil to the spot. She lowered the coat, letting the hem pool on the floor. Nils was still turning about erratically. 'They took it off me; I couldn't stop them, I couldn't . . . but then she . . .' His breath failed for a moment. 'She stood there.' He stepped towards the door. 'She was looking at me, and then she walked away. I called her name, but she didn't wait, and I . . . I was tied up; I couldn't follow. And then, when I was free, she had gone . . .' His feet stilled finally, and he stared outside at the storm before turning to Lil like a bewildered child. 'Did you see her? Did you see the way she went?'

Lil looked into his eyes and couldn't find him. Any words she might have said were knocked aside by his belief that he had seen Effie. His expression changed as she watched. A new thought surfaced, throwing a pall over his face. He looked at the window. His mouth worked as if he would speak. Eventually, he whimpered, 'She has gone to find *her*. Yes!' He was loud suddenly, and tall. Great dread and resolution spread across his features. 'That is where she is waiting for me.' He made for the door.

'No, Nils! Stop him.'

Nils was bigger than Haxton and possessed of a certainty that lent him strength. He wrenched himself free from them both, as if they were children, and rushed back outside. Lil went after him, still clutching his coat. Her lungs burned with the cold and effort. She shouted uselessly, blundering into gorse as she followed him up the hill. Tripping, she nearly lost her footing and dropped the lamp. The darkness became enormous. Snow flurried around her, icy and drenching. She reached the top of the mound, sweat and melted snow running into her eyes. Nils was at the edge of the central trench, head thrown back. *'Come to me!'*

Lil peered into the darkness, almost believing she could see something, a figure, *her* figure. Haxton caught up with his own lamp, and Nils pitched forward into the hole. *'Have you gone to her?'* He clawed at the soil below them for a few moments before falling back on his heels and lifting his face to the relentless, plunging snow. Lil jumped down and draped the coat over his shoulders. She managed to get one arm into a sleeve before he was up again and peering into the night. His gaze grew sharp. There was nothing but darkness and chaotic flecks of white ahead, but he pointed into it and began climbing out of the trench. The dreadful smile returned. *'Wait!'*

There was no way to hold him. He lurched out of their grasp, dragging the coat behind with one arm still in place. Lil scrambled out, and they charged down the north side of the brae. She tried to remember how the land lay: a boggy field, then trees, another slow descent through farmland, eventually the river. Her foot caught in a rabbit hole or rut, and she felt the horror of falling without knowing what was beneath. She landed with a grunt onto snow-blanketed grass. Nils had disappeared. She screamed his name.

Nothing but the night-time and the storm hissing around her. Her skin was numb. Flakes hit her eyes, stinging like grit before melting away. Her heart still pounded, the blood thudding in her ears. She was alone. There were no Samhain fires still alight in this weather. The night of the dead, the old new year, was passing by without protection. She became aware of the silence beneath the wind. It was an emptiness that pressed in, remorseless and without light. She shut her eyes. In her mind, she saw Nils's face again as he pointed into the darkness, and all at once, with a certainty that seemed carried like a voice on the wind, she knew.

When Haxton found her a few minutes later, she was still curled on the ground with her hands against her ears and her elbows clamped together to shield her eyes.

14

Lil wouldn't go to bed. Not with Jenet still fluttering between life and death, and with Nils out in the storm and out of his mind. She consented to blankets, once she had re-bandaged her face, tentatively testing the swelling all around her eye, and wiped the blood from her wrists and neck where the gorse had caught her. She sat with Raube and Haxton in the kitchen, the three of them scattered about on chairs and benches, mostly in silence, sometimes joined by the doctor, who accepted a dram and frowned at the floor, also without speaking. Lil felt her body settling with exhaustion, ticking and whining internally like a steam engine come to rest. Hidden injuries from her fall down the stairs in Edinburgh and all the knocks she had suffered since were starting to reveal themselves in deep aches and sudden twinges.

When he wasn't looking at her, she looked at Haxton. Outside in the field, when he had stumbled across her, he had simply lifted her up and half carried her back to the house. He hadn't asked what had driven her to the ground with her arms wrapped around her head, and she hadn't spoken of it. She didn't dare think of it yet. His eyes turned to hers, and she looked away.

Her gaze landed on the things around her: gleaming copperware, a rolling pin, a basket of logs, and it slowly dawned on her that they were hers now, or would be. All of it, the stone flags, door hinges, supporting walls, and – she felt a strange, painful jolt in her core – the burial mound, the standing stone. She shifted in her seat and looked at Raube. He offered her a quiet smile.

Heir. He had tossed the word out so carelessly earlier. Did she want it? To be mistress of the kettle and door jamb, the three floors and many chimneys, the servants and tenants? He had been born to it, all the rules and customs of a society that she had studiously avoided in her proud and marginalised life with Effie and Nils. A life that was now over. It would mean freedom to excavate wherever she wished, and the museum fellows would have to take her seriously, or pretend they did. But was it worth the weight of the name, the burdens it would bring? She dropped Raube's gaze.

Haxton went out twice, looking for Nils. There was no sign that he had returned to the cottage. The snow had stopped by four in the morning but not before it had covered any tracks west of the mound. Nils's coat he found iced stiff on the ground, not far from where Lil had lost sight of him. He brought it back to the house and hung it over a chair by the range. Looking at it, Lil told them how, in Norway, Nils would break the ice to swim in the winter and not even shiver. Haxton listed stock sheds, hay stores, nearby farms – plenty of places where shelter might be found. They fell silent. Raube rubbed his hand over his chin. 'Does it look like the wet nurse will make it through tonight?'

Haxton shook his head. 'They'll not set out 'til first light. It will take some time.'

'The baby's taking cow's milk.' Lil offered the drop of good news. She had been to see Jenet's son, unable to stop herself, although she went no closer than peeping in at the doorway of the office. The fire had been built up and a basket found to serve as a cradle. The midwife's helpers were taking turns to watch and feed him. Snoring in a corner was Jenet's husband, limbs flung out like a colt's. Asleep, he looked no more than a child himself, but Lil remembered how his eyes had turned to her, knowing what Mudie meant to do. Staying at Pitcarden meant she would have to deal with people in all their mess and unreason. There could be no sliding, untouched, past the lives of others, pulling their strings for finite ends and moving on. She would be exposed, and all her behaviours watched. Her exhaustion deepened, and she felt a sudden sympathy with the older Raube, her grandfather, for simply withdrawing behind his scorched walls and ending his days as a despised recluse.

―――――――

A chair scraping against the floor woke her. Others in the room were already standing, and she was on her feet instantly. Sunshine streamed through the kitchen's high windows, disorientating, the lateness of the hour frightening. Raube was shaking the doctor's hand. 'Thank you.'

'I'll return later. I've left instructions. Don't move her.' The doctor tipped his hat at Lil before walking out.

Lil's voice was hoarse. 'Jenet.'

'Stable.' Raube sounded terse. 'For now, at least.' When he turned, Lil saw it was exhaustion. He looked ill and weak as he sat back down. 'She made it through the night; we must keep our thoughts on that.'

'Where is Haxton?'

'Raising a party to search for Jensen.' He looked at her again more closely. 'We'll know soon one way or the other. The waiting will be over.'

She needed the privy and excused herself to look for one. The cold air outside the kitchen was welcome against her skin. She thought she would like to go outside and lie down in the snow, let it numb her against everything, news of Nils, and also the other thing she knew was coming. It arrived sooner than she expected. When she returned to the kitchen, the old housekeeper was there, talking to Raube. The roads were passable, and the cart had drawn up with the wet nurse finally. 'There's another come with her, asking for you, Miss Vincent. From Edinburgh.'

Lil understood. Her body received the blow, drawing the truth into her very bones, like the stunted hawthorn on the hill absorbing the full fury of the storm.

The wet nurse was in the passageway, being shown into the office. Lil continued outside to where the horse and cart were being turned around. Everywhere was white and light, sun and snow, a shining loveliness that seemed innocent of the night that had delivered it. Lil squinted against the brightness, felt the air sharp in her throat like a beautiful blade.

Standing where she had alighted, dressed neatly from head to toe in black with a travelling bag in hand, her head raised to take in the house, was Bina. Lil stopped, yards away, and their eyes met. Neither offered to speak. Eventually, it was Lil who gave the slightest nod and walked on at a wide angle towards the path that led up to the brae. Behind her, she could hear Raube's greeting and Bina's deferential request to speak with him. She carried on walking, not believing the sound of her own breath or the rasp of her skirts. Snow clung to the sides of the Carlin stone like a shroud. She was at the foot of the barrow when her knees gave way and she fell forward, grateful at least to surrender to the whiteness, welcoming the sting of it against her face and hands. There was a blankness there between her warm breath and the freezing snow that shut out for the moment the terrible thing. She dwelt within it, not knowing or caring how much time passed, only keeping herself small, too small to be found. Warm breath, cold snow, warm breath, cold snow. But the terrible thing was not shut out.

Effie was dead. Lil's body yanked in the next breath as if the fact were ice-cold water closing over her head. Snow filled her mouth, and she rolled onto her back, coughing. She had thought it was Madelyn who had rejected her as a daughter. She had thought herself safe, that she could never again be thrown to a man like Lachlan as she had been to Lambert. But Effie had done it. And Effie was gone.

Lil's love for her rose up, billowing outwards, as vast as the sky, and was rent on terrible, implacable thorns. Her mother. Cries swelled in Lil's throat. She had believed that nothing could be more painful than not knowing. 'I want you to be alive.' She pressed her fingers into her eyes. 'Be alive, so I can hate you.'

Something landed beside her. A sigh and shifting of limbs told her who.

'A few more minutes. Then back inside. You can greet in the warm.' Haxton's voice floated into the dark, cold place behind Lil's hands. She shrank from it.

'Leave me alone.'

'You'll catch your death. Pitcarden can't afford to lose another Raube just yet.' She was silent, which he took as a question. 'He told me while you were asleep.'

It was nothing, of no consequence to Lil, and she didn't speak again. Haxton shifted more and cleared his throat. 'We found Jensen.'

She opened her eyes. He spoke quickly. 'He's alive. Found his way into a stable. They'll bring him to the house when they've warmed him up.' His expression didn't match his words, and Lil sat up. 'He's in the same state as last night, Lil. His mind . . .' He raised his hand to his head. She started to scramble to her feet, but he closed his fingers around her wrist, making her look at him again. 'There's something else that you don't know yet. About Jensen.' He looked past her to the top of the mound. His lips parted, but he seemed to hesitate. 'At the house,' he said at last.

She stared, searching for some clue in his eyes, but saw what she had never seen in them before: pity. It frightened her, perhaps even more than watching Nils pointing into the darkness.

She recoiled, snatched her arm back and, climbing to her feet, hurried away from him towards Pitcarden.

Bina and Raube stood up as soon as she entered the kitchen. Tea things had been placed between them. Lil saw the same unbearable pity in Bina's eyes as in Haxton's. 'What is it? Nils has been found, but what is it I don't know?'

Bina glanced at Raube and then at the table. She picked up a sheet of paper, a letter. Raube retreated to the settle and sat with his hands on his knees, gazing down.

'Sit, Miss Vincent, dear.'

'No. What's that?'

Bina sat down herself, blinking, and placed the letter on the table with her hand over it. After a moment to settle herself, she began.

'A few days ago, I found her trying to burn this letter in its envelope with a candle. She caught her fingers in the flame and dropped it, and her shawl nearly caught light. I don't know what . . . if I hadn't come in just then.' She gave a little shake of her head. 'I stamped out the sparks and took the envelope from her. She was very distressed. I've rarely seen her so upset. I said I'd burn it for her, if that's what she wanted, but properly, in the fireplace. You know she couldn't see the fire very well, with the sofa where it is. I don't know what made me do it, Lil, but as I was walking away from her, I slipped the paper out and tucked it into my collar. By the time she'd pulled herself around to watch, there was only the envelope left to burn, but she thought it was all of it. She watched until nothing could have survived, and then became quiet as a lamb. I felt terrible. I put the letter in my sewing box. I had no intention of reading it, but something told me I should hold on to it, that it might be important. And then, yesterday . . .' Bina's face seemed to grow unstable. She made an effort to bring herself under control. 'I didn't understand why she summoned that doctor. She promised me they would only take you away for a short while. She said it was the only way open to her and you wouldn't be hurt by it. I knew it was wrong, Lil.' Her mouth pulled down at the corners, and her eyes began to swim. She took a heavy breath. 'I'm so glad you got away.' She raised a handkerchief to blot the tears. 'After you'd gone, she . . .' Bina pressed her lips together.

Lil moved forward. Effie's last hours that she could never witness herself were playing in Bina's mind in front of her. Bina cleared her throat. 'She was anguished one moment, and the next seemed to find it all . . .' She raised her hands. 'Well, she laughed until I worried she would hurt herself. As time went on, it was clear she was falling into a delirium. She started talking about the past as if it were now, and calling out for Maddie. I sent for the doctor, and it wasn't very long after he came that she was quiet, and . . .' She stopped again briefly. After a moment, she nodded to herself and reached for a more matter-of-fact tone.

'I wanted to sit by her after, and fetched my sewing, when I remembered the letter. Her behaviour towards you was so strange, and as she had passed, I decided I would read it.' She looked squarely at Lil. 'It's from Mr Jensen, Lil. He sent it when you were in Edinburgh with us.' She lifted the letter from the table and held it out. Lil remembered Madelyn holding out the reference to her, the sense of something being offered that was like a key turning. To take it was to leave one room for ever and enter a new one. She reached out.

My love, forgive me. You must tell me what to do. A terrible accident has happened. It is as you said and feared it might be – SHE has found us, she came here looking for L. She has been attacking the site. Every night it was her who came, disrupting the work. I found her this time. She was hitting the stakes with an axe at the edge of the central trench. The men had only repaired it today. I tried to stop her, but she screamed at me and would have hit me too. I had to take the axe and push her away in the dark. She was biting, scratching. I only pushed her away to stop her attacking me. She fell into the trench and her head hit the corner of the cist. That was all – my God – that was all. The stone against her head. I was greatly shocked. I didn't know what I should do. I broke the stakes and pushed the earth back in. I covered her – I covered the trench. My love, I am sorry. I am sorry with all my heart. You must tell me what to do, Effie darling. Write soon, my love. N

Lil read it through three times and sat down. A small sound escaped her. She saw Haxton, moments earlier, looking past her to the top of the mound. She remembered Nils's insistence that they didn't dig there, his strange behaviour when she returned from Edinburgh. It was to the central shaft, in his madness, that he had followed his vision of Effie, where he had clawed at the ground. *Have you gone to find her?*

'Madelyn.' She had not said her name aloud in twelve years, not even when she'd spoken with Agnes. Hearing it in her own voice concertinaed time again, just as stepping into her bedroom had, and the real woman was vivid before her. The real woman, who was buried a few hundred yards away beneath a trenchful of earth, and had been for days. *New bones over old.* Lil's spade must have dug within inches of her. She made the small sound again and sagged in her chair. Bina was watching with an expression like wringing hands. She stood and walked around the table. Drawing Lil's head against her body, she held her and stroked her hair. Lil let her.

It was Bina who helped piece together the most likely chain of events. They sat in the kitchen together, chopping vegetables or polishing anything that came to hand, and talked, more words passing between them in a week at Pitcarden than in all the years they had lived in Effie's house. Lil recalled how Bina had clouted Lachlan's henchman with the china shepherdess, going against Effie's wishes, and found herself looking for reasons to be near her. She listened intently as Bina told her what she knew.

Madelyn had known what old Raube's death would mean when she read his obituary. She had known Effie would do anything to retrieve the brooch – a symbol of her triumph over the world, longed for and cherished since they had first read about it in the orphanage. She couldn't bear that the older Raube had buried it again. And Madelyn's own belief in the curse had driven her all the way to Pitcarden to sabotage the dig, cutting the ties and axing stakes. It had transformed her into the myth herself, the hag that haunted the site. She was probably the strangely familiar figure Lil had glimpsed on top of the mound when she had found the plaque. Her faith in the spirit world had been real after all. Even after twelve years, even without Lil's forgiveness, she had loved her enough to fight for her in secret.

Lil realised that Effie had read Nils's letter in front of her at the breakfast table. She had watched her learn of her darling Maddie's death before Lil herself had even known they were connected. The shock and grief of it, the effort of bearing it silently, must have weakened her, in Bina's opinion. Still, she had sent Lil back to Pitcarden, perhaps worried about Nils's state of mind. He had sent telegrams to Effie that week. Bina hadn't read them, but he must have been warning Effie that Lil was determined to dig out that trench, that Raube was letting her continue, and then about Agnes's letter.

And Effie. Effie did what she had always done, moulded circumstance to her will. She had manipulated Dr Lachlan, planning to tidy Lil away at least until the weather made it impossible to dig. And if Lil had returned from London knowing enough to suspect Madelyn was at Pitcarden, her words would have been as light as air in the asylum. Raube may have been right too, that Effie had intended to use Lil's disappearance to pressure him about the brooch.

    Lil was grateful to be working with her hands. She kept her mind on each task as a way of grounding each memory, working them into the shine of a handle or slice of a knife. Bina remained adamant that Effie would have kept her word and quickly snatched Lil back from Lachlan once Madelyn's remains were secure. Lil said nothing and doubled her efforts on a discoloured candlestick. She remembered Effie talking about paying the price in those confused final moments with her. Had she meant to make Lil pay with her freedom to keep her innocent of Madelyn's death? She had said something else that only came back to Lil once everything within reach had been prepped or gleamed and her hands were still. She had said Lil was dearer to her than anyone alive. It was the 'alive' that hurt. Lil might have been Effie's daughter, but it was Madelyn, already dead, that Effie had called for as she lay dying herself.

15

They buried them next to each other in Balcraig's kirkyard. Lil was certain neither would have chosen the setting, but Agnes was ignorant of Madelyn's wishes, and if Effie left instructions with Nils, he was incapable of recalling them.

Police came. Raube insisted on it. But the letter was compelling, as were character witnesses, and Nils's health made him unfit to answer any charges against him. Pneumonia scraped away at his large form until his bones stood out. For a while, Lil thought she would have to bury him too. He sat in front of the fire, and later, when the seasons changed, in the sunshine of Pitcarden's newly tended gardens, saying little and refusing books. Lil sometimes wondered if he had returned to himself more than he was admitting, choosing instead to dwell in the quiet space alone, as she had for that short time between her warm breath and the cold snow.

Her own grief was a second winter come upon her. It raged inside. She moved through the days as if through fog. The activity at Pitcarden seemed at a distance, its sounds muffled. Raube lost no time in starting improvements to the estate. Haxton was given free rein; he began mending roads with stones that were cleared from the fields, and ash collected from coal pits further south; crop rotation was to be increased to a seven-shift system, dropping potatoes altogether, and he made plans for rearing cattle at Mains Farm. Raube courted the good will of his tenants and workers by increasing wages, reducing rents and updating machinery. He became an expected presence in the hamlet, listening to anyone who would talk to him, learning children's names, promising a return of Pitcarden-hosted fetes and holidays. Lil accompanied him on his rounds, standing stiffly in cramped kitchens and failing to put anyone at ease. She went to the Free Church to be seen to be normal, and mumbled her way inexpertly through hymns and pleasantries. At the house, the office became a kind of war room. The three of them plotted benign incursions into the surrounding area.

Lil retrieved the goddess plaque from the storeroom and kept it with the other artefacts. Its blank expression no longer frightened her. It seemed instead to hold a space for all the contradictions and paradoxes of her grief. Sometimes, when she felt brave enough, she took the plaque from its wrappings and thought about Effie and Madelyn. They were as open to interpretation as the figure itself: was one unnatural or progressive? The other deluded or inspired? There were times, staring into the gold until her vision swam, that she could allow them to be both.

No more talk of the curse was heard in Balcraig, or of burying the hoard. Mudie was shunned by many. She sensed an unspoken collective shame hanging over the night that Jenet's baby had been born. The feeling was complex and unsettling, and her heart began to melt towards her neighbours, although she struggled to show it. She couldn't make sense of her own contradictions. Her journey from hated outsider to mistress of Pitcarden was a steep climb for everyone.

It became easier once Jenet was well enough to walk with her, and Lil could inhabit a less formal role with tenants. The girl's unselfconscious chatter and evident ease with Lil probably did more to pacify them than Raube's money. Lil became tolerated, a figure that was not too familiar, not too remote. Her new status thrilled Jenet without making her shy, and her constant questions and comments soothed Lil like a rushing stream. She often went to sit by her. Even the baby was a welcome distraction from the whining ache of her grief. Her superstitious fears of harming the child lifted clean away at some point in the wake of so much loss. She took to holding him after he was fed, when Jenet was still too weak, finding comfort in the ferocious determination of his little body. Their heartbeats ticked along next to each other as he slumbered against her chest, and it was as if her own troubled heart were taking lessons from his newly minted one. The fear itself didn't leave her, but it settled into its true home, a place she couldn't have guessed at before she knew who she was. For her, the curse remained real enough, but it wasn't out on the brae or in the artefacts; it resided in her own blood. The Raubes' sickness was hereditary. It was her own children she threatened.

Children. They came to her sometimes as the night-mare. Not only as the small boys of before, but as monsters that screamed out of sight, pulled her hair, crawled up walls. Vicious, malevolent creatures. It seemed fanciful, now, that the visions had anything to do with Mudie; her hopes that it would leave her in peace, as it had after she'd escaped Lambert, evaporated. Not even the truth had freed her. It was as if the night-mare's home was Pitcarden itself. There were times she thought about leaving.

Days and weeks passed without her making any clear decision. She wandered the upper rooms of the house, beset by generations of Raubes, their books and trinkets, furnishings and pictures, collections of moths and shells. The portraits eyed her darkly. As she roamed, she toyed with the locket at her throat. Bina had brought it back with her from Edinburgh, dropping it silently into Lil's palm one day. Madelyn and Effie still lay within, folded against each other. It was the only thing Lil felt she truly owned. Her father also seemed more comfortable downstairs, preferring to stay close to the office even after the dustsheets were cleared in the rest of the house. They often ate with Haxton in the kitchen, hashing out plans between mouthfuls, or while riding out to inspect some corner of the estate. It was Bina who felt most at home. She took over from the aged housekeeper and went about turning out rooms and hiring staff as if she had never worked anywhere else.

Snow fell again in January. Returning from a visit to a sick tenant who, she suspected, would have felt better if she hadn't, Lil came across Haxton straining to shift the cart out of a drift. She waited, unnoticed. Since all her woeful secrets had spilled out, he had adopted an air of gentle respect around her. It was the one thing that came close to making her laugh out loud that winter. She lanced it with coarse language, deliberate contrariness, and a habit of letting doors shut in his face. In the lane, he leaned his shoulder against the cart for one final push and, as it rolled forward, lost his cap. She picked it up and offered it to him, but before he could take it from her, she threw it high over his head into a rowan tree with a whoop. He gave her a bewildered look, and she felt suddenly, incomprehensibly, exasperated at them both. She walked on but glanced back when her name was called. Something hard and stinging struck the side of her face. She gasped, not immediately understanding it was a snowball. It punched through the fog, and for an exhilarating moment she was able to breathe. Haxton was regarding her without a smile, arms folded. When she didn't move, he shrugged and bent to gather more snow.

From then on, a silent battle raged. Tea was salted, chairs disappeared from underneath sitters, jam found its way into pockets. Raube was occasionally baffled by abandoned meals or sudden departures, but they met his enquiring looks with blank faces. Each prank was a benign assault, a tender ambush. Lil learned to fight without cruelty.

On a cold day in early April, Raube joined her by the mound

to talk through ideas for resuming the dig. Lil had kept away when they had dug up Madelyn's body, only requesting the trench be filled in with fresh earth afterwards. She made herself walk up a few days later and found a simple wreath of yew, ivy and Michaelmas daisies laid on the bare ground. It hadn't come from the house. Someone from the hamlet had done this for a woman they had never met. Perhaps it had come from the same place as the protective rowan twigs; a different kind of offering.

Raube was so layered up against the spring air, he was sweating. The winter had not been kind. Fevers had frequently laid him low, and he had ventured out less as the months wore on. They discussed how to excavate the mound in a way that would minimise the damage done by Nils in his frantic search for the brooch. Lil felt her blood pumping again. She had worried that returning to the dig would be too painful, but the passion still burned, and she became warm as she talked. When she stopped, she found that Raube was looking at her. He pushed his walking stick into the soft earth.

'You know, when I first heard you talking like this, I felt desperately relieved, even though we were strangers who had only just met. The legacy of this place, the curse, what it did to my father – it was hanging over me all the way from Australia. And then there you were, already up to your neck in it, consumed in an entirely different way. A wonderful way. I felt as if you had taken it off my hands. It makes me proud that you will inherit Pitcarden. You have worked this land. You belong here.'

Lil felt herself gently rocked by the word. It half frightened her. She cleared her throat. 'It's early to talk of inheritance, isn't it? You could marry again. Have a son.' She threw the word down like a gauntlet.

Raube laughed. 'A son?' He shook his head. 'Sons of the Raubes don't fare so well. I should know, being one. I've never been healthy, and I'm not going to improve now.'

She looked at him sharply. 'You're not used to these winters. You need sun.'

He shrugged and looked over the fields towards the river. 'Difficult to say if I miss the heat or only like the cold less. But the sounds, the light. Yes, I do miss it.' He seemed lost in a memory of Queensland, but when he spoke again, it was about Pitcarden. 'There is the next generation to think about too. That will be your decision.' He eyed her. 'There are different paths open to you. You could marry, yourself. I think you made a conquest last night.'

It was Lil's turn to laugh. 'Mr Finnie?' She remembered shining, admiring eyes from the night before. Raube had been hosting dinners in recent weeks, wishing to restore relations with neighbours and relatives, and had been invited in turn to suppers, shoots and tennis matches. To her surprise, Lil had enjoyed herself on the occasions she'd joined him. They had agreed he would introduce her as his daughter, long since returned to London to be raised by relatives after his wife had died in Australia. No one questioned it. The older Raube's reclusiveness meant any news of his son had been infrequent and incomplete. If anyone recalled the rumour that Raube had eloped with his father's fiancée, all mention of it was kept behind closed doors. They were regarded with an intense and wary curiosity, which Lil was more than comfortable with. She wondered if she weren't after all happiest when feeling an outsider among equals. Here, she was understood to be different, but accepted as Raube's daughter. It gave her space and licence to be an oddity, which she didn't have with the tenants and workers of Pitcarden. There, she still struggled to find a tone that felt natural. Her responsibilities had never extended to people, not in a legitimate, serious way. She needed a guide, someone who understood both her and them. Mr Finnie, she recalled, was a widower, master of a thriving estate some miles to the east.

He knew the territory, but he had regarded her with a sort of delighted bafflement.

'I like him,' she told Raube, 'but I think he would find me highly unsatisfactory as a wife, and I would have limited use for him as a husband. No.' She headed Raube off before he could talk about children. 'I shall marry our factor.'

She waited for his reaction, ready with sarcasm and a caustic smile. Anxiety curled in the pit of her stomach. Beyond a slight pursing of his lips, Raube's expression didn't change. He thought for a moment. 'Does *he* know that?'

Laughter erupted from Lil, and she smiled at him. 'I have given him some time to think about it.'

Raube returned the smile, regarding her as if she had just exhibited an unexpected talent for yodelling or gymnastics. 'You seem hopeful.'

She was. Something in Haxton's disappointed look when she had explained her terms told her he had already accepted. He only needed time to become accustomed to the idea and to forgive her for saying what she knew about him. And also, perhaps, to recover from the manner of her proposal, a peremptory statement not even directed at him, while sprawled in front of the office fire, her feet on the scuttle and solicitors' letters spilling from her lap. Lil had surprised herself. In the depths of her own private winter, she had been slow to grasp that their silent games were a kind of courtship. He sometimes caught her eye and either looked away too quickly or held her gaze too long. Curious, she continued to watch him one time as he turned awkwardly to some business with a ledger, and recalled – or at least her body recalled – the deep thrill of their first encounter. It was like a stiff wine cork suddenly popping free; no amount of effort could restopper it. He began to haunt her thoughts, and a different sort of silence grew between them. She considered reaching for him as she had before, but the kind of untrammelled liaison she had embarked on elsewhere was impossible at Pitcarden. Secrecy was corrosive. The thought of reenacting her own parents' illicit meetings repelled her. And an open affair was equally impossible; they would lose the trust and respect they had only just begun to build within the estate.

Marriage. It kept leaning into her peripheral vision like a pamphleteer. The big decision was upon her. If she committed to Pitcarden, it had to be either entirely alone, or in legal partnership with a man who was willing to take her on her own terms, night-mare and all. And there was only one who might do that. The alternative was returning to an itinerant life without Nils and Effie, to chance encounters, independence, belonging nowhere.

She had been prodding again at the marriage idea in her mind, thinking of Effie and Nils, but also considering that there were dangers for a woman in any such contract, when Haxton, who was seated behind her at a desk, cleared his throat. The sound, familiar enough to her now, brought her back into the room. She thought of the muscles moving in his neck and how he would have unconsciously licked his bottom lip afterwards. The fire crackled comfortably. Her feet were on the scuttle, and she felt the delicious weariness of her limbs after their earlier ride. They were already behaving like family, like equals. Something would have to change, and if she didn't choose what, the decision would be taken from her. Haxton couldn't propose himself in his position, not to her, but one day he might ask someone else.

'We should get married.'

The words had startled her, that she had said them aloud. There was silence behind. She sat up and craned around the side of the chair. Now that it was said, the proposal seemed to pull something else up from the depths of her, something potent and urgent. Haxton's expression suggested, all the same, that she should have begun differently. Nerves made her want to laugh, and she rose to perch on the edge of the desk next to him. He strained back in his chair, as if to put distance between them, frowning. She resisted the urge to touch his forehead.

'We work well together. We understand each other more than most. You will have greater authority over the estate reforms. I shall continue with excavations and won't have to worry about Pitcarden or . . . or my father, when I'm away.' An expression passed over his face that she couldn't name. 'We shall be faultlessly respectable in public, but also respect each other's freedoms.'

The slightest smile teased one side of Haxton's mouth. She waited a moment before continuing. 'There is one condition that might decide you against it.'

'One, is there?'

She was too nervous to hear his humour. 'You know the history of the Raubes. Their sickness is hereditary, and I don't know if I carry it.' She bit her lip. 'I won't have children.' It was then that she saw it, the falling behind his eyes. His face became serious. She hurried on. 'We can fill the house with orphans if you like, but I won't have my own. That's . . . that's not something I will change my mind about.'

They were silent for several moments. Haxton stared at the letter on the desk. 'I am not one for marriage.'

'Nor I.' Lil watched him closely. 'This would be a different sort of partnership, one of our own making. We understand each other enough to make room.'

He shook his head, still not looking at her. 'You've said that twice now, but I'm not so sure I understand you, and you don't know me as well as you think. Marriage of any kind isn't a state I want to be in.'

'Truly? Or is it something you've decided not to *allow* yourself?'

The question was so genuine, so surprisingly gentle coming from her, it seemed to stall whatever had been in his mind and left him speechless. She leaned forward slightly, heart thudding harder. 'I would never ask you to change or to become something you're not, but I can help you carry who you are.' For a moment, she thought she saw a yearning rise behind his eyes. 'I can help you carry your guilt.'

He jerked as if she'd struck him. 'Guilt?'

'Yes.' She sat back again and took a breath. 'For starting the fire that killed your brother.'

His face became a battleground: shock, denial, rage. He opened his mouth, but no victor came forth. Lil folded her hands in her lap. 'It's all over you; I can see it weighing you down. And it's in the choices you've made – fighting so hard to leave Balcraig and then deciding to come back. What was that? The hope of making amends, or to punish yourself? Both, I suppose.'

She tried to take his hand, which was gripping the arm of the chair, but he snatched it away, rage winning in him. Her fingers clutched each other instead.

'And . . . And I would not refuse help in carrying my own guilt.' She tried to pinch a smile out, amazed at how heavy the words were. 'I have plenty of my own. The life I lived . . .' And all at once, it was as if she had lost her footing and was being dragged under. She stood and stepped back from the desk. Her heart screamed to flee from him, from Pitcarden, from the past six months, run like an animal to a place of safety. She was her child self, trapped in a box and expected to perform, to pull all the right strings, all alone. 'That's what I have; that's all I can do.' She flung it at him, her face tightening, and then she did run, tearing through the house and frightening the housemaid, who was closing curtains on the landing.

After that, he wouldn't meet her eye. Their conversations were polite and short and only ever about the estate. She thought of a ship, too far offshore for people on land to tell if it was coming into port or sailing away. The game was dropped, of course, but two days before her conversation with Raube, she had reached into her workbox, and instead of a dead spider or sprig of gorse, found a posy of daffodils. She had put a cigar she'd stolen from Raube's desk in his coat pocket, and just that morning had received in return a knotted ribbon she knew the girls in the hamlet tied for their sweethearts.

A week later, Haxton appeared in the old still room, where she had relocated all the dig finds from the cottage. She was using a needle to remove tiny flakes of dirt from the patina of a bronze ring when, without a greeting, he began listing reasons against marrying. It would distance him from his neighbours and family; she would be isolated from the rest of society; Pitcarden would be laughed at. He didn't look at her, delivering his objections to the floor, until Lil slid off her stool and put a finger to his lips. He made a sound as if winded. She studied his face, surveying it as if it were an ancient landscape, and had a sense of what the years might reveal to her, an intimation of happiness. It was only for a moment, and then he had grasped her hand, pressing it to his mouth, and then his mouth to hers.

Over the next few weeks, she let him lead, relinquishing the need to dictate what happened or to rush headlong in a blind fury of want. He surprised her by refusing to be in a hurry. At first, she took it for prudishness, but soon learned he possessed a gift for absorption that she herself reserved for grave goods. She found herself being slowly and gently unearthed like something wondrously precious and too-long buried. He never spoke a word about children.

Not so Bina. As soon as the engagement was announced, she twinkled and fussed and began making sideways remarks about letting out dresses and concocting remedies for nausea. On a sunny afternoon in May, she was helping Lil plan accommodation for friends of Haxton who were staying for the wedding, when she suggested redecorating the nursery for the children. Her head tilted coyly. 'It might not be long until you need it yourself.'

'Oh, Bina.' Lil slapped her hand on the morning-room table. 'Don't start. There will be no children; I've told you this.'

'I only think—'

'It's not your place to think.' Lil snapped it savagely, her old resentment erupting. To her surprise, Bina didn't lapse into wounded silence or meek apologies. She sat more squarely in her seat and fixed Lil with a furious look.

'If you don't want them, that's one thing, but to deny yourself and Mr Haxton because of a possibility, a chance . . .' Her fingers flickered in the air. 'No parents have any certainty, and many are grateful for the time they're given, however short.' Her eyes grew fiercer, and Lil realised she knew nothing at all about Bina's life before Effie had gobbled her up. She had never thought to ask. Bina remained stern. 'It's not for you to decide what will happen.'

'No.' Lil spoke more gently. 'But my blood might, Bina. Hereditary illness is so little understood. It might not have come from the Raubes but through my grandmother's family. She and her sister were healthy as far as anyone knew, but nearly all their sons died. It's possible I have inherited it through her, but it's my children who would suffer.' She lifted a hand vaguely in the direction of the kirkyard. 'All the Raube boys, all of them, and my father's health is so weak . . .'

'And you'd wish him away, is that it? Decree he should never have lived at all?' Bina was caustic. '"Might have", "It's possible", "As far as we know".' She all but spat. 'Mr Haxton is as strong as an ox. And what about daughters? It's a terrible, terrible thing to—'

'I can't lose anyone else!' The words exploded out of Lil. She gripped the table as if she would fall, and looked at Bina with pleading eyes. 'I can't.'

Bina's expression turned in an instant from anger to pity. 'Oh, my dear.' She hurried around the table to take the chair next to Lil and folded her into her arms as naturally as a mother would her child.

The night-mare grew worse and more frequent. She became certain that its nature was informed by Pitcarden itself. The small boys and old man, the terrifying screams, they seemed to reflect the tragedies of the place, its lost children, its great sorrow and violence. Was she to carry it all around with her like the taint of the Lilith myth, ever to be hounded by a vengeful Mara-like figure? Where did any of these stories even begin? If the Pitcarden curse was truly as old as the hoard, then it had survived for innumerable generations, connecting everyone at Balcraig to people more ancient even than those who had built the brae. Every person living – that had ever lived – was so *new*, the oldest barely awake for a moment. It was as if the true inhabitants of earth were these ancient myths, enduring for millennia, while all mortal beings were merely conduits, each one spent in turn like a heartbeat or exhalation, cells dying and renewing to sustain something too vast to comprehend.

She took to walking at night again, trying to put off sleep, and succeeded only in adding exhaustion to the terror. One morning, a baby perched itself at the end of her bed, grinning horribly. When it pounced, jumping with unnatural agility onto her legs, she closed her eyes and gave in. She wouldn't fight. The thing crawled up her body, and she waited, unresisting, for hair-pulling and sharp nails. She heard instead the sweetly laboured breaths of a small child concentrating. Tiny fingers landed on her cheek, but they didn't scratch. With infinite tenderness and care, her face was stroked and patted. Tears welled up and streamed from the sides of her eyes. The baby hiccuped, and the gentle breaths drew close enough for her to feel them on her skin. Her eyes squeezed shut more tightly. She wouldn't look. 'I'm sorry.' She whispered it in her head. 'I'm sorry. I can't.'

Nearby, the laughter of an older child bubbled up. As if she'd said the funniest thing.

16

October 1887

Lil pulled on boots and an old overcoat and trudged along the passageway past the kitchen, waving at the new cook as she did so. The old cook had grown tired of her peculiar mistress traipsing mud across the floor on her way to the still room and helping herself to pots of tea and sandwiches at all hours. A man with a large satchel was disappearing through the side door ahead of Lil, and she ducked into the office. 'Post?'

Pen in hand, Haxton patted a pile on the desk without looking up. She still thought of him as Haxton; 'Hugh' was held in reserve for intimacy and arguments. Searching through estate business, dinner invitations and periodicals, she stopped at a fattened envelope with American stamps, and groaned. Haxton put down the pen. 'Agnes?'

She decided to get it over with and seized a letter opener. With Madelyn buried, Lil had gifted the London house to Agnes, who had promptly sold it and sailed to America to make her fortune as a medium. It was going well. She wrote long, impassioned letters, always signing off, *With the love of the spirits.* Lil grumbled every time, knowing she would be devastated if the letters ever stopped coming. She read aloud to Haxton now. Agnes had met a couple recently emigrated from Edinburgh and was asking if Lil knew them. 'More victims; they'll be dragged into a séance.'

'Willingly, perhaps.'

Lil rolled her eyes. 'They won't know she's trying to dig up dirt on them so she can astonish them with insights from the spirits.'

Haxton pushed his tongue into the side of his cheek briefly. 'It's one way to pass an evening. I expect there are people who would find it quite fun.' Lil opened her mouth but found she was unable to think of a word to say. Haxton smiled. 'Besides, I thought digging up dirt was what you did?'

Lil put down the letter and regarded her husband gravely. 'I've told the new cook you adore potatoes.'

Early October had burnished the drive, now weeded and levelled, with beech leaves. Everything green was returning to the earth, settling back into the dark, damp underground work of winter. They should plant bulbs, she thought; she would talk to the gardener. Servants were a feature of life that she was still getting used to: managing, instructing, cajoling, avoiding. But for now, she was free. Rosehips grew bright and fat in the hedgerows. Bina was making enough syrup out of them to feed the kingdom. Lil picked a few handfuls for her as she climbed the slope, slipping them into her pocket.

The burial mound was transformed. As so much of the site had been degraded and she already knew where the primary burial lay, she had cut a wide trench straight through the middle. When the top stone of the cist was finally lifted off, she had found the unburned skeleton of an adult man lying on his left side, his head in the east, with his legs drawn up under his chin. An ornamental urn stood by his shoulder. In the north-west corner, laid out on a stone, was a gold disc, only the second discovery of its kind in Scotland. And next to this was another skeleton: an infant, very young. Another child taken, passing an unimaginably long time ago. But it wasn't fear that Lil had felt with the discovery. She'd run a hand unconsciously over her belly. Once, she had dug up bones to chase away the spirits that lived in her head. Later, she had told her father she was unearthing these ancient people to learn something from them. But when she looked into the grave, she had wondered if either thing were true or even possible, or if, in intruding on these sacred spaces, she was really only looking for a reflection of herself. Gently brushing away the dirt from the remains of the child, all she had felt was love.

Once the centre had been excavated, she had worked south again, looking for and finding later interments, until half the mound had been cut back to the subsoil. Then she had dug down, as far as the rock would allow, finding new pits. She took her time, working with her own hands alongside a handful of trusted men, and Jenet, whose interest in 'treasure' had only intensified since the drama of her son's birth. Her fingers were as precise and careful with prehistoric pots as they had been cleaning brass. Lil was pitched into the role of mentor and teacher, and discovered reserves of patience within herself that she would never have suspected. It made the part she was soon to play in shaping a new life a little less daunting. In return, she found herself picking up more Scots words and phrases. She began talking naturally of *skelbs* of flint, *dreich* weather, shovelling *clarts*. Haxton roared with laughter and made her repeat her daily lessons endlessly, but Lil felt each new word was a tiny hand taking hold of her. They were slowly and gently helping her settle into place. The cottage was improved, and they offered it to the young couple. It was good for everyone to see Jenet happily digging the brae and living so close to it with her thriving child.

As Lil reached the top of the path, she saw a figure next to the standing stone. There was a flicker of fear – the night-mare still came at times in its old shape – but it was her father. His presence surprised her. He had barely left Pitcarden since the wedding, spending much of his time with Nils, who had recovered enough to talk of returning to Sweden; the National Heritage Board in

Stockholm had asked for his help, and Lil knew he would be unable to resist. She listened to the two men exchanging fragmented stories of mining and archaeology. Raube recalled the thunder of the stamp mills, the seas of calico tents, the fortunes prised from rock and chance. Nils spoke of folklore, of puzzling finds, the thrill of a new site. She often wondered if they were talking to themselves only, and not listening to the other at all. They were not so different from her, tearing at the earth to find something solid to hold. She had once asked Raube, 'Why gold?' and he had said it was the one thing that everyone trusted – over words, over each other, even over God.

She approached him, smiling, and tucked her arm into his. Voices came from behind the gorse, and Jenet appeared with her son Angus. His arms reached up, hands clasping at a jackdaw that flapped noisily away. She waved and pointed out Lil and Raube to him before wandering over to where the large stones still traced the south-west edge of the mound. They waved back and, after a few remarks about the success of the dig that year, fell silent. Two geese honked high overhead, and Raube lifted his gaze.

'I have been thinking, my dear ...' He hesitated for long enough to pull Lil out of her own thoughts. 'I shall return to Australia.' He looked from the geese to her, but she didn't look back. A shard of ice had sliced through her. He squeezed her arm. 'You were right. I am not used to these winters, and I have spent so little time at Pitcarden, even as a child. It is not my home.'

But I am, and you are mine. The thought rose to her lips and stuck there – too painful, and too late, she suddenly felt, to form into words.

'I have been away too long. I thought I had had my fill of the mines, but British investment has only just started, and there are reefs to find further north. It seems the gold fields have a hold on me still.'

'But I thought you came back to Pitcarden to make it your home.'

'Not permanently. I never wanted to live in my father's house. He never forgave me for killing my mother in childbirth, and then I stole his second wife from him too. There is too much bad blood here. I had a duty, but now you and Hugh are running things, I've really done everything I can. I'm surplus to requirements.'

Lil didn't speak for a moment. The colours seemed to drain from the landscape until everything she could see looked dead and grey. 'I don't want to do this without you.' She still wasn't looking at him. He turned her to face him, leaning his stick against his body so he could take both her arms.

'You already are. With Hugh.' He put an unsteady hand to her face. 'You're a miracle, Lil. This year has been a miracle.'

'We'll come with you.'

He smiled at her. 'And leave your pots and bones? Take Hugh away from Balcraig? Neither of you would survive it. You belong here, both of you, and I belong there. I shall sail in the new year.'

She had known it, she realised; deep down, too deep to see. It had never been his intention to stay. She clung to him like a child for a long time. Autumn sunshine warmed her tears, filling her eyes with golden light. She stood back from him finally and wiped her face with the heel of her hand. 'You're worse than Nils. I won't forgive either of you.' A smile sharpened the corners of her mouth. 'Don't imagine we'll miss you.'

'Of course not.' His own eyes were wet. 'I won't think of you at all.'

Lil wanted to tell him he was leaving her as he had left Effie, knowing it would wound him, knowing it wasn't true. Her impulse to draw blood had been blunted in the last year, but not entirely. His stick, forgotten, fell to the ground, and she bent quickly to pick it up, to head off the impetuous words. While she was crouching down, her eye travelled across the ground to the cist, and beyond it to the north half of the mound, still standing proud. A small patch of earth had fallen in from the wall. She wouldn't complete the excavation until next season, and the thought that Raube wouldn't be by her side to share in the finds nearly pushed her to the ground. Family seemed to crumble away the moment she could name them.

She rose and handed him the stick. His hand closed over hers. 'We shall write. We are in each other's lives now; there is no going back to how we were before, even if we wished it.'

'Of course I don't wish it.' She thought she would cry again and looked down, biting her lip. The impulse to tell him her news as a way to influence him rose and fell. He released her.

'I didn't have a very good night. If you'll excuse me, I'll return to the house.'

'Are you not well?'

'A little tired, that's all.' Smiling, he squeezed her arm before turning away. He looked pale and tense, but she let him go. As he walked towards the path down to the house, his head was turned to the burial mound. Finally, she saw him make a small, dismissive movement with his hand, as if he were from that moment done with the place.

She looked across the site herself. It had meant such different things to different people over so many years. And could any of it be said to reside anywhere but in their own minds? Jenet was showing it to her boy, slowly moving along the perimeter stones. What would it mean to him in years to come? He was almost walking by himself now, taking heart-in-mouth steps between his mother's hands. Lil was grateful for Jenet's involvement. She wanted the excavation to be something the people of Balcraig could feel proud of and a part of. Their work was already being written about and attracting attention, many of the finds properly displayed in the museum in Edinburgh. She picked her way carefully across the site, between pits and past the cist, to put her hand to the earth wall. Next season was already pulling at her;

they might have stopped only a few inches short of something extraordinary. Perhaps there would be another tiny soul to show it to then. For now, there was much still to write up. One day, when she had finished the north side, she intended to restore the barrow as faithfully as possible. She wouldn't rob Balcraig of its brae. Perhaps its living inhabitants would help.

The small heap of soil had fallen from a spot a couple of feet from the surface. She passed the toe of her boot through it. Something small and too uniform to be natural surfaced and was covered again. Squatting, she felt for it with her fingers and pulled out a ring. She blew some of the dirt away and rubbed a section clean. Gold flashed in the sunlight. She was still for a moment, her breath short, and then she began working urgently, spitting on the ring and scraping at it with her nails until she could see clearly. She wiped it on her dress and held it up. A gold band, a wedding ring.

The sun went in, throwing a shadow that seemed to penetrate her skin. She was at a distance from where the rest of the artefacts had been found. The ring must have been buried at a remove on purpose, making this last piece harder to find. But the hoard was complete now. The thought went through her like a shiver. She remembered pulling out the first of it, the gold goddess, and something slithered in her gut, as if a monstrous, unsuspected parasite had awoken. Dig up all five objects and the hag would come; she would come for the youngest. One hand went instinctively to her belly and the other to the wall to steady herself. Jenet and her child were still at the edge near a gap in the boulders. The deepest trench on the site ran across it, tunnelling along the inside to see if the stones were anything more than a boundary wall. Lil watched as Jenet straightened to stretch her back and, at the same time, a jackdaw landed on the cist. The boy spotted it. In a sudden burst of excitement, his legs carried him forward towards the gap, and Lil saw what was going to happen. A cry ripped from her throat. She flung herself towards him across the site, not minding where she stepped. He was too far away. The jackdaw took fright and flapped off towards Pitcarden. Lil's foot plunged into a pit, and with a cry she fell her length on top of a deposit of calcined bones. Her voice was hoarse with terror. She raised her head, making herself look. Jenet was standing at the edge of the trench, her face wide open with shock. In her arms was her son.

'Are ye hurtit? Mrs Haxton?' She called it over Angus's rising wail. Lil stared, unable to believe, and then she was scrambling up and running again. She jumped down into the trench.

'He's— I thought he— I thought he fell.' She sobbed up at them, her words mangled.

'He's awricht.' Jenet seemed awed at the sight of her. 'He gied me a fricht an-aw tho. Did ye no, Angy?' She kissed his cheek and jigged him up and down. 'You're meant tae walk afore ye run.'

'He's all right, then?' Lil was too frightened to be ashamed of her tears.

'Ay, he's jist fasht he cannae catch Jackie ower yonder.' Jenet crouched down with him to be level with Lil. 'See. Look wha it is, Angy.' Angus was unimpressed and bawled louder. Lil tried to smile, her cheeks still wet with tears, and reached up to pinch his chin softly.

'I thought he fell,' she said again. The force of the relief made her feel faint. 'There, now.' She took his little hand in hers, and he gripped her finger tightly, as if to take out his frustrations on it. His fierceness helped calm her breathing somehow. The ring was still in her other hand. She slipped it into her pocket so she could stroke his hot cheek and wipe away the tears. Her gentle proddings started to distract him, and he stopped crying to frown at her. She smiled more convincingly and glanced up at Jenet for a witness to her success, but Jenet was staring over her head, her face clouding.

'Mrs Haxton.'

Lil looked quickly behind and around but could see nothing. Jenet stood up, lifting Angus with her. 'Lil.' She was more urgent now. Lil pulled herself out of the trench and followed Jenet's pointing finger. In the grass on the east side near to the standing stone, a thing. A low hump of tweed, the sole of a boot, a hat knocked off. Lil ran. No breath at all. She reached Raube and fell to her knees beside him, one hand on his back and the other lifting the length of scarf that had fallen over his face. His eyes were open, staring towards the Carlin stone, but it was as she had known it would be.

Lil was aware of the mutterings. They skittered around her like dry leaves before a coming storm – at the funeral, during her visits to the hamlet, among the servants in the house. They whispered how Raube had died beside the brae, how his health had failed living close to it, how Lil had never been able to stop digging, just like her grandfather. She had told no one about finding the wedding ring except Haxton, and her heart blanched at what would happen if it became known. Raube's death had unsettled estate relations once again, opening fissures in the fragile trust he had worked to build. Fear ran into the cracks like icy water. Men refused or were forbidden by their families to come back to the site, even to cover it for winter. The curse was spoken of again.

She knew she had to act quickly and boldly; she could not allow her grief to seal her up in Pitcarden House. Raube's legacy, at least the only one he cared about, lay not in his land, but in the people who lived and worked upon it. He had been content that she should inherit only because he had seen her dig Pitcarden soil with her own hands. She understood now. *You belong here.* Effie's voice came back to her too; *Courage, dear one.* To her surprise, she found she drew strength from it.

She made sure Haxton locked the office door before lining up the artefacts on the big desk. Plaque, torc, candlestick, brooch, ring. Her fingers trembled. *One, two, three, four, five.* Haxton was watching over her shoulder; he reached around for her hand and drew her against his body, kissed her neck. 'His heart was weak. It always had been.'

'I know.'

'It was a coincidence. It doesn't mean . . .' He spread his fingers over her middle.

'I know.' It didn't mean the curse had caught up with him at last. She looked at the treasure. It was the find of a lifetime, her name in books across the world. 'I want to bury them.'

He rested his chin on her shoulder. 'If you sold even one to the museum, it would pay for . . .'

'No.' She shook her head. 'We must end this.' He was silent, but she could hear his thoughts. She put both her hands over his. 'It's not about believing in the curse. We need to show that we believe in *them*. And in Pitcarden.' She turned her head so she could see his face. 'You know that better than me; it's why you didn't want us here to begin with. This hoard has caused so much division; it can become a symbol of unity instead.'

Haxton looked down at it and cleared his throat. 'Then let Balcraig decide.'

She stared at him and then at the gold. 'Give them the choice to bury or sell?' All at once, it was the most obvious thing in the world. She smiled suddenly. 'You know what they will do?'

He nodded. 'But it will have been their decision.'

'In that case,' she kissed him, 'I know what to do about John Mudie.'

Raube's words guided her: *If I can't make peace with him, I'll keep him close.* She thought of poor Mrs Andrews; if it was impossible to like a person you have injured, perhaps it was also impossible to remain enemies with someone you have helped.

Mudie still made her uneasy; it was not so simple to forget how far his hatred had carried him, the fear he had instilled in her. But she stood in his small cottage, ignoring the baleful stares of his wife and son, and came straight out with it. 'I am here to ask for your assistance, Mr Mudie.'

She told him about the wedding ring falling from the side of the brae and the choice she was offering the community. 'I would like you to organise the ballot, if you agree. I shall leave it to you to decide whether to tell them about the ring or not.' His wife, she noticed, had grasped their son's hand when she spoke of it.

Mudie remained surly but couldn't hide his shock at having the mistress of Pitcarden under his roof suggesting such a thing. His neighbours had kept their distance since the violence nearly a year earlier. She saw him calculating how far this request made of him by a Raube might go in restoring his position in the hamlet. He agreed with little enough grace, and Lil waited anxiously for news that he was using the ring to stir up trouble again. Nothing happened, and a few days later, he delivered the result of the ballot. It was overwhelmingly as she had expected.

On Samhain, the day of the burial, Mudie was at the front of a long line from the hamlet, strolling into the yard as if he owned it. She nodded to him, and he nodded back; the first exchange that hadn't begun with a snarl. The hoard was to be buried under the foundations of the new stable block. She wanted it clear finally of the brae and the excavation, and safe from treasure hunters. People had worn their best clothes, she noticed. They became silent as they assembled, the atmosphere solemn and expectant. She stepped up onto a mounting block and looked at their faces: friendly, suspicious, curious, wary. Some were there purely for the spectacle and promised Samhain feast, others for salvation. It occurred to her that she was in the séance room again, creating a little theatre, a little magic, helping people make peace with the dead. The thought calmed her nerves, and she spoke simply about Raube and his plans for the estate, the gratitude she had felt over the last year, and her hope that this act of burial would mark a new era in the fortunes of Pitcarden and all who lived there.

'The legend demands something personal and of value be added to the hoard.' She pulled the locket from under her collar and undid the clasp. 'This was my mother's. Gemstones and gold, but its value to me is far greater than its material wealth.' She held it up, the sixth piece. 'May this be the last precious thing any of us has to bury.'

She let the silence that followed deliver up its dead for each of them. Nothing moved; even the cold air was still. She was about to step down towards the waiting casket when a harsh voice broke through.

'Hoo div we ken it's the rael gowd?' It was Mudie, his malignant grin breaking out like a gargoyle at the front. Lil's heart clenched. A scattering of voices murmured support. She stared over their heads, and the harsh words that were rushing to her lips faltered. It was her father who had interrupted, as surely as if he had waved to her from the back of the crowd. She saw his bloodied lip again, the forbearance in his expression. A smile slowly bloomed across her face, and she called out to the gathering.

'If I can satisfy Mr Mudie that there is no skulduggery here, will you be content? There is a hog waiting to be eaten, and I for one feel it's been a long while since dinner.'

Laughter released them. She stepped down and waved him forward to the casket, throwing back the black cloth that covered the artefacts. He stood at his full height, looking down his nose at them, but she saw the shock that went through him at so much wealth laid out. Doubt crept into his face. He glanced at her sharply as if she had tricked him out of a fortune. She gestured. 'Handle them if you wish.'

He hesitated before reaching a hand towards the gold plaque.

His fingers hovered for a moment above the female figure, and then he snatched his fist back, curling it into his body as if it had been burned. His eyes were troubled as they met hers, questioning. She held his gaze. 'They will believe whatever you say.'

He could have started a riot, ruined the ritual out of sheer malice. After another moment, he nodded and threw a hand up. 'It's thare awricht.' He marched back to the crowd and was made room for. Someone clapped him on the back.

Lil placed the locket next to the wedding ring, pausing to rest her fingers against it. She would never know for certain what had stayed his hand. The female figure gleamed innocently. Lil took one last look at it and replaced the cloth.

EPILOGUE

She woke up. There was a hissing in the air, pressure on the top of her head, but she didn't even try to move. It had been a while. She wondered who it would be, what they would do. At the end of the bed, she saw the bottom half of a figure, indistinct but with a glow flickering around it like sunlight reflected off water. Effie or Madelyn, perhaps, as they had appeared in the orphanage photograph. They had come before, giggling and tickling, jumping out at her from corners of the room. Their laughter had been like bubbles of light, so full of possibility they lifted her off the bed. Once, Madelyn had come alone as a young woman and simply lain down next to her, wrapping her in a soft, warm embrace. With Effie, it was a voice usually, clear and close to Lil's ear. *Courage, Lily Pad.* Sometimes she was simply a sensation of strength, a gathering of will. She had turned up bodily only once, with snow falling around her. Lil had felt the flakes soaking through her sheets, wet and cold, and wondered if this was what Nils had seen and what it meant.

The horrors never returned. Every time she woke to the hissing, she chose to let go of the terror and darkness, and in their place came curiosity. She remembered the time at Madelyn's when she had given in to it in the hope it would kill her but instead had heard a voice that was achingly, lovingly familiar. Madelyn had been right in a way – the night-mare grew worse when she fought it, and helped her when she didn't. Not to warn her of a figure in the outside world, though. Only the dead and the dying, safe between their end-papers, ever showed themselves. The dead, the dying, and perhaps the unborn. The child asleep in the nursery and the infant that had patted her face so tenderly when she had given into it a second time: were they connected? She couldn't say, but it occurred to her that she herself was somehow choosing what came, that the forms – both shadow and real – were decided by forces deep within her, beyond her own understanding.

The figure at the bottom of the bed was closer suddenly. Lil heard springs creak. The golden shimmer grew brighter, flickering around the shape so its features were never clear together. For a moment, she was reminded of the head of the night-mare hag in Edinburgh, swinging on its stretched neck, and a spike of fear shot through her. This thing was new, unrecognised. It moved up her body until it was hovering above her own face, and with a jolt, she understood. The gold figure on the plaque. Her body jerked, for the first time fully afraid. She shut her eyes to try to calm herself, but the weight on her chest was crushing her lungs. Panic closed in, threatening to break through, when she remembered what Nils had said, the story he had told. The hag-goddesses of folklore come in different guises, not all of them malevolent. She opened her eyes. The golden face was all she could see, blazing above her, larger than life. She made a choice.

'You are the Mara.' She spoke the words in her head, but they seemed to take voice in the room. The blank metallic eyes of the figure began to open. Pure light flooded out.

'You are the Mara.' Louder. She heard another voice saying it alongside hers. The mouth above her stretched as if it would smile or speak. Lil tried to scream but made no noise at all. The third time.

'You are the Mara.' Light exploded, swallowing everything in the room. And it was gone. Lil could see. She was no longer on the bed but above it. Looking down, she saw her own terrified face. Her mouth was forming words, and even as she watched, she could feel her lips moving.

I am the Mara.

It came to her then. Sudden and complete, it settled within her, deep in her bones. She glowed with it, wanting to laugh, knowing the sound would spill out of her as light.

I am the Mara.

All the shadows shrank to nothing. She beamed down at herself, cascading love, waiting for herself to catch up.

I am the Mara.

And there she was, dazzlingly illuminated, laughing light. Reflected in her own wide-open eyes was the goddess.

Acknowledgements

Most of my research involves reading books and skulking about places by myself, but for key elements of *The Night Hag*, this wasn't possible or, often, legal without the kind assistance of other people. I am indebted to Professor Stephen Driscoll and the team excavating Govan Old in Glasgow for allowing me to wield a trowel for three days, and for answering questions about a hypothetical site while they were busy co-ordinating a community dig. Professor Ian Ralston was immensely helpful with the elusive details of nineteenth-century archaeological practices, finding invaluable texts that my hours in libraries and bullying ChatGPT had failed to unearth. Dr Jacqueline Cahif at The Royal College of Surgeons of Edinburgh was very generous with her time and expertise, both over email and in person. I couldn't have approached the Scots dialogue in the book without the help of Dauvit Horsbroch, who also pointed me to sources I hadn't considered. Any inaccuracies – archaeological, historical or linguistic – are all my own doing.

For immersing me in the complexities of Victorian spiritualism and the lives of the extraordinary women who made it their own, I am particularly thankful for two excellent books: *Out of the Shadows: Six Visionary Victorian Women in Search of a Public Voice* by Emily Midorikawa, and *The Darkened Room: Women, Power, and Spiritualism in Late Victorian England* by Alex Owen.

Heartfelt thanks, always, to my agent, Juliet Mushens, for her unequalled vim, and to the passionate and hard-working team at Mushens Entertainment. Also to my exceptional editor at 4th Estate, Katie Bowden, and to Lola Downes for her astute reading; their combined insights illuminated strands of the story in ways I could never have seen for myself. Charlotte Webb and Amber Burlinson provided much-appreciated fine-tuning. I am deeply grateful for the vital support of the whole team at HarperCollins, including Hope Butler, Eve Hutchings, Nicola Webb and Becca Heselton, whose beautiful cover design proved inspirational in itself.

Thanks finally to my friends and family for their ongoing love and enthusiasm, especially to early readers, Rebekah Lattin-Rawstrone and Tom Collinson, who were so generous with their time and feedback; to John Berry and Megan Bastick for letting me loose in the family archive; and to Holly Fleming, whose experience of sleep paralysis first alerted me to the phenomenon and made for some wild breakfast conversations – and who also designed my website.